THE LAST ENEMY

The Ninth Century Book IV

M J Porter

Copyright © 2020 MJ Porter

Copyright notice
Porter, MJ The Last Enemy
Copyright ©2020, Porter, MJ Amazon Edition
All characters and events in this publication, other than those clearly in the public domain, are fictitious and any resemblance to actual persons, living or dead, is purely coincidental. ALL RIGHTS RESERVED.
No part of this publication may be reproduced, stored in a retrieval system or transmitted in any form or by any means without the prior written permission of the author, nor be otherwise circulated in any form of binding or cover other than that in which it is published and without a similar condition being imposed on the subsequent buyer.

Cover design by MJ Porter
Cover image by Dreamstime ID 126224382 © Tomert. Dreamstime.com.

This book is dedicated to my Dad, MJC, on his 75th birthday.

Thank you for all the maps:)

CONTENTS

Title Page
Copyright
Dedication
Map of Mercia in AD874   1
Prologue   2
Chapter 1   24
Chapter 2   45
Chapter 3   58
Chapter 4   65
Chapter 5   83
Chapter 6   91
Chapter 7   106
Chapter 8   126
Chapter 9   132
Chapter 10   143
Chapter 11   176
Chapter 12   194
Chapter 13   211
Chapter 14   223
Chapter 15   253
Historical Notes   270

Cast of Characters	272
Meet the author	276
Acknowledgement	279
The Ninth Century Series	281
Books By This Author	285

MAP OF MERCIA IN AD874

PROLOGUE

"We're going to attack together, in a long line, one after another. We run them down, and we hunt them down. They don't have horses or shields. Lyfing and Gyrth found all the shields' on the ships. They have seax and war axes, and a few have spears. They'll try and run for their ships. We'll follow them. Once they get there, they'll have no means of escape, none, and we can scythe them down, as though it's the harvest."

Edmund scowls at my words, but I expect him to do so. I turn to Pybba, weighing his response. It'll be far more telling. He doesn't grimace, but neither does he look overjoyed. Rudolf, on the other hand, grins with delight. Was I ever as young as him? Were the rest of my warriors? It seems impossible, and yet, we've had our reputation for longer than Rudolf's drawn breath, and back then, we must have been young. Well, they were. I was off, elsewhere, my brother leading them. What I concerned myself with is not really important.

"When?" Hereman asks.

"Now, mount up. Let's do this, and do it quickly. I'd like something to eat that's actually spent some time close to the fire."

Hastily, everyone mounts up, even Ælfgar. Some sleep and some mushrooms have reinvigorated him. Even I don't feel quite as achy as I did, although my body thrums with wounds that I've yet to discover.

"I'll take the rear," Icel informs me. He doesn't ask for permission. I want to refuse him, but I don't, perhaps because Edmund glimmers with rage at the audacity, or maybe just because I don't want to upset Icel.

"As you will," not so much as an agreement as an acceptance.

Above my head, far above the nodding heads of the trees, the day is moving quickly, the air temperature beginning to dip. Soon, I imagine, darkness will begin to fall, and this needs to be done long before that.

"Come on, boy," I aim Haden where I wish to go, only for Rudolf to come beside me, Dever angled differently.

"This way, My Lord. That way, you'll end up in the middle of the woods searching for your arse in the darkness."

A chuckle from Pybba assures me that others have heard Rudolf's cheeky response. If he were my squire, he'd be the one on his arse, but he's not.

"Were any of you going to fucking tell me?" I demand to know, only for more laughter to ripple around me.

"You're daft bastards," I huff, Haden eager to make his way in front of Dever.

"This way?" I point, just to be sure. Rudolf nods, eyes alight with mischief. "Then you have my thanks," I condescend to offer him, inclining my head, and now he stills in seriousness.

"Aye, My Lord." His voice is firm, no hint anymore of the strange trills and dips that affect all youths as they become men.

"Come on," I give Haden his head, fixating on a tree in the far distance, from which a thin line of smoke seems to emanate. Provided I keep my eyes on it, and I'll not go astray, not again.

Weapon to hand, I ride easily in my saddle, Hereman directly behind me. I spare one look, to make sure that everyone is obeying me, and my eyes alight on Samson. The horse eagerly follows those before it, his patchwork covering making it appear as though he moves from darkness to light, although he does nothing of the sort. I blink and clear my eyes of the illusion.

Turning back, I realise I don't need the trail of smoke to guide me anymore, because I can see the ship-men now. I watch how some bend low over games, while a few shelter around a fire, sticks showing where they roast whatever fish or beast they've managed to slaughter for their meal.

Rage ignites within me. Once more, the fuckers have made themselves at home in my kingdom. How dare the bastards? Do I travel to Denmark or further north? Do I rush to steal their land and resources, or do I remain in Mercia?

I would wish I had enough warriors to reverse these attacks, to make them worry for their families, their women and their grain and harvested goods. I would wish I had the warriors to do as much. But I don't, and even if I did, could I afford to risk their lives in such a way? I don't think I would.

I squeeze Haden tightly, encourage him a little with my heels, and soon he's spurred to a quick canter, and then ever faster. And yet, none of the ship-men seems to hear us. Only when Haden's gait changes, his legs outstretched as far as they can be in the woodlands, galloping towards the camp, does anyone even look up.

A cry of surprise reverberates around the enclosed space, panicked eyes seeking me out in the gloaming, the sky cut off overhead by the trees, despite the late season, the ground deeply matted with the leaf matter of years. It's too late for those who are supposed to stand a watch to take any sort of action. Haden leaps the small flames, and my seax takes the dazed ship-man to my right, his eyes wild, as my blade slices deep into his neck.

I leave the other three for those who come next, and direct Haden towards the central part of the camp, wildly hacking as I go. Fragments of blood flee through the air, the cold holding them for the blink of an eye, before allowing them to tumble to the floor.

Haden allows me to take two more ship-men on my right before I'm forced to slow him for fear of galloping straight through the camp, and out the other side.

I want whoever shelters at the centre of the camp, within the dirty, stained canvas, only a flood of ship-men have rushed to protect it. I can see nothing beyond their bodies, and certainly not whoever is within. The tip of the structure seems to taunt me, and I growl with frustration.

Those furthest from our point of entry, have abandoned all of their possessions, and rush to make it back to their ships, the dubious chance of survival, encouraging them to greater and greater speed. Haden follows them, even without my command. He knows what I expect from him. He's not exactly new to winning such attacks.

Another two men fall victim to my cuts and jabs, and then I'm directing Haden back toward the main body of the fighting.

Hereman has impaled a man on his long spear, but the swaying body refuses to slip free, even as his foe's eyes lose all focus. With disgust, Hereman discards the weapon in favour of his war axe, the long handle wobbling where it's wedged within the dying man, his hands gripped around it, while blood flows liberally. Rudolf has had more success, his blade moving in a whirl of motion, first one ship-warrior and then the next, tumbling to the floor.

But my focus is on the tent, and I'm not alone in being so consumed. Edmund and Icel are the same.

A good number of our opponents have all rushed to protect the inhabitant of the tent, even those who could have made a bid for freedom toward the ships. That arouses my intrigue. I also notice that here, at least, they have some shields, if not enough for one each.

But, I can't get to the canvas, not yet, because three ship-warriors face me. I have time to focus on the three men. I can see how strong they are, their upper bodies heavily muscled, necks wider than I might imagine, and fury in their eyes. They don't wear byrnies, but they do have thickened tunics, perhaps needed for the cooler weather, and whereas a shield-warrior might wear an emblem of Thor or Odin, perhaps even an inked image running along their arms, these men have none of the same embellishment. I think it a wise decision. Why risk a chain around their necks to weigh them down should their ship sink?

Lyfing grins at me from behind my foes, the imprint of the dent he obtained fighting Sigurd, just about visible on his iron helm, for all a seasoned blacksmith has hammered out most of the damage.

He lashes out with sword to take one of the ship-men keen to attack me, leaving me just the two. I spare a quick glance for Ælfgar and realise that he wars beside Gyrth. I hope the two look after one another. But then I focus on the task at hand.

I have two opponents. That doesn't overly concern me.

The one swings a long war axe toward Haden's front leg, and the other holds a seax he wants to stab at my legs. The pair of them broadcast their intentions so broadly that it's easy to counter them both. I force Haden closer to the seax ship-warrior, the war-axe man's swipe going wild. I thrust my seax handle into the first ship-warrior's nose, blood budding immediately, to drip over his gaping mouth, and it's easy to thrust the blade inside.

The scrape of iron over teeth is a sound few should hear. Abruptly, Haden rears, and I'm obliged to grip his reins tightly, my hands on the saddle, as he kicks out with first one leg, and then the other, to leave the first warrior a crumpled mess on the floor. It seems the fucker pissed off my temperamental beast. He really should have known better.

Edmund and Hereman direct their attention towards the mass of ship-men surrounding the tent. I hunger to join them, but Pybba and Ingwald are engaged in a heavy attack, Pybba somehow unhorsed, and I know that he must be the priority. Either that or Rudolf will never forgive me.

And Rudolf can't help his ally, not at the moment, as he expertly beats back a wild-eyed ship-warrior who's armed with both a seax and what seems to be clumps of horse manure. I admire his attempts, but he probably doesn't realise just how impervious to the stuff my young warrior has become, as they thump against his byrnie. I wouldn't be surprised if Rudolf could no longer scent the stuff.

"This way," I point Haden toward Pybba, and my horse eagerly rushes forward, not bothering to avoid the bodies he tramples. A cry of pain, and a sharp snap, and I turn aside and spit the bile from my mouth. I almost know a flicker of pity for the poor fucker.

Only then Pybba's cry of pain seems to bring everything to a standstill, all apart from me. Haden spurs to such a turn of speed that I'm aware of weapons flying slowly through the air, as others battle for their lives. Somehow, Haden makes it beyond the three opponents getting ever close to Pybba, turning to stand between the man and the enemy.

Sharp movements see me impale one of the men on my seax, even as Ingwald directs his sword into the back of one of the others. That leaves just one, or it should, but a sudden rushing sound, has everything snapping back into the real passage of time, and now there's another opponent to defeat. Somehow, he's closer to Pybba than I am.

"Mount up," I roar, fear making me shout so loudly, they probably hear me in Northampton. But Pybba can't mount up. His missing hand is normally no impediment, but one of the fuckers has managed to land a blow on his remaining, left hand. Even I can see how deep the wound is, the flow of blood making his hand too slick, the pain making it impossible for Pybba to retain the hold on his seax.

"Shit." I jump from Haden's back, a thwack on his back to force him to shield us. I don't like to risk my horse. Neither will I allow Pybba to be skewered by the prick whose found a spear. Trusting Haden to protect himself, I concentrate on Pybba.

He turns pain-hazed eyes my way, a look of utter despair on his lined face, even as he desperately scrabbles for Brimman's back.

I shake my head at the bastard who tries to deprive me of one of my most valuable warriors. I'll not have it. I really fucking won't.

"*Skiderik*," I bellow at the man, keen for him to see me and be distracted so that Pybba can either escape, or at least, attempt to, but the bastard is fixated on my injured warrior, giving no indication that he's even heard me.

"Bastard," I try, bending to flick a lump of green horse shit at his ear, but still the ship-warrior doesn't turn aside, even as the shit hits his neck.

"Is this really the hill on which you wish to die?" I demand to know, but of course, he doesn't understand my words, and they have fuck all impact on him.

I rush him then, seax on my weapons belt, not prepared to have it turned against me in the coming fight or to have the foe's spear any closer to Pybba or Brimman.

I thrust my fist into the ship-warrior's lower back, and as he buckles, I deal the same to the back of his neck, reaching around him with my left hand to wrestle the spear from him. Even as he falls to the floor, he keeps a firm hold on his weapon, and I admire him. It seems I was hoping for the sort of knee-jerk reaction that hauling an oar stops a man from doing.

Despite being splayed on the floor, the spear is still levelled toward Pybba, where he's held in place and unable to move, perhaps an enemy coming at him from the other side of Brimman as well, I just can't see.

"Fucker," I snarl, keen for the man to be dead, as I fumble for my seax, crouching low, and prepared to hold him with my knees if I must.

But he's just too damn fast. He rolls before I can react, seeming to bounce back to his feet, the spear a mere hands-width from Pybba's chest.

"I wish you'd just fucking die," I huff.

I lash out at his back, my seax eager to shed yet more blood, but even though I gouge a sizeable chunk from his byrnie, revealing a slither of skin, he still doesn't turn to defend himself.

"What the fuck have you got against Pybba?" I question, wishing that Pybba would move and that the bastard would turn and face me; that Ingwald would reach Pybba before me.

I think he'll skewer my friend, only then he thrusts back with his arms, and I jab my hand through the arch that his elbow makes. I hold it there so that even as he tries to land a killing blow, he can't. He jams my left arm as he attempts to stab forward, and it hurts like a bastard, because he's strong but, just as before, when he didn't react to my attempts to defeat him, it doesn't stop him from trying. Time and time again, he jabs forward, and I feel as though my arm is caught in a vice.

"Fuck's sake," and I manoeuvre from behind him so that even though I'm half bent, I can stab upwards, towards his face.

He doesn't even flinch, even as his other hand fumbles for the almost useless spear, and I finally manage to land a blow, on his broad, flat nose, so that blood erupts from it, fountaining down his chin. But the bastard doesn't even seem to notice. Certainly, it doesn't slow him down.

I can't risk looking up, to check on Pybba, but I sense he might have finally moved. I hope he has because this bastard isn't going to give up. I wish I knew why he's directed so much rage at Pybba, but it doesn't matter. All that's important is stopping him.

With my right hand, I again aim my seax at him, hunting for the flashing skin beneath his tunic. It reveals itself quickly, but I can't quite reach it, not wedged as my arm is.

"This better fucking work," I growl to myself, as I slip my arm free from the vice of his grip. I rush around to the front of him, angling my seax down so that it easily pierces the skin, and then burrows as deep as the hilt, and still, the bastard, able to move his trapped hand once more, lunges with the spear toward Pybba.

I half-turn, angle my elbow back into his chin, feeling the snap of his teeth crashing together, catching sight of a whirl of fabric, that I take to be Pybba, grateful when the relentless fuck finally stills in death.

Not, it seems, that I've killed the ship-man. Instead, he's skewered, having the same done to him as he tried to inflict on Pybba.

"Hereman," I shout, both wanting to thank and berate the lucky bastard, but he doesn't respond. And I'm not surprised. I don't know where they've come from, but the number of ship-warriors seems to have swelled.

"Get on Brimman," I hastily instruct Pybba, thrusting him upwards, trying not to look at the mess of his remaining hand.

"My thanks," he huffs, even as sweat beads his face, and an anguished shriek erupts from his lips as Brimman takes his weight, his arm brushing the saddle.

"We need to get you out of here," but as I hastily take in the view, I know it's impossible. While many of my warriors still surround the tent, the enemy has slipped in behind them. There are few enough of us not trapped, and I think they might be leaving Pybba alone because they realise he's half-dead anyway.

How the fuck did this go so wrong?

Mounting Haden, I flick my gaze around the clearing. We've made a good number of kills, and so far, all of my warriors yet live, although Lyfing and Gyrth are hard-pressed as they fight off at least seven ship-warriors, weapons glinting with menace.

Other than that, Edmund, Hereman, Icel, Ælfgar and Wærwulf are all trying to assault the ship-warriors who protect the structure at the centre of the camp, while Rudolf and Ingwald attempt to get to them, to add their skills to the attack. I can't call them back, it would be too risky, but neither can I watch them all being overwhelmed.

"Fuck," Pybba's face is white and drained, blood dripping from his wound.

"Here, I'll bind it." I reach across, and as gently as I can, I strap it tightly together using a piece of fabric from Pybba's saddlebags. The deep cut runs down the length of the back of Pybba's left hand, and I'm sure that the tip of his middle finger is missing. A lucky attack by the bastard, but one that's going to be painful to heal.

"Can you move it?" Sweat drips from his nose as Pybba tries to do just that, but his hand moves only a little, and his fingers tremble with the exertion.

"No, then." This leaves me in a quandary, and Pybba knows it. I need to support the rest of my warriors, but Pybba can't defend himself, not without the use of his hands. Not that he won't have some success with Brimman's hooves and his own feet.

"I'll be fine," he huffs, but I've not just risked my life to save his, only to abandon him again.

"No, stay with me. I'll fight for both of us."

"You can't fucking do that," Pybba mutters, but I can already see that the knowledge I won't abandon him has filled him with resolve.

"I can do what the fuck I want, remember. I'm your damn king."

"We're going to Lyfing and Gyrth. I'll kill the fuckers, and then we can help the others." Without giving him time to argue, I knee Haden forward, aiming for the smouldering remains of a fire, trusting Brimman to follow behind.

Lyfing and Gyrth fight side by side, and they're winning, but it's too damn slow. I need them now. I ride Haden into the fray, trampling one ship-warrior beneath Haden's heavy hooves, and taking another through the neck as he turns to aim a war axe at Haden's right front leg. I can hear Pybba attacking someone behind me, the huff of his air making me wince, because it's ragged with agony, and yet he persists, all the same, using his feet, and his elbows, and probably his head as well.

I sight the reaching hand of a foe coming from behind Lyfing and lash out with my seax, the satisfying sound of the weapon falling to the floor, followed by a heavier sound, and gushing blood falling through the air. I wince as I realise my blow was poorly aimed, and the warrior is now missing a hand. Taking pity on him, I persist, taking him with a well-aimed blow through his neck. It'll be quicker than bleeding out through his missing hand. I'd have hoped some fucker would have done the same for Pybba if we'd not been the victors.

By the time I've finished with the handless ship-warrior, Lyfing is checking on Pybba, while Gyrth is on the floor, stabbing down to end the life of one of his foes who twists in agony, his hands trying to hold his belly in. It seems I'm not the only one who takes no joy in prolonging the suffering of my enemy. Better dead, than half-dead. There's just more finality to it.

"Now we need to reach Ingwald and Rudolf."

I turn Haden to face the mass of ship-warriors, trying to determine how many of them there now are. Perhaps I was mistaken about there being more enemy than there was. Or maybe not. It's impossible to tell. It's possible I just felt overwhelmed with Pybba threatened.

Rudolf has managed to force a path through the shield-warriors. I almost wish he hadn't, because now there are more of my men with enemies at their backs as well as in front of them.

"What now?" Pybba asks.

"The shield-warriors don't want us to reach the structure. Look. They're all protecting it now. We can focus on that. Pick the bastards off one at a time. Pybba, stay close to me."

I ignore the searching look from Lyfing at my insistence that Pybba fights on. He should know that I have fuck all control over what my men decide to do. I'd like him to retreat. Chance would be a fine fucking thing.

"Let's get this done as quickly as we can." We've done nothing but leave a trail of bodies since we left Northampton, and it's far from over yet.

I slick my seax through my gloved hand, keen to remove as much of the sticky blood as possible. I grimace at the torrent that pours to the ground, the scent of the leaf-litter combining with it to make a smell that speaks only of the slaughter-house.

Pybba, as I knew he would, directs Brimman close to where Rudolf labours. I spare a glimpse for him, marvelling at his skills. He doesn't seem beset by fatigue, and more often than not, he lands his attack, even while turning Dever to prevent the ship-warriors from attacking his animal.

I choose the most awkward position, beneath the reaching arms of a low hanging branch, where it makes it difficult to swing my seax well.

Lyfing and Gyrth take the rear of the canvas, and then I lose sight of my men, my focus exclusively on hacking my way to join my warriors, relying on them to stay alive, until we can all fight side by side once more.

But I'm worn out by the constant battling. Haden lashes out with teeth and hooves, even on one occasion, thrusting his arse into one of the bastard's faces and emitting a foul-smelling fart that makes him gag and then cough. It's almost too easy to stab down, through the top of his exposed mane of brown hair. But I feel the strain in every part of my body.

Maybe I'm getting too old for this shit.

Perhaps it's time for me to sit in Worcester, with my ealdormen and bishops surrounding me, and direct other men to fight for the future of Mercia.

The sound of battle, of men and some women, fighting for their lives, slowly recedes from my consciousness, and my movements become instinctive. Thrusting, cutting, slicing, protecting my horse, and myself. Not that I remain unhurt. Far from it. I feel cuts open on my legs, particularly just above my high boots, and along my forearms, and even one fucker who manages to slice a chunk from my cheek, but I know I'm slowly diminishing the number who attempt to stop me.

And then I find myself with my seax dripping wetly down Haden's black and white side, both of us, chests heaving, but with no enemy to fight.

I risk removing my helm and under-cap, wiping the sweat and blood from my face, wincing as the rough fabric of my tunic brushes the cut, while I consider how the rest of my warriors fare.

Pybba still lives, thank fuck, and he fights side by side with Rudolf, kicking and spitting, and using his elbows to stun those who try and attack him. It must hurt like a bastard, but he doesn't stop.

Hereman and Edmund are close together, just a thin layer of ship-warriors to get through before they reach the tent the enemy have all been labouring to protect. Lyfing and Gyrth have no more than five warriors battling against them, while Icel and Wærwulf have only a few more. Ælfgar has retreated behind them, face white with pain, and I appreciate that he's

13

done all he can, for now. I can see where his byrnie has darkened with blood, and I hope the fucker hasn't done too much. My men. They'd fight even as their bodies wept their blood into the ground.

Only then, with such a thin band of the enemy to protect the solitary structure, does someone emerge from it, just as a piercing whistle echoes through the air. I glance to the person who's stepped from the now open doorway, even as I'm listening to see if the sound means anything. Are there more ship-warriors out there? Will they come running at the noise, or is it entirely unrelated?

I thrust my helm back onto my head, not prepared to take the risk, as I instruct Haden so that I can see the enemy more easily.

Who is it? I think I've never seen them before, but perhaps I have. It's impossible to tell when warriors wear their war gear. And certainly, they're dressed for battle. An elaborate helm covers their head. It glints both gold and silver, but more impressive are the bristles sticking from its crest. Not red, as my ceremonial helm which the bishops placed over my blond hair, but black as night, and they're much shorter. Yet even I can see the shape of the animal being depicted. An ugly boar, snout over the warrior's nose, with thick silver plates that cover the neck.

"Who the fuck is that?" I hear Pybba demand to know.

"I wish I fucking knew," I reply, licking my lips and thinking that whoever kills such a foe will be wealthy for the rest of their lives. The byrnie, rather than being made of leather, glints with the skills of a metalworker whose managed to weave iron as though it were no more taxing than stitching a collar, and the legs are sheeted in iron as well.

Whoever this is, they have the best equipment I've ever seen, and that's before I even consider the sword that glints maliciously from the weapons belt or the seax whose hilt is similarly covered with silver with an animal depicted on it. I can't make out the details from where I stand, but I'm sure it must be a boar as well.

The figure beneath the armour is strong and well-built, eyes glinting blackly as he surveys the scene before him, the hint of amusement playing over the small parts of the face that are visible.

I don't know who this warrior is, but they show no dismay at our endeavours, and that, even more than the immaculate warrior's garb send a shiver of worry down my sweating back.

He oozes confidence, and that can only come from believing a battle won, even before he's lifted his sword or seax. Even with so many of his ship-warriors dead, he still thinks he can win.

I knock aside an opportunistic slash with a blade from one of the shield-warriors who bleeds profusely from a wound that's opened up his tunic from shoulder to elbow. The man stumbles and falls to the ground. I don't know what killed him but imagine a poorly discarded seax or sword was to blame, that, or he carried another injury that I'd not seen. But I keep my gaze focused on the warrior before me.

He lifts his sword high, and my eyes travel the length of the weapon, even though I don't want to be distracted. The small skirmishes have all come to an end. Now all of my warriors face just the one man, and yet, there's no fear or unease on that face, as another piercing whistle echoes through the suddenly soundless woodland.

What is this?

"Who the fuck are you?" I demand to know when none of my warriors speaks, not even Edmund.

Slowly, the head turns and settles it's gaze on me, the superiority in such an action making me swallow down my question. Why would a warrior of such renown fight only with ship-men? Surely, such an outfit calls for mounted warriors, and more than a hundred people to protect them?

Only then do I detect the thunder of those missing mounted warriors, and I force my gaze away from the disdain of that contemplation, to peer through the tree trunks and try and determine from where the riders are coming. It's evident to me that they must intend to rescue their beleaguered leader. But from where?

Haden moves unhappily beneath me, his ears alert to the same sound, as do the rest of my warriors. My breath is harsh in my parched throat, my stomach complaining that mushrooms and berries are not enough to maintain this long-drawn-out fighting. Edmund meets my eyes, and I feel the heat of the searching glances of the others as well, but I'm watching someone else.

Icel has brought Samson to just the far side of the open space. His byrnie is sheeted in blood, his saddle shimmering darkly, his helm wedged slightly to one side, but it's the look on his face that's arrested me. I might have no idea who the fucker is that struts before me, like a peacock, but it's evident that Icel knows who it is only too well.

He slips from Samson's back, the horse not even seeming to notice, and takes calculated steps toward the warrior. And the Raider seems to welcome his scrutiny, a smile still playing around his lips. I swallow my unease, trying not to focus on the threat of more mounted Raiders coming toward us.

I know I should order my warriors together, perhaps even try to achieve a quick escape, but I don't. Icel consumes me, and I'm reminded of the words Edmund composed about my friend when he thought him dead. They've never seemed more apt than the way Icel reveals himself to me now.

He stands alone, but seemingly shrouded by more and more manifestations of himself. I see him as I first knew him, not young, but not aged either; as he has been when facing the usurpers of Mercia during the long hot summer, and then as he is now; changed but the same. I hear Edmund's words, even though he doesn't speak them.

"Bitter in battle, with blades set for war.
Attacking in an army, cruel in battle.
They slew with swords, without much sound.
Icel, pillar of battle, took pleasure in giving death."

"Jarl Olafr," Icel's knowledge of the man's name has no impact on him. It's as though the stranger expects others to recognise him.

"Who is he?" I demand of Icel, but I get no reply.

"Form up," I belatedly instruct, wanting my warriors closer to me, even if we linger behind Icel, prepared to support him because one thing is obvious. Whoever this man is, Icel has a personal connection with him, and this battle will be fought between the two of them. I dare not interfere.

"Riders are coming," Lyfing worries.

"I know, but if their leader is dead, it will not matter." Icel's voice rumbles with the sound of falling rocks, and although I feel myself the object of Lyfing's stare, I hold my tongue.

"Hurry the fuck up." Hereman has no such compunction, and yet Icel doesn't seem to notice the words. Neither does our enemy.

Jarl Olafr stands, surrounded by the dead and dying, all he once laid claim to becoming nothing, and yet he doesn't even seem to notice. Instead, his keen eyes are fixed on Icel, although I sense no recognition there. How then, can Icel know who this man is? And then I understand.

"Fuck," but it's too late. Icel has taken six steps forward, and with his seax ready, begins his approach. I don't expect him to rush. This is something that's been driving him on since his recovery. This is something he will savour.

"My Lord," Edmund questions my decision without even voicing it.

"This is Icel's fight," I assert. "Stay alert for the Riders." The instruction doesn't please my warriors, but nor does the clang of iron on iron as Jarl Olafr and Icel finally clash, sword to sword. The sound seems intensified between the tree branches far overhead, and the matt of bodies and leaves below, making it sound as though giants battle, and not mere men.

Icel moves quickly, his sword almost a blur, as Jarl Olafr counters each move with languid ease. I can't tear my eyes away. I have to watch.

Jarl Olafr has a shield to hand, and he uses it against Icel's every other blow, and in between, the two swords shimmer and strike one another. Icel has no shield, and I wish he did. Jarl

Olafr's has been bleached white, an image of a boar depicted in detail on it, and when Icel pauses between blows, Olafr thrusts it outwards, forcing Icel to sidestep, unbalancing him. But Icel is determined. No trace of exhaustion marks his movements, which are fluid and determined, even as his opponent attempts to unsettle him.

"My Lord," Rudolf shouts for me, and I flick my eyes toward him.

"Bollocks," Pybba's eyes have rolled in his head, and he slumps over Brimman's back. I make to go toward them, only for Lyfing to demand my attention once more, his voice filled with worry.

"My Lord, they're coming." I know what he means, but Pybba isn't fit to fight, whereas Icel does fight.

"Hereman."

"My Lord?" He surprises me by speaking softly.

"You have Icel's back," I inform him. Of all my warriors, he's the one with the most similar build to Icel. Should Jarl Olafr succeed in felling Icel, which I just can't envisage, Hereman will fill the void. I feel Edmund's seething frustration that I'd risk his brother, but really, what choice do I fucking have?

Pybba and Ælfgar are wounded. Icel engaged in a battle that will only end with his death or that of Jarl Olafr's, and I have few enough men as it is.

"Ælfgar, get the other side of Pybba. Assist Rudolf. Wærwulf, protect them all."

That leaves me with Edmund, Ingwald, Lyfing, and Gyrth. It's not many, not to counter the threat about to emerge through the gloom, but it's all I have to offer.

I force my warriors close to me, ensuring the rest are shielded. I vow then that we'll all ride from this fucking woodlands. All of us, or none of us, but all of us is my preferred option. Obviously.

"Fucking fools," Edmund curses, and I don't know whether he means us, or the Raiders, and I don't want to know either.

Behind me, I can hear Rudolf speaking to Pybba, trying to rouse him, and the response is weak, reedy and barely heard above the clash of weapons and the approaching thudding hooves.

I straighten my shoulders, prepare to once more wield my seax in support of all that I hold dear, and only then risk glancing to where the others look. I can see the horses coming towards us not by the glint of metal or the flash of piebald or chestnut, but rather by the darkening of the ground as they gather speed.

They don't come in a long line, but rather between the tree trunks, so that it all merges to double the number, and I can't look away, even as I hear Icel's grunts and his enemy's answering snorts.

"Kill them," I instruct, dredging resolve from deep inside me. I could curse my luck. I could demand to know why this is not easy? I could even rail at my God for sending so many of the cursed bastards to infect my realm, but what would be the fucking point?

I can only thwart what's happening. I can only do my fucking best, and then the riders are before us. Rather than screaming for my warriors to oppose the attack, I feel a furrow of consternation forming over my eyebrows, and I turn to Edmund, the question half on his lips already.

"What the fuck?"

Before anyone can reply, I perceive the sound I've been dreading, the cry of anguish from Icel, a rare enough occurrence, and one that I won't allow. Not even the realisation that Hereman has already hurried into the fray, as instructed, can stop me from rushing to his aid.

With concise movements, I dismount from Haden, and stride to where Icel is bleeding into the ground, desperate to get to his feet, a deep wound exposing too much of his thigh. The boar warrior exudes arrogance and confidence, even as Hereman blasts him with his sword, racing from left to right, from left to right.

"No," Icel screams, his face tight with pain where his helm's been knocked askew.

I offer Icel my hand, taking all of his weight as he stumbles back to his feet. I can't see the bone, in my swift examination of his wound, but the flood of maroon is enough to make me realise that Icel will struggle to stand straight even when it's healed.

Yet, his furious steps take him beyond me. To my amazed eyes, he lashes out at Hereman, hooking him around his upper arm and pulling him away, the action only just not resulting in Hereman being the next to feed Jarl Olafr's blade, as he batters the other warrior aside.

"What the fuck?" Hereman roars, and I move to restrain Hereman, one arm around his neck so that he has to stop fighting or risk being choked by my hold.

"I don't fucking know," I gasp. It's all I can say. "I don't understand. But Icel needs this."

"Fuck that," Hereman defies my orders, wriggling free from my grip because I'm distracted by Icel's current predicament. Hereman goes to Edmund's side. He shakes his head, spittle flying through the air, and we can all hear his words, even if he has only offered them to his brother.

"Fucking mad cunt."

I do not disagree with him, and I turn to meet Rudolf's horrified eyes. This is not our way. It has never been, yet Icel is once more attacking his opponent. His movements quicken, and while I watch, Jarl Olafr seems visibly to weaken. For a moment, I worry it's a ruse, but it isn't. It seems Icel isn't the only one to carry an injury.

Pybba calls weakly to me from where he too watches what's happening.

"My Lord, help him." But I shake my head.

"He needs this," I call, swallowing the distaste the words form in my mouth.

I've never seen such rage, such fury, such naked need to accomplish the death of another.

I've fought a lot of fucking bastards, all of them seeking my death, and yet, rage is never the way to go, not if you want to live through the battle. And what boils my piss, is that Icel knows this. If anything, he's the fucker who taught the most valuable lesson I've ever been made to learn.

Fight with skill, fight with precision, but not with the fury of a personal vendetta. It's why we've always managed to beat our enemy. They've always hated us, despised us for being better, for being meticulous with our movements, for killing as easily and quickly as we can.

But that's not what Icel is doing.

Yet, his opponent is faltering. The boar shield seems to rise only so high now; the sword blows that Icel thunders against his foe's blade, making the straining arm tremble. All the time, those swipes reach ever closer to their target of ending the man's life.

Only then, the thundering hooves that we've been hearing for some time come to a complete stop. Jarl Olafr finds some new incentive, his attack even speedier than before, his chest heaving beneath the weight of iron that he carries, and my ears pick up a conversation taking place behind me.

A conversation, not a battle.

I risk a glance, a smirk stealing over my face at those I encounter there.

They're not the fucking Raiders. It couldn't be further from what I thought. Instead of twenty or even thirty mounted Raiders, there are eleven Mercians, led by Wulfsige, a look of contentment on his face for finding his king. I'd go to him, give him my profound thanks, both for turning up just when we need him, and also for not being our enemy on mounts; only Rudolf shrieks my name.

"Coelwulf." The sound rings too loudly, seeming to repeat, even though Rudolf's mouth is closed as I twist my body, unsure what I'll see, but knowing it will be terrible.

And it is. Icel is down on the ground once more, his leg flailing uselessly beneath him as Jarl Olafr hammers him with a war axe, Icel's sword discarded on the ground. Blood and flesh pollute the air, and each blow makes me wince, even as I scurry toward the pair of them.

I can hear others doing the same, Hereman's voice the loudest of all as he rebukes, "the daft bastard." But I'm going to get there first, I know it. I was the closest, and I'm also the quicker of Hereman and me.

Icel's arms are in front of him, no longer attacking, but defending himself. I see his flesh open under the onslaught, bloody running freely down his arms, where he tries to protect himself, but his foe is getting closer and closer. Any moment now, I expect the killing blow to land, depriving me of Icel one more time, and this time forever.

I run so fast that I feel as though I'm almost out of control, hand on my seax, ready to counter the fucking bastard who batters against Icel. Only, it's all happening too quickly and too slowly. I see the war axe take more flesh from Icel's forearms yet, and then they slump to the ground, perhaps a muscle torn or wrenched apart, something so terrible, Icel can no longer prevent the attack.

His bloodied leg flails on the ground, as he attempts to find his feet, his boots moving in a mesmerising circle, but he can't get to his knees, let alone stand. He's too weak, and the enemy too strong, and then Icel arches backwards, the seax impaling his undamaged leg, and at that moment, I know what the Raider will do because Icel's neck is exposed, his helm almost touching the ground.

"Fuck," I huff, the sound spurring me on and on. There's only one option available to me, and I have to do it. If I don't, Icel will be gone, for all time, and I'm not about to allow that. Not when it's within me to stop it.

My seax in front of me still, held rigid against my chest, I thrust myself between Jarl Olafr and Icel, even as I hear Icel's cry of outrage.

I feel war fluid covering my hands, and know that my blade struck true, but suddenly there's too much blood, the scent sweet, my hands sticky. My head feels too heavy for me, and something is tugging at my throat, a pain so raw I have no words to explain it. I try to move my head, ensure that Icel is well, that

Jarl Olafr is dead, but I feel as though I'm being ripped in two, and my vision fades into spots.

I form words in my mind, but they don't make it to my lips.

And then I know nothing else.

CHAPTER 1

Three weeks earlier

"Where the fuck have you been?" My eyes rake in Icel, looking for wounds, and when I don't see any, wondering just what cuts he does have that we can't see. As far as he's concerned we left him to die, or rather, Edmund and the rest of the men who travelled with him, did. What he thinks about me, I have no idea.

"It's a long story," Icel rumbles, and I try not to watch my Aunt as she grimaces at me from behind Icel, her eyes fierce, her lips tight and filled with frustration for my clumsiness. It seems this isn't the correct question to be asking.

"I'm overjoyed to see you," I try instead, infusing my voice with the warmth that's been missing since his death, but even this earns me a gentle shake of her head. I try not to focus on the lines around her eyes or the silvery-grey threads of her hair.

What does she want me to say to him? I have so many questions, all of them seem urgent, but perhaps they're not in the grand scheme of things. Maybe it just better to accept his return and leave it at that.

"Come, we should get inside." In the distance, I can see that the Raiders have been dispensed. All that's left to do is pick over the rapidly-cooling bodies, taking anything of value. I take a step toward where the warriors of Northampton guard the new, hidden doorways, only I've forgotten about my hard-won injuries, and I stagger, pleased when Rudolf catches me before I tumble to the ground. What a sight that would have been? I can see how my Aunt would have reacted.

"Come on, old man," Rudolf comments, and I'd cuff him around the head, but fuck, it's good to be alive to be called 'old.' I'd not appreciated, before, just what it truly meant to live such a long life. All those young men I've slain, taken before their time. It could so easily have been me.

"Did Haden make it?" I ask then, remembering my beloved mount because I would wish he were here to sustain me, rather than my aching legs.

"Yes, looking sorry for himself." Rudolf's voice tells me all I need to know about the state in which Haden arrived at Northampton. I spare a thought for that daft horse. He's the most disloyal loyal animal I've ever met. I consider whether he knows to chastise himself for leaving me behind, or whether he's really not at all concerned. I hope for the former, but I imagine it'll be the latter. Certainly, he'll have made an entrance, no doubt striking fear into all those who witnessed him arrive under his own control.

Behind me, I can hear the soft murmur of conversation between the reunited men, and I know a moment of fear. Should I have left Icel and Edmund alone? What will they say to each other? Will Icel blame Edmund? Will Edmund still think himself culpable?

I turn, forgetting that Icel has his mount, and immediately, I'm bumped from behind, by the animal, no doubt keen to return to the stables and the promise of warmth on this cold day.

My Aunt has remained behind. I don't know if this is her first battle site. She's healed the sick all of her life, but has she ever seen the carnage of the dead and dying, those who have no chance of survival? I pause, consider the best way to prevent her from peering too closely at the marbling corpses, the blue-tinged veins of death more prominent than in life. It's not a pretty sight; it has never been.

"Pybba," I hiss his name, not wanting to draw attention to my worry, and he grunts at me as though I disturb him from some great reverie, his wise eyes seemingly far away.

"My Aunt?" I state, eyebrows high as I jut my chin toward her, and he understands immediately, even though there's incredulity in his understanding.

"I think she knows herself well enough," Pybba offers, not wishing to be distracted from his reverie, but I grit my teeth, all the same.

"At least stay with her. Just in case."

"Fine," Pybba condescends, clearly unhappy with the instruction, as he drops back to the rear of the line of my warriors.

Rudolf wisely keeps his opinions to himself at my side, even as my eyes take in Edmund and Icel. Icel stares straight ahead; his eyes fixed on the tall wall surrounding Northampton. Edmund merely focuses on his feet, his shoulders hunched, his misery clear to see. I could do with Hereman at his side, but he's not there. Fuck. I'm overjoyed to have Icel returned to me, but it's evident it's only going to cause more problems, all of them entirely new.

And then we're walking down the steep ditch, weaving a path through the sharpened stakes and puddles of water that glisten darkly from the depths, hinting at all sorts of crap. I feel my legs teetering, the muscles too tired to support me down the sharp incline and then up the other, equally steep, side. But, I have to go that way, because that way lies admission to Northampton itself.

Then I'm being directed toward the small tunnel that's been used to come to my assistance. I try to focus on it, but I'm exhausted. Rudolf is slightly in front of me, and because the tunnel is so narrow, the light of day is momentarily blocked, and it's as though I walk through daylight to dusk.

All the same, I can see the ingeniousness of the hidden tunnels for myself. I want to stay and explore the engineering of the secret entrance but now isn't the time. It really fucking isn't. Glancing above my head, I see gleaming, brown mud, but also thick pieces of Mercian oak. They must hold the upper layer of the defences clear of the carefully constructed gap. To either side of the tunnel walls, a thin slab of stone has also been worked into the mud, and I confess, it feels safe and secure, for all it is fucking strange. Perhaps I wouldn't want to linger there, with the worry of the weight of such construction work over my head, but I'm grateful for its existence.

Walking once more into the daylight of Northampton, my arrival is greeted with cheers, and they startle me. How many warriors are there within Northampton? Were they all here when I left to chase down the Raiders in Grantabridge?

It feels as though at least fifty men cheer my return, all of them dressed for war, weapons belts gleaming and byrnies shimmering in the morning sunlight.

I raise my aching right arm to take the acclaim, even as I turn, trying to determine how the tunnel can be closed from the inside. Surely, they've not left it open, relying only on the fact that any enemy wouldn't know it was there? Only people are waiting to greet me. I'm forced to turn aside, but I vow I'll look later. I need to know. I need to understand how such ingenuity functions.

"My Lord King," a grizzled man calls out to me. His right cheek shows a long-healed wound, but the gash must have been deep, and it's puckered-pink and angry, even now. No doubt he has a lover who delights in tracing such a mark of honour when they lie curled around one another, on a winter's night.

"What's your name?" I call to him, surprised by the fatigue so evident in my voice.

"Gundulf, My Lord King."

"Tell me, where did you earn your scar?"

"A battle, in the east, against the bastard Raiders."

"Then you have my thanks for keeping Mercia safe." And he beams, showing that his two front teeth are also missing.

More and more men, and more than a few women, also call my name, and I wish I could stop and speak to them all, but Rudolf's grip on me is growing ever tighter, and I know I need to sit down, perhaps lie down, probably sleep, before I fall. What a fucking fine sight that would be – the Mercian king, victorious against impossible odds, only to stumble over his own damn feet.

"The king will make time to speak to you all, when he's rested," Rudolf surprises me by shouting, his voice joyful, for all I must be a heavy weight for him where I press against his shoulder. Immediately, the press of bodies steps backwards, clearing a space for me, so that I can limp onwards, to where, if my memory serves me, the main hall is located.

There's a sudden hush. I turn, surprised, only to be greeted by the image of my Aunt on her horse, Icel in front of her, walking his beast forwards. I would gasp as well if I didn't know who she was. She rides with all the poise of a queen. She's such a fucking natural at this, and I can't deny that I'm envious. It speaks of her excellent birth and even better upbringing. I had the right birth, but I became a man in very different ways. This is all so strange to me, even now, even when I've worn Mercia's warrior-helm and taken the acclaim of the bishops, the ealdormen and the nobility.

"Come on," Rudolf huffs, a thread of annoyance in his voice, and I turn aside, allow him to guide me. It suddenly feels so far, and I wish I had a horse to ride. In fact, I should check on Haden; I know I should.

"He is well, My Lord, I assure you," Rudolf complains when he realises my intent as I try and hobble toward the stables. "He's well cared for, and you need the same. Stop being such a stubborn bastard."

Abruptly, Edmund is on the far side of Rudolf.

"You look like you're more likely to fall on your face than make it inside," Edmund huffs. I can't see his face, because he's supporting my left arm. I wish I could. How must he feel on seeing Icel returned to him? I wish I could ask him, but I won't, not where Rudolf and his eager ears might hear.

"Make way," Pybba is abruptly in front of me, no doubt dispatched by my Aunt. The doors of the great hall are open, beckoning me inside, a wave of heat threatening to undo me, but then I remember the wounded and stop my slow forward motion.

"They're inside," Pybba announces, again understanding my thoughts. "All of them. Inside, being tended to, which is where you should bloody be." His voice is gruff, and I glance at him, but he avoids my eyes. I thought we'd resolved our problems. I'm not sure why he's being so difficult.

"All of them? How is Gardulf? Leonath? Where's Hiltiberht?"

"Will you just get your arse inside, and then all your questions will be answered," Edmund wheezes with annoyance. I glance at him with surprise. Rudolf isn't struggling anywhere near as much.

"I'm going, I'm going," but I'm so slow. Everything seems to hurt, and that's just right now, with the heat of battle still thrumming through my body. I dread to think what it will be like when I've slept. In fact, no, I don't dread it, I know it'll be fucking awful. Maybe I'll stay awake. Sleep is for the weak. Perhaps as Mercia's king, I can cast aside such requirements.

Above my head, the sunlight dims, and then the smell of the hearth reaches my nostrils, and I shiver.

"Fuck," I complain. Rudolf feels the movement and looks at me with consternation.

"I'll be fine," I offer, although I don't know if I will be. It's not like me to feel the after-shock of battle, but then, while I face each attack as though it might be my last, I genuinely thought that this one would be my last. There's nothing like facing my demise to make me weak and pathetic.

"Here you go." I slide from Rudolf and Edmund's shoulders, and on to the waiting stool. My eyes rake the room, and I see prone bodies, and also a few looking at me in surprise, Hiltiberht amongst them. I try and find a smile for him.

"Fuck, don't do that, you'll scare the boy." I don't appreciate Edmund's comment.

I notice my Aunt has beaten me, as if I needed a greater proof of how slow I've made my way here.

"Thanks," I mutter. But she's busy, her hands checking my face, and my chest, and even crouching down to run her hands down my legs, without so much as a wince for the state of my ruined trews.

"You need to get all this off," and she looks not at me, but at Edmund and Rudolf. Rudolf jumps to do as she bids, trying to tug my tunic from me, his eagerness a shock. My arms feel as though they weigh heavier than the rest of my body, and Rudolf struggles.

"You might do better to cut it free," I advise, my voice laboured. I swallow and taste only old blood, salt, and sweat.

"Drink this," my Aunt commands. The wooden beaker is filled with something noxious, glimmering with all the appetite of the latrine pit, but I swallow it. She won't take any complaints, so I'm not going to waste my breath. I try not to gag, even as the warmth of her mixture starts to percolate through to my tired limbs. I hand the beaker back. Edmund takes it, not my Aunt, and I realise I'm missing something, but I'm too damn tired to care.

"Lift your arms," Rudolf huffs, and I see he's determined not to cut my tunic.

"I am," but I'm really not.

"Help me," and Edmund rolls his eyes, refusing to accept my frailty, just as I was surprised by his, before roughly grasping my hand.

"Fuck," I complain.

"Seriously," Edmund's head is abruptly before me, his remaining eye flashing with ire. "Seriously?"

"Yes, fucking seriously," but my words are muffled as the tunic covers my head, and that's probably for the best. Damn bastard.

When the light of the fire once more floods my world, I'm conscious of six or seven sets of interested eyes looking at me, most of them with a wince of sympathy on their faces.

"How did you get that?" Rudolf points and I look down. My chest is crisscrossed with shallow cuts.

"Well, I was fighting quite a few warriors," I shrug and then groan. Even such a small movement hurts like fuck.

"A few?" Rudolf's voice is filled with a strange combination of respect and disgust. I would smile at him, but I remember Edmund's warning about my previous attempt.

"Well, were you watching?"

"No, not all of it. I was a bit busy, escaping and stuff," Rudolf huffs, but it's with annoyance and frustration. I can't imagine it was easy on any of them to realise what had happened and to appreciate that despite all their recent and ancient oaths to the contrary, they left me there, to fend for myself. It doesn't matter that I wouldn't have wanted it any other way. They need to learn to live with what happened.

"Out of the way," my Aunt bustles between Edmund and Rudolf, her lips rigid as she concentrates. I expect no sympathy from her, and I don't get any.

"Warm water," she calls over her shoulder, and I wish I knew who obeyed her words, but I can't see.

I shiver again.

"Get him a cloak, for when I'm finished with him," my Aunt also commands, while Rudolf is busy trying to undo my boots. I try to lift my legs, to aid him, but it's impossible.

"A proper mess," my Aunt objects, peering at something on my left arm. I try to turn my head, to see what catches her attention, but she firmly grasps my chin and pulls my head back to the front.

"Stay still," she hisses, holding my eyes with hers, to ensure I understand the instruction.

Edmund glances at me appraisingly.

"Well, I think you win the competition for the most wounds on a man who lived through an attack."

"Is there a prize?" I ask, hissing again, as my Aunt begins to clean my wounds, the pinch of the warm, slightly salted water, assuring me that I'm in for an unpleasant time of it. She's efficient but never gentle.

I catch Pybba's eyes, and Icel's, and also Ealdorman Ælhun's.

He nods at me, and I grunt because I don't want to move my head. He too watches me with respect.

"What's happening?" I ask Edmund.

"Fucked if I know. I'm here, tending to you."

"Who's on the defences?" I demand to know, only my voice lacks all force, as I try not to wince at my Aunt's less than tender ministrations.

"Wulfsige and his men, but there are no Raiders left. They're all dead. I don't think any lived to return to Grantabridge."

"How many warriors are here?" I ask Ealdorman Ælhun, but he's already moved away, no doubt busy with his own injured.

Rudolf takes pity on me.

"Your Aunt brought more men with her. Northampton now boasts nearly a hundred warriors."

"So many?" the number astounds me, but I'm impressed that Rudolf has already discovered so much in such a short space of time.

"How long was I fucking out there?" I demand to know.

"More than long enough to earn a reputation for being Mercia's mightiest warrior," my Aunt advises, but her tone assures me that it's far from a compliment. "And mind your language." I expect a slap on my arm, but my Aunt seems to realise that would be too cruel, and instead taps her finger on my nose, and my eyes cross as I focus on it.

"Remember that not everyone needs to express themselves in such a way."

So much for me being Mercia's mightiest warrior when my Aunt can chastise me in such a way. I see the smirk on Edmund's face, and glare at him, trying to quell him with just a look, belatedly realising that he'd already been watching his tongue.

"How are the others?" I'm sure they should be receiving all this fuss, and not me. I'm just shattered, and with a few cuts here and there. The bruises will come later.

"Gardulf and Leonath are settled. Gardulf needs sleep, Leonath needs to be watched carefully, but Siric is doing that. He knows much of what needs to be done. The others are all being stitched up or encouraged to sleep. Really, nephew, of them all, you're the most difficult."

Again, Edmund smirks, but my Aunt must realise what's happening, and her head snaps around, fixing him with her icy glare. The smile slides from his face, to be replaced with mock concern, and I wish I could punch him—damn bastard.

"Where did you find Icel?" I ask my Aunt, but she shakes her head.

"That's not my story to tell," and I know I'll get no answer from her, or seemingly from Icel. He's settled some distance away, with Pybba at his side, Penda leaning forward, head rested on his elbows, while the 'old men' talk. Tatberht joins the small group. I consider sending Rudolf to listen, but I need him here, with me, although it should be Wulfhere.

"Where's Wulfhere?" I ask, suddenly realising that I've not yet seen his face.

"With your damn horse," Rudolf complains. "Haden is as difficult as you are."

"Was he wounded?" I'm half rising, even though my knees shake, and my Aunt manages to push me down with only the firm touch of one hand. That shouldn't be possible.

"Not really, just, well, you can see for yourself. But he's fine, just, well, I would say sheepish," Rudolf seems to be struggling to explain the problem.

"Sheepish?"

"Yes, that's the best way to describe it, sheepish. I think he realises that he left you behind."

"Ah," I'm not entirely sure how to react to that.

And then I'm distracted by my Aunt being handed a long needle, thread tangling from it.

"What the fuck's that for?"

"Language," she snaps once more, and then says nothing else, as she moves behind me, and I grit my teeth, ready for the horrific sensation of my skin being knit together.

I focus on my men. Those who've still been busy with the aftermath of the battle are making their way into the hall, their eyes seeking me out, perhaps to reassure themselves that news of my survival is correct, before finding somewhere to congregate, checking everyone is well. I notice Sæbald, Ordheah, Oda and Lyfing as they join Wulfstan, Eahric, Wærwulf and Goda. I consider where the others are.

"How's Hereman?"

"Sleeping."

"What about Siric?"

"His arm has been bound. I hope it will heal."

"What of Gyrth?"

"He needs to rest."

"But does he know who he is yet?"

"Well, he knows who I am," my Aunt confirms, as though that's the most important thing.

"What of Beornstan?"

"I've stitched his wound. It needs to be kept clean, but it should knit together well."

"And what of Ingwald?"

"I've bound his foot, after making sure the wound was clean. Again, it should mend, but he'll need to learn to walk again. Losing a toe is no small wound to grow accustomed to."

"And Penda?"

"Again, his wound has been cleaned, but I can't stitch it, not so close to his eye. He'll need to be careful with it."

"What of?" But my Aunt cuts me short. I can sense her ire, even though she's still behind me.

"I've tended to all of your men. They should all, with the correct care, recover. For some of them, it will not be quick or easy, but they shouldn't lose their lives. Now, stop asking questions, and let me attend to your wounds, or you'll be the one with wound rot, and then it won't matter about the others, will it, because they'll have no one to lead them into battle and worry about their little scratches and cuts."

I snap my mouth shut, determined not to ask more questions. Rudolf settles on a bench before me, licking his lips, before pouring himself water and drinking deeply. He wisely holds his tongue as he watches his oath-lord, and king, being berated as though he were no more than a child who'd shit himself because he's not learned to control himself yet.

"How did you do it?" Rudolf asks instead, and I know he means 'stay alive', but I have no real answer for him.

"I wasn't about to give up," I would shrug, but I remember my Aunt's labours behind me and don't. I know she'd blame me if her stitches weren't straight, or needed to be redone.

"Did you honestly believe you could beat them all?" he asks, his curiosity compels him to speak, and I shake my head, cursing as it rings with the movement.

"No, but I wanted to give it a, *damn*, good go," I hesitate before damn, using it to replace the word I wanted to use, but realise I daren't.

"Why didn't you call us back, to protect you?" Edmund shakes his head at Rudolf's questions. It amuses me that Edmund knows me well enough not to ask. He might well question all of my decisions, but he knows better than to try and understand my motivations.

"I couldn't allow everyone to die when they were truly only after my death."

Rudolf nods, as though my argument makes sense, but then his lips purse, and he stands.

"I'm going to check on Wulfhere," he advises, and I watch his slight build wind a path through the crowded hall.

"I think you may have lost your hero worshipper," Edmund comments. "I think even he realises what a reckless bastard you are."

My Aunt hisses but doesn't chastise Edmund and my eyes open wide with outrage. Edmund grins, and then a long groan fills the hall, and he's on his feet.

I would recognise Hereman's tone anywhere.

"That man can't be felled by anything," my Aunt complains, standing in front of me, hands on her slim hips.

"Penda," she calls the lad to her side, and he skips to her side, only a slightly wistful look on his face for being called away from the chattering 'old men.' I eye his wound. It has been cleaned well. The skin already seeming to knit together. Just another example of the advantage of youth.

My Aunt makes herself busy with a selection of herbs, steeping them in a wooden beaker of gently steaming water on the table she's evidently claimed as her own.

"Take this to Edmund. Ensure Hereman drinks all of it. Don't let him spit any of it out."

The lad nods eagerly and scampers away. I admire his litheness. In fact, no, I'm jealous as fuck, but I hold my tongue.

"We need to check your legs," my Aunt states, and I peer down at my bloodied, stained and ripped trews. "I'll just cut them loose," she explains, handing me the cloak to drape around my naked shoulders, and no doubt to protect my modesty. Not that seeing me naked would surprise her. She's not made a name for herself as a skilled healer by refusing to look at the bare flesh of a man or a woman.

"When did you arrive?" I think I might get an answer to that one question.

"With your warriors," she confirms, the sound of her knife cutting through my trews almost making her words inaudible.

"Why did you come?" I'm determined to try my luck now.

"I came with Icel." That doesn't answer my question, not at all. "And I brought more warriors. You'd been gone a long time. I wanted to see what was happening for myself." This sounds more like my Aunt. "You're lucky I arrived when I did."

"How's Werburg?"

"She'll recover, in time. She's a feisty woman. I approve of her, but no woman should ever endure what she's been through."

"Does she remain in Kingsholm?"

"Yes. She'll probably never leave."

My legs are bare before me, and even I wince at the number of jagged cuts, and bruises already forming. I feel as though everything hurts, and that's because every part of me has been attacked in some way.

"You've been bloody lucky," my Aunt cautions, and I wait for her argument about how it's unseemly for the king to be involved in such a battle, but she remains silent. Her hands and cloth are busy, cleaning all of my cuts, checking that they're not about to become infected, while I huddle inside my cloak, feeling vulnerable, exposed as I am for everyone to see.

"There, you'll mend. Now, drink this," and she hands me another beaker of the foul mixture, but as I'm no longer shivering, I knock it back quickly, trying not to gag.

"Find some clothes, and then get some sleep. You'll ache like a bastard tomorrow," she informs me, and my mouth hangs open, as she winks at me, a rare smile transforming her into a woman thirty years younger. Damn her.

"I have more patients to attend. Summon your squire if you want anything else."

What I want is to stand and walk amongst my wounded men, but I know I can't. Not yet.

"My thanks, it's good to see you."

"Yes, I'm sure it is." I watch her walk away, and only then does Icel lumber towards me. I watch him keenly, noting as I do that his black beard is rimmed with iron now. It seems we've both transformed in our time apart.

I'm not sure I'm ready for this conversation yet, but I do want to know what's happened to him since I last saw him. It feels like years ago but was only months; long months when I feared him dead and lost to me.

"My Lord King," he bows to me, and I swallow back my immediate objection. He didn't witness my coronation; perhaps he needs to do this.

"Icel, sit with me. We should talk." But Icel looks away, refusing to meet my eyes.

"It doesn't need to be of anything important, if you don't want," I offer that, even though I can feel my curiosity burning inside me.

His vast shoulders shrug, but he does sit on the seat that Rudolf's vacated.

"There's little to talk about, and none of it important. I'm just pleased to be reunited with you and the rest of the men."

"You went to Kingsholm?" I think he could at least tell me this.

"I went for my horse." His eyebrows are high as he makes the statement, and I feel the slither of a smile playing with my lips.

"Well, Samson has missed you."

"They tell me that Edmund was riding him."

"Yes, for a while. His horse was stolen from him, but Jethson was quickly found."

"Hum," his response offers me no way to extend the conversation, and I can see what he's thinking. We found Jethson, but not him.

"You should put some clothes on," Icel instructs me, already standing to move aside.

"Icel, sit, talk with me. Tell me how I did in the battle?"

He hesitates, and I think he'll go, but then he sits again.

"As I said, I've fought similar battles in the past, I've been overwhelmed by a far superior force. I confess I came away with injuries similar to yours." He points his chin toward my chest. "But I killed the enemy rather than let them ride away."

"I thought no one survived?" I'm looking around, trying to decide who I can ask about Icel's assertion.

"I believe someone escaped," Icel's tone doesn't broker an argument.

"Then we'll need to prepare."

"For what?" his forehead is wrinkled in thought.

"Well, the Raiders won't let it end like this? Will they? They'll come at us again."

"They surely can't number enough to mount an attack on a settlement of this size, and with defences such as these?"

"I killed Jarl Guthrum's sister, and maybe a brother or uncle as well. I can't imagine the jarls will let that go without a response."

Icel stills at my words, a momentary reaction, and yet I see it all the same. I lick my lips. I don't want to push Icel to speak of his time away from me, but I'm curious. Has he been fighting with the Raiders? Was he healed by them, or is his survival pure luck, and it's simply taken him this long to be well enough to ride to Kingsholm.

"Then, yes, you should probably prepare for some sort of retaliation, but do you truly think they'll attack Northampton? I've never seen a place so well defended before. They can't attack via the river, or over the bridge, and they can't get through the stout defences of the mud wall, ditch and ramparts."

"Do you think that would stop us?" I ask him, made curious by his belief that we're safe. I wouldn't expect him ever to believe such a thing.

"No, but I don't think we'd try and attack somewhere so well fortified, not when we could merely launch an assault elsewhere, and draw them out."

This was my intention when I hunted down the Raiders. Is it likely that they'd reverse the tactic on us? It's not impossible, I suppose.

"I don't want them to go elsewhere. I want them to come here."

"Yes, but what you want, and what you get are rarely the same thing." And I concede that Icel is correct.

"They tell me that Eoppa died. That his body is still out there, unburied."

"Yes, it is. We couldn't bring him back. Not when we were being hunted."

"I'll go and get him," Icel rumbles, but I'm shaking my head.

"You can't, not when there's the potential for retaliation."

"I'll go alone, risking only Samson and myself, and one other horse, to bring back his body."

I swallow heavily. This sounds like something that Icel isn't asking my permission to do. He will go whether I agree or not.

"His horse is missing as well. I imagine Poppy will be close. Find her, bring her back."

"My Lord King," and Icel bows his way from me, and I watch him go, with more than a flicker of unease. Icel is, well, changed. And I don't much like this new Icel. I want the old one back, the one who would never have asked for such a task. That I understand it, doesn't help. Doesn't he know that we went back for him, but that he was no longer there?

"Fuck," I complain, reaching forward for more water, only for my cloak to slide down, and my newly stitched back to painfully twang. But it's not those things that cause the true grievance. No, it's Icel. I wish he'd not asked for such a duty. I yearn for him to tell me everything that's befallen him while we've been apart. But desiring something won't make it fucking happen.

I look around the room. Men and women watch me, as I struggle to cover my nakedness, their eyes raking in my bruised and bloodied body. Perhaps I should expose it to them, show them all what fighting for Mercia truly entails, but I don't believe any of them don't understand the burdens we've placed on ourselves.

I wish I didn't feel so weak, but I do. I need to sleep. I know it, but there's too much to do.

And then Rudolf walks into the hall, his eyes wide, as he leads Wulfhere before him, coming to a stop in front of me. Something about his stance alerts me to the fact I've erred in some way.

"Did you give Icel permission to ride out?" Rudolf's whisper is not a whisper at all and edged with fury.

"He didn't ask for my consent," I try and deflect, wary. "But I didn't refuse him, no."

"Fucking hell, My Lord King, don't you know."

"Know what?" I ask, but Rudolf doesn't have the time to answer, because Pybba is before me, all puffed up and filled with bile, and I wish I'd known more before Icel spoke to me. Why didn't my Aunt talk to me if there was some huge problem? What was with the evasiveness?

"Where the fuck is Icel going? He can't go out there, alone. Don't you know anything?"

"Pybba, talk to me. I don't understand. Tell me what's happening."

"This is fucking ridiculous," and Pybba storms from my side.

"Where the fuck has he gone?"

"After Icel," and Rudolf dashes away, his legs faster than everyone else's.

"What the?"

"What's happening?" Edmund is before me.

"I wish I knew," and I fling my hands up high, forgetting about my injuries.

"Bloody bollocks," I protest, but there's no one to hear me because Edmund has gone as well.

"Wulfhere," I beckon the lad to me. He comes closer, and I note the vivid bruising across his nose. It must hurt like hell.

"My Lord," he speaks deferentially.

"What's happening?" I demand from him. I wish I could bloody stand. I wish I weren't half-naked.

"I'm not really sure," Wulfhere confesses. "I've been with Haden, My Lord. He took some settling."

"You have my thanks for that. Good lad. Could you? Would you mind going to the stables, or wherever Icel, Rudolf and Edmund have gone, to find out what's happening?" Wulfhere looks unsure, but then stands tall and bows to me, formally, taking my words as an order, not a request.

"Of course, My Lord. I'll return shortly."

I watch him weave a path through the mass of men and women, my lips curled in envy.

"What's all this?" Tatberht settles before me, his gaze fixed on Wulfhere's retreating back.

"I wish I fucking knew. Icel wants to retrieve Eoppa's body, and now the others have run off as though I've done something wrong."

"So you don't know then?"

"Know what?"

"Ah," and the older man looks at me, almost with pity in his remaining clear, blue eye.

"Icel."

"What of him?"

"He's sworn a blood vow."

"To do what?" Although I have a sneaking suspicion.

"To kill the Raiders. He's not going for Eoppa. He's going to Grantabridge."

"What, alone?"

"Aye, My Lord. Alone. Your Aunt has managed to keep Icel close with careful management of him. She won't thank you for this."

"How was I supposed to fucking know?"

"Well, you're the king. Aren't you, omnipresent, or something like that? Is that the word?" Tatberht looks at me for confirmation, but I don't know either.

"What does that mean?"

"That you know everything, or see everything, or hear everything. I don't know. It's something like that. The holy men say it about their Lord God."

"I'm only a bloody man. I've only just bloody got here."

"Be that as it may, you should still have thought a little more."

I don't much like being lectured to by Tatberht, and I think he realises.

"Can you go and stop him?"

"I could try, but, surely, those three will manage."

"Well, could you go and check?" Tatberht ambles to his feet.

"Aye, My Lord. I'll do what I can."

"Sæbald," I find him amongst the crowd of others and raise my voice to summon him. With Wulfhere gone, I need to do it myself.

"My Lord. You look like shit."

"Thank you. Can you go after the others, to the stables? I think they're trying to stop Icel, and I want them to succeed."

"Stop him from what?"

"Leaving. On his own. Hurry. I want him back."

"I'm on the way," Sæbald confirms, but he moves so slowly. Again, I wish I could stand. In fact, I brace my hands on the side of the stool and try to lever myself upwards. Sweat immediately glistens on my forehead, and before I know it, the stool totters, forcing me to one side, and I land on the floor in a welter of noise and pain, my air pushed from my body.

"Fuck."

"My Lord King," my Aunt's voice echoes her outrage, at my position and my words.

"Help me up, please, help me up. Icel is trying to leave."

"What? And you gave him your blessing?" Even my Aunt sweeps from me without even trying to help me up from my position on the floor.

"For fuck's sake," I explode. I'm the damn king. Why does no one listen to me, or even offer me the respect I'm due?

"My Lord?"

"Ah, Penda, can you help me. Please."

"Of course, My Lord?" His young forehead is wrinkled with consternation, but at least he doesn't dash off and leave me floundering on the floor.

It takes too much effort, but eventually, I'm seated once more, the sheen of sweat festooning my body, the cloak discarded because I'm just too damn hot.

"What was Icel talking to your grandfather about?"

"Oh, it was a bit strange," Penda confirms, handing me a beaker of water, as he absent-mindedly tidies the mess I've made, picking up bits of herbs that my Aunt's left behind. He rolls a band of linen around his hand, and I appreciate that this isn't the first time he's helped my Aunt.

"Yes, but what was it?"

"He spoke of waking from his wounds. He spoke of revenge, and sorrow and, I confess, My Lord, I found him very much altered, not at all the man I remember from Kingsholm, although that's perhaps because I'm too young to have ever truly known him."

"And what did Pybba say to him?"

"He told him to bide his time, not to worry because you were hale and that he should speak to you before he decided anything."

"And what did Tatberht say?"

"He advised him that revenge wasn't always as rewarding as he might think. They both seemed to be trying to talk him out of something, although I'm not sure what."

"Bloody bollocks," I explode. Why didn't my Aunt warn me when she was tending to my wounds? All this could have been avoided then.

"My Lord, are you okay?" Penda's voice is rough with concern, his hand on my lower arm, no doubt chosen because it might be the only place that doesn't have a cut or a bruise.

"Yes, yes, apologies." I've almost fallen asleep, my exhaustion weighing me down, even though I'm worried about Icel, and the others. And why my Aunt has gone as well, I just don't know.

"Here, Edmund is back," Penda informs me. I look toward the door, hoping to see something that assures me that all is well, but his posture tells me everything. His shoulders are slumped, and I know then, that Icel has gone.

"Fuck," I explode, the force of the word, causing too many curious eyes to peer my way.

CHAPTER 2

"You need to sleep?" My Aunt's voice is laced with concern, and I'm not used to hearing it.

"I need to go after Icel."

"Oh, and what use would you be? You're more likely to fall off your horse than catch him."

"Why didn't you warn me?"

"I didn't believe he'd even suggest such a thing. He's been quiet, on the journey here, I won't deny it, but I didn't believe him capable of this."

"Why couldn't you stop him?"

"He was already mounted, and half out the tunnel before we even found him." Edmund sounds furious, and Pybba won't even look at me, as he hooks a seat close enough to me to hear, without having to look at me.

"Then you've done your best. I'll go after him."

"No, you won't." My Aunt speaks deliberately, as though to someone slow to comprehend instructions, and for whom total clarity must always be given to avoid misunderstandings.

"I must."

"No, not yet. You need to heal. Icel has gone. We'll have to accept that, and hope he returns in good time. Maybe he has simply gone to retrieve Eoppa's body, as he said. It's an honourable endeavour for a man who believed himself left behind by his allies and friends." The words sting, I can't deny it, but I don't believe they're aimed at me, or even at Edmund. I think my Aunt merely speaks as Icel has explained it to her.

"But Tatberht said he'd gone to Grantabridge, and not for Eoppa at all."

"Maybe he'll come to his senses." But my Aunt's words are not the reassurance they need to be to keep me inside Northampton.

"I can't see that happening," Pybba finally speaks, his words doom-laden, for all he still refuses to meet my eye. "There's nothing to be done for now. He's gone. We could rush after him, but all our mounts are exhausted, and so are we. We'll have to leave the daft bastard to himself. Maybe tomorrow we can send a few men to track him down."

I don't like the idea, but I nod, all the same, trying not to wince as even that hurts. I don't want a mutiny on my hands if my warriors believe I've abandoned Icel for real this time.

"Right, we'll all get some rest and decide what to do at first light."

Grunts and unhappy 'yeses' greet my words. I'm the same. I don't want to wait, and already, I'm hatching a plot to follow Icel once my Aunt sleeps.

"Here, drink this," she hands me a beaker of steeped herbs, and I drink, looking forward to the renewal that thrummed through my body last time she gave me such a brew. Only this time, I feel my eyelids grow heavy, and I'd curse her, only, it's all I can do to slump to the floor without hitting my head, again. The egg-shaped bump is still prominent.

"There. Sleep, My Lord King, and tomorrow will come soon enough for a solution to be found for Icel's desertion."

I want to argue, but the faces of Edmund, Pybba, Rudolf, Penda and Sæbald are swimming before my eyes, and I'm forced to close my eyes or vomit all over their shoes. I might quite enjoy that, but it wouldn't be overly kingly.

I startle awake, already trying to rise, only for a white hand to appear from out of the darkness to force me back down.

"Peace," my Aunt's voice is gentle, but brokers no argument.

"Fuck," all of a sudden, my injuries make themselves known, and tears come unbidden to my eyes.

"Peace," my Aunt says once more, a beaker in her hand, pretending not to have heard my foul language. I look at her with wary eyes.

"It's water. And anyway, you needed to sleep. Your thinking was muddled."

Gratefully, I swig the cold liquid, and as it enters my stomach, it seems to crash against an empty void. Once more, my Aunt is in front of me, taking the beaker from me, and replacing it with a bowl of warm pottage, the scent of honey, promising much-needed sweetness.

"Have you been awake all night?" I ask between spoonful's.

"No, but I've been tending to my patients, and waiting for you to wake, filled with resolve and fury."

I eat, rather than try and convince her that wasn't my intention.

"Icel," she says, and I'm startled that she speaks about him first.

"I should have warned you, but I thought there was time. Damn the man." That's the closest my Aunt has ever come to outright blasphemy, aside from yesterday, and I'm so startled, I almost drop my spoon. I can't quite see in the shadows, but I imagine another rare smile touches her lips. Her two hounds are curled around her feet. I can hear their breathing, and also see her stroking their heads in the dark.

What would she be without the two beasties, Wiglaf and Berhtwulf? They're ideal companions for her; fiercely loyal and biddable to her every wish. She certainly doesn't get the biddable part when she interacts with me.

"Tell me?" I ask when she lapses into silence. "I need to understand."

"We all do," she offers, her words edged with sadness.

"He came to me at Kingsholm. His wound was healed. Whoever did it was a master of their art. I don't even think I could have stitched such a huge wound together, even with the aid of the monks and the women at Kingsholm who sewed your banner. Did you like it?" That she has to ask, speaks volumes of her worry about it, and my oversight in not mentioning it before now.

"It guided me to safety," I acknowledge. "Thank you." I infuse my voice with gratitude.

"Good, then it's fulfilled some of its purpose already. But, his wound, it must have run from neck to buttock, and it was deep. The skin around it now is puckered and can look angry if he does too much. I know it pains him, the skin has been drawn together tightly, perhaps too tightly, but I don't believe he risks it splitting open once more, provided he doesn't exert himself."

"So who saved him?"

"He doesn't know." And she pauses, as though considering the wisdom of her next words. "I suspect it was a Raider." I hiss, and she shakes her head.

"They can't all be murderers. I don't believe that our God would put so many men and women on this earth to merely have them kill others."

"Whoever it was, they took him away from the site of the clash in which Edmund believed him killed. That's why his body wasn't there when you went back for it."

"Does he blame us?"

"He hasn't spoken of any blame. None at all. But he is driven. I believe he means to find either the person who healed him, or perhaps, whoever this person wants dead. I'm not sure. It's something like that. He's spoken little of his time being healed. I don't truly believe he remembers much of it. I imagine he was unconscious for huge amounts of time. He would have needed to lie, prone, and on his front, for weeks, if not a full month, to mend as well as he has. Whoever helped him, spent a great deal of effort ensuring he was whole once more. And then they simply disappeared, leaving him a horse to make his way back to Kingsholm."

"So, he's truly not gone for Eoppa then? He's gone to find whoever healed him, or whoever betrayed the person who healed him?"

"I believe so, although I can't be sure. But no, retrieving Eoppa's body is not his main motivation. That was merely an excuse for him to leave. I saw the hunger in him, even as Ealdorman Ælhun's men were felling the Raiders. He wanted to be out there. He wanted to be killing them all."

"Icel has always wanted to kill the Raiders."

"Perhaps, but now he's even more motivated. I fear for him," and I try and rise once more. "But it is for him to do. Icel needs to find his peace, or he'll never be able to ride with you and your men again. His loyalty shouldn't be doubted, though."

"Fuck," and I ignore my Aunt's hiss of annoyance.

"Edmund wanted to seek a man he believed to be Icel, regardless of what it might cost him. Now Icel wants to hunt as well, no matter the risks."

"And you?" my Aunt adds, her words softened to take away the sting of them. I hardly thought it needed saying.

"I need him back."

"I can't stop you going after him, but I don't believe you'll find him anywhere other than at Grantabridge."

It seems my Aunt has learned of all our exploits. I'm far from surprised.

"You need to rest for a few days more yet before you do anything. I had hoped to keep Icel close, but it can't be helped that he's evaded my watchful eyes. Don't blame yourself. There was no way you could have known."

"Can I have more water?" I ask, rather than replying. I am culpable. I always am, and my Aunt knows that.

I swallow thirstily, the pressure in my bladder growing, but I haven't finished my conversation just yet.

"I saw a single Raider close to Repton. I suppose it's possible that they tracked us to Torksey, or perhaps, crossed the Thames, and tracked Edmund and Icel. But I don't understand why they'd have healed Icel. If they wanted revenge against someone, why not take it themselves."

"Perhaps they couldn't."

"Perhaps?" I ask, her sigh tells me that she's withholding information.

"The person, and Icel doesn't know whether it was a man or a woman, was only sighted in one eye, and walked with a terrible limp, and had fingers missing on their right hand. Whoever the person was, they've been badly wounded themselves. I imagine they can't carry out the revenge that they crave."

"So you believe Icel has been, what, bewitched by this person?"

"No, not bewitched, but he feels oathbound to do this for them."

"Bugger," I resort to, not wanting to hear my Aunt's objections again.

"He's gone rogue then?"

"More than likely."

I can't blame her. I can't blame anyone.

"I can't just leave him out there, alone."

"I don't think you have much choice. You can't risk more of your warriors to rescue Icel, no matter what you, and they might think."

And then our conversation is interrupted.

"My Lord King," I recognise the man who dashes into the hall as one of Wulfsige's men.

"What is it?"

"There are Raiders, emerging from the woods."

"Fuck." For once, my Aunt doesn't complain and even hands me a pair of trews before aiding me to find my feet. It hurts like fuck, but I'm pleased to be upright, even if I hobble, and even one small step, has me gasping in agony.

"Can you wake Edmund and Pybba for me?" She nods, handing me a fresh tunic before moving away, leaving me to muster myself.

"Wake Ealdorman Ælhun?" I instruct the messenger, and he nods and turns.

My bladder throbs, and it's the impetus I need to shuffle forward, biting my lip, determined not to be found with wet trews. I leave the tunic behind. I can't imagine the pain of trying to thrust my arms inside. My back already tugs with each breath, my stitches pulling tight. I take the cloak with me, though. There's a chill wind blowing through the slightly open doorway, and I can almost taste the frost that must have formed while I've been asleep.

Not that my progress is particularly quick. As I hear the groans of my men being woken, I try to find more speed. I don't want to be seen pissing against the wall when they come to find me.

"Bloody bollocks," it's even colder outside than I suspected, and I'm forced to regret the decision to leave my tunic behind, as I huddle into my cloak.

As quickly as I can, I shuffle to the latrine, and then on, to where I can hear a burble of conversation coming from the defences. Ealdorman Ælhun quickly catches up with me, his hand rubbing his face, as though it might wake him more quickly. I notice his lack of hair, even as I realise that he and Icel must be a similar age. Could two men be more different and yet also the same?

"My Lord King," he bobs his head. "Good to see you up and about." I'm not about to tell him that each and every step pains me. I imagine he suspects all the same, and although he'd been rushing, his steps quickly fall in line with mine.

"They might have come for the bodies," the ealdorman suggests, hope in his voice.

"Did we leave them?"

"Yes, but we made sure they were all dead. I know it's not your way, but, there wasn't enough time to bury them all, not before darkness fell."

I would probably have made the same decision, so I hold my tongue.

"We pillaged them, ensured they were dead and not about to spend the night crying out for aid, and then we returned inside and closed the tunnels."

I have many questions about those passageways but now isn't the time. I want to know how they work. I want to know how they've been blocked, but Ealdorman Ælhun seems confident as he speaks, so I must assume that every potential problem has been considered.

"Well, let's show our faces, and see what's what."

It's still dark outside. I'm impressed those on guard duty have been able to detect anyone on the field of slaughter, but I don't deny that they have.

Pybba and Edmund join me.

"Morning," Edmund's voice is laboured, laced with fatigue. I wonder how much sleep he's had.

"Is it?" Pybba's complains, and when neither of them asks, I feel compelled to speak.

"I'm feeling fine, thanks for asking."

Edmund eyes me in the dankness.

"You look like shit, and it's bloody cold. Where's your damn tunic?"

"I couldn't get it on quickly enough," I feel compelled to answer. Admittedly, that excuse is poor.

"Daft bastard," while he lopes away in front of me, Pybba stays beside me.

"Morning," he grumpily offers to Ealdorman Ælhun.

"How is everyone?" I ask, trying not to hiss with each and every slow step.

"Ask your Aunt." And Pybba rushes ahead as well and is quickly swallowed by the darkness.

"You can go," I instruct Ealdorman Ælhun, not wanting to hold him up any longer, and appreciating that he won't just go, unlike my warriors. "I'll be there as soon as I can get up the damn steps." They're built into the side of the defences, and while they look nice and smooth, the planks of wood new, they also look bloody steep. I can already feel my calve muscles aching just at the thought of what I need to do.

"As you will," and he inclines his head, and takes the first step, and then the second, by the time he's reached the fourth, I'm panting just with the thought of what I need to do.

"Fuck," I give myself the time to come to terms with what must be accomplished, aware that while it's bloody cold, sweat is beading down my back. I can feel the tightness of my Aunt's stitches again, and I want to scratch them, but know I can't risk pulling them apart.

I plant my foot on the first step, tensed for the screech of agony, and I'm not disappointed.

"Fuck, fuck, fuck," I utter the word for every step I take, hoping it will somehow dispel the agony. It doesn't, but it makes me feel fucking better, all the same.

By the time I'm close to the others, the gloom has started to lift. Without speaking, I shuffle beside them and peer out onto the site of my, already famous, last stand from yesterday.

"Bloody bollocks." I knew that we'd cut down many Raiders, but I hadn't appreciated just how many.

Now, figures snake between the dead, bending to see if they live or not, and I swallow against the unease that's building inside me, at the realisation of just how close I came to meeting my death. There must be at least two hundred marbled bodies out there. The hint of the night's frost, seeming to enshrine the wounds, highlighting the maroon of the many cuts, the grey of sliced skin, glimmering with the promise of silver, the ruby of fine wine, liberally sprinkled over the winter-short grasses.

"Do they mean to attack?" I ask. I'm not convinced that anyone is in a fit state to fight today. I'm certainly not, and why would warriors take a chance on death if their leader won't?

But my question remains unanswered; all eyes focused on the scene playing out before us.

I imagine I know who the Raiders surround, bringing a fine black mount to the side of the splayed body. I want to know how they got here so fast? Even if there was a bloody survivor, it should have taken them days to reach Grantabridge, and that can only mean that while I thought we'd killed all of the Raiders encamped outside Northampton, we simply hadn't.

Unless, of course, more warriors left Grantabridge after we

did. That possibility offers some comfort. Only my eyes are drawn behind me. I can't see the bridge that crosses the Nene, but I can see the thread of smoke that floats into the crystalline day. The farmer's dwelling.

"We should bring them inside the fortress," I muse, aware that it would be too easy for them to be attacked by the Raiders.

"My Lord King?" Only Ealdorman Ælhun seems to hear my words.

"As a precaution, we should bring the farmer and his family, and his oxen, inside the compound, and reinforce the bridge with more men. It's not easy to cross it, but they might try, all the same."

My heart is suddenly hammering in my chest. I imagine people can hear it. This is what I wanted to happen, but now I feel entirely unprepared, and out of control. I don't fucking like it, not at all.

I'm about to instruct Edmund or Pybba to arrange it; only Rudolf has appeared, his hair tousled from sleep, his eyes keen and alert. He doesn't even seem to limp or be in any pain. I pity the youth when he reaches my age. It'll be a bloody shock. It fucking shocks me.

"Get Sæbald, Eahric, Goda, Wærwulf and Lyfing to accompany you. Make sure they're all capable of fighting. Go and gather the farmer and his sons. Tell them to hurry, but try not to panic them. You better bring as many of the animals as you can." I'm turning, trying to see the distant river where our horses have been crossing, downstream of Northampton, but the light is still too low.

"It's clear," Edmund offers, even though I've not asked.

"Have Tatberht, Ælfgar, Eadulf and Wulfred reinforce the bridge, while you're gone, and ask Wulfsige for a further ten men as well. We'll take the bridge down if it comes to it."

Rudolf offers me the briefest of bows before he turns and scampers down the steep steps. That doesn't leave me with many of my men who can fight, but there are a few of us, and they'll protect my Aunt if it comes to it, and of course, she's brought her own Mercians with her. They are loyal to me, I'd never deny that, but first and foremost, they are her warriors. She's very welcome to them.

"Do you think they mean to attack?" Ealdorman Ælhun hasn't turned aside from watching the Raiders.

The body of Jarl Guthrum's sister has been levered off the ground and is now slumped over the black horse. It doesn't seem to appreciate its burden but is behaving, for now. I hope it's not the same horse that we made her ride back to Grantabridge, trussed up and tied to the saddle, complete with the dead body of the warrior who led the scouting party.

I look for the tell-tale glint of weapons and see them easily enough, but the Raiders are staying a respectful distance from Northampton. They seem wary, and that pleases me, even as I search the hinterland, looking for signs that Icel might have been caught. I hope the stupid bastard hasn't ridden straight into an ambush. The person that healed him won't appreciate being repaid in such a way. And neither will I.

"Do they mean to strike?" Ealdorman Ælhun still muses, and I'm thinking the same thing.

"Surely, they would have come upon us in the dark if they meant to do that."

I can't fault Pybba's logic. Last night, we would have been blind and exhausted, and of course, the Raiders I met in the woodlands, believed they had a secret way into Northampton. I can't imagine these Raiders don't share the same information, even if it is now out of date and likely to see them killed even more quickly.

"They've come for the dead," I confirm. "Or rather, they've come for certain of the dead."

"But where did they come from?" Edmund asks, no doubt his thoughts are running similar to mine.

"I'm not about to bloody ask them," I confirm, pulling my cloak tighter and tighter. I'd like to stamp my feet to drive some warmth into them, but I know it would send ricochet's of pain up my legs. I do wish I was more adequately dressed.

I turn, my attention caught by noise from inside Northampton, but it's only my men, with Rudolf, streaking across the thin wooden bridge that crosses the Nene. I watch their backs, hoping they're careful and don't walk into a trap. I wait, watching my breath plume before me, as they disappear into the grey area between the bridge and the woodlands, and then I can't see them anymore, because they're too low down, and the walls of Northampton, built to protect it, block my sight.

I try to relax, crack my neck from side to side, but the silence of the muted air is unnerving.

"What are they doing now?" It's Pybba who asks, a hand over his eyes, as though it's too sunny, which it isn't, not at all, the clouds hanging low and menacingly.

"I think they're leaving," Ealdorman Ælhun suggests, only for Edmund to sigh.

"No, no, they're not. They're making camp."

"What?" Immediately, I try and seek out the movements. Still, I just can't see as well as Edmund or Pybba, no matter how close to the fortifications I stand, shuffling forward, even leaning over the top, trying to ignore the agony that flees down my back, as my stitches stretch, and along my legs.

"Why would they do that?" Again, it's Ealdorman Ælhun who asks the question.

"I think they're making it clear that they're watching us."

His startled eyes suddenly meet mine, as I give up on my attempt to see for myself.

"This isn't over, is it?"

"Not at all," I confirm, my mind already planning what needs to be done. Who needs to do what, and whether I should remain in Northampton, or attempt to leave the place, and retreat further into the heartlands of Mercia.

"Well," and Edmund turns to me with a glint in his eye. "There's only about fifteen of them. I don't think we've got much to worry about, not yet." And he looks upwards. "And it's going to piss it down any moment now. I pity the poor fuckers. Look, the rest are leaving."

And Edmund is, of course, right. The remaining warriors, complete with their grizzly cargo, are beginning to trudge back towards the woodlands, to where I hope Icel is hiding.

But it seems that the Raiders have one more task to complete. I'm just about to leave the ramparts when Edmund calls me back.

I follow where he points, and then I groan.

"Bastards." I don't know from where, but they've cobbled together a banner that looks similar to the one my Aunt has stitched for me, an attempt made to emulate the rich colour, if not the stitches, and as I watch, flames lick along its length. No doubt they've been forced to douse it in oil to make it burn. I'm sure it wouldn't on its own, not in the dank air.

"Daft fuckers," I complain, trying to dispel the thick tension that's fallen between us all. The Raiders have made their intentions clear, but they're not the ones inside a sturdy fortress, with ramparts all around them, and food enough to last through to the warmer months.

I decide then that I'm going to remain in Northampton. I'm not going to be scared away, and neither will my warriors.

If the Raiders want a fight, I'm content to give them one. But first of all, they've got to get to me, and that isn't going to be fucking easy.

CHAPTER 3

"There's no one out there," Rudolf confirms, his mouth downcast, as though disappointed he didn't get to kill a Raider today. I've not heard him, Sæbald, Eahric, Goda, Wærwulf and Lyfing return with the oxen, but it's evident that they have. His face is flushed with exertion, and his clothes are sodden and damp from the rain that's started to fall heavily, just as Edmund warned.

"That's good," I state. I've made my way back inside the hall, and my Aunt has assisted me into my tunic, having checked my stitches are clean. Somehow, she's even managed to stop herself from rebuking me for rising from my sickbed without her agreement. She's now busy, seeing to her other patients, leaving me to my problems.

"Maybe. What are they doing out there?" Rudolf inclines his head to where he thinks the Raiders were. I'm not sure he's quite got the direction correct, but I understand his intent all the same, as I slowly chew the bread I've been presented. I'm so hungry, I need to be careful not to swallow my tongue.

"Taking the dead, and some of them, no more than fifteen, have made camp. Did the farmer come inside without problems?" I don't want to talk about the Raiders, but rather the Mercians. It's they who are my main concern.

"He did, yes, but I don't think he's pleased about it."

"Would he sooner be dead?" Edmund complains, settling beside me noisily. Ealdorman Ælhun has found some urgent matters to attend to, and I'm grateful to have some time to think. Ideally, I want to check on Haden, but with the thunderous rain overhead, I'm prepared to wait longer yet. I can't imagine my Aunt would take too kindly to be being sodden, as well as injured.

"We couldn't bring all of his supplies with us," Rudolf explains.

"Once we know there's no chance of an attack, he can go back, if he wants." I don't want to be responsible for his death, but equally, if the Raiders only mean to watch, there's no immediate threat to the family. Even if they aren't protected by Northampton's walls, there's still the matter of the Nene to cross.

"Well, I don't want to have to help him get the bloody oxen back across the bridge. Stubborn buggers and one of them half-stamped on my foot." I can imagine the scene, but I beckon for Rudolf to sit down. My warriors, well, those who are awake and well enough to sit upright, have gathered around me, Sæbald, Eahric, Goda, Wærwulf and Lyfing amongst them.

I know that Tatberht, Ælfgar, Eadulf and Wulfred still guard the gate, alongside the men that Wulfsige sent to assist them. There's also heavy guard alert on the ramparts. The bridge is our greatest place of weakness, but necessary, for the time being at least. I'll order it dismantled if I must.

"We need to extend the rampart closer to the bridge," I'm making plans, more speaking out loud than anything else, even if it appears that I'm talking to Pybba and Edmund.

"Surely they wouldn't risk an attack there?" Ealdorman Ælhun comments, startling me because I thought him still elsewhere.

"We can't think that anywhere is truly safe. We need to take whatever precautions we can, which reminds me. How do the two tunnels work?"

"Ah," and Ealdorman Ælhun's face flushes with pleasure. "It's quite ingenious. Essentially, if the Raiders try and attack through them, if they even know of the existence of them, then we can collapse the tunnel on their heads. It means we won't be able to get out that way, but they won't be able to get in either. We thought that was more important."

"And what happens when they're not being used?"

"An iron fence is forced into place. There's a knack to it. Only some of the men can do it. You've got to be strong. It's embedded into the sides of the tunnel, and it can't be pushed inwards by any would-be attackers. And I wouldn't want to be the one putting it in place either. It's not easy, not at all and bloody heavy."

"So, is the iron fence there now?"

"Yes, both tunnels have been hidden and protected. I don't anticipate needing to use it any time soon."

"And we have enough food if we make a stand here?"

"We do yes, but don't you worry the Raiders will travel around us, and into Mercia?"

"No, I don't think they will. They want Mercia, I know they do, but this feels personal. They want me to pay for what happened at Repton and Torksey, and for the death of Jarl Guthrum's sister as well, no doubt. Daft fuckers should have made sure we couldn't take possession of the fortress they were building."

"Then we just wait?" I didn't expect to be having this conversation with Ealdorman Ælhun, but it makes sense to include him, now that he's here.

"For the time being. My warriors need time to convalesce. I need time to recover, and the weather is on the change. It'll be full winter storms soon enough, with only a small amount of daylight each day. The Raiders are welcome to attack, but hopefully, we won't need to do much to keep them at bay."

"What about you, Lady Cyneswith?" Once more, I startle. I didn't realise my Aunt had joined my impromptu council of war. It's Ealdorman Ælhun who asks the question.

"What about me?"

"Do you need to return to Kingsholm or Worcester? Does Bishop Wærferth require your presence?"

"Not until everyone has mended and then it'll depend on

what the Raiders decide to do next. Better to keep their focus here than elsewhere."

As ever, my Aunt speaks with careful thought, and I admire her clear-sightedness.

"The bishops know where we are. The other ealdormen as well. If we can keep the bridge in place, then that'll help with communication. But, what we need to do is plan for the better weather, when they try and assault us because they'll be spending the winter getting reinforcements. They're not going to give up."

The words are spoken faintly, but they reverberate around the hall, and I swear, every single conversation falls silent, even that of the two mice, squabbling over a piece of cheese close to the door. I'm amazed they've not been trampled on or caught by the cat. But then, as I've learned, sometimes it's easier not to be seen in plain sight.

I nod all the same. My Aunt speaks truthfully.

"For now, we keep a firm guard on the bridge, and we watch what they do. We need to be careful at night. If they did decide to risk a confrontation, it would be then, especially because soon it'll be dark for a lot longer than during the summer." My mind takes me back to the long line of brands that bordered Grantabridge's quayside, and also at Torksey, now I think about it. Maybe we need something similar to quickly light the path if an attack is feared.

"Tomorrow, we need a party to go and forage in the woodlands for fuel. We need to gather as much as we can. We don't want to be fucking cold. It'll set men against each other."

"I'll arrange that," it's Wulfsige who speaks, and he brings with him the smell of damp and the pinch of cold.

"And if the family wish to return to their farm, then they can, but only if they're aware that if there's a raid, they need to get here quickly, or they might have to swim across the Nene, oxen and all."

"Anything else?" It's Ealdorman Ælhun who asks.

There's an expectant silence, but I have nothing.

"Not right now. I'll speak to my Aunt about the wounded." My warriors take it as the dismissal it is, even Edmund, which surprises me, but Ealdorman Ælhun lingers. I watch him while my Aunt moves closer. I'm pleased she's realised that I want to speak to her privately. But Ealdorman Ælhun hasn't.

"My Lord King."

"Yes. What is it?"

"Do you think it's the right thing to be so open with everyone? Shouldn't there be some attempt to keep some of your plans secret?"

"Not with my men. The moment I do that, I'll lose their trust. Remember, Ealdorman Ælhun; they pledged themselves to me long before I thought I might be a king."

"Hum," but he sounds far from convinced.

"Do you routinely keep secrets from your warriors?" I'm genuinely curious.

"I'm the ealdorman. They don't need to know everything I have planned." I find I don't have an answer to that, and sense, rather than see, that my Aunt is smirking at me. It wouldn't be like her, but, well, she's surprised me more than once in the last day.

"Well, we'll have to agree to disagree," I try to make my voice brighter. "My warriors need to rely on me, and I need to rely on them."

"Yes, My Lord King," but Ealdorman Ælhun speaks in such a way that I know he's uneasy, even as he walks away once more.

"How are they?" I ask before my Aunt can comment on the ealdorman.

"They'll all mend, as I told you. It'll take time. Of them all, I'm most worried about Siric and Hereman. Neither of them makes good patients. Siric's arm concerns me. If he doesn't rest it, it won't knit together correctly, and he might lose much of its function. I've told him that a one-armed warrior is little good to the king of Mercia, but he's not of a mind to listen to me."

"And Hereman?"

"He's frustrating." My Aunt's huff of annoyance almost makes me smirk.

"I know," I agree, to lessen the tension, but she still looks aggrieved.

"Gardulf will be fine. The fever has already abated. It just needed the right herbs. You really should have had them with you."

I open my mouth to argue, but she's right.

"I wasn't actually with them when he was wounded."

"That doesn't matter to me. Someone should have had some sense." I can feel one of my Aunt's stringent conversations coming on, and I would rather not listen to it. Not right now.

I stifle a yawn, aware that exhaustion is starting to sour my overly-full stomach.

"You need to drink this." Again, I eye the beaker of water, trying not to let her know that I'm sniffing it.

"It won't make you sleep, not this time. I don't think falling asleep will be a problem for you," but I have my suspicions all the same.

"The men didn't ask you about Icel?" She watches me, and the satisfaction in her eyes, as I swallow the contents of the beaker assures me that she's put something in my drink, although what it is, I'm unsure.

"No, they didn't. But then, they seemed to know a lot more than I did."

"Well, they weren't as busy as you were, being heroic and all that. Now, eat this, and then sleep. Nothing is going to happen today, and if it does, we'll wake you. Well, Rudolf will wake you. That boy can't allow anything to happen without tattling to you." Her lips are once more compressed, and I shrug, only to regret the action as pain lances down my back.

"And watch your stitches."

I swallow all of the herb-laced water while my Aunt watches me.

I don't even consider the actions of the Raiders. For now, there's fuck all I can do about them. Neither do I have the inclination to continue yesterday's battle. I might not be able to lift my seax or war axe for some time, and just considering the heft of my shield, makes me judder, which only strains my stitches again.

I watch the men and women within the hall, thinking of the blood-slaughter that took place when we conquered Northampton. I'm sure we're not as arrogant as the Raiders. I know we'd never leave so few to guard the bridge, or even leave the rampant to the rear, so exposed. But, I can't find as much comfort as I might hope.

No doubt, we'll have overlooked something. Just what that might be, I'm unsure, but, as I settle on the floor, close to the hearth, rolled once more in my cloak and on a bundle of fleeces that have materialised from somewhere, I hope some fucker realises what it is and that they're Mercian and not a bastard Raider.

CHAPTER 4

"There are more of them. The camp grows almost daily."

I turn to Rudolf, unable to mask my surprise. He's sheltering beneath a sealskin cloak, the water running from it quickly.

"Really? But, look at the weather." I point upwards, just to make my point. It's currently almost raining. By that I mean, the clouds are hanging so low, it's as though the air is simply thronged with water. I'm wet already, and I've not been outside for long. My face is slick, and I could be cold if I allowed myself to be.

"Aye, My Lord, but well, maybe they're used to it, you know what they say about the northern kingdoms" He leans in, and winks, and I would laugh at him. When did he learn so much? No doubt, his devious ears have heard far more than they ever should.

"How many of them are there now?" I don't want to be drawn into a conversation about the Raiders. I know only too well what hardy bastards they all are.

"It's hard to keep track because they keep coming and going. It might just be that they come and stick another canvas up, and then bugger off, but I don't think it's empty. There are too many cook fires for that."

"They mean business, then?"

"Looks like it."

It's been two weeks since we retreated inside Northampton, and what a bloody interesting two weeks it's been. Well, it hasn't, but I wish it had. The tedium grows every day. I think myself lucky because I've only just fully healed, and I'm busy trying to ensure my seax arm hasn't lost any of its force. For the others who arrived here uninjured, the daily bouts have become the only source of excitement, and even then, just about everyone has taken on everyone else. We all know each other's strengths and weaknesses, and the daily wagers have fallen by the by. No one will bet against a warrior they've already watched disarm a man in three or four moves.

Rudolf has surprised most of the Mercians. They look at him and see a boy, not one of my warriors, and that, alas, has been their downfall, time and time again.

Gyrth has also made himself a decent-sized haul of anything men and women will wager, from leather belts to pots of honey and even some coins, emblazoned with our previous king's image. I really should see about having my image struck onto the new coins. No doubt my Aunt makes such arrangements already.

While the farmer and his family, and stubborn oxen, have returned to their home, few others leave, unless to collect wood for the fires in the woodlands where we sheltered, earlier in the year. From there, any Mercian cut-off from Northampton could retreat to London, or Warwick, the Watling Street is close.

I feel as though we're well prepared for whatever the Raiders have planned, but as of yet, I don't know what that is. I believed they'd retreat to Grantabridge for the winter, but that doesn't seem to be what they're doing. And of course, Icel hasn't returned, and that's making me uneasy as well. I want him back, where I can keep an eye on him. I wish I'd never let the old git go on the first place, but the time for recriminations is long gone. I can only live with the decision that was made.

"I'm coming to look," I inform Rudolf, and he nods.

"I thought you would. Edmund's up there, waiting for you."

Now that Gardulf is over the worse of his wounds, Edmund rarely leaves my side. Hereman spends most of his time with Gardulf. Leonath, as my Aunt said, is already up and about, and it's Siric who's causing the most concern. His arm is healing poorly, and he knows it. It's made him ill-tempered, and only my Aunt can bring him to reason when he lashes out as those who try and aid him. He's certainly not as accepting as Pybba was when he lost his hand. Although. Well, perhaps it took Pybba some time as well.

I've told my Aunt to leave, but she won't. I knew it before I said it, but I felt I had to try, all the same. A small part of me thinks that she might just be enjoying this. All those years of being made to tend the wounded at Kingsholm, and now she's here, on the front line of the battle for Mercian survival. I think she'll welcome the coming confrontation as much as my bored men.

Yet, it feels as though there are too many of us inside Northampton. If we're not careful, there'll be a battlefield inside the ramparts, not outside it.

For the first time since I returned to Northampton, I make my way up the steep steps to the wooden walkway that crests the fortifications without wincing. Rudolf hovers behind me, and I know he's impatient, but I take my time, listening to him huff behind me with annoyance.

"Edmund, what's happening?" I call when I draw level with the wooden walkway and can see him.

There are ten warriors on guard duty, but not all in the same place. This spot has become the place where Ealdorman Ælhun and I often congregate, peering into the distance, to stew over the same words that we've been speaking for nearly two weeks. The Raiders mean to perplex us, but while we feel safe and secure, it doesn't unduly concern me. Only the worry of just what they might plan plays on my mind, but I can't decipher the future. I'll just have to fucking wait.

My Aunt's banner is still proudly displayed, no matter that the Raiders burnt a replica one. Some might think it foolish to proclaim my presence, but I hope it keeps them here. I don't want the Raiders going elsewhere in Mercia. I want them dreaming of overthrowing me. I don't want them to think of Repton or Torksey, or any other river site they might fancy in the interior of Mercia. Better that the bastards are where I can find them.

"Fuck knows," Edmund's voice drips with scorn, and he doesn't even turn away from his scrutiny of the enemy to look at me.

"How the bloody hell can you see anything?"

Beyond the ramparts, the cloud seems to have gained greater form. Certainly, I can't see much beyond the muddy foreground, where the ditch flashes wetly, the sharpened stakes offering anyone a death filled with agony.

"Because I can," Edmund has no sympathy for my poor sight. I notice his words are clipped. It's Edmund's turn to be a niggly fucker.

"What are they doing?"

"Getting wet, for the time being, but I think they plan to construct a wooden building or some such."

"Really?" I know I want the Raiders to stay here, but I'm surprised they'd make it so permanent.

"Either that or they want to build an obstacle course." I don't much appreciate Edmund's sarcasm, but I let it pass, all the same. I can't see it. I'll have to rely on what he reports to me. Really, I should have stayed in the hall. At least I'd have been dry and warm in there.

"It certainly seems that way. I counted at least four carts, and maybe as many as thirty more Raiders."

"There'll soon be more of them than there are us if they carry on like this."

My doom-laden words hang unanswered. I'm not surprised. I'm the one who decided to remain here.

"They're certainly persistent, although they've done nothing but watch us, so far."

Edmund's right. The number of Raiders might have been steadily growing before this fresh influx today, but the camp is a good distance away. And, we've not even seen anyone scouting out Northampton. They've come to watch, but not to menace. The lack of a presence from the other side of the Nene, close to the farmer's steading, assures me of that.

I expect it will come soon enough, but I'm not convinced they can do anything. The rampart that crowns Northampton is well built. But, they'll know that, because they began the work. With the closure of the gateway that spits travellers out onto the ground they now occupy, there's nothing for them to try and ram open. The mud sides of the wall are sheer enough that they'll be almost impossible to climb, even if the walkway on the interior, wasn't crammed with Mercians just waiting for them to try such a tactic. And despite my worries, the dank, damp weather, is having no impact on the integrity of the walls either.

I know the flaw in our defences remains the bridge over the Nene. I also appreciate that measures are in place to reinforce it, or, if need be, to topple it into the river.

The worry that there's another weakness persists in nagging at the back of my mind. And I've conducted my assessment of the defences built by the Raiders before we killed them all. I've found nothing. And neither has anyone else. But, I still don't rest easy. I will not be the sort of leader who feels so secure, that the enemy sneaks in under the floorboards.

I know that the Raiders will have something planned. What that is, remains a mystery.

Their blatant watching of us has also perplexed me. I know from experience that an enemy will be less prepared if they're caught unawares. I also understand that the absence of the Raiders would have left me uneasy. This is too brazen.

"Do you think they're going to attack?"

"At some point, they must be," Edmund confirms. Again, we've had this conversation before.

"Oh, you look better," Edmund startles, finally dragging his eyes away from our foe, so that he looks at me for the first time that day.

"Well, I can't malinger forever." Chance would be a fine thing. "I wish I knew what was happening at Grantabridge."

"Maybe you should go and see," but I know Edmund doesn't mean it. When I did suggest that a small party travelled back that way, no one agreed with me. I was met only with angry stares and furious silence. The wounds from the recent attack on my warriors are still too raw, the loss of Eoppa far from accepted. And of course, Ealdorman Ælhun doesn't have men who are as skilled as mine at keeping out of sight.

His warriors are for fighting a very obvious enemy; perhaps in a long line, shields held one against another. They've not engaged in the hunt, as my men have. I doubt they'd know what to do, and that would make them useless.

"I wish I knew where bloody Icel was." I shouldn't be hoping that he might be able to answer my questions, but I do, all the same.

"My Lord King," Wulfhere is before me, chest heaving, cheeks pink with the cold, his hair stuck to his forehead. "There are Raiders at the bridge."

"Fuck," I turn, trying to gaze through the wet gloom, but of course, I can't see them, because there's a bloody great big gate in the way.

'How many are there," my hand goes for my seax, even though I'm too far away to strike.

"Just four of them. A delegation, I think they called it."

Edmund looks at me. "What sort of trick is this?"

"I have no fucking idea. Wulfhere, get my Aunt and Ealdorman Ælhun. Is there a party in the woods, collecting fuel for the hearths?" This I direct to Rudolf. His youth makes it much easier for him to keep track of everyone, or so I console myself because I can't always remember everything, the similarity of the days blending one into another. My Aunt observes the feast days of the saints, but it's no way for me to keep track of time.

"Yes, under Wulfsige's command."

"Well, let's hope he checks carefully before trying to come back." Wulfhere scampers away, and I face the steep steps with a grimace.

"Bastard things."

Edmund moves to come with me.

"No, stay here. I want to know if anything happens while I'm away. They might have something prearranged."

"Like what?" Edmund's forehead furrows, but he turns aside all the same, and the fact that he agrees with me, is strangely reassuring.

"Right, now to get down the bastard steps." I purposefully take my time. The Raiders have come here unannounced. They can bloody well wait.

Every downward step hurts, but not as much as it has, and by the time I hit the level ground, I'm not drenched in sweat, and that feels like a victory.

Wulfhere rushes to me, a fur cloak over his arms, folded twice, so that it doesn't drag in the many and varied puddles on the floor. It's been cold for days, but crystal clear, the hint of ice meaning the morning frosts have taken a long time to thaw. But, today is entirely different. Today speaks of near-constant drizzle and dampness. I sniff the air. It has that special tang about it that speaks of mud, misery and an inability to get warm and dry, once cold and damp.

"Your Aunt said to put this one."

"Of course she did," but I allow Wulfhere to help me into the new cloak, the old one, wet and stinking, a pleasure to discard, even as it drags in the puddles I've been trying to avoid.

"She'll meet you by the gateway," Wulfhere confirms, turning to dash away with my ruined cloak. I waste a breath watching him and wishing I owned legs as young as his.

In the last two weeks, the ramparts have been extended to the bridge. There's a small entrance there now, a gateway, and a wide ditch to the other side of it. Anyone attempting to attack via the Nene will first have to clamber out of their ships and up the bank. And then down the ditch and then back up the rampart. It'll be exhausting, and hopefully, my warriors, and the men and women of Mercia, will be there, just waiting for an opportunity to impale the fuckers on the end of their spears.

There's an expectant hush as I walk passed the main hall, and then the stables, and across to where I can see a small collection of people congregating. The horses shuffle in the stables, those forced to find shelter beneath the long over-hanging roof, standing sullen in the damp air.

Somehow, and despite the fact he's sheltered far inside the building, I still catch sight of Haden's inquisitive black and white-nose hanging over the stable door. He must recognise my footsteps or some such. I wouldn't like to think he's just been standing there, waiting to see me.

We've made our peace with one another. It was not a pleasant reunion. He tried to kick me, and when I neatly side-stepped him, my bruises aching like a bitch, he stepped on my foot. I have another bruise now. It's evident that he blames me for becoming separated from him. Equally, it's apparent that he feels some guilt for that—damn brute.

The smell of horse manure is rife. For the last few days, it's been too cold for the scent to travel far. I'll need to think of a means of getting rid of it all. Perhaps I'll order the ditches liberally sprinkled with it.

Or perhaps not. I don't want to have the smell overlaying everything else. Or maybe I do.

No, it's a bad idea. It'll just have to be taken to the farmer, and then he can decide whether to use it or not in his fields, after all, that's what the Raiders did when they had control of Northampton. It'll be an unpleasant task for someone. Perhaps the next Mercian to argue about shit will be given the task of dealing with the crap. I'll make the punishment fit the crime.

"Right, what do the fuckers want?" My Aunt grows rigid as I speak, but, wisely, does not comment as I come to a stop before the gateway. Sometimes she surprises me with her understanding of the way the mind of warriors works. And other times, she just doesn't. It almost makes me smile to realise I've been allowed such behaviour. But then, I sober. I'm a grown man. I shouldn't be rejoicing in something a small child would.

"They asked to speak to King Coelwulf." It's Pybba who speaks into the tense silence. His eyes are keen as they take me in. Like Edmund, it's evident he finds me much restored to my usual self. I stand a little taller, and this brings a wry smirk to his lips.

"What about?" It's my Aunt who asks the question.

"They wouldn't say." Pybba doesn't shrug as Rudolf might have done in the same situation,

"Great," I interject. "And there are four of them?"

"Yes, just the four, but only two came across the bridge." This surprises me. Two on the bridge, two to watch their backs. I'm not sure there would be room for many more on the planks of wood.

"Men, women?"

"A man and a woman."

"And they're just waiting for me?"

"Yes." I peer at Pybba, but he has nothing further to offer. I can't even tell from his face, whether he's surprised or not at this development.

"They'll want to reach an accord with you," Ealdorman Ælhun sounds hopeful. But my Aunt shakes her head.

"No, this isn't about that."

I eye her, wondering what she knows, but as she doesn't offer anything further, I hold my tongue.

"Right, let's do this." The decision made, I turn to face those around me. "Aunt, Ealdorman Ælhun, come with me, but I'll do the talking. We'll make no immediate decision, no matter what they say. Edmund, Pybba, Rudolf, stand at my back, and look mean, and the rest of the guard detail as well." I meet the eyes of the other Mercians. I know them all, even if only by sight.

I indicate that they should open the gate, and as it swings wide, I try not to glance forward with too much interest. This is just another of those kingly duties whose skills I lack.

As one, the three of us walk forwards as soon as the gate is open, Pybba directing the guards to line the cramped walkway. There's only just about enough room to get the hay cart through. With a warrior to either side and me walking between them, I can almost hear their hearts beating as they face our enemy, expressions as blank as they can make them.

At the far end of the bridge, the small collection of Raiders is waiting. As they see me, two figures detach themselves from the group, walking, one behind the other, toward me. I hope they've not deciphered all of the defences that have been added to the bridge. But it's too late to worry about that now. I peer behind them, noting the thread of smoke being emitted from the farmer's steading. It lies low, mingling with the dankness of the day. I take it as a sign that they've not been molested.

I wait on my side of the bridge, where a small walkway allows admittance over the deep ditch. It's retracted every night, leaving people nowhere to go but the deep ditch or back the way they came. I sniff the air, detecting the ripeness of the water. I'm not about to step onto the bridge and make myself vulnerable.

The first person who comes towards me is undoubtedly a woman, her hips swaying with every step, as she quickly makes her way. We've left a small space for them to stand side by side. Behind me, I'm aware of my Aunt and Ealdorman Ælhun's presence.

"King Coelwulf," the woman's voice is sharp, and I meet piercing grey eyes that are only a few inches lower than mine. She's tall, for a woman. "My name is Estrith, and this is Asbjorn." Her accent is sharp, the words seemingly spoken with some effort.

"Well met," I incline my head, but make no other show of respect. I have no idea who they are. None at all. Estrith is dressed in a sealskin cloak, wrapped tightly around her body, with leather boots reaching to her knee. They are surprisingly clear of mud; I can't see that lasting for long. Asbjorn is taller than the woman, his face devoid of a beard and a moustache, his naked head flashing in the gloom. He's entirely bald and has been for a long time because I detect no difference in the colour of his skin, as I might see on someone who'd shaved their head.

"Thank you for agreeing to speak to us."

"I haven't, not yet. I'm merely here to listen to what it is you want to say." I hope my Aunt approves of my words. I hope they're the bloody right ones.

"Then, my thanks, all the same." It seems the man isn't to speak, and I gaze at him.

He shares the same grey eyes as the woman, but they're much less sharp. He's not the thinker in this relationship, whatever that relationship is.

Estrith is undeterred by my less than helpful reply.

"I've come to beg for your assistance. I. Well, to put it bluntly, I left something behind in Northampton, and I would like to claim it back. I have the coin. I'm prepared to pay." She fumbles beneath her cloak as though to bring forth her great wealth. I'm already busy thinking. It seems this woman is nothing to do with the Raiders on the far side of Northampton.

"Why would I give you back something that is now mine by right of conquest."

"Ah, My Lord King. I don't believe that you will want to keep it. It's probably causing more problems for you than you'd like to admit." This piques my interest, even though I don't want to admit as much.

"What exactly is it that you discarded in Northampton?" But I think I know what she's about to say.

"A child. Well, a baby really, not long out of the womb. I left him here, and I should dearly love to hold him in my arms, and have him back."

I hear Ealdorman Ælhun's sharp inhalation, and I wish I could caution him to silence. Does this woman genuinely think we would hand over the child if it weren't already dead?

"How would we know the child is yours?" My Aunt speaks, for all I cautioned her against it.

"Well, I would recognise it," the woman states, as though the question is ridiculous.

"And how would such a small child recognise you?"

"What?" Estrith's sharp eyes snap to me, and I shrug, ensuring that the weapons on my belt make a soft clunk of noise as I sway from side to side.

"How would we know that you're the mother? Tell me, does he have any marks that would identify him."

I see a flicker of fury on Estrith's face, while the man beside her, shuffles on his feet, although his eyes remain downcast.

"Did you leave him in the care of another woman? Surely, such a small child would need his mother to feed him?" My Aunt speaks once more.

I think the woman will just give up. Surely, she must realise that she can't just come here and retrieve the child. I consider who she is, perhaps the child's Aunt, keen to claim the baby's inheritance.

She surprises me; she really does, with her reaction.

Tears begin to fall down her face; her body wracked with sobs. How I consider, has she gone from fierce-faced warrior to sobbing woman between one breath and the next.

Now the man speaks.

"Would you deprive a woman of her child?" His voice is rough, as though he rarely uses it, although his delivery is smoother than Estrith's.

"I have no means of knowing if the child belongs to her," I state blandly, not at all concerned by the sobbing noises which are slowly increasing in sound.

"I could examine her," my Aunt offers, her voice devoid of all emotion. "I would know if she's recently birthed a child."

The words hang heavy, and I believe my Aunt would do such a thing. I also know that this woman has not brought a child into this world recently, but I'm curious to know who she is.

The fact that the woman doesn't immediately submit to such an inspection only reinforces my belief that this is all utter bollocks. But, I've had enough of the tedious exchange.

"Return this evening. I'll have an answer for you."

Such a flurry of emotions covers the woman's tear-stained face that I hardly know what she makes of such a statement. Does she truly believe that I'd just hand over a child? If Werburg was still here, and the child still lived, would she not have something to say about it? I want to speak to my Aunt and Ealdorman

Ælhun before we do anything. For now, I'll give Estrith some hope, even if it's futile.

"My Lord King," and she bows her head and turns, as though to move away.

"There's also the matter of the child's wealth," she twists her head to state.

"Wealth?" I feel my forehead furrow at the statement.

"Yes, yes, there should also be a chest, filled with coins. They belonged to the child's father. It would make his future much more secure if I could also have the coins back."

This doesn't quite match with her assertion that she could pay for the child, but I simply nod.

"This evening. I'll make a decision and meet you here."

I watch the woman and man walk back across the bridge, noting that her sobs have stilled and that she walks with the poise and fleet-footedness of a warrior once more. This woman is a liar, but I don't want to dismiss her immediately. Not just yet.

"Come on, let's return inside," I instruct my Aunt and the ealdorman, and the three of us make our way back inside the gate, nodding our thanks to the men who've guarded us so well. I wait for everyone to return inside, and for the gateway to be sealed closed once more.

"You did well. You have my thanks," I inform my men and the Mercians, and tight smiles cover strained faces.

As I make my way to the hall, the silence between my Aunt, Ealdorman Ælhun, and myself is heavy. It seems we all have much to discuss.

"Rudolf."

"My Lord." He's before me, eyes bright, keen to assist, as always. By rights, I should call on Wulfhere, for this task, but I don't.

"Go into that room, hunt for this chest. I've seen nothing like it, but if it's here, I would be curious to see what it contains." The room where Werburg was found is abandoned. No one uses it. The knowledge of what happened in there is too powerful.

A smile plays around Rudolf's lips at my command, and I

know he'll get Wulfhere and Hiltiberht to assist him.

"Well," My Aunt speaks first as we settle close to the hearth. "Who is that woman?"

"It must be the child's aunt, or someone clever enough to know that the child could be wealthy, with the death of its grandfather and uncle."

"The bloody presumption," Ealdorman Ælhun is scandalised by what he's seen and heard. His face is almost puce, and I hide a smirk as my Aunt hands him a goblet of wine to calm him.

"Why didn't you just tell them that the child was dead?" My Aunt asks the question, but Ealdorman Ælhun nods beside her. He's thinking the same.

"I'm curious as to who they are, and what they might be able to tell us."

"I doubt they'd offer anything."

"Maybe, but, I didn't want to just send them on their way. It might be a coincidence that they arrived with the reinforcements, but I'm not at all convinced."

"Coelwulf," Edmund rushes into the hall, calling my name. I'd lost track of him on my return to the hall.

"What is it?"

"There's more of them, and they're coming towards Northampton from the landward side."

"Ah. Let's see what this is all about then."

I stand quickly, almost pleased to be distracted from the mystery of the woman demanding back Werburg's baby. Certainly, there are no other small babies inside Northampton who could be the focus of this woman's demands.

It's almost easy to struggle to my feet and take the steps back up to the wooden walkway. I feel more able than I have for days, and that seems to perk me up even more.

Those on watch duty are alert, but not concerned, and that surprises me until I look out at the view.

There are ten mounted warriors, slowly riding toward the place where the gate once stood, which is now blocked up tightly, and with the deep ditch in front of it. I imagine there are so many because they're trying to determine how we managed to escape inside Northampton even though there's no visible entranceway. Maybe they believe we had the aid of sprites or goblins.

Leading them is a man I know to be Jarl Guthrum. He's shrouded in a thick fur, and yet his arms are uncovered. He's determined to reveal his owl tattoos, even though it must be uncomfortable. But I can't decipher the details; it's his auburn hair that gives him away, that and the fact that Jarl Oscetel's face is covered with serpent sigils. I know who this man is. I imagine he comes to seek payment for the death of his sister, and possibly his brother, or Uncle.

The party comes close enough that it's possible to hear the snorting of the horses and the heavy impacts of their hooves over the rapidly muddying surface.

"Lord Coelwulf." Jarl Guthrum turns his head upwards to bellow for my attention.

"King," Edmund retorts immediately, and I almost wish he hadn't, when a small smirk touches Guthrum's cheeks.

"Jarl Guthrum. What brings you and your warriors to Northampton?"

"Restitution."

"For fucking what?"

"I think you know, Lord Coelwulf," Guthrum's eyes flicker to Edmund's puckered face, and I wish I were close enough to Edmund to caution him. But I'm not, however, my Aunt is, and I watch her as she reaches out to touch his back. They're so close, I doubt anyone else notices the movement, but I do.

"The murder of my sister and my Uncle."

"They died in battle. They knew what they were doing. They didn't have to fucking fight. They could have come running back to you. They chose to take a chance on death. There's no wergeld due."

"Ah, but there is. You kidnapped my Aunt."

"But she died in battle."

"Why don't you come here," Jarl Guthrum taunts, his finger

indicating the ground in front of him. "This conversation is tedious when we must shout, one to another."

"No, it's not," I state. Even now, it seems that Jarl Guthrum doubts my intelligence. It's fucking infuriating.

"If there is no wergild, then I'll have no alternative, but to attack Northampton, claim back the price of my sister's life. She was my only sister."

"You think your sister's wergild is the value of Northampton?" I confess I laugh as I speak, pleased to see the swift flicker of fury on Jarl Guthrum's face.

"Yes, well, it will be when I also factor in the lives of the men and women who served me here. I assume they're all dead as well."

The mortal remains of the three bodies I had on display outside Northampton have disintegrated to little but empty pieces of cloth, still, I would have expected Jarl Guthrum to realise what they were.

"Jarl Guthrum, there's no wergild due for your sister and Uncle, or your lost men and women. We conquered Northampton. Your sister and Uncle died in battle. Our conversation is at an end. Good day."

I don't turn my back on him, but I do step away so that it appears as though I've dismissed him.

"Lord Coelwulf," his voice thrums with menace. "If you'll not negotiate with me, then I'll fucking take what I'm due." Fury masks his words.

"And that would be fucking nothing." I step back to the wall to deliver my final statement.

I'm rewarded for my words, by the noise of the jarl and his warriors, turning their mounts. The thunder of hooves, filling the air. It sounds as though there are a hundred warriors out there, but I know there aren't.

"The fucking cheek," Edmund explodes.

"He's all hot air and bile," I caution everyone on the wooden walkway. "He's just told us what he plans to do, but now we need to decipher what he's going to fucking do." My words get the attention of everyone, and I'm pleased.

"We need to remain alert, even more than before. We're safe inside Northampton, but only until they manage to find a way inside. Anything strange, any half-heard noise in the night, anything, needs to be reported to me, or Ealdorman Ælhun. No matter how small and inconsequential. I don't trust the bastards. Not at all. Whatever they do out there, with the reinforcements and the tents, it's merely to distract us from their true intent. Remember that. But, we will beat them, again, when the time comes. Remember that as well."

I turn aside then and make my way down the steps.

I'm not sure how Jarl Guthrum plans on reclaiming Northampton, but I know that he does, and that means that I was right to stay here. Now, I just need to work out what it all means. My mind returns to the worry of who the traitor within Northampton might be, because I know they're still here, somewhere, hidden in plain sight.

"Fuck," I complain, over-stepping as I belatedly realise there's a muddy puddle before me, sending a shuddering pain down my right leg.

"You should watch where you walk," my Aunt offers, no hint of sympathy in her voice, as her stride matches mine.

"Thank you," I seethe, and she laughs, the sound reverberating around the enclosed space of Northampton.

"I hadn't realised how enjoyable spending time with you would be," she offers. "An enemy at the front gate, and one where the rear gate used to be, both of them clearly up to something that seeks to undermine you."

"Yes," waiting for her to say more.

"Is it always like this?" she asks, almost eagerly, and I feel my lips pull down.

"No, there's normally others as well, and there's always someone trying to kill me."

"Lucky for you that I'm here then. I can heal you from anything but the most mortal of cuts."

"How would you suggest that I proceed?"

"I'm here to watch you at work, not to interfere. I'll mop up the bleeding cuts, and see to the injured. I have no advice for you." But I know she doesn't mean that, far from it.

Great, I think, now I have to second-guess myself, and consider what my Aunt wants me to do at the same time.

Fucking wonderful.

CHAPTER 5

"There are three young children inside Northampton. You'll have to come and decide if any of them is your son. The women who care for them are adamant that they belong to them."

The woman startles at my words, turning to peer back to where the two other riders wait for her on the other side of the bridge. I've had the gateway opened once more, and my Mercians are alert as they stand to attention.

The scouting party from the woods have returned, and I've had the farmer and his family brought inside Northampton as well, the oxen as well, much to Rudolf's disgust. I'm not prepared to risk anything, not yet. I still think this might be a two-pronged attack, for all the Raiders on the far side of the Nene must have made themselves scarce after our earlier discussion on the bridge. I wish I knew where they'd been, but Wulfsige was unaware they'd even visited Northampton when he returned with a wagon piled high with wood of all shapes and sizes. It will last us for some considerable time, and that pleases me.

"Can you not bring the children here? I would know my son as soon as I saw him." Estrith looks perplexed by my words, and also, deeply uneasy. I try not to notice the consternation on her face at my statement that there are multiple children. Does she suspect the falsehood? She'd know I lied if she'd ever been inside Northampton before.

"No, the women will not allow such, and neither will I. Even if you determine on which child is yours, there's still the matter of proving it. It won't be easy. You can bring your companion with you." I offer that because the man is already trying to back away and to speak of him, draws the woman's sharp attention, and he reluctantly returns to her side.

My Aunt and Ealdorman Ælhun await me in the main hall, and so I stand alone on the bridge, although surrounded by my warriors.

"What assurance do I have that nothing will happen to me."

I've been expecting such a response.

"Here," and I push between my legs the chest that I think she wants. It contains little, and also much. She's welcome to it.

"My chest?" the woman only just stops herself from pouncing on the item, made from rich, dark wood, in her eagerness.

"Take it, but this is your only chance to come inside and find your son."

I can see that she's torn. Does she still mean to pursue her claim to a child or is the chest that Rudolf, Wulfhere and Hiltiberht discovered, enough?

Her hand caresses the darkness of the chest, and then she stands and faces me.

"I'll come alone. There's no need for anyone else to come with me."

"As you will," and I stand to the side to allow her entry. Behind me, Sæbald and Goda are protecting the open gateway. They're adorned with as many weapons as we could hang onto their weapons belts, their byrnies clean and shining, and I know how intimidating they look, and equally, how they're trying not to cut themselves on so many blades and edges.

"Wait for me here," the woman commands her man, handing him her weapons belt. I try to ignore the way he licks his lips, as though considering whether to stay, or leave, his eyes flashing to the chest with a look of wanton lust. I suspect he'll go.

"Keep an eye on everyone," I inform Lyfing, who has the command of the gateway and bridge. "No one is to leave here." I raise my voice as I speak, and the man startles. The fool. He should make his thoughts less easy to discern.

The woman walks passed me, head held high, the scent of her, making me wrinkle my nose. She smells of blood and pain.

Inside the gate, Sæbald and Goda flank Estrith and I, although there are only a handful of other warriors in sight. I don't want her to count my strength. If she's come here on the instructions of Jarl Guthrum and Oscetel, I want him to be disappointed with what she reports.

"Where is my son?"

"In the hall, by the hearth, keeping warm. It's a bitter night." And it is bitter. The rain that's fallen all day has given way to a crystalline sky, no clouds in sight. By the morning, I imagine there will be ice in the puddles.

I walk beside her, aware that she could attack me at any time, although I doubt she will. I didn't ask her to cast aside her weapons belt, but she did so all the same, that speaks to me of someone with more weapons hidden on their person. Otherwise, she would not have been so keen.

I don't miss that her eyes try and peer into the shadowed recesses of the stables, or even that she seems to intentionally stop and fiddle with her leg bindings, even though they're tight enough. I know that Rudolf and Edmund are watching her carefully. Anything that I miss, they'll see.

At the entrance to the hall, Tatberht and Wærwulf observe our passage with uninterested eyes, holding the door open, with a respectful nod of their heads as they spot me. They too shimmer with blades and wear thick cloaks flung over their shoulders, so that Estrith can see the weapons they own. I confess, I admire her fierce resolve. A pity she's going to be disappointed.

And then we're in the hall, the warmth of the hearth licking around my ankles, as the door shuts behind us. Now comes the time for my ruse.

My Aunt sits by the hearth, as though she holds an infant, her arms cradled in front of her. She has her back half turned to the door, Ealdorman Ælhun beside her. The majority of the men are absent, either on guard duty, or just waiting elsewhere. They didn't object to the tactic to keep our expanded numbers a secret.

"Where are the other women?" Estrith demands to know, her forward momentum suddenly slowing as she realises that there are not three women and three children waiting for her. Frantic eyes look my way, but I shake my head.

"You should sit," I advise her. "It'll go better for you."

"You tricked me!" Her voice is a screech of outrage, her hand fumbling for a seax at her waist, only she's left it at the bridge.

"And you didn't try and deceive me? Now sit, and this can still go the way you want it." Estrith looks like a trapped animal, left with no option but to jump over a cliff edge or submit to the arrows aimed at it. Behind me, I feel the presence of Sæbald and Goda, as they follow me into the room. I wouldn't want to go against them, not unarmed.

Reluctantly, I watch Estrith decide to take the offered seat, to the side of my Aunt, and placed alone. There is no one close to her. My Aunt remains in position. I need Estrith to think that the child still lives for this to work.

"Are you an ally of Jarl Guthrum?"

"Who?" her eyes bore into me. I would think it the truth, but I'm not sure.

"Jarl Guthrum. About my height, auburn hair. Really shit tattoos of owls on his arms." That she tenses as I speak tells me more than her shake of denial. She at least knows who Jarl Guthrum is, but whether she's an ally or not remains to be seen.

"Why are you so much in his debt that you have to risk your life in such a way?"

Stoney silence greets my words, and I think that she'll not speak, only then she does.

"It's not Jarl Guthrum who's my ally, but his sister. And you, you fucking bastard, killed her." Spittle flies from her mouth to land near my boot, although still a reasonable distance away, as her finger jabs toward me.

"She tried to kill me," I offer, a faint shrug of my shoulder. I'm pleased the motion no longer pains me as it did when I first returned from my heroic last stand.

"So what, now Jarl Guthrum has sent you to Northampton? As some sort of punishment."

"This is nothing to do with Jarl Guthrum, you daft bastard." The malice in the final two words, finally convinces me that her arrival hasn't been planned to coincide with that of Jarl Guthrum and Oscetel to the rear of Northampton.

"Who is the child to you, because you're not its mother?"

"What?" She doesn't like being caught with her invention.

"I know you're not the child's mother. Tell me why you want it?"

Again, I think she'll stay silent, but with a lick of her lips, and a hunger in her intelligent eyes that I despise, she speaks.

"The child is the heir to Ealdorman Wulfstan. With it, I'll hold a claim to his lands." The rampant need in Estrith's eyes is unsettling.

"That's not how landed inheritance works in Mercia." Ealdorman Ælhun enters the conversation. "The child will not give you what you want."

A squawk, almost like an animal in distress, rips from her mouth, to be followed by a heavy silence, punctuated only by her gasping breaths.

"Then it's all for nothing," she admits, the longing in her eyes dissipating, as her shoulders slump. I've put her out of her misery, but I have a final question for her before I allow her to leave.

"Do you know if there's a traitor within these walls?"

"What?" She appears dumbfounded, perhaps even angered by the knowledge that there might have been someone who could help her, had she known about them. "We found Raiders, camping in the woods in that direction," I nod towards Grantabridge.

"I know nothing of them," but again, her voice quivers.

"They're all dead," I continue, watching her reaction. The knowledge upsets her, although she tries not to show it. Her hands are gripped tightly, one inside the other. Her eyes look anywhere but at me, or the longed-for child.

"I don't know anything about that." But I know she's lying, even if she's a competent dissembler.

"The child is dead," I inform her, aware the words are callous, as my Aunt drops her pretence of holding a child close.

Estrith gasps in horror, as my Aunt turns to face her. There's no compassion on my Aunt's stern face, none at all.

"Did you know they trapped the woman beneath the floorboards?" My Aunt demands to know. Her voice is flecked with rage. It's immediately evident that Estrith did know. That she doesn't try and deny it, earns her a flicker of my respect.

"And the woman?" There's an element of hope in her voice, but I don't give the satisfaction of an answer. I won't imperil Werburg, even if she's safe in Kingsholm.

"Now, I believe our meeting is at an end," I nod to Sæbald and Goda, and then come forward, waiting beside Estrith's chair. That she doesn't immediately stand, puts me on edge.

Did she come for the child, or something else?

"You can leave now," I speak, just to break the suddenly tense atmosphere. If my Aunt had access to a weapon, I'm sure she'd slay this woman. It's for that reason that I've kept Rudolf and Pybba far away from this strange meeting. I wouldn't be surprised if they did the same, even though Werburg was only amongst us for a matter of weeks.

"Why would you let me go?" This seems to surprise her, as Estrith finally stands.

"I do not need to kill you. You say you're not an ally of Jarl Guthrum or Oscetel. The child is dead as well. Are you a threat to me?"

"No, no, I'm not," she assures me quickly, perhaps the promise of survival when she expected to be slain, making her speak the truth for the first time during our meeting.

"Then you can leave. I'm not a cruel man," and the taunt is enough to make her move, even though she winces as though I've whipped her.

I watch her walk away, flanked by my men, and I settle on a

chair, letting out a huge sigh.

"Fucking bitch," Ealdorman Ælhun explodes, and I feel my eyebrows jump into my hairline. I'm not used to him reacting in such a way.

"How could a woman treat another woman in such a way?" my Aunt asks, her voice soft, shaken perhaps. Such cruelty from one to another always comes as a surprise to those who've never witnessed it before.

"Well, that was a waste of fucking time," I complain, only for my Aunt to fix me with her firm gaze. My hand extends towards Ealdorman Ælhun, who's escaped censure, but she shakes her head at me, the disappointment clear to see.

"Perhaps not," it's Edmund who speaks, only as I open my mouth to ask him what he means, Wulfsige rushes in behind him, the door barely closed after Estrith's departure, before it's opened once more.

"An attack, My Lord King, on the old gateway."

"Fuck," but I'm already on my feet and rushing for the door.

"Stay here," I caution my Aunt, but I know she'll do exactly what she wants. Still, I have to offer the caveat.

I take a moment to peer toward the gateway at the bridge, pleased to see it closing, Estrith sent on her way, Goda and Sæbald remaining there to ensure that nothing untoward happens in the coming moments when we're at our weakest.

Ealdorman Ælhun is close behind me, my Aunt hovering in the still-open doorway.

"Everyone, weapons ready," I bellow, pleased to see faces emerging from doorways and other hideouts. At the same time, the men at the bridge gateway, startle and quickly turn to reinforce the gate with long pieces of wood, prepared for just such an eventuality, slotting them into the catches made by the blacksmith. He's much in demand.

I can smell smoke, and turn frantically to look to the wooden walkway above the old entrance, visible even from where I stand, relieved to see men streaming up the steep steps. At least it doesn't burn.

"How many?" I demand to know of Wulfsige.

"Impossible to say. But at least fifty, maybe more." Damn the fuckers for deciding to attack now, in the dark. What can they hope to accomplish?

"Some are mounted, others are not. They seem determined to reach the old gateway."

"Um," that doesn't surprise me, not when I think back to my conversation with the Raider in the woodlands. He thought there was both a traitor and a weakness inside Northampton. It seems I'm about to find out whether he spoke the truth or not.

"Right, well, we need to reinforce that area and the new entrances. Edmund," and he's beside me immediately. "Take half of the men and guard there. I'll be along shortly." I want to look at what Jarl Guthrum and his men are doing beyond the palisade. "The rest of you, join Sæbald and Goda at the bridge. I don't want to throw all my weight behind the obvious attack when there might be another one planned."

Edmund uncharacteristically rushes to follow my instructions, leaving me with Wulfsige, Ealdorman Ælhun and my Aunt.

"Send men to watch every length of the wall. I don't trust the bastards." And then I'm dashing through the street after Edmund. I veer to mount the steps that felt too steep earlier and now disappear beneath my feet without so much as a second thought.

Three brands are lighting the palisade, but no others. Not that I need them, for Jarls Guthrum and Oscetel have lit enough on the far side to make it appear as though it's day, not night.

"What the hell?" Once more, I'm astounded by my enemy. What the fuck are they even doing?

CHAPTER 6

Below me, there are eleven mounted warriors just to the far side of the deep ditch. They've formed some sort of protective ring around a group of twenty warriors, all carrying items.

"What are those?"

Wulfsige risks a glance.

"It looks like ladders to me."

"So, they weren't building shelters with all that wood?"

"It appears not, My Lord King." Wulfsige's voice is steady as he replies.

"Can you ensure none of the ladders allows anyone inside?" I turn to meet his eyes then, hoping to see his firm resolve.

I wish I'd not sent my men to the most obvious places now. I would have appreciated Goda and Sæbald on the palisade, Lyfing and Tatberht as well. They're steady men. They'd not have panicked. Perhaps even Hereman, with his unfailing ability to hit an enemy with his spear, even if he takes unacceptable risks, but he's still recovering. I hope the daft fucker is protecting my Aunt, as well as Gardulf and Siric. I expect everyone else to be fighting.

"Yes, My Lord King. We'll die trying." Wulfsige's words are a bit dramatic, but I appreciate the intent behind them, despite that.

"You have my thanks."

But as I turn to rush back down the steps, a whoosh reaches

my ears, and I'm already crouching low, keen to avoid the arrow. It skips beyond me, but I can smell its passage. Was it a lucky shot? Surely it must be. How could they have known where I'd be, and when?

"Bastards." It seems they're going to try every means to destroy Northampton. I doubt the flame will catch on anything, it's too damn damp after the day of rain, but such weapons might skewer my warriors, and it wouldn't be a pleasant way to die, far from it.

The arrow lands harmlessly in the middle of a muddy puddle below the palisade, and I watch its glinting flame sizzle and die out, a flash of bright light in the darkness. It might have been helpful once the ice had formed, but it's not yet cold enough for that,

'My Aunt brought four archers with her," I inform Ealdorman Ælhun when I reach him. My Aunt has left his side, and I hope it means she's following my instructions. "Have one of them brought here, and given the same. We'll see how the fuckers like flaming arrows flying back at them."

I'm grateful then for the wall that the walkway juts out from. The walkway might be wood, but the embankment is mud, damp mud, the smell assaulting my nostrils. It's not going to burn. Not anytime soon.

"Get some shields up there as well. The men might need them."

Only then do I leave Ealdorman Ælhun's side, a glance toward the bridge gateway, showing me nothing, because there are buildings in the way, and it's too damn dark, anyway.

"Ah, Wulfhere," the young lad stands before me, all eagerness. "Stay close, but not too close. If I need you to, I'll rely on you to deliver messages to the gate or the men guarding the walls. But first, run and check on the horses. The main stable door needs to be closed but open all the stalls. I'll not risk one of these fire arrows hitting a target. My horses won't perish."

"My Lord," his eyes are alight with enthusiasm as he speaks. For a moment, I wish he wasn't here. I wish no one were here other than my warriors and I. I don't like to consider being responsible for more unnecessary deaths, but no, I'm the king of Mercia, and everyone here fights willingly for a future free from the Raiders.

"Your Aunt wants you to know that she's ready for the injured. Hereman's with her. He's not happy being inside."

"I doubt he would be, but he's no good to me out here. He's weaker than a new-born foal. Now, stay out of trouble, and go to the stables," and I rush to where Edmund is busy arranging the men under his command, just in front of the twin tunnels.

Tatberht greets me with a wry smirk, his clear eye, bright in the flames from a brand.

"Does it never stop?" he asks, and I clasp his forearm in greeting.

"I think you know the fucking answer to that," I retort, as Wulfstan chuckles beside him.

"Come now; we nearly had two weeks without a fight. That might be a bloody record."

Edmund has also included Ælfgar in his selection of men, and Pybba and Rudolf stand close together, both checking the other to ensure byrnies are well fastened, and they've done all they can to protect against injury. They don't yet wear helms, but they have them ready if they're needed.

"Why do they attack here? There's no bloody way in?" Rudolf's voice reflects his confusion at facing a steep wall of mud, a deep ditch to the far side, and little else besides. There's a thin line of churned mud before the ditch, but not enough for a horse, or even a warrior, encumbered with sword and shield.

"I just have a feeling," I advise him, slapping his back as I make my way to Edmund. He and Wærwulf have hands against the muddy slope. It's been reinforced with wooden boards, to hold the mass upright. Without them, I might fear that the quantity of rain and moisture in the air, would force the mud wall to slither, either inwards or outwards. But, like Rudolf, I don't see a way for the Raiders to get inside.

"Any weaknesses?" I demand to know.

"Not a fucking one," Edmund's voice is rich with assurance, his empty eye socket, turning to glance at me, although his hands remain busy checking the surface of the wall.

"I just don't think they could come this way."

"Neither do I, but this is where they've chosen to attack. It must be for a reason." Edmund's grunt tells me all I need to know. He thinks my worry misplaced. I wish I could be as confident.

"What about the other entrances?"

"They're closed. They have been for two weeks now. I can't see that they'd even know they were there. The fact they attack the old entrance, makes me believe they didn't even realise the ruse when we rescued you."

"Perhaps, but maybe not."

"Pybba, Rudolf," they both lift heads from their preparations. "Guard the new tunnel. Wulfstan and Tatberht, you take the one to the right. Wulfhere is running messenger duty. Keep him informed of anything, and I mean anything, that's strange or just doesn't sit right with you."

"Coelwulf, seriously, this is stupid. You shouldn't waste us here. We could be up on the rampart. We could be killing the bastards."

"How? It's not like we can ride out and run them down. We have few enough arrows, and I'm not going to throw good iron spears at them, which I might never get back. They'll wear themselves out with this stupid attack, but just in case they don't, we need to cover everything."

I can see he's not fucking happy.

"What do you want to do?" I feel stung into asking.

"Not crouch here in the fucking dark?"

"Then, light a bloody great big fire," and I stalk from him. What does he expect me to do? I didn't tell the Raiders to attack now.

The rest of the settlement is strangely quiet, nothing but the occasional whinny from the stables, and the soft murmur of men and women talking. It feels bizarre. Beyond the defences men and women try to beat us, but how can they possibly expect to win? It's that, more than anything, which makes me wary. That, and the knowledge that the Raiders I encountered believed there was a traitor inside Northampton.

"All quiet here?" I call to Sæbald when I'm close enough to the bridge gate to be heard.

"Nothing, My Lord, nothing at all. What's happening over there?" and he inclines his head towards the wooden platform. The fires of the Raiders backlight the far reaches of the settlement. I can see the men on the wooden platform but only as sticks.

"A fucking lot of piss and bile, and not a lot else. What are they playing around at?"

Sæbald shrugs his shoulders.

"What the fuck's happening with the daft bastards?" Of course, Wulfred makes an appearance.

"They've got a few fire arrows and some ladders, or so it seems. I think they mean to climb the walls although they won't be able to, not from there. Ealdorman Ælhun's men will meet them."

"Are they only attacking by the old entranceway?" Sæbald's forehead is as furrowed as mine, the brazier close to the gate offering light to enable us to see.

"Yes. But it makes no sense. Mercian warriors line the rampart. The Raiders would need a ladder to get up there, and one to get down on the interior as well, or face marooning on the bloody top."

"Daft sods are just trying it on," Wulfred announces, turning aside. My men are close to the tightly closed gateway, hidden from sight. It's as though we fight the dark and nothing else.

"It smacks of desperation," Sæbald agrees, Goda grunting along.

"Just stay fucking alert," I caution them. "Just because it seems futile right now, doesn't mean that it will be all night. Fuck, it's cold." I've removed my left hand from its glove to wipe my sweaty forehead, but immediately, the cold attacks it.

I thrust my hand back inside the warm glove.

"If anyone gets wounded, anyone, get him inside. This cold will kill more quickly than a knife cut. Don't chance it."

I press my hand against Sæbald's shoulder, pleased to have his steadying presence here. With Icel gone, and Hereman still not healed, I need good men who will keep their heads when all around them seems madness. I missed Sæbald when he was wounded.

"Wulfhere is running messenger. Use him if you need him."

"What are you going to do?"

"I'm going to watch the fuckers and try to determine at what they're playing. Damn pestilent bastards."

As I make my way back the way I've come, a few arrows fly through the air, coming to land in any variety of sodden puddles, as though they can only aim for them. I would laugh, but my unease is growing. This all feels very wrong.

"My Lord," Wulfhere appears before me, bent double, hands on his knees, as he pants.

"Over there, My Lord. Over there," and he points, not toward either of the entrances, or the wooden platform, but rather to a dark patch of shadows behind some of the dwellings. Immediately, I understand what he's trying to tell me.

"Fuck. Get Lyfing and Ordlaf, from the bridge. Send them after me."

I'm almost running to where Wulfhere indicated. It's impossible to see a great deal, but the light of the Raiders fires has made visible something that troubles me. The damn bastards. They are going to try it with the ladders, only not where I expected them to do so. How much damn wood did they collect?

"Come with me," I run into a selection of the warriors my Aunt brought with her from Mercia, and recognising their leader, Turhtredus; I bark my instruction at him.

Lyfing and Ordlaf jog to join me, just as I come upon the men sent to guard this section of the wall. There should only have been two of them, but now there are eleven. No doubt, they've called others to aid them as they've realised what's about to happen.

"Get back to your positions," I order, surprised by how easy I'm finding it to give instructions. "I've men to reinforce this section. But be wary, the damn fuckers might try this anywhere."

"But how will they get down?" There's almost wonder in the voice. The wall towers over the main hall, and the steadings of those who made Northampton their home, look like children's toys. While it might be easy to lean a ladder against the wall, on the thin strip of land that remains between the deep ditch and the wall, how they're going to get down is beyond me. Unless they have another ladder. Is it even possible? Could they climb up the ladder, and then move it to the interior of the wall? Would it not be too heavy, too unwieldy, threatening to tumble them into our spike-laden ditch?

Above, I see a leg appear, illuminated by a burning arrow, and immediately, I wish I had more archers than just the four my Aunt brought with her. And then another leg appears, seeming to mount the top of the wall, and yet, what will the Raider do now? The interior walls are just as sheer as those on the exterior. Will he just dangle there? Or will he risk falling?

And then I see a piece of rope snake down the wall, and I know their plan.

"Wulfhere," I bellow, and the youth is there almost before the word leaves my mouth.

"They're going to use ropes. Tell the others."

His glance upwards, perhaps to assure himself of what's happening, brings a sort of strangled cry to his mouth.

"Tell my Aunt to send out any remaining men. We need to guard all of the walls. All of it. Inform Sæbald and Edmund. Have them redirect some of those with them."

He nods and rushes away.

I lick my lips, reach for my seax, keen to kill this Raider, who attempts to sneak inside Northampton. The damn fucker.

Only Lyfing is quicker. Before my eyes, he snatches up a piece of wood and thrusts it into the brazier close by, wrapping a piece of fabric torn from his tunic around the wood. Without pausing to consider his intentions, the flames are against the dangling rope. While everything else is damp and soggy, the rope must be bone-dry, because the flames streak skywards, as though a piece of hair, and the warrior screams, letting go of the flaming snake he holds, tumbling to his death.

The jumble of bones and flesh as he hits the floor beside us even brings bile to my throat.

It's not a fitting way for a man to die.

"Fuck." The Mercians closest to the wall jump backwards, trying to avoid the pieces of flesh that flee through the air. I snap my mouth shut. I don't need to taste that.

"Bloody bollocks."

As one, all eyes travel from the ruin of the Raider upwards. There's another warrior there, highlighted against the glow of the fires outside Northampton. His white face is too easy to see, as our gazes turn from him, to the second rope, just swinging into view before us.

"Fuck, quickly," but Lyfing is already there, his brand taking only moments longer to catch. This rope must be dry as well. But my eyes are on the Raider, as he scrabbles, desperately, to reach the safety of the ladder that allowed him to climb the wall. Only, of course, there's another Raider there, no doubt trying to balance on the thin pieces of wood which are all that separate him from crashing to the ground.

With no thought for the other Raider, the man attached to the flaming rope shoves hard, desperate to have something to grab hold of, as the flames climb higher. To my mind, the fire travels more slowly than the first time around. At the last possible moment, the Raider cuts himself loose from the rope, and it's the only object landing on the floor with a soft snap. There's little enough of it left.

But now the two Raiders are seemingly stuck on the top of the wall.

I find a smile on my lips.

"What the actual fuck?" I muse.

"Stupid bastards," Ordlaf offers, and I'm grunting an agreement, while we're transfixed by the action on the top of the wall. The first warrior, who nearly fell to his death, is back over the wall, only his head keeps reappearing, while the other, marooned, Raider looks around in confusion.

He's not seen what's happened to the first man. He doesn't know why his comrade is trying to escape.

"Light the fucker up," I instruct Lyfing, and he does, throwing the brand to the ground. It quickly catches on the Raiders clothes, a brief inferno covering him, the stench of singed hair, and the smell of roast pig almost making me gag again.

Of course, the Raider on the wall glances instinctively to the source of the flames.

"*Skiderik.*" He shrieks, trying to follow the first man off the wall, but again, there's nowhere for him to go, because there are now four heads there.

I lick my lips, wishing Wulfhere was still beside me. I'd appreciate an archer about now. I'm not the only one to have the idea, and in the quickly guttering fire of the dead man, a selection of items are thrown skywards. The clang of a stone hitting one of the helms is greeted with a roar of approval. I'm even tempted to join the game, but I want the damn bastards off my wall. Now.

There's a scurry of activity above, and I wince as the inevitable happens. There's just not enough room for all the Raiders to keep hold of the ladders. There was always going to be an argument when they tried to return to safety.

The man falls with a screech that could wake the dead, but the thump as his body hits the hard ground is just as fatal as the first man. Three pairs of angry eyes glance down at me fearfully, and I shrug.

"I'm not even fucking doing anything," I bellow, my amusement rippling through the words.

"What are they going to do now?" Ordlaf queries.

"If we're lucky, the lot of them will fall to their deaths, but preferably on the other side of the wall. Less mess to bloody clear up."

Lyfing has rushed forward, patting down the body of the man who's dead, but unburnt, but he stands, shaking his head.

"Just weapons, nothing else."

"Well, take them. It's always good to turn a man's blade against his allies."

And then Wulfhere has returned, his eyes wide with shock at the sight before him.

"Arseholes," Ordlaf offers, as though to take the sting away from the sight of a gently smouldering body, and a broken one.

"Your Aunt has redirected the men. Edmund is checking the far side. Ealdorman Ælhun and his men are still on the walkway."

"Any reports of anyone making it inside."

Wulfhere shakes his head and then realises I'm not looking at him.

"No, My Lord. But everyone is armed."

"Good, what do you have?"

Wulfhere's hand goes to his weapons belt, not quite as well provisioned as it should be.

"Here," Lyfing hands over the seax the dead man was carrying, and in the glint of the scant flames, I see no details on the holster, although I imagine it'll be a decent enough weapon. Anyone prepared to take such a direct route into Northampton, was probably a nasty bastard when it came to killing his enemy. They'd have needed good weapons.

"Look," and Ordlaf recalls me to the men on the wall. I'd expected the foolish fuckers to give up, but they're persistent shits.

"He's trying the rope around his waist, and the other is going to help him."

"He must be a mean cunt if he thinks he can take on all of us and live through it. Wulfhere, go and fetch me an archer. I've had enough of this farce."

The lad once more scampers away, and I consider removing my seax from my weapons belt, but there are enough Mercians to fell the man if he makes it to the ground. I'm sure I don't need to get involved.

I'm aware that I shouldn't just be standing here, watching, but I'm speechless. What are the Raiders trying to do? Is it all a means of distraction? I would think so, but I'm not at all convinced they're not just the victim of some half-cocked idea by Jarls Guthrum and Oscetel. Do they know the appearance of the interior wall? Or do they simply not give a fuck in their desire to reclaim Northampton, to crack it open so that I'm left with no choice but to leave the safety of the interior?

"Lyfing, Ordlaf, remain here. Make sure the arseholes aren't successful. I need to check the rest of the settlement, make sure no one else has snuck inside."

"Very well, My Lord," Lyfing rumbles, and I turn aside, only to pause.

"When the archer gets here, have him shoot them off the wall. This has gone on long enough."

But I don't go directly around the walls, but rather back to the bridge entrance, keen to ensure all is well there. I know it's the area of greatest weakness.

They still only have the one fire to see by, and it takes me a moment to work out what everyone is doing. My hand is on my seax when Sæbald steps into the light.

"We're just taking it in turn to rest up. I think it's going to be a bloody long night." That then, explains why not everyone is standing. One of the clever sods has hauled the hay cart from the stables, and now Eadulf and Wulfred are lying on it. Not that I think they're asleep, not in the real sense of the word, but they're still, sometimes that just has to suffice.

"Crazy bastards are trying to climb over the walls," and I point back to where I've just come from, but of course, it's impossible to see, because it's too damn dark and there are buildings in the way. "Make sure they don't try and climb over here." Sæbald grunts, as though the news is no surprise.

"Wulfhere mentioned it. I'm as alert as I can be. I've also had Eahric and Osbert checking the buildings close to us. I wouldn't put it beyond one of the bastards to be hiding rather than attacking. I pity the poor fucker who makes it when his comrades don't."

I hadn't considered that.

"He'll be desperate, might do anything," I agree, contemplating whether I need to direct my men elsewhere, ensure my Aunt is protected. But, in all honesty, I'd be more worried about the Raider than my Aunt. With her knowledge of healing, she'd be even more deadly than a warrior who'd lived through twenty years of battles.

"It might be a long night, yes, but we can sleep tomorrow when the wankers won't be trying to assault us. Hopefully."

"Did the woman leave?"

Sæbald nods. "She did, but not quickly. I could hear voices raised in argument long after I'd have expected them to be gone."

"Let's hope she runs into some of Jarl Guthrum's warriors. I don't imagine it'll go well for either of them."

I turn and head back into the interior of Northampton, determined to make a half-circuit before returning to Edmund, and the wooden walkway overhead.

For all that I can hear jeering from where the four men tried to gain entry over the top of the wall, it feels eerily quiet as I walk away.

Here, there are no lights at all, but I've paced the route a few times before, and with the wall at my right, I hope not to fall over my own bloody feet.

But the going is surprisingly slow.

The first two men I encounter hear my footsteps.

"Who goes there?" a deep voice calls.

"An ally," I reply, not wanting to give away my identity, just in case.

"An ally, you say?" I feel someone creeping up behind me, and I place my elbow ready, my seax in my hand.

"A fine Mercian, from Gloucester," these words settle them, and then the one calls to the other.

"It's the bloody king, you damn fool. You nearly had me attack the sodding king." A horrified face emerges from the gloom, eyes wide with shock, and I force a smile across my lips.

"Better to be bloody wary, than dead. The Raiders have been trying to get over the walls, using ropes." I recognise the two men as I step closer, and I can smell their fear.

"Call for an archer if you see anyone up there," and I point upwards, but the light from the fires doesn't reach so far, and all I can see is my pluming breath and the crystalline stars high overhead. I can feel the frost starting to settle over me.

"My Lord," the one agrees with a bow of his head, and I feel compelled to reach out and grip his forearm.

"Stay alert, and all will be well. But it's going to be a long night." And then I walk on, every so often looking up, alert to every strange sound. Even the scurrying of the rats in the rafters forces me to pause, as I make my way to every two-person guard around the periphery of the wall.

It's only the first two who threaten me, but all of them have different means of checking my identity. With relief, I appear before the old gate, almost walking into Edmund.

"Any spiders?" I ask, but Edmund's forehead furrows in confusion.

"Any Raiders trying to come over the wall?"

"No, no, not here. Why are they wasting their time trying to do something so fucking stupid?" Edmund demands to know. His voice is tight, and his face is pale. All this not knowing when he'll see the first blade is no good for Edmund. By now, he should have killed a couple of the fuckers, and be hitting his stride.

"There's something else going on, I'm sure of it, but I just don't know what yet."

"Bastards," Edmund whines and I grunt an agreement.

"Not that we didn't know that. What's Ealdorman Ælhun been up to?"

"Just been watching. No one has tried the ladders there."

"I'm going up to see," and I stride away, taking the steps quickly. It might be cold, but the threat is keeping me bloody warm.

"What news?" Ealdorman Ælhun turns to glance at me.

"A lot of titting about," his face is downcast, not so much a grimace as frustration. "It's just a distraction."

"I agree. Did Wulfhere tell you about the Raiders and the ropes?"

"Yes, he did. I take it they're dead?"

"Two of them were. An archer was going to deal with the remaining two."

Abruptly, a cloud of flames erupts from the other side of the wall. The smoke that follows is thick and black, making it impossible to see. The heat and the smoke are just too damn viscous.

"Bastards," I cough, spitting ash from my mouth, and when I can finally see, I'm unsurprised to find the Raiders and their horses gone.

"Fuckers," Ealdorman Ælhun surprises me by offering, but I'm peering out, making use of the remains of the fire that still burns. The Raiders have seemingly disappeared.

"Run back to their camp, or so it seems."

"Stay vigilant, though. It might just be another damn trick." But I've caught sight of something, the look of which I don't like. I'm already running back down the steps, to where Edmund and the rest of my warriors are looking around, confusion on their faces.

"Check the wall," I urge Edmund, walking close enough to speak quietly. I don't want there to be mass panic.

"What am I checking for?" he demands to know.

"Heat. I think they're trying to dry it out, not burn it down."

"So that's the purpose of the fire. It makes sense," Edmund admits, and I run my hands along the wall, lower and lower, and as I do, the wall gets warmer and warmer.

"What do you think?"

"I agree. There's more warmth at the bottom. No doubt about it."

"Crafty bastards."

"But, if they dry it out, and then try and knock it down, it'll fall on them."

"Unless they hope it's just going to fall and leave us with nothing."

"Hmmm," I can see that Edmund is considering my words.

"We should build an inner wall." I'd not realised that Rudolf was close enough to hear.

"What?" Edmund is about to scold Rudolf, but I raise my hand.

"Another wall?"

"Yep, join it to the rest. It's the weakest part of the structure anyway, and it's not as if we don't have the fucking wood and mud to do it. We even have an ample supply of horse manure to hold it in place."

I grin.

"A clever little fuck, aren't you?"

Rudolf nods.

"Well," and he pitches his voice so that he sounds remarkably like Tatberht. "With age, comes great wisdom."

"And with youth, comes great strength," I chuckle. If the Raiders are hoping to gain entry through stealth, I'm going to make sure they have no joy, none at all. No matter what it takes.

CHAPTER 7

"Whose fucking idea was this?" Wulfred exclaims. His face is sheened in filth and muck, and in all honesty, I'm not enjoying the work of digging either. My muscles ache, my recently healed wound tinging with each shovel, and I'd like nothing better than to sleep. But, there's no time. None at all.

"Ah, shut up and get on with it?" Pybba retorts. He's watching, because he can't use a spade one-handed, and no matter the complaints, he refutes them all. If I didn't know better, I'd think him proud of Rudolf. Not that Rudolf is enjoying this new activity much either.

"Bloody bollocks," he stands, stretching his back and looking at the rather pitiful ditch and the wall that's under construction. "Wish I'd kept my bloody mouth shut."

No one's had much sleep. Not that the Raiders attacked again. But of course, there was always the possibility throughout the extended hours of darkness, that have served to lower the temperature so that those who dig appear to be wreathed in smoke.

"Better to be digging, than dead," Edmund retorts. There are about fifty of us, all crammed into the tight space where the old entranceway has been blocked off. There's no room for anyone else. But I confess, I thought we'd have accomplished more than this by now.

In the cold light of day, I inspected the wall, along with my

Aunt, Ealdorman Ælhun, Edmund and Pybba. All of us agreed that despite the freezing temperatures, the wall was showing some stresses, visible in stick thin cracks in the dark mud, forming in the space where the old gateway had once stood.

There's little to hear but the sound of petulant warriors, and the scrape and scratch of iron digging into the earth. It was difficult to break through the top layer of ground, heavily trampled down by the passage of hundreds, if not thousands of feet, but we've achieved it. It might be about all we manage today before I send everyone to get some food and sleep.

"My Lord King," Ealdorman Ælhun stands back from the mess, a slight look of dismay on his face for the confusion of activity he's witnessing.

"Might I speak to you," he asks, and I nod, wiping the sweat from my forehead, handing my shovel to Wulfhere, waiting patiently to have his turn, and stride away. I wish I could be as keen as the youth to fulfil such a tedious occupation. He doesn't even look tired, and we've been awake for most of the night.

"Ealdorman Ælhun?"

"I've had men scrutinising the camp, as you suggested. There's been very little activity, but we've just noticed more logs being dragged towards them."

"Do you think they mean to build more bloody ladders?"

"It makes sense to me."

"Yes, me too. I think they mean to distract us, until the old gateway cracks open, and then they hope to overwhelm us. If I didn't hate the fuckers so much, I might be impressed with such a ploy."

"What shall we do?"

"We just need to watch them, make them believe that they're winning. Tonight, we'll set double guards around the perimeter, with only a token number of men up on the walkway. Make them think that we believe what our eyes are telling us. Any idea what caused the explosion last night?"

"It looks like there might have been some barrels flung into the fire they'd already lit. Maybe they contained oil."

"Hum, I would have thought so. Certainly, something had to make it flare so much, and cause so much damn smoke." I can feel my sweat lying cold and slippery on my arms. It's fucking cold as soon as I stop moving. It's clear overhead as well. The day will be much colder than the previous one, and the night perhaps even cooler.

"Three horses came close earlier, well, closer, not close. But not close enough to see who they were."

"It'll be fucking Jarl Guthrum again. He wants Northampton back. I'm not surprised. It'd give him a good position in Mercia if he could hold it. Perhaps even better than Repton and Torksey, especially now we've finished the defences they began."

"Do you think this second wall idea will work?" The doubt in his voice worries me, but then, he's an ealdorman, not a warrior. He's not spent most of his life living on his quick reactions, as I have.

"It's worth the effort," I confirm, without saying whether I think it will work or not, infusing my voice with resolve all the same.

I take the steps up to the walkway, nodding a greeting to those on watch duty.

There are few enough of them; after all, it doesn't take many to watch so little.

I peer into the distance, wishing I could see more, cursing the low-lying cloud that seems to work for the Raiders advantage. Without it, I might actually be able to see what they were doing.

And only slowly do I realise what it means, and then I grin.

"Fucking bastards," and I'm rushing back down the steps, keen to speak with my warriors. Everything has suddenly become much clearer to me.

"Fucking ridiculous idea," Pybba is the first to speak, his eyes hazed with exhaustion and also disbelief. I should probably have let him sleep first, but I can't keep the crazy grin from my face, hoping it's infectious enough to get the rest to agree. We're inside the hall, alone, apart from a few lucky buggers wrapped in cloaks, snoring on the floor in the far corner.

"Why is it that when I come up with a mad idea it's ridiculous, and yet when you do it isn't?"

Pybba almost cracks a smile at my aggrieved tone.

"Because I'm a wise old man and you're a daft fucking bastard."

"Just a touch of envy then," and Pybba shakes his head, but there's the hint of a grin on his face. I think his comment is more because he won't be able to take part. Not in what I plan.

I turn to look at Edmund, but his mouth is opening and closing, although no sound comes forth.

"I like it," Hereman rumbles, and I know then that Pybba is right to brand it fucking ridiculous, but I also know it stands some small chance of working.

Still, Edmund doesn't speak.

Rudolf's face is flooded with excitement, but if he thinks I'm going to let him take the risk, he's mistaken.

Goda's chest rumbles with laughter, and as I face all of my warriors I see what I need to see to know that they'll do what I ask them to do, no matter what they honestly think of it.

"So," Edmund begins, and I nod.

"So," and I'm nodding furiously, waiting for him to say something useful.

"Fucking bollocks, Coelwulf. This is cracked. It really is."

"Well, it might be, but the Raiders have set their sights on Northampton, and, despite it all, I don't much like the idea of spending the winter here, with them attacking us every bloody night."

"When would we do it?"

"It has to be when the weather is perfect."

"And when will that be?"

"No bloody idea," I acknowledge cheerfully. "But we need time to prepare. And then, we can do it when the weather is favourable."

"Are you going to tell your Aunt and Ealdorman Ælhun about this?" The caution in his voice surprises me, as does the threat that he might 'tell' on me.

"Yes, but only just before we go. I don't want to be listening to any objections beforehand."

"Where will we get so much rope from?" Wulfhere queries, his voice almost hesitant, and I turn to look at him. Has it taken Wulfhere to find the flaw in my plan?

"I suggest you get looking," but I'm also looking at Rudolf, and almost at the same time, we speak.

"The farmer."

"There's your answer. I think he wants to leave anyway. We'll escort him back, and help ourselves to his fine hemp rope."

"And when do we get to bloody sleep?" Eahric grumbles.

"When you can," I offer, far from sympathetic, even though we're all feeling the bite of so little rest the night before.

"Ealdorman Ælhun's men are digging for now. I need no more than five of you to escort the farmer, and the rest can sleep."

"Well, I want to bloody sleep," and Eahric stands, and walks away, before finding a space to lie down and wrap himself in his cloak.

"Volunteers?" I ask, unsurprised when it's the younger men who're keen to go, Rudolf, Penda, with Hiltiberht making himself obvious in the background. He shouldn't be there, and yet he is, and I will use him if I must.

"I'll go," Hereman mutters. "I could do with some practice." I'm sure he shouldn't be included in this, but for the time being, he seems to have evaded my Aunt's censure, and I know how freeing that can be.

"I'll go as well," Sæbald agrees, and I grin at them.

"Well, I wish you luck, not that you're going to need it. If the woman and her men are still out there, give them a scare. I don't want them hanging around."

With that, everyone disperses to their task, as I suppress a huge yawn.

"Get some bloody sleep," Edmund aims at me. "Otherwise you'll be asleep at your post tonight, and that would not be a good show of leadership."

"I might just do that," I chuckle, keen to find my own spot to sleep.

"This is all there was," Rudolf sounds disappointed, even though he's adorned in rope. It's as though he's wrapped it around himself so that only his head is visible. I'm not entirely sure why. Surely it would have been easier just to carry it?

"Won't that be enough?" I ask, realising I don't know the answer to that.

"Hereman says there might be enough for five of us, but no more." I risk looking at Hereman. I see the tension of residual pain on his face and appreciate why he's not the one speaking.

"Well, then we'll have to go over in groups of five."

"But what if there's an attack and we need to get back."

"Then we'll just have to fight it out."

I refuse to let the idea go to waste. It seems too good to ignore.

"Don't you think," and it's Sæbald who speaks, "that it's a bit reckless?"

"Seriously, Sæbald, when did we ever do anything that wasn't reckless?"

His head wobbles from side to side as he considers, and his failure to resume his argument, assures me that I'm right. Reckless, but with just the right amount of caution, or so I like to think.

"Ah, you're awake," my Aunt stops dead, gazing at the rope Rudolf has coiled on the floor, as he's worked himself free from his entrapment.

"No," she says, without so much as even asking. "And I want to speak to you. I have a better idea than that," and her hand waves toward the spirally mass.

"Fuck," but Edmund is grinning at me, whereas Hereman seems to be trying to calculate just how much rope there is by laying it out on the floor of the stables. I can see Haden watching him, and I can sense his impatience. He wants to be out of here. I thought the daft sod would appreciate the warmth of indoors for the coming winter, but it seems he doesn't wish to be contained.

"You look terrible," my Aunt begins, but then waves aside her comment as though she wishes she hadn't spoken it aloud. "I think we should send a force around the back of the Raiders, hem them in between the walls of Northampton and another force."

"Who?" I'm trying to reason, and not be surprised by her hardened battle talk. "Who would you send out there?"

"The Mercians. They're as keen to prove themselves as your warriors. Surely fifty warriors would be able to take on that rabble out there?" Now her hand indicates where the Raiders have made their camp. Her sense of direction is much better than Rudolf's.

"We don't know how many there are, or how many more might come from Grantabridge."

"No, you're right, we don't. But, even you don't know how many warriors there are in Grantabridge, and you've been there."

I accept that with a wry twist of my lips.

"I didn't go inside Grantabridge," I feel it essential to make that distinction. "If I were having this discussion with my warriors, I'd label the idea, 'shit or bust.'"

"You can call it what you want," my Aunt offers, her eyebrow arched high into her iron-grey hair. "I call it progress and worth it. Get these Raiders gone from Mercia. I don't care if they retreat to Grantabridge. I just don't want them here," and now she points down toward her feet.

"It might work," I admit, thinking that combined with my other schemes, we might have a real chance.

"It will work," she informs me, and I grin, as she almost dips her head respectfully before walking away.

"What a bloody woman," Edmund offers from behind, and I turn, unaware he'd even been listening.

"She should have been born a man," I offer, not for the first time.

"Maybe, maybe not," and he chuckles, and turns back to

watch Hereman. "What's the foolish fucker up to?"

"Leave him to it. He's fucking happy."

"He's fucking weird," but there's none of the usual disdain in Edmund's voice, and I see Gardulf watching his Uncle as well. Nothing like near-death to heal old wounds. Daft bastards. How easy it could all have been if they just appreciated each other a little more.

"It's started," I'm eating, the beef pottage rich with onions and spices. Wulfhere's cheeks glint pinkly in the light of the hearth. It's bastard cold out there. I'm pleased to see he's wearing both of his cloaks, and that his hands are encased in a ragged pair of leather gloves that are probably too big for him, and make me think he wears two pairs and not just the one.

"Early tonight lads," I lift my voice high, keen for everyone in the hall to hear the scorn in my words. It's the fourth night of near-constant attack, and it's becoming tedious, even as I ready our offensive.

"Wulfsige is directing the men."

"Tell him I'll be there shortly. I need to finish this and check on Goda and Sæbald at the bridge." Wulfhere dips his head and rushes from the warm hall.

The number of wounded hasn't grown by more than a handful, despite the Raiders continued attacks. My Aunt has full control over those who are injured, and even now, I can see her moving amongst them, and tending to Siric. His arm still pains him, and I know he worries he might never have any use in it again, but my Aunt is persistent. Now, his forehead is sheeted in sweat as she has him clasping and unclasping his hand around a wooden beaker. Poor fucker. Perhaps it would be better to have just lost it.

My Aunt catches my eye as I stand. She knows what I'm about.

Outside, it's bitter, and I mean fucking bitter. My breath doesn't so much plume as become ice shards before my very eyes. Winter has come early and hard. I almost pity the Raiders and their temporary camp. It can't be much fun for anyone, even with the enormous fires they've been building night after night.

Since that first night, no one's attempted to get over the walls again, but I know it's coming. Every night, they build their fire close to the old gateway, and every night, they disappear in a cloud of reaching flames, hot ash, and explosive oil, and the cracks in the defences become ever more significant. I'd be concerned, only our new, inner wall, nears completion. Even now, if they managed to forge a path through, they'd be met by nothing but another wall. It amuses me when I allow it to.

"Bloody bollocks," I mutter to myself, pulling my gloves tight, and looking around, keen to assure myself that everyone knows what they're supposed to be doing. As ever, there are only just enough lit brands to light the path I need to walk around Northampton without fear of bumping into buildings that only loom from the darkness at the last possible moment. And beside each brand now rests a barrel of water, probably half-frozen, if not entirely frozen, but there, in case any of the damn fire arrows connect with one of the grass roofs. So far, any that have struck firm have sizzled themselves out in the dank conditions. But still, the Raiders keep trying.

I don't allow anyone to be complacent. The Raiders might just be trying it on, hoping that we'll leave the arrows alone, only to launch something far more combustible. It wouldn't surprise me.

"All quiet?" I ask Sæbald and Goda. They also have Penda and Gardulf, healed enough for this duty, as well as Lyfing and Tatberht. It's only right to have experience mixed with a bit of inexperience. How else will the youths learn, and how else will the older men, start to feel their age?

"Quieter than the fucking grave," Sæbald mutters scathingly. For the past two nights, he's been with the men closer to the old gate. This duty must feel tedious to him, and I sympathise.

"You know what these fuckers are like. They might just surprise us."

"I bloody doubt it," but all the same, Sæbald stands a little taller.

"Keep the fire going. It's only going to get bloody colder." And then I walk along the length of the wall. I've taken to checking it as often as possible. During the daylight, as short as it is, I have men and women examining the walls for any signs of cracking or heat. I know the Raiders couldn't torch them without using flames, but all the same, I'm wary. I've realised I'm not good at being locked up. Like Haden, I wish I could be bad-tempered and kick my way free from the stables. If we can just defeat the bastards, then that'll be possible. But not at the moment.

I call greetings to everyone I meet, keen to see them all alert. The exhaustion of the first night and day has given way to men and women eager to sleep whenever they can so that they don't feel the long nights dragging at their eyelids, risking the safety of all they hold dear.

"My Lord King," Wulfsige dips his chin to me when I crest the steps onto the walkway.

"How's it going?" I ask, careful not to step too close to the edges. There's no point in making targets of ourselves. The glow from the fire to the other side illuminates the immediate area without the need for any braziers on the walkway. But there's one, all the same, just in case the Raiders try something different, for once.

"Nothing different, the shields, the horses, the few ladders."

I can't help thinking the Raiders are as fed-up with this tedium as we are. The ladders, which we thought would be so lethal, are nothing of the sort. Even if they manage to climb the haphazard things, there's nowhere for the Raiders to get inside the walls, not since the rope fiasco, and the splattered men. I still shudder to think of the state of the two dead men. Poor bastards, and I've never had sympathy for any Raider's death before.

We had to scrape them up in the daylight. Scrub them up and then fling them onto a funeral pyre. I wasn't going to risk moving beyond the walls to bury them.

"Well, tonight might be different. Hopefully not, but maybe." And I make my way to where Edmund, Pybba and Rudolf are standing, close to the tunnel on the left. Wulfred, Eahric and Osbert have the one to the right.

"Anything happening?" But Edmund shakes his head. His face is pale but not as blanched as usual. He knows an attack might be successful, but it's becoming increasingly unlikely, as each night passes. I half suspect the Raiders might stop their tedious and useless attack. But of course, they're not to know that we're on to them.

"Maybe the weather will be kind."

"I wish it would bastard warm up," Pybba grumbles, and I can see how his lips are pinched with cold.

"Stand closer to the bloody brazier."

"I'm fine," Pybba offers, his voice rigid, his pluming breath too rapid.

"If you get too damn cold, you won't be able to fight, when an attack comes."

"I know what I'm doing," he retorts, while behind him Rudolf shakes his head at the pair of us. He has no idea what it's like to feel ice running through your body, instead of the fire of youth. I pity him discovering that.

"Tell him," I order Edmund, but Edmund shakes his head as well.

"If the old man loses his other hand because he's too fucking stubborn, it's not my fault, is it?"

"Pig-headed old fucker," I complain, noticing as I do, that Pybba takes half a step closer to the brazier after all. Maybe the old fool will listen to reason after all. Edmund winks at me with his one remaining eye, and I'd chuckle, only something is happening, somewhere. It begins not so much as a rumble, but rather as too much silence. It's hard to explain, but all of us hear it and startle.

"What the fuck now?" Edmund complains.

"Stay here. I'll find out," and I'm scurrying toward where the noise has come from, and of course, it's not from the heavily defended places, but rather from the bridge, or so it appears.

I'm not the only one to hear, and Wulfhere dashes toward me, his breath showing the path he's taken as it hovers in the air behind him.

"The bridge. There are ten of them, mounted, down there."

"Right," and I march toward the stables and Haden. I can hear kicking on the stable door and immediately know that it's Haden.

"Get Edmund and Hereman, and Rudolf as well."

Wulfhere swallows quickly and rushes on his way. I'm envious of the lad's speed.

"Calm down," I'm already talking to Haden, rushing inside his stable, and reaching for his saddle and reins. "I know, I know. It's been bloody tedious, no need to go on about it." I think he might bite me, but he takes the bit easily enough, and then I'm strapping his saddle in place, the movement so familiar it's soothing. I hear the others coming to join me, and I pop my head over the stable door, as I reach for my shield.

"Ten mounted warriors, by the bridge. We'll give them a fucking scare," I inform the others.

"Are we going out there?" Hereman asks.

"Well, some of the way. We'll chase them off, or kill them. I'd rather kill 'em and take their horses if you want my personal opinion."

"I was just fucking asking," Hereman grumbles, but even his voice thrums with excitement. It seems I'm not the only one to resent being locked up. I thought we could all do with the safety and security, but I couldn't have been more wrong.

When I mount Haden and steer him away from his stable, I'm aware that the silence has been filled, not with the roar of battle, but something else, perhaps a strand of battle. I don't know. Certainly, I can sense the anticipation of all who watch Haden, and I erupt from the stables, as he kicks out with his back legs, keen to scent freedom.

"Calm down," I advise him, enthusiastic for the others to join me.

In the distance, I can see that the bridge gate is closed, Sæbald and the others ready for whatever comes. But it hasn't arrived, not yet. I thrust my helm over my head. I'm taking no risks, other than the main one, of riding into the enemy.

"Come on," and Haden makes short work of reaching the gate. In fact, it's an effort to keep him under control. Perhaps it wasn't such a good idea to involve him after all.

At that moment, a fire arrow arcs over the gate, a flash of bright flame almost blinding my eyes, and causing Haden to rear, a whinny of unease, before it sizzles to nothing in a half-frozen puddle.

"Ten of them?" I ask Sæbald.

"It seems that way. There might be more in the woodlands, but I can't see that far. It's too bloody dark." And it is dark because there's no moon overhead, and while the brazier shows the area the men patrol, it doesn't extend over the bridge because there's no need. Every night the gate is closed, and it doesn't reopen, if it does reopen, until it's light enough to see if our enemy lurks there.

"Do they just have arrows?"

"And bloody horses," Penda offers. "They've been rushing the gate, or making attempts to rush the gate."

I see now that the two extra pieces of wood used to reinforce the entranceway are in place. It appears as though the single piece we usually use has buckled under the pressure.

"Using a horse as a battering ram. I'm not sure I fucking approve."

"Sounds to me like the horses don't much approve either."

Now that I'm close enough, I can hear the voices of the Raiders, including the slap of whips on horse hide.

"Fuckers," I spit, and I'm not alone in looking dismayed at such treatment.

"Right, when I say, you're going to open the gate, and we're going to hunt the bastards down."

"What, four of you against ten?" Gardulf asks, his voice reflecting his worry. I bite back my initial comment, accepting it's not cowardice that makes him speak in such a way, but rather, worry for his father and Uncle.

"Yes, any more, and we'll block the bridge and get nowhere.

Four of us."

Abruptly, the sound of a horse travelling at speed reaches my ears, and I grin.

"Quick, open the gate. We'll hack the fucker down and then go after the rest of them."

With swift hands, Sæbald and Lyfing throw the two bars to one side, and just in time, the gate swings open. I grin to see the look of shock in the eyes of the Raider, his mount galloping out of control.

As the Raider sweeps before me, I extend my seax, bringing Haden as close as possible to the path the horse is going to take. I need do nothing more. The Raider slices his own neck open, blood sheeting the air, to stain the clouds of his past breaths with the fatal wound.

The Raider drops to the floor with a dull sound, but I'm already moving, Haden's rear legs bunching beneath me, as I set him loose.

The cries of the surprised Raiders reach my ears, and I'm grinning, even as Haden picks up speed. He rides much faster than the horse who made it inside Northampton because he wants this just as much as I do.

With my shield over my left leg, protecting Haden's side, as well as mine, I rush toward the milling riders.

There's little light, but I don't need it to see by, because the frightened eyes of the horses are too easy to see, white rims, glowing brighter than flame.

Only one of the Raiders manages to get his mount to obey him in meeting my headlong dash. But by then, I can hear more hooves over the wooden bridge and know I'm not alone.

I direct my seax at the rider, noting that he carries a blade that glints in the reflected glow of the brazier inside Northampton's gate, but it's not in his hand, instead on his weapons belt. Before he can so much as get a hand to it, I thrust my seax through his throat, Haden's incredible speed, meaning I don't have the time to yank back my weapon. But I'll get it when the rest of the bastards are dead.

I grip my war axe next, the weight comforting and as Haden ploughs into the next horse and rider, I thrust sideways, knocking the man's helm, a dent already forming as his eyes lose focus. I manage to keep hold of the weapon this time, and tightly turn Haden, hitting the same rider on the other side, so that he's stunned, but not falling. Quickly, I lash at his chest, tugging open his byrnie and laying bare his tunic beneath. Gripping his weapon from his lifeless hand, I propel it through his chest, and leave it there, eager for my next target.

As Haden turns again, his heavy hooves drumming on the ground, I catch sight of Edmund. He fells his first attacker. And then I see Hereman, his spear running through not one rider, but two so that he has to drop the weapon rather than risk being toppled from his saddle by the excessive weight.

Rudolf is hollering at the top of his voice, his blade busy severing first one hand, and then the next on the rider who keeps his seat. The remaining four are all trying to turn their beasts, but the horses are terrified, the stench of iron and salt heavy in the air, and it's almost too easy to slice a huge gash down the leg of the man closest to me. While he bends forward, his bearded lips open in a cry of pain, I thrust my war axe over his helm, and he drops to the floor, the horse keen to be done with its rider.

Edmund and Hereman take the remaining kills. Only then do I realise how much my chest heaves. Fuck, it feels good to shed blood. And there's a great deal of the stuff, and nine very confused horses.

"Is that it?" I demand to know. This battle is over too quickly; I need more of them to kill.

Sæbald peers through the still open gate, Lyfing at his side, while in the background, I can see that Wulfhere has taken command of the stray horse, pulling it to one side, away from the dead warrior, calming the beast.

"Is that fucking it?" I roar once more, a taunt to anyone who might be hiding in the shadows. But there's no one else. Not even the hint that others might be hiding in the woodlands that start in the near distance.

"Fuck. This feels good," I leap from Haden's back, bending to run my hands over the body of my last kill. It's too dark to make out much, but the equipment seems adequate.

"Bring a brand," I bellow. Tatberht steps forward, having cautioned both Penda and Gardulf from their over-eager desire to be the ones to light the path for me.

Carefully, he walks across the bridge, holding the brand high and to the side of him, so that he doesn't obscure his night vision.

"Bring that here," I instruct, and he scampers toward me, almost as keen as the youths he's left behind.

In the warm glow of the flickering flames, I examine the body in more detail, noting the cut to the leg, extended in front of him, while the other is crumpled beneath the body.

"It could have been a tidier cut," Tatberht offers, surveying my work.

"It could have been, yes. It's difficult with a moving target."

"You probably need some practice with that," Tatberht confirms, and I'd knock the smirk from his lips, but I don't want this feeling to dissipate, not yet.

"Perhaps you could show me?" I ask, eyes raised, making him follow me to examine another of the dead.

"Nothing to say who they were."

"Nothing at all, but look," and I crouch on my haunches, and peel back the sleeve of one of the men's tunics.

"Perhaps there is then," Tatberht confirms as I reveal the small owl tattoo. Nothing like Jarl Guthrum's, but he probably wouldn't like that.

"Nothing like a bit of appreciation from your warriors." Tatberht's words surprise me, and I startle. Do my men have such trophies on them? I'd never considered it before.

"This one has it as well," Rudolf offers, bending to examine my first kill.

"Well, we have our answer. Come on, gather the horses. We'll leave them for the morning."

Gardulf and Penda have escaped the confines of Northampton, and now they move amongst the stray horses, reaching for reins to bring them closer. Tatberht watches them, his lips half-open as though in a warning, and I share his sudden worry because it's fucking dark, and the lads move in and out of the darkness. Anything could be waiting for them out there.

"Come on, hurry up," my voice snaps sharper than a whip, and Edmund startles from examining Jethson, and quickly goes after Gardulf. Hereman does the same with Penda, and I'm relieved when they're once more walking over the bridge. I mount Haden, Rudolf once more on Dever, and we slowly walk the horses backwards, even though they don't much like it, eyes peering into the gloom, just daring any fucker to appear.

The gate shuts with a resounding thud, and I slip from Haden's back, a thwack on his shoulder for his endeavours.

Sæbald and Lyfing are lifting the heavy bars back into place, one at a time, and I move to help them.

"What were they fucking thinking?"

Only, no sooner have the words left my mouth than I hear a cry from somewhere else inside Northampton.

"Where did that come from?" I demand to know, as a sudden burst of flames shows me only too well.

"The walkway," and I rush to Haden, leap into his saddle, encouraging him forward.

"Keep the gate secure," I holler over my shoulder, aware that Edmund, Hereman and Rudolf are following me with their mounts.

I keep my eyes on the flames, watching them as they seem to grow and then contract, as though buffeted by the wind, but there's no wind, none at all.

"What the fuck?" I hear Edmund's complaint, but I don't know the answer.

The space between the great hall is empty, not even my Aunt poking her head outside to see what's happening, and then we're moving through the tighter thoroughfares, and I don't even have time to hope that no one is walking along them.

"Fucking bollocks?" Haden rears under me, as I bring him to an abrupt stop, fearful of running down those who're in the open space before the walkway up ahead.

"They threw a barrel over?" Ealdorman Ælhun calls to me, his eyes white with fright, although his words sound calm enough.

"Bastards," there's little remaining of the wooden walkway. I can see someone gripping tightly to the top of the wall, but my eyes focus on the smouldering remains of the wooden structure, and the few broken and twisted bodies I can see.

"Wulfsige."

"Here, My Lord King," his voice is filled with sorrow and remorse, and I'm already shaking my head, to deny him the guilt.

"Can we get that man down?" I don't know how, but I can't leave him there, not while he lives.

"How?"

"The steps. Can you swing to reach the steps?" But the man seems unable to hear me even though I'm shouting. I'm not surprised. The sound of the fallen walkway reverberates around the space. I wouldn't be surprised if the man's hearing has been temporarily affected.

"The steps," I roar, and others take up my cry, but the warrior does nothing other than try and hold on for dear life.

"Quick, bring me some barrels and anything else we have that we can stand on," I order.

The man swings, higher even than the great hall. If he lets go, his end is going to be as awful to witness as that of the Raiders who died from their impacts with the ground. He must know that.

Hastily, I jump from Haden, rushing to find a barrel, and begin wheeling it toward the wall.

"It's too late," Wulfsige almost sobs in anguish. This must be one of his warriors.

"It's not too late until the fucker's dead," I grit my teeth, grateful for his help, even as he despairs. Someone brings the cart, being used to ferry the wood to the second, inner wall, and I bend, keen to lever the barrel on top. Ealdorman Ælhun continues to bellow at the man, but I don't risk looking.

"Come on, more." I'm standing on the barrel, on top of the cart, as Hereman single-handedly thrusts another barrel onto the cart, and then the building begins. A piece of wood meant for the new part of the wall, and then a ladder, found from fuck knows where, and I'm resting it against the wall. I can feel the heat from the fire, a few flames still smouldering, but I'm not about to let a bit of heat stop me from rescuing the man.

"Here, take this," Rudolf thrusts a coil of rope into my hands, and I've no idea why until I see the loop around the one end.

"I can't throw that accurately," only for one of my Aunt's archers to join me, her lips pursed as she considers the next move.

"My Lord King," her hand outstretched for the rope.

"Take it, take it," I think I know what she's going to attempt. The arrow thuds into the wall close to the stranded warrior, and he cries, as though under attack, but then horror-filled eyes look down at what we're doing, and he appreciates that it's a rescue attempt.

"Grab the rope." I bellow.

Rudolf has scampered backwards, and I have no idea what he's about to do. Beside me, the archer takes another arrow and shoots again. I almost screech with outrage, but the arrow lands unnervingly close to the rope, and I turn and grin.

"Keep on doing it." The man turns, reaches for the first rope, and I jump down from the barrels on the cart and rush to help Rudolf.

More and more of the warriors are hurrying to grab hold of the rope, while the archer sends another arrow thudding into the wall, a little lower down, and now the stranded man has his hands on the rope, walking them one over another, as the others take the strain.

"Come on, fucking come on," I'm chuntering under my breath.

It seems impossible that the tactic will work, and yet painstakingly, the warrior is making his way down the steep wall.

"Direct him to the steps," I bellow when it seems that the archer plans on leading him all the way down, and all of us are straining on the rope, desperate to hold it taut. We've come so far. We can't allow him to fall now.

"To the left," Pybba is standing almost directly under the teetering warrior, roaring at him, and I smirk. Nothing will stop Pybba, nothing.

"To the left you daft cunt," Pybba's bellow almost has me moving to the left, but it finally does the trick, and the warrior, with a reaching foot, finally touches solid ground. He bends at the knees, as though to recover his breath and all I see is the flash of his terror-filled eyes before there's an ominous creak from the wooden steps.

"Get down," I roar, "hurry."

And then the warrior is down, and the rope hangs slack between our hands, and so do my plans. How the fuck can I do it now?

CHAPTER 8

"Well done," I incline my head toward the archer, and she grins, the relief evident in the way she puffs out her cheeks and wipes sweat from her brow.

I make my way to the survivor, and he startles upright at my approach.

"You must have the strength of a bear to hold on for that long," I praise, with a slap to his back, which probably leaves him winded.

"Sorry," I apologise, but he grins at me, the relief of being alive when he thought he'd be dead, earning me forgiveness for my lack of care.

"Right," and I turn to the mass of eyes watching me, Haden amongst them. "We need to get another walkway up there as soon as possible. I know it's been a long night already, but we're blind without it."

A few look at me as though I'm mad, but more nod in agreement. In their number is Wulfsige, who's making his way to his warrior, no doubt to reassure himself that the man hasn't sustained any lasting injuries.

"There's more than enough wood, and more than enough of us to share the workload. Those who are too exhausted can sleep, but we need as many as possible. The bastards have made a lucky strike. Let's not allow them to have any great benefit from it."

I glance to Ealdorman Ælhun, and belatedly he realises that I want him to lead the men. I need to get Haden back to the stables, and then decide what to do next. My plan is in ruins, and with no way of communicating with the Mercians already on their way to circle around the back of the Raiders, I fear they might be in even greater danger than they were when I agreed to my Aunt's plan.

"Lucky fuckers," I mumble to Haden. He's placid enough beside me as we make our way to the stables, but I can sense his desire to be liberated from Northampton, to stretch his long legs and run free. If only it were that fucking easy.

Edmund, Hereman and Rudolf follow me with their mounts and of course, Pybba as well, never one to miss out on such conversations.

"What now?" Rudolf is blunt with his question.

"We'll have to wait, and hope the others realise what's happening."

The news doesn't sit easily with any of us.

"It was always possible that the weather wouldn't be favourable. Kyred's sensible enough not to take any risks."

"He might be, but what about the rest of them? That Turhtredus is an impatient git." Hereman speaks sourly, and I don't want to ask how he knows the warrior so well. My Aunt brought a hundred warriors with her, some led by Kyred, others by Turhtredus and yet more by Eanulf. I'm hoping that the three men are working well together, but I don't know. My Aunt raised no concerns, but then, she might not know their true natures when lives are threatened.

"Let's hope he values the lives of his men over his desire to seek battle-glory. Better to have the opportunity of living to fight another day, than fucking wasting it all."

The mood is sombre; I can't deny it. We've been attacked from the other side of the Nene, and now the Raiders have destroyed our vantage point. And all of that on a night I thought too fucking cold to do anything but stand and watch, stamping our feet to keep some feeling in them.

"We could use the hidden tunnels," Rudolf offers, his hand rubbing Dever's nose now he's free from his saddle and reins.

"It's too great a risk."

"Oh, and hanging over the side of the fucking walls isn't?" Of course, it's Edmund who argues with me, his tone rife with derision.

"Hanging over the fucking walls only risks our lives, not everyone else's."

"A pretty excuse," Edmund huffs. His face is rigid with cold, and I can see that he's working on getting some feeling back into his stiff fingers.

"Where are your bloody gloves?" I demand to know.

"I took them off, to haul on the fucking rope." It doesn't answer my question, but I'm relieved he's not spent the entire night without them.

"What? You'd rather take the risk?"

"If the weather is our ally, then yes, we shouldn't delay. Four nights of these fuckers, and I'm bastard tired, and I've had enough. We need to end this, sooner rather than later."

When no one disagrees with his words, I'm forced to reconsider my decision.

"It's a gamble."

"All of this is a damn risk," Pybba is virulent with his reply.

Hereman shrugs his massive shoulders. I'm not at all sure he should be fighting the Raiders, not until he's completely healed. But of course, the fucker won't allow me to say that.

So slowly, I don't at first realise, the rest of my warriors file into the stables, well, all those other than Sæbald, Lyfing, Goda, Penda and Gardulf who still guard the bridge entrance, although I notice that Tatberht is here. I wonder who summoned him, and why the others voted for him to attend this spontaneous gathering.

"Fine, if the weather is our ally, we'll use the tunnels. Is everything prepared?" I seek out Wulfhere and Hiltiberht amongst the crowd of older men. They're the two who've spent the most amount of time running around to ensure we have everything we need.

"Yes, My Lord," Hiltiberht's voice wobbles and then firms as he speaks. He appreciates what I'm asking him. While my warriors will always check their weapons, it's the two squires who've cobbled together the packs of supplies that will go with them. If there's a mistake, it'll be theirs to answer for, and they know it.

"I'm fucking going, and you can't stop me," Pybba stands tall and rigid before me, his stump on display. He couldn't have managed the ropes, but he can handle the tunnels, and he knows that I know that.

"But we won't be able to pull you back inside if the tunnels become impassable."

"I know," and there's such finality in Pybba's voice, that I swallow heavily, and merely nod.

"I would welcome your expertise," I offer, but then meet the eyes of others who probably wish they'd spoken before Pybba.

"Half of you will go through the tunnels, five to either side. You know where you're supposed to go. And then wait for the command. It might not come tomorrow night. Remember that. Piss your trews if you have to, but don't give away your location. The other half will remain inside Northampton, hopefully, on the other side of the wall to you. There will be ropes if we need them. It'll be a proper fuck on, but it can be done, we've seen it."

I caution everyone in the gloomy stables with my gaze, unsurprised to see Haden fixing me with his warm brown eyes. Damn that beast. He dares me not to return just as much as my warriors do.

"When we're gone, ensure that my Aunt and Ealdorman Ælhun know what we're up to." This I direct at Tatberht. He inclines his head, the mop of white hair almost covering his eyes, but his one good blue one holds my gaze. In that look, I see his trust, and not his doubt. Damn the old fucker. Can't even he speak out against such an audacious plan?

I blame myself. I've made all of my warriors careless of their lives.

Fucking bastards, all of them.

"Right, hop to it," and I stride through them, back toward Haden. I've got a few words to share with my surly horse.

I wait, allowing the conversation of my warriors to peter out, and for the silence of the stables to shroud me.

"Do as your told, if I don't return," I direct him. I swear the animal understands everything I say, and the kick of his front left leg on the stable door at my words doesn't surprise me.

"My Aunt will care for you, and Rudolf," I don't tell him that Rudolf will also be risking his life. That would be too cruel, and yet, I have to say something. "And if not Rudolf, then Wulfhere and young Hiltiberht. Be kind to Hiltiberht, he's only small now, but he'll grow."

I crouch beneath Haden's head, reaching up to run my hands along his long nose. How many times, I consider, have I done this before facing my enemy? I can't even count the number of Raiders I've killed, or Wessex men, or even Gwent Welshmen. I've lived the last ten years fighting for what I believed in, trying to outrun the loss of my brother at the hands of the Raiders.

I've claimed many lives in retribution, and yet none of them has brought him back to me. None of them. Neither have they salved the wound to my soul.

Fair enough if I despised my brother, but fuck the bastard who took him from me, leaving me with only the memories of lost opportunities.

"Stay safe," I step from Haden, and he watches me, his eyes far too intelligent. He knows what I mean, and I swallow heavily.

"I'll be back," but I stop short of promising or pledging him my oath. I'll not lie to him. I never have before.

Outside, the sound of industry greets my ears, as does the glow from the fires they've had to light to be able to see. My Aunt is standing there, seemingly waiting for me.

"It's ridiculous," she objects. "It's beyond stupidity."

I open my mouth to argue, but instead, she steps toward me,

throws her arms around me, and pulls me close. The embrace feels as though I'm encased in iron, and yet it's welcome for all that.

"Stay safe," her words mirroring mine to Haden, and then she marches away, and I watch her with a dawning new realisation. This is as hard for her, as it is for me. Each and every time I take to the trackways of Mercia, she must wait for news, or for me to return. It can't be easy. Not when she knows how fucking reckless I can be.

As I stride toward where I know my warriors will be massing, I'm dismayed to feel the dampness of the night air descend. This is what I wanted. Not the cold, clear night where the stars and moon are visible, but rather this haze, as though the very ground smokes from unseen fires.

This is what I wanted, and yet I'd have happily not taken it. Not tonight. I can feel exhaustion weighing me down, and I would sooner have tried this wild exploit tomorrow. I walk, shoulders bowed, through the gathering gloom, and only just before I come into the area lit by the spluttering flames, do I straighten my back, find the inner assurance that's always led me so unfailingly before.

"Right, you daft cocks, let's get on with this."

Nineteen sets of eyes look my way, even Siric's, and I incline my head to him. His face is pale, his arm strapped tightly to his side so that he appears lopsided, but I'm not about to send him back to the hall, to be tended to by my Aunt. She must know he's here, and so I'm not the one to deny him.

I swallow and then find a tight smile.

"We've done crazier things in the past," I offer. A few heads nod, a few of my warriors' grunt. "But, of course, they've always been Pybba's ideas, so, if this one gets fucked up, we know who to bloody blame." And there's laughter, a bit too hard, a little too harsh, but laughter, and then we get ready once more to kill the fucking Raiders.

CHAPTER 9

"I'm fucking sick of digging," I share Lyfing's protest, but I don't voice it. Sweat beads my face, and I'm cursing this endeavour already.

"Why, if we were going to do this, did we fill in the tunnels so bastard well." His voice is little more than a whisper, but it echoes back to me quickly enough.

When the Raiders burned down our wooden platform, they made it difficult for us. It's almost as though they knew what we had bloody planned.

"It's not much farther," Ingwald mutters. He's at the front of us all. He's got the most challenging task of all. All we're doing is shovelling what he hollows out, passing it back until it can be piled to the side of the tunnel. If I'd thought to keep our intentions a secret, that idea is long gone. Instead, the remaining Mercian warriors are queueing up to help us.

The blacksmith has been inside the tunnel. He had to force the iron mesh out of place. It wasn't easy, but I'd ordered the entranceway entirely filled in, and so we've had to dig out the other side as well.

I didn't think it would take so long to burrow our way out; I truly didn't. I wish I hadn't been quite so virulent in my demand that the tunnels be closed up tight enough that no Raider would even know of their existence.

I've been helping, but also forcing my way back into the forecourt, testing the weather, checking the light. There's no point in breaking through if we can't make use of our tunnels, and will only expose ourselves.

But abruptly, there's a change in the sound of Ingwald's advance, and hands reach back to touch faces, demanding silence. Now, we're at our weakest. Now, all could be undone.

"Ingwald, get back here," I hiss. He doesn't have his weapons with him; neither does he wear his byrnie or even tunic. For all the weather is freezing, the tunnel is too warm.

I sense a hesitation in the men in front of me, but then they follow my commands, and for a final time, we all eye one another, white eyes, full pupils. This is it. There's no going back once we break through the tunnel so that we can sneak around the exterior of Northampton's wall.

I slap Ingwald on the back. He grins, his body covered in the darkness of the earth, for all his chest shimmers with sweat. We started trying to dig out both tunnels, but it was just too labourious. Now there's just the one. It both increases and decreases the threat.

"Good man."

"Aye, you can always rely on me to be good at shovelling," but he grins to take the edge from his voice, swigging liberally from a water jug that Wulfhere holds out for him.

"This is it. Remember where we're all going." I aim this at Edmund, Hereman, Goda, Lyfing, Sæbald, Wærwulf, Pybba, Gyrth and last of all, Rudolf. I really shouldn't be letting him get involved in this, but I know what he'll do if I don't, and this just seems the safer option.

Rudolf shoots me one of his jaunty grins, and I fucking wish I could open my mouth to caution him as though he were my squire, but of course, I can't. Not anymore.

"If the fuckers are waiting for us out there, pull the stones out," this I direct to Tatberht and Eadulf. They're not the strongest of my men, but they're the least likely to panic if a Raider pokes his fucking head through the tunnel.

"Don't even think of waiting for us to return." Tatberht nods first, his white hair flickering in the gloom, but he knows what I expect from him. Eadulf is more reluctant, but he gives his agreement eventually. It's either that or he's assigned another task. He surely knows that.

"Good men."

"Right, everyone behind me. Stay silent. Stay hidden. Until you hear the signal, whenever that is."

"Leonath and Beornstan, you have the first watch. Ælfgar and Osbert, you have the second and Ordheah and Eahric, you the third. Make sure you change around, get some rest. Whoever is in the tunnel needs to be alert."

I don't wait for any further arguments, but grab my shield and a small pack containing a water bottle and whatever food Wulfhere and Hiltiberht thought would survive the longest. I proceed into the tunnel, ducking my head to avoid the flat pieces of stone wedged overhead. Now that I know how they're supposed to interact, I hesitate to trust them as I first did. I don't much fancy being buried beneath layers and layers of soil and muck.

At the end of the tunnel, it grows lighter, not darker, and I pause. This is it, the moment of truth.

Northampton has been made as impenetrable as possible, but if I step through the tunnel now, right into the path of the Raiders, it might all be for nothing. And it's impossible to know whether they're there or not since we lost our viewing post.

I try to calm my harsh breathing, desperate to listen for any sound that might show that Raiders are waiting to get inside Northampton. Only it's impossible with my men behind me. I should have made them wait, but if I did that, who would know either way?

"Fuck it," I mutter under my breath, and with my war axe, I open up the hidden entrance, filled in for the last few weeks, allowing the mud and muck to pool around my feet. As the grey light of dawn illuminates the space before me, at first just a shaft of light that grows bigger and bigger, I poke my head outside, a glance to the left and right, in front as well, but the dank fog hangs heavy here, and it's impossible to see much beyond my nose.

There's light, yes, but it's not much fucking use. It probably makes me visible while casting any potential enemy into darkness.

I make myself pause, focus on dark shapes in the foreground that appear insubstantial, but could be anything from a bush to a Raider. Only then do I step through, back pressed tightly to the wall, as I beckon my warriors outside. I breathe deeply, almost choking on the stench of burnt oil while Wærwulf emerges, eyes cautious. He has the furthest to travel, almost to the bank of the Nene. But he has the advantage that if he's caught, he can just about get away with pretending to be a Raider, as in Repton. Perhaps we should all learn to speak their tongue.

"See you later," he grunts, and I nod, keen not to speak. I've no idea how the sound will travel in the fog. It might stay close to me, or it might echo through the low hanging cloud. It might alert the enemy just because it's a contrary bastard. I'd sooner rely on my men than the bloody weather.

Hereman is the next to appear. His eyes are clear, for all I can see where his wounds aren't yet entirely closed on the left of his face. Crazy fucker. He should stay in Northampton, but I'm not about to try and argue with him.

He nods at me, just once, his gaze defiant. I swallow the words that would have seen him sent inside. I have to trust that he knows his mind.

Hereman, with his back close to the wall, heads off in the opposite direction to Wærwulf. He too must travel until he meets the Nene. I've told the pair of them to swim for it if they come under attack, but I know they won't.

Pybba follows Hereman. I'm not sure when they sorted themselves out into this order, but I'm pleased they did so. It means we don't all have to reorganise ourselves, potentially drawing the eye of the observant. Not that I think we are being watched. Certainly, I don't feel as though we are.

Pybba places his hand around my forearm, an acknowledgement that this is a risky manoeuvre, and then he disappears along the wall. Within only a handful of steps, I can't see him or hear him. Rudolf trails Pybba. His face is flushed from being in the confined space of the tunnel, and I expect a cheeky comment from him, and it disturbs me more when he holds his tongue, expression pensive.

"Keep Pybba safe," I growl at him, feeling my nerves stretched too tight. I shouldn't be doing this. I shouldn't be asking my men to take such chances, and yet, I know they understand the hazards, just as I do.

I turn then, licking my lips, considering that of them all, I'm the one who's being irresponsible in not going directly to my place of concealment. One man alone could probably be dismissed as a figment of the imagination, but two, well, the Raiders are going to look much fucking closer if they think there are two.

Edmund materialises before me before I make my move to my chosen location. I think he'll say something to me, some objection concerning the absurdity of what we're doing, or maybe just a half-hearted attempt at humour, but he doesn't. Instead, his movements are slow, still, composed, his face missing its usual paleness.

"Fucking bastards," he whispers, before turning to shadow Pybba, Rudolf and Hereman. Lyfing and Goda disappear between one blink and the next. Knowing that Sæbald and Gyrth will be the last two to appear, I turn to the right, following Goda, alert for any sign that we've been detected. But it's silent, only my breath audible. There's not even any bird song.

Quickly, I stride around the edges of the settlement, labouring to stay upright and not slide down the sloping ditch that's filled with wooden stakes and all sorts of other atrocities meant to dissuade the Raiders from a closer attack.

The grass is damp beneath my feet, still too long, despite the weeks that have passed since the summer, and my trews grow damp quickly. I grimace. I don't much like having wet feet. Not anymore. And they're going to be wet, potentially, for quite so time. I scowl, only to grow still, a noise coming to me on the dank air.

I clamp my mouth shut, breathe shallowly, just trying to hear whatever it is. But the sound doesn't repeat, and even though I squint into the fog before and behind me, I can see nothing.

"Fuck it," I huff. If I'm jumping at shadows now, what am I going to be like when I've spent the day in the godforsaken ditch?

And that's it. I find a tight curve for my damp cheeks, my gloved hand failing to absorb any of the moisture, and begin the descent into the ditch. I know to be careful. We've not been filling it with sharpened stakes, and any old bits of discarded pottery we can find, to descend into it without trepidation.

I don't want my own defences to fell me. Not here.

At least, I consider, finding a place on the far side of the ditch, through the sharpened stakes, rising like twisted half-burnt branches from the embers of a fire, we didn't fill it with shit and dead bodies, or the horse manure. That would have made the task deeply unpleasant. If still necessary.

For a final time, I glance all around me, just checking before I make this my temporary camp, but seeing nothing, other than the grey veil of cloud pressing in all around me. I crouch down, on the gleaming mud, not wanting to risk the grasses, hoping my trews will keep me dry, but knowing they probably won't. Then I pause and listen again.

But there's nothing. I can't even hear anyone inside Northampton, and there's got to be over a hundred people inside. Sound is entirely muted. It's just possible that a Raider could appear above me, and neither of us could hear the other until one of us stepped onto the other. I shudder at the thought, hand ready and close to my seax. I'll kill any fucker who tries that.

I lick my lips, taste the salt of my exertions during the night, and feel my head thud forward, impacting my chest. My eyes open.

"Fuck," I hadn't even realised I'd fallen asleep. My hand lies lax on my seax, but the crick in my neck and ache in my back, make me appreciate that I've been asleep for a not inconsiderable amount of time.

"Bastard fool," I chastise myself, cricking my neck from side to side, sitting upright so that the ache in my back pulses for a moment longer, and then begins to fade.

"Shit, shit, shit." I can't imagine I'm the only one of my men to have fallen asleep. We did too much last night. I should have waited another night between digging the tunnel out and using it. But then, we'd have been more vulnerable. I shake my head. I can't win either way, and I know better than to argue with myself. I'll never win. I never do.

Yet, the gloom hasn't lifted. Northampton's walls are just about visible, as they menace high above me, but I can't see them. It's more an idea that they're there, silently doing their job, of protecting those inside Northampton. It's a damn sight more reliable than I'm proving to be.

I crane my head backwards, keen to see if there's even the chance of the gloom lifting, but there isn't. It hangs so thick, it seems almost as solid as the wall surrounding Northampton.

I swig tepid water into my mouth, swilling it around my mouth, before allowing myself to swallow it. I've no idea how long I'll be here for, and already the inaction is clawing at me, and it's been but moments. I'm unsurprised I fell asleep. I am surprised that I've woken to find myself unmolested.

Why haven't the Raiders left warriors to watch the walls more closely? Have they given up already? Do they realise they stand no chance of getting inside? Have they decided to employ a new tactic? I wish I knew. But my choice has been made, and there's no turning back from it. I'll wait, and I'll wait, provided I can keep my damn eyes open.

I could use the time to consider everything that's happened to me since King Burgred fucked off to Rome, but I don't want to do that. It'll only be a never-ending accounting of Raiders I've killed, seemingly without cease, coupled with grievances about bastard Burgred abandoning his people. There are better ways to spend my time.

I could think about Icel, and about what he's been through,

and about where he's gone, but that's another useless activity. Instead, I clear my mind, focus only on the sounds around me, and find a spot, out there in the glooming on which to focus. It's the only way.

I've no idea how much time passes, but slowly, my hunger sneaks up on me, and I reach for my bag of supplies and pull out a chunk of cheese. It tastes delicious, and I appreciate just how hungry I am, even as I force myself to return half of it to my bag, and not to touch the bread, or pieces of meat, wrapped tightly inside a linen. I might be here for days.

I hope I'm not here for bloody days.

At some later point, I reach for the other half of the cheese and eat it slowly, savouring the tart taste, another swig of water keeping my throat from becoming too dry. The rain still hasn't materialised, and that's both good and bad. If it rains, I'll be drenched in no time at all, but the damp, cloying mist, is accomplishing it almost as quickly. While it remains fog-shrouded, I don't expect the Raiders to attack.

But maybe they will?

I consider what might be happening inside Northampton itself? I try and decide what time of day it is, or if night has fallen, the difference indefinable in this strange half-light. Only the thud of an object hitting the ground close by startles me, and I tense, hand hovering over my seax, as I peer to where I think the sound emanated. A grim smile steals over my face as I focus on a rolled package, and that, more than anything else, tells me that I've been outside Northampton for far longer than I thought I would be.

It seems a full day has passed, and these are my supplies for the next one.

I shuffle forward, crouching low, the hint of smoke mingling with the grey gloom to make it even more impenetrable, as I quickly lift the leather bag, and take it back to my other supplies. The swish of more water in the bottle is enticing, and I promptly remove the stopper, sniff it, to make sure it is water, and then replace the plug and pour the remaining water from my first water bottle down my throat.

It barely satisfies me, but I'm not going to risk drinking this second bottle. Not yet.

The heat of something linen-covered encourages me to unwrap it, and hungrily, I stuff the cooked pork into my mouth, savouring the juices. There's also another lump of cheese, and some fresh bread. I fill the empty void of my stomach with the new bread before focusing on my surroundings once more.

For a moment, I think the thick fog is going to clear; only it doesn't. Instead, a figure emerges from the swirling gloom, and I find a grin for my face.

Has the enemy finally come to play?

I watch the warrior, impossible to tell whether it's a man or a woman, although whoever it is, rides a fine stallion, the animal's forelocks glinting whitely. The Raider is so close to me, I can hear the horse breathing, and yet they've emerged from the gloom without warning. It seems as though sound is still playing tricks on me.

The figure pauses, staring upwards at the wall, their thoughts on the impediment, impossible to decipher because they wear a full helm. The chin is fully covered, with only the hint of eyes. My hand stays close to my seax, but I don't believe they can see me, not from where I'm crouched close to the ground, mist swirling all around me.

And then another mounted warrior joins the first. To begin with, there's silence, and I think nothing more will come of it.

Only then the newcomer begins to speak, the voice low and almost bored-sounding. I recognise it, for all I don't understand the spoken words. Jarl Guthrum.

I don't think the other rider will respond, but then a surprisingly youthful sounding voice erupts from their mouth. I wish I knew what they were saying.

The conversation doesn't last long, but I watch them, through narrowed eyes as Jarl Guthrum listens carefully, while the youth gesticulates. I might not understand the words, but I do the intent. It seems our tactics have caused confusion, and now, if I'm right in my interpretation, the youth is trying to decipher how we've made it in and out of the settlement when there's no entranceway. I hope the youth won't solve the riddle, and I seem to get my wish, as the two horses retreat, and slowly disappear from view.

It must be morning, the whole night passed reasonably peacefully, and Jarl Guthrum has come to reassess what must be done. They didn't attack last night. That intrigues me. Maybe they were dissuaded by the fog.

I lick my suddenly dry lips, hoping that this means they'll mount an attack shortly, only for the drum of rain to reach my ears.

Ah. This will dispel the fog, and then, perhaps, I can begin my grizzly, if necessary, work.

I pull my cloak tight around my shoulders, keen to keep as dry and warm as possible, as I watch where the Raiders have gone. I expect them to return quickly, even more so when the view opens up before me, almost between one blink and the next. The gloom is gone, the muted sound of fog being replaced by the heavy drumming of the deluge hitting already saturated ground.

I taste the rain, tongue extended out beyond my nose, enjoying the clear tang of it, so different from the water in my bottle. My eyes sweep one way and then another, experimenting with just how well hidden my men are. I see no sign of them, but I know they're there.

At the same time, the sense that I'm being watched steals over me. I turn again, first left and then right, and then in front of me. But nothing moves, other than the rain, and it's so intense now that any shape would be watery to me, exposed more as an idea of what it is, than what it actually is.

I pivot my head slowly, looking toward Northampton itself, and it's then that I see a pair of furrowed brows looking at me from the end of the hidden tunnel.

I want to hiss at them to be gone, but it's as though they hear my words anyway because the face disappears. I wish I knew who'd broken my orders, but there's no time for that. Above the drumming of the rain, another sound reaches my ears. It's this that I've been waiting for. It seems the Raiders have finally bestirred themselves.

CHAPTER 10

I keep low, regardless of the water sinking into my clothes, despite my seal-skin cloak. I don't want to be discovered by the Raiders.

They've come on horseback. I can't quite determine how many of them there are. Even just a handful could sound like a hundred when four hooves per rider are factored in. But I don't think there's a hundred. Neither do I believe there are only one or two.

Not that they rush to make war. Instead, I would almost hazard a guess that Jarl Guthrum has brought more of his swornmen to scout out the place. Surely, after the days and nights of unrelenting attacks, they've seen all they need to. I'm surprised at such persistence. I would have expected them to give up long ago. But perhaps this is personal, and family honour needs to be upheld. It wouldn't surprise me.

The rain continues to fall, and yet the sky grows lighter, not darker. This seems to excite the Raiders, and I hear the drum of more and more hooves over the soggy morass, and suppress a smirk when a screech and then a loud squelch reaches my ears. I imagine one of the riders has dismounted, quite unexpectedly.

I hear the laughter of others, the words that accompany them beyond my understanding, although the intent is not. I would laugh as well, especially if it were Icel or Hereman, or even Edmund, that ended up head first, in a muddy puddle.

I want to glance upwards, take a risk on watching what the

Raiders are doing, but I'm sure it'll become clear, soon enough.

From inside Northampton, I can hear the sound of wood being chopped, and I consider whether the wooden rampart might be rebuilt that quickly. But perhaps not. Maybe they simply chop wood for the hearth. I don't know because I'm not there to see it.

More horses come ever closer, encouraged by their riders, and again, I hold myself as still as possible, not wanting to be seen, to give away the knowledge of our intended ruse.

The smell of burning, not just the scent of smoke, trickles passed my nose, and my forehead furrows. What are they doing? Do they mean to burn more oil, during the day? That would surprise me. I begin to grow impatient, my mood not helped by a need to piss because of the heavy downpour and the groaning of my stomach. I've just fed it. What more does it want?

Only I think some time has passed. I can't see the sun, not yet, but it's almost as bright as day if I can only see beyond the thick raindrops. Maybe they're merely preparing for tonight's onslaught.

Still, I wait, my bladder growing more insistent so that I'm forced to shuffle deeper into the ditch, turn over, and risk peeing into the steadily growing pool of dirty water. I need to remember that's there, when I return to the hidden tunnel. Either that or I'm going to be bloody wet.

The sound of my stream hitting the other water seems overly loud, but when I'm back in position, not one of the Raiders has come to investigate. Impatience getting the better of me, I risk moving upwards, elbows digging into the soft ground, head low. What are the fuckers doing?

The view that greets me almost makes me cry out in surprise.

I expected them to be arranging lines of attack, of tying horses up out of the way, of sharpening blades. What I don't anticipate finding is the Raiders camp, moved from the far distance, to just beyond the ditch.

A vast array of tents greet my curious gaze, burning fires sending damp smoke into the air, while men and women shelter around their dubious heat, the scent of meat angering my stomach.

A grin slips onto my face.

Could they make it any fucking easier for me?

As soon as it's dark, I know what I'm going to do. But still, I'm curious, as I slip back down to my hiding place, why have they come so close? Do they have something planned, or is this just another part in their game of intimidation?

I don't believe it really matters. I can't help but think that I've already won the coming battle, without my enemy even being aware of just how bloody close danger lurks.

I wait for darkness to tint the sky. I expect the Raiders to attack, but that doesn't concern me. In fact, I want them to assault the walls once more.

I do spare a thought for the obviousness of their actions. Are they, just like I am, really planning something else or are they being blatant because, somehow, they still expect to win? Not that I can do anything about it. Not now. I've made my decision, and unless I'm one lucky fucker, I can't backtrack. I need to continue with my plan, even if I have to change it now.

As full dark descends, I feel a stirring of action from the camp and know that this is my time to get to it.

I've eaten my fill, determined to quiet my noisy stomach. I'm not the stealthiest of men, but a growling belly will give me away just as easily as a misplaced step.

With a final glance behind me, just on the off-chance that the wooden platform might have been rebuilt already and my allies might be searching for me, I crest the ditch. I move forward on elbows and knees, keeping myself low, ignoring the dampness that leaches into my trews and tunic. I've left my cloak behind. I can't risk it becoming stuck underneath me, making it impossible to move forwards or backwards.

The string of fires burning inside the camp temporarily blinds me when I glance up to see where I'm going, and I'm forced even lower, the smell of the damp grass tickling my nostrils, as my eyes adjust—bloody fool. I should have considered that. Maybe I should have come to the camp from a different angle.

I can hear instructions being given inside the camp, the Raiders calling one to another, as they force themselves into byrnies and clamp weapons belts in place. They also have shields, although I can't see that they'll be used for anything other than protecting their heads from whatever might be thrown from inside Northampton. It seems they don't know that the wooden platform is little more than a broken ruin on the floor. It means that they'll be wary of objects falling from above, and not from behind.

When I can see again, my eyes no longer returning bands of light every time I blink, I resume my forward momentum. I want to get to the rear of the camp. While they're busy lighting the massive fire in front of Northampton, I want to be moving steadily backwards. I consider whether the rest of my men will have had the same thought, and decide that it's possible, even though I told them not to move from their designated places. I can't see Hereman, Edmund or Pybba doing as their told, not if another opportunity presents itself. After all, I'm hardly one to fucking talk. If they knew what I was about, none of them would be happy about it.

As I shuffle forward, I try to keep a reckoning of how many tents make up this new campsite. I should like to know how many enemies I face.

But, no sooner have I begun counting, than I'm once more forced flat to the ground by the sound of heavy footfall coming toward me. I'm exposed if the enemy decides to look down. I can't even reach for my seax, because it's wedged between my body and the cold, wet grass.

A voice follows the sound of boots, and I think I might have to make myself known far sooner than I'd have liked, only for the voice, and the boots to fade away, perhaps remembering something forgotten.

I heft myself up on my elbows, resume my passage, only realising when I'm level with some of the campfires, that I've failed to count the number of tents. My focus is exclusively on reaching the edge of the campsite, not on how big is it. I don't even risk looking behind me. I don't need to see what the Raiders are doing. Not yet.

I'm surprised to discover that the camp is not protected to the side and the rear. Nowhere, in the darkness of the night, the clouds scudding quickly overhead as a gentle breeze blows, do I see the tell-tale sign of small campfires used by guardsmen. Even when I reach the temporary paddock for the horses, there's no sign that anyone is protecting the valuable horses. And they are priceless.

With the stench of horse manure rife in my nostrils, I heave myself up from my squat position, dusting down my trews although I don't know why I bother. They're drenched, the chill surface adhering to my skin with an unpleasant clamminess. But, at least I'm on my feet.

I turn then, trying to determine what's happening at the front of the campfire.

The sight of Northampton's impregnable walls fills me with a thrill of excitement, and a crazy grin slides onto my face. I might be a mad bastard to be attempting my plans, but the Raiders are surely even more so. How do they expect to topple such a colossal edifice?

A massive fire burns outside Northampton's walls, smoke spiralling lazily into the air, where it's tugged and twisted by the breeze, before trailing its way ever more skywards. The fire might allow the Raiders to see, but it illuminates much more for me.

I can see, even from where I stand, that the lower wall, their first line of attack, does seem to be cracked in places, tendrils spiralling ever upwards, crossing and re-crossing each other, a temptation that's too good to miss. The Raiders evidently don't know that we've realised the problem and have already acted to remedy it. Not that they seem happy to allow it the time it might need to dry and collapse. Instead, as I watch, another barrel of something highly flammable is flung onto the fire, and I close my eyes against the sudden inferno that spirals shockingly high into the night sky.

There's a rumble of cheers at the action. I can see the backs of heads, most of them glittering with iron and I accept that my enemy might well be worthy of me, but I have no intention of allowing them to fucking beat me.

With steady hands, I move amongst the horses, dismissing what's happening closer to the wall. I slip horses lose from their harnesses, encouraging them to move away with soft slaps to their rumps. Some seem keen to go; others merely return to tugging at the damp grasses. I allow them to do what they must. If all the horses abruptly disappeared, someone might get suspicious. This way, a casual glance will show that the horses are where they should be.

On the far side of the mass of horses, at least sixty of them, I stop and stare about me, trying to see if there's anything else that I need to know. Have the Raiders been planning this for the last day or so, is there something meant to trick me if I ever brought my horses free from Northampton? But there's nothing, not even a single guard.

Cocky fuckers, I grimace and then turn back to face Northampton.

I can feel the stirrings of excitement from men and women who live only to make war. They've finally realised that there's no retaliation from inside Northampton. It's evident in the way they've gone from standing around watching, hands useless, to standing alert, just waiting, hands hovering over weapons belt. What do they expect to happen? I imagine I have an idea and take comfort from the knowledge that it won't work. No matter what they think.

But my focus is on something else.

For all those waiting to fight, there are others, I hope, sleeping inside tents, perhaps those who laboured all day to erect the camp while others slept.

Choosing my first target, I step on light feet, well, as light as they need be when men and women jeer at those trapped inside Northampton, and with a furtive glance over my shoulder, I'm inside the first tent I come upon.

It sags with the dampness of the day, and there's little or no light to see by once I'm inside. I pause on the threshold, trying to hear whether it's occupied or not, but it's impossible with the exterior noise and the ripe smell of damp and rot.

"Fuck it," I complain to myself, seax in hand, striding forward purposefully, prepared for whatever I might encounter. My foot kicks something wooden, and immediately, my seax hand stabs down into a mass of furs, but nothing else.

"Empty then," and I turn to move outside, the dancing flames from a central fire illuminating the path I took inside the tent.

Perhaps there's no one sleeping, after all.

The next canvas is no more than twelve paces away. I pause on the threshold, peering into the blackness that extends towards where the woodlands begin, far in the distance, and only then step inside. This time, I sense, rather than see, that there's an occupant. A grin touches my damp cheeks, and my blade is against the prone body before I can consider what I'm doing. The blade cuts deep and true, the soft exhalation of air followed by a more rapid gurgle, the only indication that I've made my first kill.

Confidence restored, I leave the pungent smell of rust and determine my next target. The stillness of the camp surprises me, but it probably shouldn't. Why would the Raiders expect there to be anyone here? They think us all trapped inside Northampton. They believe they sent riders to the far side of the Nene to force us inside. It's an arrogant assumption to believe such a small force was successful. And, to my thinking, there's nothing to stop the Mercians taking advantage of the same grey gloom that the Raiders have to get so close to the walls.

I don't like to underestimate an enemy, but sometimes, it seems I overestimate them as well. I would not act the way that they do. That much is evident.

The next two tents prove to be as empty as the first. By now, I'm almost drawing level with the central campfire at the centre of the spirally mass of structures. There's some sort of order here, but I'm not entirely sure what it is. Not yet.

The Raiders have taken no further action at the walls of Northampton, but their cries are becoming more and more raucous. They're building up to their attack. I wish them fucking luck with it.

I peer toward the horses, noticing with relief that the vast majority of the animals have started to make their escape, the mass of shadows lessening, even as I watch. That'll prevent a quick retreat for the Raiders when they do realise what's happening to them.

I pause, consider what to do next. One kill seems little reward for the peril I'm taking, and yet even one less Raider attacking Northampton has got to be a good thing.

I step back toward the rear of the camp, determined to continue with the next line of tents, only I sense that I'm no longer alone in the darkness. Holding still in the lee of one of the saturated buildings, I stop, wishing I'd wiped the blood from my seax, because it drips down my leg, the smell overly sour despite the pervading stench of dampness. Not that I could be any colder, but the scent is a sure giveaway to a seasoned warrior.

Risking it, I poke my head free from my hiding place, but I can see no one. I shuffle backwards, not prepared to take the gamble, not yet, and feel cold iron at my neck.

"You little fucker." The breath is hot and stale, and I almost choke on it, but I recognise the voice.

"Hereman, it's me," I gasp against the cold blade, fearing to turn in case he cuts me, the movements instinctive despite my words.

"Coelwulf?" Surprise marks his rasping voice, but the blade drops away, as he turns to gaze at me.

"Fucking hell. I nearly slit your throat," he gasps, relief flashing in his eyes, although I can't see the colour of them, only the reflection of the fire dancing within the black pits.

"Are you alone?" I ask, voice low.

"No, Edmund's here. Obviously," and Edmund materialises, as

though conjured by the words, a wry smirk on his face.

"See, I knew we wouldn't be the only fucking ones to do this."

"It was still worth it," I confirm, not wanting to argue here. "Did the others stay at their posts?"

"No fucking idea," Hereman comments, his eyes peering into the gloom all around him, "but someone cut the horses free."

"I did that," I confirm, and I have the illusion of his head bobbing up and down.

"Then, I think there's just us three."

"What are they doing here?" It's Edmund who asks, his chin jutting toward the Raiders as they bellow at the people inside Northampton.

"Doing what we're doing, only not as fucking well," is the only explanation I give. I don't know what they've got planned. They certainly didn't need to come so close. Perhaps it smacks of certainty. They expect to enter Northampton quickly. Although, if they do, why have they bothered to erect their tents.

"What do we do now?"

"Carry on. But now there's three of us, rather than one."

"Make that four." Icel's sudden appearance almost has me stabbing him with my seax, as his face erupts from beside us. "And I've been harassing them for much longer than you."

I peer at the other man's face, looking for something that I don't find. The shadows make it impossible to focus on him truly. I'm beyond grateful that he's returned to me.

"That's why they're here. They suspect something strange is happening. I can't decipher what they say, but I believe they think we've already abandoned Northampton."

"That must be why they attempted to attack over the bridge. Although, there were few enough of them."

Icel shrugs his massive shoulders. He might not know that they did so.

"The river is full. It's impossible to cross without taking a huge detour." I arch an eyebrow at the knowledge and turn back to Icel.

"What the fuck have you been doing to them?" I ask, opting

for a light tone. I want to know if he found Eoppa's body, but now really isn't the time.

Icel shrugs again, almost smiling, although the amusement doesn't quite reach his hooded eyes.

"The odd item has gone missing. A few horses have wandered away, a few pans from over the fire. The occasional dinner pit has spluttered and gone out. You know the sort of thing. Just enough to make them feel as though something's not quite right."

"Oh," and he pauses. "I might have left a few bodies here and there, and I believe that Jarl Oscetel might be missing a finger." His rumbling tone is contrary to the actions he's taken.

"Fucking bollocks," Edmund is watching Icel with incredulity. "You're one ballsy bastard." But even hearing such praise from Edmund doesn't have any impact on Icel's unperturbed expression.

"Jarl Oscetel has retreated to Grantabridge. He took about forty warriors with him. Guthrum wasn't best pleased."

The news delights me.

"What have you been doing?" Icel questions.

"Killing them while they sleep."

"Too much for you while they're awake?" Icel's attempt at humour falls a little flat and yet I chuckle, and so too does Hereman, while Edmund merely looks furious.

"What do you suggest now?"

"Here," and Icel passes me a byrnie, stained with another man's sweat and blood, and I wrinkle my nose.

"I've got two more of them. None of them fit me, but you three can pretend to be Raiders if you want. Well, maybe not Edmund."

Again, Edmund bridles at the words, but there's too much truth in them. Edmund is also easily identifiable with his missing eye.

"Where did you get these?" I demand to know, my voice little more than a hiss.

"Well, there's no fucking point killing the men and leaving

them in their byrnies, is there. What good will it do them?"

"Hereman, are you up to this?" I ask, unsure whether I want him to say yes or not.

"You know me. Always fucking happy to assist," and Hereman is already tugging his byrnie free, and forcing himself into the other one. I can see why Icel has taken the time. These byrnies, while similar to the one I usually wear, have Guthrum's emblem depicted on them, the flashing owl eyes seeming to follow me, as Hereman settles it over his chest.

Edmund has his arms crossed tightly over his chest, and I know he's pissed at being left behind. But Icel is right.

"And what the fuck do you want me to do?" Edmund fumes. I pause, consider the suitability of my reply, but then mutter it anyway.

"Get back to where you should be, in the ditch. Let the others know what's happening along the way, if you can. Icel, are you up to doing the same on the right-hand side?"

I'm mirroring Hereman's actions. I thought I stank, but it seems the Raider who once owned this byrnie really did stink. I thought the bastards were supposed to be fond of bathing. This fucker surely hasn't, maybe for years, not just months. No doubt, if I could see better, I'd see the salt stains of sweat under the armpits and around the neck.

"Yes. I saw you leave Northampton. I know where to go." His statement astounds me.

"Fucking bollocks, did you," Edmund all but cries, Hereman silencing him with a shake of his head, and a tight hand over his lips. I'd be worried we might be heard, but it seems nearly everyone is close to the ditch. No one wanted to miss the opportunity of cracking open Northampton's walls.

"I only speak the truth," Icel rumbles. "It's a good idea. I would have done the same."

"How many did you see?" I ask, just to be sure Icel speaks the truth.

"Ten of you. Everyone disappeared into the ditch, apart from Coelwulf. I thought you'd seen me, but clearly not. I killed the

Raider on watch duty. Whatever he saw, died with him, so the Raiders have no idea of this development. They only sent one man to watch. Fools."

I nod, displeased to realise that we'd been seen, and yet unable to thank Icel, all at the same time. I thought I'd be so damn fucking clever, but evidently not.

"Okay, so Hereman and I will infiltrate them from the back. Icel and Edmund, you return to positions in the ditch and let the others know if you can. The Raiders are expecting the wall to fall, that's why they're here. They'll get a nasty surprise when it gains them nothing. Hereman, you and I will kill as many as we can, while they think that we fight with them, not against them."

"Any problems, retreat to the ditch."

"The wall to fall?" Icel queries.

"Yes, they're burning it, hoping to dry the mud out so that it collapses. We've built another wall inside. Whatever they're doing now will gain them nothing."

The news that we know what they're doing doesn't seem to surprise Icel.

"Are the tunnels open?" he asks instead.

"Only one of them, but they're heavily guarded." This seems to please him, and he asks nothing else.

"Remember, the other men are still circling from behind. I'm not sure when they'll attack."

I hunt for something to say that's inspiring, but there's nothing.

"Just kill the bastards, and stay the fuck alive," I find myself stating, only to be greeted with a disgusted huff from Edmund, a nod from Icel and a grin from Hereman. At least he's pleased about what's about to happen. I'm not sure the other two are.

"Right, let's stop fucking talking about it, and do something."

With that, I bend low, grip a handful of wet grasses and run them over my seax, before jamming it back into my weapons belt. I'm not leaving that behind.

Hereman is already striding away, his eyes focused on what's waiting for us, and I hasten to follow him, my gaze glancing upwards again. But there's no one inside Northampton looking out. How could there be?

As I get closer and closer to the fire, I try and take stock of how many Raiders there are. Backs greet me, and nothing else. I hear the slither of a body tumbling lifelessly to the floor, and appreciate Hereman has already begun his tirade, whoever was too slow in their approach to the ditch, his target.

I admire his dedication, even as he tramples over the body, not even bothering to hide it. I would caution him, but what's the fucking point.

The Raiders focus is exclusively on the walls of Northampton. I don't think they'll be treading this way any time soon. The dead body will never be found. It seems that despite Icel's little games, the fuckers still believe themselves invincible. It's always a shock when they discover that they can die just as quickly as anyone else.

Marching beyond the second to last line of the tents, I encounter one of the Raiders rushing to fasten their weapons belt, eyes looking anywhere but at where they should be going.

Quickly, my seax is in my hand, and then it's stabbing upwards, under his armpit, and the gurgle is drowned out by a sudden roar of acclaim from the Raiders. I take the time to place the body to the side of the tent. I don't want to trip over it if I have to make a sudden retreat. Only then do I look to see what's so excited the Raiders.

One of the daft fucker's has skipped through the ditch, evading all of the stakes and the foulness at its bottom, and now cavorts in front of the wall, two flaming brands in his or her hands. It's impossible to tell if it's a man or a woman. I would think a woman, but I could be wrong. Some men are as light on their feet.

And they're not alone. At least another ten suddenly join them, while yet others throw flammable items at them. It seems the fire that already burns is not enough. They mean to build a funeral pyre for Northampton's crumbling wall. Fuckers.

I spit to the side, a swift glance showing me that Hereman mingles with the Raiders. I can't see his blade, but it must be there, because someone stumbles to the ground, hands outstretched although they grasp nothing.

"Trying to fucking beat me," I huff, moving my neck from side to side. Immediately, I pick my target. A broad back, slightly bowed legs and a curl of hair down the neck, is all I see of the enemy, as I once more drag my blade across an exposed neck.

The air seems to shimmer with the stench of shed blood, and yet no one notices, even as the body slumps first to its knees, and then to the well-trodden ground.

Everyone's attention is on the rapidly building fire before the wall. I've not seen it from this side before, but it's vast and quickly growing.

I can scent my enemy, and I wrinkle my nose, hooking another Raider away from the rest of the party, a hand over a mouth, even as my blade caresses another throat. I wince as a splatter of blood falls onto the exposed neck of the Raider in front of my target, and when they turn, to see what's happening, I'm sure they'll notice the pooling blood, but they simply don't.

"*Skiderik*," the Raider grunts, eyes alight with the killing frenzy as a rush of flames roars through the night, dragging the man's attention back to the fire.

"Fuck." And I dump the body I'm holding up, the limbs landing one after another, as though drumming the ground. Stepping over the carcass, the man with the blood on his neck is my next victim, and he succumbs to a blade slicking into his armpit. An easy way to kill a man, if not always possible in the heat of battle.

I'm still at the back of the leading group of Raiders, and yet I'm sure that someone will notice what's happening, sooner or later. Rather than take any more significant risk, I move along the line, wishing to end the lives of them all, but knowing I can't be too obvious. At the end of the ragged column, a solitary enemy sways, no doubt too pissed to wield his weapon, hanging limply in his hand, and it's easy to stab high on his back, and then drop him into the yawning chasm of the ditch, as he buckles before me.

An exclamation makes me peer along the trench, and I expect to see the eyes of Icel, but there's no one there. Not that I can see, and I move to the next Raider. They turn, perhaps surprised to realise they're the end of the group, and I grin, licking my lips clean of the brine of my exertions, and nod toward the fire. The Raider looks that way, and as he does, my blade slices into his armpit, encountering more resistance than I'd like, so that he half turns, his eyes peering at me in consternation. I hammer the blade home, and the light dims from his eyes, a question on his half-open lips.

"Fucker," I offer, ensuring he too falls forward into the murky water below.

While the fire climbs higher and higher, I move to the next group of Raiders. There are more of them here, four or five of them, standing so close together it's impossible to tell the exact number.

Their voices boom as they jeer at their comrades, fists raised. And then one of them disappears before my very eyes, without so much as a squeak. I realise I do have an ally below. I hope I didn't just send two bodies on to them. That wouldn't make me very fucking popular.

One of the Raiders turns confused eyes my way, as though feeling the disturbed air of their fellows departure, and I shrug my shoulders, a wry smirk on my lips as if to say, 'what can you do.' He turns aside, and my blade snakes between the joins of his byrnie and his body, and I slice open his belly. I tip him forwards, a swift thought for my ally, and then I'm amongst the group of Raiders.

There were five of them, I note, and now there are only three, but they think there are four because I'm beside them. I consider whether it's Icel, or Edmund assisting me, and decide it must be Icel. Edmund would have been forced to make his presence known. It's just his nature.

The flames from the fire, suddenly double in size and I'm forced to look away because it's just so bright in the black of the night. Clouds scud overhead, making it impossible to see the moon or the stars.

When I look back at the group of Raiders, there are only two of them. It seems that Icel hasn't let the leaping flames bother him.

The man closest to me stinks of burnt meat and fat, and I wrinkle my nose, trying to breathe shallowly. I don't want to taste the bastard. He holds his shield in one hand and an axe in the other, and he bangs them against one another, the sound a discordant cacophony. If there were a beat to keep to, this man wouldn't be able to do so. He sways, and I realise he's drunk far too much ale. Yet, the fact that he's armed himself gives me pause for thought. Might this man be capable of defending himself?

I'm still considering it, when I notice a hand reaching over the lip of the ditch, gripping the man's right leg. Only, he doesn't stagger forward, but instead glances down, malice turning his face to haunted shadows.

"*Skiderik,*" he exhales. I can feel him inhaling air to shout. Quickly, I step close to him, back to the fire, trying not to suck in his putrid air, and while I point at the fire, distracting the Raider who stands just beside him, I headbutt the inebriated Raider, knocking him off balance, catching him, and then shoving him into the ditch.

"Eilifr?" The remaining warrior from the group speaks with an edge of surprise as he looks for his comrades. I shake my head, turn to glance behind me as if that's where his missing ally has gone. As he turns aside, my seax slashes widely across his throat, exposed by his twisting motion, and another falls into the ditch. This time, I hear the thud of the body falling into the pit, wincing and hoping that a splash does not follow it, but it's at least five steps to the next group of Raiders, and they're fixated on the fire and the individuals frolicking in front of Northampton.

I don't know what these fuckers have imbibed before beginning their attack, but it's made them too confident of their abilities, even as it's inhibited them.

I bend, grab some grasses and slick the blood from my blade once more. The Raiders make it almost too easy, and yet I know better than to think that all of it will be quickly accomplished. At some point, someone is going to stumble over one of the bodies or realise that the horses are missing. It's just a matter of fucking time, but until then, I feel no compulsion to stop and wait.

I slither up to the next group of Raiders. Here, they're more tightly packed, some not seeming to want to be close enough to see everything that's happening, but rather content to have the false comfort of not standing at the fore. Poor fuckers.

Their faces are lit by the roaring flames, slashes of orange seeming to warm them. I blink away the image of reaching blackness that superimposes itself on them. I need to kill the fuckers before I can dream of watching their bodies blacken and turn to ash in the heat of the fire.

I think it should be both easier and more difficult to deliver their deaths. Only, before I can get any closer, there's a sudden roar and a few shrieks of shock and triumph, and I focus on the flames, wincing as I watch the undermined section of the wall crumble under the onslaught of the super-heated conflagration.

"*Våben.*" I'm not sure who shouts the command, but I hear it easily enough. And then the man to my left is rushing forward, seemingly undaunted by the ditch before him. It takes me a moment to realise why.

"The fuckers," Icel is beside me, blowing hard, his gloved hand pointing to where pieces of wood have been flung over the ditch. It's not quite a bridge, but it's not far off.

"Crazy fuckers," I take the time to watch, mouth almost open in shock.

I've done some pretty fucked up stuff in my time, but I think this might be even more perilous than that.

The fire burns on the opposite side of the ditch. The tongues of heat reach to find more and more combustible material now that everything offered to the flames has been consumed. The Raiders run the gauntlet of the fire, rushing through it, or around it, and often over it, before my very eyes. And all before the dust from the tumbled wall has settled. It's almost impossible to see what they run into, the smoke from the fire, mingling with the rising dust.

I settle my seax in my weapons belt, fold my arms, and just step back, prepared to watch. I don't want to get mixed up in this fuck up.

"Where have you been?" I ask Icel, and I think I'll get no response.

"I buried Eoppa. It had to be done. I found his mount. As I said I would."

"How long have you been hounding the Raiders?"

"A while," and I'd press for more details, but I can't drag my scrutiny away from what I'm watching.

"What the fuck?" I can't help but ask.

In front of me, the Raiders perhaps realise that not everything is as they believe it will be.

The fire still dances, the heat almost too much to withstand, and I'm a fair distance from it. The number of Raiders close to the fire is starting to grow, more and more of them either rushing across the make-shift wooden walkway or trying to find somewhere to plant themselves in the thin strip of level ground between the ditch and the broken-down wall. Other than that, there's nowhere to go, other than into the deep trench with all its secrets.

The second, interior wall, which they don't know is there, must be doing its job, and while the number of Raiders on my side of the ditch has diminished, they can't move forward, as they thought.

For all that, a voice encourages them on.

"*Rykke, rykke.*"

I hunt for the owner of the voice, unsurprised to find it belongs to a man who's made no effort to join the attack.

"Craven bastard," I spit, although I know that Jarl Guthrum has no problem fighting with his men. Well, apart from now.

Still, I would expect him to be at the fore. Surely, this should be his triumph?

"Look at them?" But I can't drag my attention away from what I'm watching. I'm forcefully reminded of Sæbald's comment that the Raiders are ants, as they crawl over the ruined wall, or teeter on the make-shift bridge or try to evade the reaches of the inferno.

"Come on. We should get the bastard while we can?" I turn to Icel; only he's no longer there. I turn, head swivelling as I seek him out, but Icel has gone.

"Icel?" I hiss, peering into the inky ditch, expecting to find him there, but it's empty.

"Fuck." I wish my warriors would stop pissing off whenever they felt like it.

"Fuck it." And I start to wind a path toward the bridge, as though I'm going to cross it. But of course, that's not my target, not at all.

No more than five hearth-warriors surround Jarl Guthrum, all glistening with weapons, reflecting the orange and yellow of the fire, eyes fierce, faces covered with iron helms, weapons belts ready, hands closed over favoured weapons. But for all that, not one of them looks behind, they all peer forwards, more than one of them lifting their voices to encourage their companions.

It's evident that they've not yet realised how trapped the warriors are. They can't go forward, and as the fire splutters, finding more and more discarded items to feed its advance, they can't go backwards either. Not immediately, not if they don't want to be burnt.

It seems they're all trapped. They just don't know it yet.

I squint into the gloom, wondering if my warriors have come to wield their weapons yet, or if they still wait, as I told them to. I can't believe they wouldn't be here. Maybe that's where Icel's gone. Perhaps he's beckoning them to join the battle.

I slip into place behind Jarl Guthrum, so close, I can see his owl tattoos on his forearms, even as they're covered with gleaming sweat. The heat from the fire reaches us, even here. One of the hearth-warriors looks at me, as he shuffles aside, but it's evident he sees nothing beyond the owl emblem on my byrnie.

I'm so close, so very fucking close. I can end this now by taking Guthrum's life. Just as all the others, I can slip my blade beneath his armpit, or across the back of his neck, or the front of his neck. Or I could stab down, into his back, or up, into the top of his leg, allowing his life-force to pool to the ground, perhaps without him noticing.

Only at that moment, I'm suddenly beset with indecision. What would be the best way to kill the bastard? I need to make sure he's dead, with no chance of recovery. I must ensure this ends, now. With Jarl Guthrum's death, that would only leave Anwend and Oscetel, and I'm convinced that Jarl Anwend could be prevailed upon to fuck off, with the right incentives. Then only Oscetel would remain, and he's already fucked off back to Grantabridge.

I shake my head, annoyed with my scattering thoughts, fearing time running too fast and my opportunity slipping away. The hearth-warrior to my right grunts something, his words too fast for me to even half understand, and I know my time is at an end.

I reach with my seax, taking the man in his exposed eye, enjoying the grate of my blade over the bones of his face. But, for all the sharp edge must pierce deep inside his head, the man doesn't just close his eyes and die. Instead, his hand reaches out, gripping the hearth-warrior in front of him. While I enjoy his lingering death, I suddenly find myself facing not one enemy, but rather two, and my seax is still embedded in the dying man's head.

"Fuck," and I raise my foot, force the dying warrior down to the ground, the surge of his dripping blood making it sound as though a torrent of rain suddenly falls.

"*Skiderik*," the roused warrior roars, more than spit fleeing his mouth. I reach for my war-axe, keen to have my next preferred weapon to hand, as I feel the prick of a blade close to my arm.

"Fucker," the dying man has his seax ready and tries to scrap it across my seax hand. I release the weapon immediately so that it falls to the floor, and the warrior totters and then falls, but by now, Jarl Guthrum and his men are all aware of my presence, and they circle me. The dying man reaches out, as though to grab my foot, and I wish that Icel were with me.

I can't even look at the ruin of the attack against the ramparts, even though I can hear outrage as the Raiders appreciate they've been tricked because I need to focus on what's happening around me.

Five men, against one. I've had worse odds. But I've had fucking better as well.

I stamp down forcefully, trapping the dying man's hand in place, aware that his other one is wedged below his body. He's not going to be able to do anything else, not unless he manages to lift his head and bite my ankle, and that's not possible, not in his current state.

"Fuckers," I exclaim, meeting the eyes of two of my opponents with an arrogant tilt of my head.

"Which one first?" I demand to know, and they squander the opportunity by looking at each other as though it's something that they get to decide. I use that infinitesimal amount of time, to step forward, and head butt the one man, stunning him with the force of the blow. At the same time, I hack into the other opponent's left arm. It hangs limp, weapon in his right hand, so it's far from an ideal attack.

The first warrior falters, his eyes seeming to cross as he staggers backwards, landing with a huff of air on the floor, his legs splayed before him.

"*Angreb.*" I can hear the frustration in Jarl Guthrum's voice, but I don't allow myself to be distracted by more thoughts of killing him. I had my chance, and I frittered it away. Now I need to fucking make good on that.

With one of the Raiders floundering, I attack the same man again, this time, chopping with my war-axe against his byrnie, and his face, aware that both are well-protected. Behind me, I sense that another moves to attack me, while Jarl Guthrum has finally pulled his sword clear from his weapons belt.

They all focus on me, five sets of eyes, all filled with hatred and malice. The fucking thrill of it surges through my body. I know what I need to do.

Swinging the axe out wide, I turn, my intention, to get as many of the fuckers as I can in just one giant windmill of my arm. I start low, dipping my knees, axe to the floor, just tight enough in my hand that I know I'll keep hold of it, provided I don't encounter an object that holds it firm, such as a fucking sliced open chin.

While my opponents seem to be weighing up the best line of attack, I'm already in motion.

The edge bites deep, sinking into the first man's lower leg where he stands with most of his weight on it. I don't witness his reaction because I'm already facing the next enemy, my blade tearing a path through his byrnie, bunched around his waist, slicing clean through his weapons belt so that it tumbles to the floor, and deeper still.

By now, the first victim is whimpering, I can hear it, but I'm onto the third man. This one seems more aware than the others, almost stepping away from the shimmering blade, but all the same, I draw blood along his right arm, where he grips his seax tightly, or at least, once did.

The fourth enemy is Jarl Guthrum. His mouth is open in a cry of outrage; only I don't hear it until I've cleaved through his chest, the broaches on his byrnie offering little protection, until the axe bites deeper, just below his chin as he tries to step away from the onslaught.

And then there's only one man left, and he, at least, has his weapon ready, and his body half-turned. He knows what's coming. I'm hardly surprised. He's had the most time to prepare.

His shield lifts, to cover his upper body, but too slowly, and my axe knocks it easily aside, to take the tip of his nose, and the strip of hair that sticks out just above it. The lucky fucker just about keeps his eyebrows, but only because he's managed to step that little bit further back.

With my circle complete, I brace for an attack, and it's not long in coming.

The first man launches himself at me, despite the weeping wound to his lower leg, and his left arm just about circles my neck, but not his right, which flails to the side, his heavy weapon moving too slow.

With practised ease, I kick back with my right foot, impacting his injured leg, feeling his grip tightening around my chin, as his balance falters. I shove my head backwards, hitting his jaw or his nose, they both crunch the fucking same, and then his hand slips away, and I stamp down, and swivel, ensuring my axe thuds into his exposed midriff.

My opponent bellows in rage, his hand fumbling for his weapon, but I'm too fast. Clumps of bloody flesh fly through the air, his comrades, ducking to avoid them, nursing their injuries. With a final cut, I sever his throat, and his air escapes in a satisfying wet gurgle.

"Who's next," I glower. But it's not the second man who steps into the fray, but the third. His right arm is a mass of running wine, and his seax is long gone, no doubt lost on the ground somewhere, but in his left hand, he holds a huge axe, its sharpened blade menacing. I know, as surely as he does, that he'll need little skill to make a kill with something so huge.

He grimaces at me, a small tongue licking blackened lips, his eyes bright with fury.

"*Skiderik*," he hisses at me, and that's his downfall.

I rush into him, not even trying to avoid the still body of his dead comrade. It's my sudden speed that has him falling to the floor. A more alert man might have just moved aside, scythed me down as I passed him. We land on the ground together, a thud jarring my hand, and yet my seax is steady, so that I stab down at the same time, staying his heart, and opening up another wound.

His eyes are already staring upwards, as I rush back to my feet.

There's three of them now. And they're angry as rutting bulls. I flick my tongue across my lips, tasting the blood of others, and while I'd typically spit it aside, I find myself savouring the knowledge that I caused it.

"Who's fucking next?" I leer, turning back to face them. Over the make-shift bridge, I catch sight of the rest of the enemy, and they're still oblivious that their leader is threatened. Hereman, is there, wrecking his fury on the enemy. I wish I could fight with such wild abandon.

Jarl Guthrum has somehow moved behind his other warriors, his venom evident on his face, for all he doesn't try and attack me himself.

"No? Both of you, then?" I ask, but before the final word has left my mouth, I'm moving forward, left foot, right foot, and I crash into the pair of them. They both grip weapons, but the one man holds his severed nose, and the other, his bleeding guts, and I can't see that either of them will be much competition.

I thrust my elbow out to ram it into the nose of the man with the bleeding guts, and as he bends double, crumbling to the floor, I eye the man with the missing nose.

"Shall I take the rest, be done with it?" I ask, indicating his nose with my hand, but he shakes his head, eyes wild, pain making him too alert.

His shield stabs out at me, the metal boss trying to impact my upper body, and I have only my axe and byrnie to stop it from doing some real damage. My arm reverberates as the wooden handle absorbs the movement, making my fingers tingle. With my other hand, I try to get my axe behind the shield, but Jarl Guthrum has finally found some stones, and he attacks me, even if it is from behind.

I feel his blade trying to exploit the weakness beneath my extended arm. Fucking bastard. With no time for thought, I drop my axe, and yank on the shield, pulling it loose, my hand on the edge. My opponent cries out as I expose him, but I don't give a fuck about him. Quickly, I pivot, shield barely held tightly, but with just enough control over it, that I can thrust it up high, turn it and grab the leather handle on the interior, before using it to batter aside Jarl Guthrum's seax.

"You should have been fucking quicker," I provoke, enjoying watching the frustration building on the other man's face. His jaw clamped together; his eyes focused only on me. He thought this would be an easy victory.

He should have known better.

But, he's not given up yet, and neither has the warrior whose shield I've stolen. He rushes to stand beside Jarl Guthrum.

The two of them finally seem determined to work together, standing shoulder to shoulder, as though two small shield walls, and I smirk once more.

I notice then that the two of them stand between me and the ditch. It's not lost on me that now I have to battle beyond them to get to my sanctuary. I'm not even sure they realise, though. They still believe that the fight is to prevent me from attacking the rest of their allies. Jarl Guthrum doesn't appreciate that he's now stuck between two lines of Mercian attack.

Only then I realise that I've forgotten about the remaining Raider.

I thought him dispensed with, bleeding on the floor, from both his belly wound, and bleeding nose, but clearly not.

I sense him rise, more than see him. My back is to him, but now I have a shield. I grip my war axe, and of course, my sword hasn't even been drawn, not yet. But there are three weapons against me. Jarl Guthrum growls a string of words, but I don't comprehend them, although the man at my back does.

I think he'll strike, take me while my focus is on Jarl Guthrum and his hearth-brother. Only he doesn't, and it's that lack which distracts me. I turn my neck, just the smallest amount, and while my eyes appreciate what's happening behind me, it's my front that's now exposed.

The single man is waiting, blade poised, ready to clobber me, but lacking the ability to continue the movement, as though time for him has slowed down, and by rights, it should have done.

His clothes hang gaping open over the wound I've torn on his belly, the fabric above and below, glistening wetly. Such an injury is almost always lethal, and I pity him such a death, even as I feel two weapons attacking my shield.

The blows are brutal; my fingertips are tingling once more. I don't wish to turn aside from my solitary enemy. A man in his death throes will do all kinds of crazy shit, because what does it matter? I'm exposed. I might have two men trying to prise a shield from me, but at least I still have that shield to slow them down.

For a long moment, indecision wars within me. Who is my enemy? Who is the weakest? Only then the man with the belly wound simply falls to the floor, and I wince as a gobbet of bloody matter lands on my chin.

"Fucking bollocks," I exclaim, but Hereman merely grins at me from where my opponent once stood, before turning to find another enemy.

Thinking quickly, I attack the man to my right, trying to ignore Jarl Guthrum, while also being aware of his actions.

I lash out at the man, my war axe making small, precise movements, as I hack at him, raising blood on his forearms and then on his chin until finally, angling the blade in such a way that my axe bites deep into his forehead. There it stays, wedged, no matter my attempts to force it back.

"Fuck," I complain, forced to relinquish my hold on the weapon. Only when I turn aside, do I realise that Jarl Guthrum is no longer there.

"What?" I turn both left and right, but he's gone, either into the fray, or, and I don't like to think it of the man, running for his freedom, perhaps toward the horses, or maybe just toward the woodlands, and the promise of safety in Grantabridge, far to the east. Fucking arsehole.

"Bollocks." But there are others to kill, and I don't want Icel and Hereman to claim them all.

The smoke and dust from the collapsed wall, still mingle, the flames of the fire licking closer and closer to the gaping hole, and all of it means, that despite the amount of time that's passed, the Raiders still don't understand that there's nowhere for them to go. They can't go forward, and expect to live.

"Stupid bastards," I grunt, wishing I had water to cool me, but I discarded my supplies in the ditch, and I couldn't find them now, amongst the smoke and the darkness and shove of angry warriors, even if I fucking tried.

The mass of warriors from this side of the ditch has diminished to only one or two, and they're either bent over clutching wounds, or stumbling, unsure of where to go, no doubt due to head injuries. I ignore them as I reach the make-shift bridge.

The fire flares, allowing me to glance into the darkened trench, and I grimace on seeing all those raised spikes, a splayed warrior skewered on one of them.

"Fucking shit." I don't want to risk such a death. It would be a foolish and wasteful way to go. But I do see other eyes peering up at me, and I find a smirk. Rudolf.

"Get back to your position," I yell at him, but he holds his hand up to me, and I grip it and help him gain the side of the ditch.

"There's fuck all happening around there," Rudolf complains, his one hand pointing back the way he'd come. His eyes are alert, a splatter of blood covering the parts of his face that are exposed, and I appreciate that he's already taken a kill.

"Daft bastards," he juts his chin toward the broken-down wall, and I grunt in agreement.

"Was that Icel?" he questions, wiping his blade on his trews to clear it of the blood.

"Yes, he's back."

I'm unsure whether this pleases Rudolf or not. The two of them were once grudging allies, but Rudolf's changed since then, although not as much as Icel. Rudolf's no longer the young squire in awe of the older man. And while Icel still seems to be impervious to even a mortal wound, he carries something else within him, and I don't know how it's twisted him, only that it has.

"Have you seen the others?"

"Yes, everyone is around here, somewhere, even Pybba." Rudolf's lips flatten as he speaks, and I'd laugh to see him so displeased with his mentor, but I don't. How quickly the master has become the apprentice, at least in the eyes of the apprentice.

"Come on. I don't like to take men in the back, but they've had their chance to retreat."

With that, I choose where to place my feet, and make it across the ditch using the pieces of wooden board. All the same, I'm not happy with just how easy it is to get across something that took a great deal of fucking effort to construct. Damn bastards.

I'm unsure if Rudolf follows me, as I sight my first victim. The Raider seems to be half-blind, floundering along the edge of the thin strip of ground, in peril of falling, or worse, heading into the fire. Already, sweat beads my forehead from the proximity, and I'd order it quenched, but it's still more my ally than my enemy, for now.

Only then do I realise I've not retrieved my fallen seax. For a moment I waver, war axe, or sword, and then my opponent slips on the edge of the ditch, his cry of dismay more a scream.

"Daft bastard," Rudolf huffs behind me, and I nod, peering down, just to be sure the man is dead. Only, he's not, but rather floundering around down there instead, the inky blackness of the water that's gathered at the bottom, looking more like pitch.

"Leave him," Rudolf states, and I agree with him. "He'll still be there, in the end. A nice, easy kill for someone. Fucking hell, it's bastard hot." Rudolf wipes the sheen from his face, twirling his seax and determining what to do for the best.

"We'll just go in behind them," I state, thinking the same. There must be about thirty or forty Raiders still expecting to gain entry to Northampton.

"Aye, and I'll join you," Hereman speaks from my left side, and

I glance to him, finding Icel and Edmund waiting as well.

"And me," Pybba stands next to Rudolf, and I don't miss the huff of annoyance that Rudolf emits. The lad needs to learn some respect, as I quirk an eyebrow at him. I think he'll say something, perhaps justify his worries, but he merely nods, accepting the commission. I notice then that the rest of my men have joined the small group, Goda, Lyfing, Sæbald and Gyrth.

"Where's Wærwulf?" I demand to know.

"Over there, fucking over some Raider bastard," Hereman offers, pointing to the other side of the trench. I turn and catch sight of Wærwulf. He's standing over a prone body, resting on the pommel of his sword, while the person beneath him twists and turns.

"He'll be along shortly," Hereman acknowledges.

"Then, let's get this done. I didn't think we'd be fighting them this way, but provided they're all dead at the end of it, what does it matter."

I realise then that all of my warriors have their shields, and that I still hold the dead Raiders shield. I'm not sure this calls for a shield wall, I'm not even sure there's room to swing a sword, but it's what we have.

"I once fought three hundred enemies, in a space half the size of this," Icel rumbles.

I feel a grin on my tight cheeks at his statement. Bastard, always trying to belittle us.

"Come on then, let's see what we can do when we have twice the room and half the number," but I'm already moving forward, keen to be away from the dense smoke and super-heated flames. Eager to have this done.

My first victim dies without even being aware that there was an enemy at his back. The second dies with a scream of warning on his lips, and the third, well, he makes some small attempt to defend himself, some sense alerting him that those he fought with are dead or dying, as his war axe clatters harmlessly against my borrowed byrnie.

Rudolf has the same success, Icel as well, but by the time the rest have arrived beside me, the Raiders are aware that their enemy is behind them, and not in front of them.

Ash-covered faces slowly turn toward us, but even then, the fuckers don't look daunted.

"*Angreb,*" two of the Raiders bellow at the same time, and despite the sounds of battle, and the roaring fire, every single attacker seems to heed the instruction.

"Stay fucking alive," I caution my warriors, even as Icel raises his sword arm and yells, "For Mercia."

The next warrior hesitates before me, his small-beady eyes seeking out something from behind me, but I don't turn to look. I know who's out there, and it's no one who's coming to aid him. If the Mercians have arrived, then they're here to help me, not the Raiders.

I lift my war-axe, keen to add another kill to my tally, only the Raider stumbles backwards, unaware of the strewn remains of the wall behind him, and he tumbles, falling on his arse. I wince and look away. The damn fucker severed his own throat as he fought for balance. I can't see that Odin will welcome such a warrior, even if he did die with his sword in his fucking hand.

I spit out the spray of blood that lands on my lips, while Rudolf chuckles darkly beside me.

"That doesn't count," he comments, amusement on his young face.

"I didn't say it fucking did," I huff, lifting my war axe to stave off the reaching blade of my next opponent who seems to know what he's doing.

He's a wiry man, long beard showing beneath his covered chin-guard, eyes glinting with maliciousness, as he darts to my left and then my right. His feet seem to fly over the ground, if they even touch it, and I almost envy his litheness.

But it will do him no good. Not against me.

Almost casually, I heft the shield before me, the man's eyes recognising the sigil of his oath-sworn lord on it. It's his hesitation that allows me to ram the rim of the shield upwards, into his nose, and then, while he stands stunned, to hack my war axe against the left side of his body, tearing his byrnie, and digging deep into his flesh.

A smile slithers on to his face at my actions, and I brace, expecting an attack from one of his comrades, surprised when nothing happens. Instead, he tries to attack me with his seax, and despite his injuries, he still cavorts before me. Perhaps his smile was merely one of joy. Meeting a worthy opponent can bring such pleasure, even to me.

I hold my shield firm, keen to fend off his assault while trying to continue my attack on his left. I can't tell how deep the wound is. The fact he still fights lends itself to the fact that it wasn't deep enough. I swing my war axe wide, hoping to gain enough momentum to have it silence the warrior, but he skips just out of my reach, the edge of my blade encountering nothing but air.

I feel my eyebrows reaching into my hairline at the attack, the accompanying slither of sweat falling into my eyes, forcing me to blink rapidly, all the while, refusing to lose my focus. I'll kill the bastard. Eventually.

My foe giggles as he evades me, there's no other name for his reaction. Mad fucker.

As he evades me, he crashes into first one of his ally's and then another, unbalancing them, and making it easier for Rudolf and Icel to take the kills. Yet my opponent still stands, and I'm aware that I'm being watched. I'd take the time to tell them to get the fuck on with it, but I don't.

Instead, I seek an advantage, again moving to swing my war axe, while thrusting my shield forward. I'm entirely protected, but the lithe warrior is not. The byrnie is slowly slipping down, revealing more and more of his skin, and I almost think he encourages me to attack him there. So, of course, I don't.

In the blink of an eye, I drop my shield, and thrust the war axe into my left hand, swinging it wide, and taking a swipe at the right side of his body. The swipe runs true, and the man seems to fold before me, his eyes dim, but only a little. His seax thrusts toward my eye, where I get close to him, and I have to veer backwards, losing hold of my war axe.

"Fucking bollocks," I huff, frustrated by the piecemeal nature of such an attack. I wanted to kill all of the fuckers, but my men are certainly having more success than I am.

I palm my sword into my hand, and lung forward, aiming for the Raiders neck with the point of the long blade.

I think he might once more dance out of its path, but the two wounds on his belly have finally slowed him. His eyes lack focus, and my sword easily slices through his exposed throat. The light of his eyes dims, even as he chokes blood onto my gloved-hand.

"Well, you made a meal of that," Rudolf laughs, and I'd berate the little fucker, but the rest of the Mercians have arrived, and they rush around me, keen to get a kill for their pains. It's taken them days to reach the battle site from the far side of Northampton. I'm pleased to step back, watch them all work, as a hundred warriors easily overwhelm the Raider force that's left.

I'm breathing heavily as I yank my war axe from the dead man, and then the sword from his throat. At the same time, the smell of piss reaches my nostrils, the scent stinging my eyes, even above and beyond the smoke.

"What the fuck have they been drinking?" I demand to know. It's rancid. No doubt, the jarls thought it would make their warriors fight better, but I think it's had the opposite effect.

"My Lord King," Kyred is abruptly beside me, his face plastered with sweat. "We got here as soon as we could." I can see blood on his gloves, so I know he's killed for his kingdom.

"I know you did. I know. You have my thanks. Make sure every Raider is dead."

The Mercians are making short work of the few surviving groups of Raiders. The battle is done.

I wish it were daylight, and I could see better, but I can't.

"My Lord?" and he inclines his head, and goes to assist his warriors. I look up then, somehow expecting to see the faces of my Mercians from inside Northampton, but there's nothing, just the edge of the inner wall that remains standing.

I suck in great mouthfuls of air, only to cough, the fire making everything taste of smoke and ash.

I think the battle over. I believe Northampton is safe, but I curse, because Jarl Guthrum has escaped, and I know that bastard is never going to believe my triumph, not until he's dead.

I catch sight of Rudolf and Pybba, bickering over a fallen Raider, Hereman and Edmund slapping each other on the back in a rare show of affection, while Goda and Sæbald laugh between themselves.

I almost allow myself to relax, to believe the battle won, only then Tatberht rears up before me, his white hair a halo around his head, as his remaining eye peers at me.

"The fuckers are attacking from the bridge side again," he roars, and for a moment I don't understand what he's saying.

"What?" I demand to know, the word sounding cracked and hoarse.

"You've been betrayed, from inside Northampton. The Raiders are there." Tatberht nods, as though to add conviction to his words, and my eyes focus on his wobbling cheeks.

"Fuckers," I huff, wishing I had more than a moment to collect my thoughts, but Northampton isn't safe. The killing isn't over. Not yet.

CHAPTER 11

"Icel, Hereman, Edmund, Pybba, Rudolf," I beckon my warriors to me, even as I move around the fire, keen to reach the tunnel that Tatberht's used to inform me of this new attack.

"My Lord?" but I don't allow Rudolf to finish his question.

"We've been betrayed. They're attacking the bridge again."

Instant comprehension settles their resolve, even as Goda, Lyfing, Sæbald, Wærwulf and Gyrth rush to find out what's happening, their eyes on Tatberht. We all know he shouldn't be there.

"Inside Northampton. Another attack, on the bridge."

"Someone opened the gates for them, killed the guards," Tatberht speaks quickly and concisely.

"Wulfhere," and my heart stills at his words. "Hid and escaped. The others are all dead, or nearly so."

I can't explain how relieved I feel at the news that Wulfhere yet lives.

And then my thoughts move quickly.

"My Aunt?"

"I don't believe they're running riot inside Northampton, not yet. Ealdorman Ælhun redeployed his warriors. Wulfsige commands them while the ealdorman protects your Aunt."

"Kyred." The other warrior hurries to me, confusion on his face.

"Stay here. I wouldn't put it beyond the bastards to have more warriors waiting."

"But there aren't," Icel rumbles, and I acknowledge that news, but it brings little comfort.

"Stay here," I fix Kyred with my eyes. "The interior is attacked. We're going back inside."

"My Lord," Kyred's confusion has been replaced with understanding, but I'm already turning aside.

"I need my fucking seax," frustration makes my words tetchy.

"Here, take mine," Edmund offers, but I shake my head.

"No, you need yours. I have my sword and war axe. It'll be enough." I'm thinking, trying to decide what to do for the best. Ideally, I want to rush into Northampton and kill all the Raiders, but I don't know how many of them there are.

"Come on," I hurry along, skirting the fire, and the dead bodies, to reach the tunnel over the thin lip of ground that remains.

Eadulf's face greets mine as he peers out of the tunnel. Behind him, Ordheah hunkers. I'm pleased Tatberht didn't take the risk of leaving the tunnel with only one warrior to guard it.

"When did this happen?" I ask Tatberht. I've no idea how long he's been looking for me.

"Not long ago. The fight out here was almost over, even as I searched for you."

"Right." I can't decide whether that comforts me or not. I know how quickly a battle can be decisively won. I hope I'm not too fucking late.

"Tell me," I duck my head into the tunnel as I speak, Eadulf moving to the outside to allow me passage, "exactly what happened."

"Ask Wulfhere. He's waiting to tell you."

The tunnel smells of the earth, but it's dry. It makes a nice change. But as I clamber through it, refusing to look at the slabs of stone above my head, holding up the huge mass of soil and rocks, the sound of another battle fills my ears.

"Fuck." I emerge, hand on my war axe, but there's no one there, other than Wulfhere, and Eahric. The two have their heads together, the older man with a hand on Wulfhere's shoulder.

"Tell me," I demand without any greeting. Wulfhere's face is bleached of all colour, and his chest still heaves, as though he's run from Warwick to Northampton.

"I was. I was," Wulfhere looks at me, and I don't miss the flicker of relief on his young face as his eyes settle on me. But he swallows and then begins again.

"I was running my usual errands, checking up on everyone. I came to the bridge guard and thought it was a bit strange because it was quiet. Only one or two people seemed to be on watch. I was about to give them a bollocking for being inattentive when I realised that the wooden struts were missing from the gate."

"I was going to look closer, but then the gate opened, and I watched a figure slip inside. I could tell they were a Raider from their helm and long hair. Another Raider followed them, and then another. Then I realised that the guards were all dead, on the ground. I ran then, found Wulfsige in the hall, and he and his men formed up and went to meet the attack."

"I ran on to Ealdorman Ælhun and then here, to tell Tatberht and Eadulf."

"So you don't know how many there were?"

"No idea, sorry, My Lord." Wulfhere sounds desperate.

"You have nothing about which you should be sorry. If it weren't for your sharp eyes, everyone could be dead, and we'd have no inkling of it, not from the other side of the wall. We'd have thought we'd fucking won, only to have Northampton stolen from us." I fix him with a stare, just to be sure he understands my words.

"Where's Hiltiberht and the rest of the men?"

"Hiltiberht is with your Lady Cyneswith. The others are all still in position, opposite where we thought the rest of the men were. What's been happening out there?"

"We killed the fuckers," Edmund states flatly. I couldn't have phrased it better myself.

"Remain here, with Tatberht and Eadulf. And I mean, stay here. I don't want you running around Northampton. Not at the moment." Rebellion flickers in his eyes, and I think he'll argue with me, but a swift glance between him and Rudolf, has Wulfhere nodding his acceptance.

I look to my warriors. It feels like we've been fighting for days already, and it's not over, far from it.

"We must do this, and do it quickly, but we need everyone, not just us. We've already taken kills tonight. We might think we're invincible, but we know we're not. Pybba, Rudolf, Gyrth and Sæbald, go that way," and I point to the right. "Gather the rest of the men. Meet me at the stables. Hereman, Edmund, Wærwulf and Goda, go the other way. Icel, Lyfing and I will go via the hall, check on my Aunt. Go quickly, and don't get fucking killed."

This time, my exhortation is greeted with grins, and not the earlier frustration. But I don't let them go, not yet, first, I meet the eyes of every one of my warriors, a promise in that look. We'll live through this. We fucking will. Or, we won't, and Edmund will feature us in one of his scops tales. I know which option I prefer.

"Now, go," and my warriors rush away.

"Tatberht and Eadulf, stay here. Don't close the tunnel, not unless Raiders come through it, but I don't think they will. Kyred and the Mercians are out there. If I need them, summon them inside. This might take every warrior we have."

"What about us?" Eahric and Ordheah meet my gaze steadily.

"Come with us. There's a place for you at the other gate."

As I speak, I consider the wisdom of leaving the tunnel exposed, but if the worst should happen, they can seal the entrance quickly enough, and I trust Tatberht to do so.

"You know what's required."

"Aye, My Lord. I do." His voice thrums with conviction, but I'm already turning. I need to ensure my Aunt is well guarded and then I can go after the fuckers at the front gate.

As I jog through the mess of earth from the tunnel, I can hear the cries of battle coming from in front of me and my heart pounds in my chest. I knew there was a traitor within Northampton. I realise then that I might never know who it was, not unless someone saw them, other than Wulfhere. The poor lad. I'm amazed he thought so clearly that he knew not to attack. In his place, I'd have probably allowed my fury to take me and ended up skewered on the end of a Raider blade.

It would not have been my crowning glory.

The path to the main hall is dark and shadowed, yet I find my way easily enough. I've walked this way far too many times.

"Who goes there?" the gruff voice of the Mercian guarding my Aunt is reassuring.

"It's the bloody king," Icel rumbles, as the man's face comes into focus.

He looks contrite, but I wave aside his apology.

"Is my Aunt well protected?"

Ealdorman Ælhun appears at my words.

"Aye, My Lord King." I think he's going to say something else, but my Aunt speaks first, her voice emanating from deep inside the hall.

"I don't need all these warriors to safeguard me."

I want to argue with her, but abruptly she appears before me, Hiltiberht trailing behind her, his face anguished, and I'm not surprised. My Aunt has found herself a byrnie, and a weapons belt, perhaps with the aid of the young squire, and she holds her seax well—a woman who knows how to use it.

"These men should be shielding their king, not the king's aunt."

"Well," I begin, only to snap my mouth shut. She has a good point.

"I don't want everyone down there, not at the moment. I've left Tatberht and Eadulf to guard the tunnel. Kyred and the rest of the Mercians are ensuring there's no further attack from the Raiders to the east, but I think the fuckers are all dead."

Ealdorman Ælhun purses his lips, and I think he'll say more.

"Then you'd better finish the job," my Aunt interjects, as a crescendo of noise crashes over us.

Anyone else might have finished that with a 'My Lord,' but not my Aunt.

"I'm going. I'm going," I assure her, rushing away.

When I arrive at the stables, Pybba, Rudolf, Gyrth and Sæbald are already there. Their eyes are fixed on what's happening down at the bridge. I turn and greet Wulfstan, Ingwald and Oda with a wry smirk. I also run my eyes over Haden. As usual, he has some innate sense that lets him know I'm close.

"Where are the others?" I demand to know, even as I gaze at events unfolding by the bridge gate.

"Fucking bastards." In the glow from the brazier that's been tumbled to the floor, stretching the flaming material over the damp ground, I can see both too much and too little. Wulfsige has his Mercians formed up tightly, presenting a wall of flesh to stop the Raiders, and it doesn't seem to me as though many of the Raiders are making it inside Northampton, not now. But, the gate is more than half-closed, and I can't determine what waits for us all. Ideally, we need to get the gate closed. Or do we? Would this not be the opportunity to kill the fuckers once and for all, if only we take the chance?

"Here, My Lord." Hereman almost sounds deferential as I seek our Wulfred and Ordlaf.

"My Lord," Wulfred's tongue snakes from his mouth as he speaks.

"Been a bit quiet in here, has it?" I ask him.

"Like the fucking grave," he retorts, hand raised to run it over his baldness before hammering his helm back in place.

"Right, what's the bastard plan?" It's only been days since I last saw him, and yet I realise I've missed the damn git.

"Kill the fuckers," Icel rumbles in imitation of Edmund earlier, and for a moment I think I might have a problem with the two of them, only Edmund surprises me by smiling.

"Aye, we kill the fuckers."

"But how? Wulfsige has it under control down there."

"Well, it might only look like that from here," Hereman asserts.

But before I can say anything else, I hear a crash, my gaze immediately drawn once more to the gate.

"Fuck," but I'm running, trusting my men to follow me.

The gate has been thrust aside, and even as I watch, the massive tree trunk used as a battering ram, tumbles to the floor, followed only moments later by the huge wooden gate falling.

Some of the Raiders are caught between the tree trunk and the gate, and their screams of agony ripple through the air.

But I'm already drawing my sword because more and more Raiders are rushing through the open space, and Wulfsige and his men are about to take a fucking beating.

I need to get that damn gate back in place, and I need to do it now.

"Hold," Wulfsige's voice ripples through the air, his implacable demand brokering no argument, as I watch the Mercians hold themselves more tightly. Some might find him a pedantic bastard, but it seems that others take courage from his steadfastness.

"How many?" I huff, hoping that Rudolf is doing his usual job of keeping count.

"No more than thirty-five," Icel responds quickly, even as Rudolf looks to him in outrage.

"Yep, thirty-five, and another eight, pinned between the door and the tree trunk." There's triumph in Rudolf's words that makes me smile. Even now, the little fucker wants to excel in the task given to him.

"Reinforce the Mercians," I instruct my warriors, my eyes on the fallen gate. If we could just get it back up, we could cut the Raiders off.

I risk a glance beyond, to the bridge, and then further. The bridge still stands, and that frustrates me. We put measures in place to collapse it if we should ever come under attack, but of course, the traitor has allowed Raiders inside Northampton without us putting up much of a fight. We need to reach the bridge to collapse it, and I need the gate back up to prevent anyone else getting inside.

"Hereman, Edmund and Icel, come with me," I'm moving to the side of the shield wall under Wulfsige's command. I want to sly my way between the man who holds the space closest to the side of the wall and make my way to the gate. But, I know better than to attempt such alone.

Rudolf shoots a glance my way. I think he understands my intent, even as he takes his place beside Pybba, to the rear of the shield wall. It's four men deep. Wulfsige has at his command more than half of Ealdorman Ælhun's combined force. And then behind them, my men are standing. I doubt they'll be patient for long, but if it gives them a brief respite from the fighting, they'll battle on for longer.

"We need to get the damn gate back up," I huff. "Lock the Raiders up with us, and it'll be easy enough to slaughter them all."

"And how will we do that?" Edmund's face is downcast, as so often the case. "It's fallen from its hinges."

"Yes, it has, but we still need to do it. We didn't build it a fail system as we did in the tunnels. We must destroy the bridge as well. First things first, kill the poor fuckers stuck beneath the fallen gate, and then we can try and get it back in position."

None of them argues with me, a pleasant change. I'm at the edge of the shield wall and looking at the warriors in front of me. They're fighting fiercely, the Raiders eager to force a path between the weapons and the mud wall. No doubt, it'll be easier than trying to fight through Mercians on all sides.

But of course, I'm there now, and I'm not about to make it easy for them. Far from it, in fact.

"Reinforce the shield wall, and when we can, we'll slip through, get the gate back in place."

It sounds fucking easy, but I know it's not going to be, and the reason I've ordered Hereman to stand by my side is because of us all, he's the one most likely to do something crazy to accomplish the task most quickly.

And he doesn't disappoint.

With practised ease, he wades deep into the shield wall, forcing the Mercians back until he takes the place of the man holding his shield against the Raiders.

"Come on, you fuckers," Hereman's words are easy to hear as he slams the shield into nose guards and under chins. And he doesn't stop there. Thrusting the shield back into the hands of the stunned Mercian warrior, Hereman strides into the attacking Raiders, seax in one hand, spear in the other.

As I follow behind him, even I wince as one Raider is spiked through the chin, the spear point just about sticking up through the top of his skull. His companion squeals as the seax is thrust just to the side of his nose, and then deep inside his head as well. Both men drop, and then I'm beside Hereman.

"Fucking easy," he breathes, but now we're faced with the mess of Raiders trapped by the fallen gate. I eye it uneasily. It's vast; it really is—only the best, heavy Mercian oak to ensure the safety of Northampton.

"We'll have to lift it," but even I'm daunted by the task I've set myself. It took the oxen and a few of the sturdier horses to heft the piece into place. I never thought it would fall. I've given no thought to how we'll right it, only the knowledge that we must do so, drives me on.

Icel stabs with his seax, and another of the Raiders lies dead. But in front, more and more of the bastards are trying to get inside.

"Grab it," I urge my warriors, the four of us all gripping the top of the gate, trying to lift it. But it's no good. We need to heft it higher than it is.

"I'll go underneath," and Hereman has slid beneath it before I can caution him against doing so.

The dark wood gleams where it rests on the tree trunk used to knock the gate to the ground, and it's slippery. The damp air has made the wood slicker than expected, and there are so many men buried beneath it. I don't want Hereman to become the next victim.

"Grab it," his voice booms from beneath, and I see what he's trying to do. Hereman is acting as the lever we need to get the gate further off the ground.

I grit my teeth, hoping like mad that Wulfsige and the Mercians have realised what we're trying to achieve and that they'll protect us while we labour.

Quickly, sweat beads into my eye, but I have my hands beneath the gate now, and I'm able to move it higher and higher, walking it upright, aware that my feet walk over dead Raiders as if the crunch of broken bones and clammy flesh wasn't enough.

Hereman scrambles to join Icel, Edmund and I, and the gate is almost upright, only it's fallen far from the hinges. I noticed before we forced it from the ground, that one of the thick black hinges, crafted by the blacksmith, is still in place. But of course, it's the fucking higher one, not the one closer to the ground. If we can just get it there. If.

I'm not the only one huffing and puffing. I'm not the only one who feels their arms growing heavier the longer they're above their heads. And I'm sure as fuck not the only one trying to work out what we do next, as my old wounds scream in protest.

"Let's just fling it over them," Edmund exclaims, the exertion meaning it takes him more than one exhalation to form the words.

"If we do that, they'll just climb over it."

I feel exposed, and not a little foolish, as the Raiders continue to attack Wulfsige's men. I'm not sure if they've even realised they might be trapped if we can just get the gate to hang once more.

"Hold on," it's Sæbald's voice I hear even above all the others. As my arms start to shake, I'm relieved of the considerable weight and turn to spot Sæbald, Goda and Gyrth shoring up our efforts.

"Now what?" Edmund won't let go of the gate, even though I've taken the time to lower my arms and shake some feeling back into my hands and fingers.

"It needs to go over there," and I point, but even I appreciate that it's going to be almost impossible to move the massive slab of wood nearly ten paces forward.

"We'll have to walk it backwards," Sæbald exclaims. "Icel, Goda, you go first." I rush to add my support once more, as the weight increases again as Icel and Goda shamble forwards, using their shoulders to move the wood.

"And now you and Hereman." Hereman is once more on his feet. I think it'll be impossible to move, and only attempt it because if Icel and Goda can do it, then so can we.

"I didn't think it would bastard work," I mutter when we've moved it as far as we can.

"And neither do the Raiders," Hereman grins, and we repeat the motion. Icel and Goda moving, and then Hereman and I, and somehow, the gate is back where it needs to be. All we need to do now is attach the remaining clasp to the hinge that still hangs there, and hope it holds for long enough.

None of the Raiders has realised what we're doing. Those inside Northampton continue to war against Wulfsige's Mercians, but as I risk a look, I appreciate that the number is starting to dwindle. Only, I can't see across the bridge. I have no idea how many wait there to come inside Northampton.

Sweat drips from my nose, and I watch it fall, all the time trying to reason out what needs to happen next. I've not come so far, just to give up now.

"Lift it," Icel's voice calls, and I don't understand what he means until I hold my head tight to the wooden gate and peer to where he's standing. He's reaching up his long arms to hook the surviving catch, and he's waiting for us to heft the door so he can slip the hinge inside it.

I don't think we can do it. I genuinely don't.

The sounds of fighting fade as I focus on what he wants us to do. Hereman has his hands to either side of the edge of the door, almost able to grip, but I don't.

"Here, make room for me," and I walk my hands down the wood, feeling for the bottom of it.

"If I can just hook my hands beneath it, I can lift with my legs."

"You'll lose your fucking hands if it falls," Hereman offers, not so much a caution as a simple fact.

"Better that than have to drop the damn gate."

"Fine, fine. Alright, men," and he lifts his voice. "When I give the command, everybody lift and try and grab the bottom like this damn bastard's doing here." I don't thank Hereman for calling me a bastard.

"Now," and I lower myself to the ground, hands reaching, and hoping, my face pressed to the side of the door that looks towards the interior. I still anticipate failure, but then somehow, I manage to sneak one hand beneath the ground and the wood and cup it, straining with all of my strength, the skin on my back threatening to open once more. Then my second hand joins the first, and I know that I will break both hands if the wood drops to the ground without warning.

"Fuck," the word is elongated, as I attempt to straighten my legs, bringing the gate with me. My eyes are closed, and I can't see what the rest of my warriors are doing, but I do feel the weight shift, and then abruptly lessen, and I know that I'm not the only one to have their hands in place.

But for all that, the massive piece of wood threatens to teeter, now that so many of us are low to the ground.

"Hurry the fuck up," I want to shout, but the words come out barely above a whisper, so much of my air being used just to power my muscles.

Only then I can't take it anymore, and I know I need to release my grip, no matter my gritted teeth, and sweating back.

"Let go," Hereman's words seem to come from a long way away.

"Let go; it's done." Although I hear what he's saying, it takes me long moments to risk opening my eyes, and even longer to entirely remove my grip.

"It fucking worked," I exclaim, even more surprised than I'd like to admit.

"Aye, it worked, now, let's get it shut, and the bastards killed." Hereman shrugs his shoulders, lifting them high and then dropping them low, no doubt trying to alleviate the ache of our endeavours. I want to do the same, but the Raiders have belatedly realised what's happening.

I'm buffeted from behind, and I spin wildly, almost slamming into the closing gate, but it's too late, the Raiders and their horses are inside Northampton. There are five of them, weapons bristling, horses wide-eyed. I step from the gate, vengeance on my mind when I recognise Estrith amongst their number.

Damn bitch.

"Close the gate," I roar, already removing my war axe from its place on my waist, keen to bring this to an end.

With the gate shut, there'll be no means of escape, or entry.

Estrith meets my eye, her expression triumphant, even as the gate begins to swing shut. I hear the screech of the remaining hinge complaining and offer a quick prayer that the damn thing holds so that we can put the locking bars in place.

Only Estrith's gaze flicks from mine to the gate, and she kicks her mount, slapping the animal's hide to get it to move in a reversal of what she's just ordered it to do.

"Oh no, you don't," I growl. "Oh no, you fucking don't."

I rush toward her horse, axe raised, determined to knock her to the floor. Her shield bats my war axe aside, and I growl, trying not to graze the animal. It's the rider I want, not the beast.

Still, she slaps her horse; only the animal is reticent to move. I'm not surprised. From the other side of the bridge, I can hear the drumming of hoofbeats. More of the Raiders are coming.

"Get the gate closed," I roar, my words rising above everything else, so much so that I feel everyone stop, turn towards the gate, even the few remaining Raiders fighting against Wulfsige's shield wall.

I'm willing it to bang shut. I can see Lyfing and Goda just waiting to drop the first locking bar in place, but they can't do it, not until the gate itself shuts.

"Get it closed," I bellow once more, not even looking at Estrith, but rather at the horses being encouraged to cross the bridge. I should have seen to that first, before coming after the woman.

"Fuck." I don't think it's going to stop the new force; I really don't. I just don't see how there can be time.

Only then there's a whirl of air beside me, and I don't believe what I'm seeing.

"Who told them to do that?" I screech, watching the gate finally close, but doing so only as Rudolf, Pybba, Wærwulf, Ingwald, Gyrth and Ælfgar rush through the small gap.

For a moment, no one moves. No one.

"Fuck, get Haden. Kill the Raiders, get the gate open, when I say," and ignoring Estrith, I'm running, sprinting, moving faster than I ever have in my entire life, Wulfsige's warriors opening their shield wall to let me through. Others join my headlong dash. I try not to focus on what I've just seen, only on what must be done, because if I don't, I'm going to stop and crumple to the floor. My warriors are surely gone, riding into insurmountable numbers of the Raiders, doing something that even I, and I mean, I, would find reckless.

"Come on, come on." Haden greets me attentively as I slide to a halt in front of him in the stables. He's saddled, and his harness is in place, almost as though Rudolf knew what my reaction would be. Only a small face appears from behind Haden, and I dredge a smile to my frozen face.

"Thank you, Wulfhere." He doesn't even smile, his lips trembling, and I can imagine his worries are mine.

"I'll get him. I'll get them," I promise, but there's such a look in his eye that even I lament my words. Wulfhere knows I've got no right making such a statement.

"I'll get them. I'll fucking get them, or there won't be a single Raider alive when I've finished with them." And with that, I'm mounted, and Haden and I are rushing back to the gate that's just taken so much effort to get back in place.

And I'm not alone. Edmund rides to my right, Hereman beside him. Icel to my left, Lyfing beside him, and the sound of more hooves fill the night, reverberating around the fastness of Northampton. I only wish I had the hundred warriors it sounds as though escort me. Perhaps then I'd stand a fucking chance.

"Open the gate," I roar, only for incredulous eyes to look my way, Wulfsige amongst them. I'm not surprised. I've just exerted all that effort to shut the damn thing, but I can't leave my warriors out there, alone.

The Mercians rush to the gate, steady hands trying to lift the heavy locking bar as hooves drum ever closer. I watch them, wiping the sweat from my face, and taking the opportunity to remove my helm, rub my damp hair, before wedging it back in place.

With a crash, the wooden bar springs free, and I can see where the brackets that usually hold it have been twisted on one side. It can't have been easy to force it into place or to rerelease it.

As the gate swings open by no more than a seax length, I catch my first sight of what's happening on the far side of the bridge. It merely firms my resolve that I'm doing the right thing.

There are Raiders out there. Too many of them, and yet my warriors are holding their own against them, for now. But all it will take is for one of them to take a wound, and it'll all be over.

I crouch down behind Haden's elongated neck, hand reaching for my sword, wishing I'd thought to bring a spear, but knowing I'm not about to stop now.

"Stand guard," I command, pleased when Wulfsige orders his men to move aside from the gate, and reform the shield wall, or at least, those who yet live do. I can see the fallen bodies of my allies, and it pains me, it really fucking does. It's a reminder, if I needed one, that the same could happen to my warriors if I'm not there to assist them in their fucked up and crazy endeavour.

Only a figure steps in front of Haden, and it's all I can do to avoid running him down, even as the rest of my men clatter through the gate.

"Watch out, you mad bastard," I roar, spittle flying through the air, Haden's chest heaving beneath me. I think to spur him on, but there's a hand on the bridle, and I meet the furious gaze of Ealdorman Ælhun.

"Let go," my voice is like iron over iron.

"I can't let you, My Lord King. You can't risk your life, and the safety of Mercia, for a handful of men, no matter their loyalty to you."

His words impact me like the edge of a blade, drawing my ire, not my blood.

"I would remind you, Ealdorman Ælhun, that I've been these men's oath lord for a lot fucking longer than I've been the king of Mercia. Without them, I wouldn't be king. With them, I can be everything you expect me to be."

"But you're the king," he fumes, and I note the red tinge of his cheeks, the jerkiness of his hand on the bridle. The damn fucker is about four breaths away from collapsing his fury is so great.

"And I'm about to do something that's kingly. I'll not shelter behind these sturdy walls while my men fight for their lives."

"But you must," Ealdorman Ælhun persists, only for another figure to emerge from the shadows.

I eye my Aunt, hoping she's not about to echo Ealdorman Ælhun's words.

She holds my gaze, and I see too much in just one look, perhaps more than I've ever imagined about her.

"Come, Ealdorman Ælhun, let the king protect Mercia. It is, after all, why he was made our king." Her hands are firm, if steady on the ealdorman's shoulders, and I nod once in thanks for her support.

"Bring them back," she mutters, before leading the enraged man away. My back stiffens, my resolve redoubles itself, even as I notice the Mercians are hesitantly returning the gate to its closed position, unsure of what to do, and no doubt fearing another incursion.

"Hold the gate," I shout, encouraging Haden on. "Hold the gate," and it's Wulfsige who stops his warriors, from shutting it, his stance aggressive, as he waits in the gap.

"My thanks," I offer, guiding Haden more slowly to the entranceway than I might like. I want to be out there, with my warriors, and I want to be there now.

"Here," and another tries to arrest my momentum, and I move to kick them aside, only to feel the weight of my seax being pressed into my hand.

"Yours, I believe." Kyred offers me my missing blade, and I know then that I'll be successful, no matter the odds.

"My thanks. Is it secure?"

"Aye, My Lord King. Everything is as it should be. The bastards are all dead; even the ones found cowering in the ditch."

"Excellent. Ensure it stays that way," and Haden and I leave the safety of Northampton, his hooves loud over the wooden beams of the bridge.

There's little light to see by, the moon shuttered behind clouds, but all the same, I can sense the ebb and flow of the battle.

"Come on, fine beastie," I encourage Haden, only to feel the bridge trembling beneath his steady gait.

"Fuck," I know what's about to happen, but all the same, I'm too damn slow to encourage him to greater speed. The creak of the bridge starting to tumble into the rushing river below me sends a stab of fear through my body, my legs momentarily numb, even as I see the way forward being denied me.

I force Haden back, and back, his movements unwilling.

"We're going to have to jump," I warn my mount, the sound of gurgling water rising to overwhelm my senses, drowning out even the roar of the battle.

"Come on, you daft bastard," I urge Haden. Abruptly, he follows my commands, only for me to once more compel him onwards to where the black expanse of the river has been exposed.

I don't even consider the length of the gap.

It doesn't matter.

We have to make it.

Haden's back legs bunch beneath me, his sudden speed, almost knocking my helm astray, and then we're airborne, and I feel as though I'm flying, even though I'm sat astride my horse.

Time slows, and I gaze down, daring the fucking river to claim us both, just fucking daring it.

"Come on, fucking come on," I exhort, something jumping clear of the water, only to return to the icy depths with a loud splash.

I hope we don't follow it.

I doubt Ealdorman Ælhun would ever forgive me.

CHAPTER 12

Haden's hooves scrabble for the ground, and I think we're doomed to a watery death, only for his balance to stabilise, as I feel his rear legs standing straight beneath me.

"Thank you," I breathe, but Haden is already moving on, as though he's not just jumped further than I've ever seen him accomplish before.

Only then do I glance around, attempt to discover the rhythm of the battle.

"Fuck." Just in front of me, my warriors are forging a path through the enemy.

I still don't know how many we face, but I can't imagine that ten warriors, including me, are going to be able to do much against so many, especially when some of the Raiders are mounted.

The thought frustrates me. I've not just spent the night in a fucking ditch, killed fuck knows how many of the bastards, to fall below a blade here. I simply won't allow it.

And it's not as if anyone from inside Northampton can come to our aid. Not now.

The bridge, as they promised me it would, has disintegrated with a few careful taps against the wooden planks that held it together. I didn't believe the wood craftsman when he assured me that such a tactic would work, and then when he went on to inform that without such taps, the bridge would stand for a hundred years or more. It seems he knew his stuff, and I'm grateful to him. But now, I have more Raiders to kill.

Edmund and Hereman are cleaving a deadly path through a crowd of unmounted Raiders, their horses, nose to tail, as they protect one another. I leave the brothers to it. They're lethal bastards, and that only increases when they decide to labour side by side.

Pybba and Rudolf have also formed a group, as have Icel and Lyfing, Gyrth and Wærwulf, Ælfgar and Ingwald. I assess them and then aim Haden towards Gyrth and Wærwulf. The two face at least seven mounted warriors. Their opponents are highly skilled, even turning their horses with just touches of their knees as they try to reach my warriors.

"Come on," and Haden canters toward the group. At the last possible moment, I give him the instruction, and he rears, legs fleeing before him, the left and then the right, as he attacks the largest of the Raiders, more waddling in his saddle, than sitting in it.

Our foe doesn't see us coming, and between one blink and the next, he tumbles from the saddle, not dead, but very definitely stunned by his impact with the hard ground. It clears the path for me to join Gyrth.

Wærwulf's war axe scythes through the air, and I duck to avoid its path, allowing it to hit another Raider. This one has not just a leather byrnie, but also a metalled tunic. Wærwulf aims for the slither of skin just above the neckline of his tunic. But the warrior ducks out of the way. The blow lands on the neck of a grey horse, sending the animal's eyes wild, as it canters from the melee, regardless of the frantic instructions of the Raider sitting atop its back.

"Well, that's one way of doing it," I grin, seax in my hand, as I thrust at the exposed hands of the warrior directly in front of me. Gyrth has already floored one of the other riders and has turned to find the next.

"*Skiderik*," the Raider spits into my face, his eyes glazed with pain, where my seax has severed one of his long fingers, despite the thick gloves he wears.

With blood pooling down his arm as he lifts it to lash out at me with his seax, he seems made of liquid, not flesh. I reverse the hold on my weapon, and plunge upwards, aiming for his neck, but hitting his collarbone instead.

My weapon harmlessly glances away, and then his blade is before my nose, and I'm forced to veer to the side, even as my hand flails to catch my wayward weapon, dislodged from my grip.

"Bastard," I return the greeting, turning my seax, probing down into his exposed thigh.

He screeches, his blade trembling in his hands. I release my grip on Haden's reins and flick his blade aside with my spare hand. Able to sit up right now I'm no longer in immediate peril, I direct my strike just above his collarbone and this time the aim is true. His blood gushes over my already stained gloves. They're sodden with the stuff, as his eyes lose focus.

I kick his horse aside, the animal eager to be away from the crush of so many other horses, and the stench of spilt blood, and horse shit.

Wærwulf has taken a kill as well, so with the stunned man still on the floor, and the other somewhere in the distance, trying to tame his frightened animal, that leaves only one each for Gyrth and Wærwulf.

Slipping from my saddle beside the man whose eyes are unfocused, I push his helm free from his head, or at least make the attempt. The damn thing is stuck, no doubt from the fall, so instead, I stab down, into his exposed thigh, and another man meets his end.

Leaping onto Haden's back, I survey my surroundings. There's little light to see by, and that which there is comes from either inside Northampton itself or from the farm buildings, which burn. I pity the family for their loss, but take comfort in knowing they're safe inside Northampton's walls.

Perhaps they should make their home inside the walls from now on. But no. I'll banish the Raiders, and then they'll be free to live their lives unmolested once more.

Sitting astride Haden, I once more try and determine the flow of the battle. Who are these Raiders? Did the woman command them, or was she merely the means by which they gained invaluable information to enable them to disable the huge gate? Are they connected with the smaller group who attacked before? One thing is sure, Jarl Guthrum isn't here, and neither, if Icel is correct, is Jarl Oscetel. Is there some new foe?

Gyrth and Wærwulf quickly join me, their opponents all dead or breathing their last, and together we survey the action.

"Everyone is holding their own," Gyrth acknowledges, and I move to agree with him, only for something to catch my eye, just behind where Pybba and Rudolf face off against the Raiders.

"Did you see that?" I point to the spot.

"What?"

"More Raiders, out there." Gyrth glares into the distance, as though such fury could illuminate the area. For a moment, we're all still, and then his response is less than reassuring.

"At least fifty of them, perhaps more."

"Bastard. Why can't this be easy, just fucking once?" But I'm already considering what needs to be done.

"Gather everyone together. We need to make a stand, close to the farm," and I point to where I mean. The place offers us the best visibility because of the blazing fire, but I know the Raiders will want to attack the remains of the wooden bridge. We need to win this battle on our terms. And, really, there's nothing to protect at the bridge. There's no way of gaining admittance, not now the gate is back in place, and the bridge shattered into pieces. The few Raiders still alive within Northampton won't be for long, and Kyred, Turhtredus and Eanulf have secured the tunnels.

If only my warriors hadn't raced out to counter this new threat, we'd be locked up tight behind firm walls. But, then we'd be the prisoners, and I'm not about to fucking allow that.

I'm the king of Mercia, and I'll not cower behind the walls, while the Raiders threaten the interior of my kingdom once more. I'm not King Burgred to allow the Raiders to make such decisions for me.

I direct Haden towards Pybba and Rudolf, sucking in a sharp breath, as Rudolf sends his seax widely high, and I think he'll injure himself, only to watch a lumbering warrior slump to his knees. I hadn't even seen the Bastard, only the blade.

The ground has been churned up by so many hooves, the dank mud promising a slip onto an arse if we're not careful. I pass Hereman and Edmund, the two enjoying some sort of heated debate, even as they cut and slice their opponents.

It's not the time for a family argument about Gardulf's future. It really fucking isn't.

"The farm," I holler at them when there's the space of a few heartbeats. I'm not sure if either of the bastards hears me, but I'm sure they'll work it out.

Gyrth has Ælfgar and Ingwald, and he leads the way through the fighting, somehow remaining unscathed, even though Raiders are rearing up time and time again, blades ready to cut. But it's as though our enemy is incapable of landing a single blow.

Lyfing and Icel face-off against a small battalion of our foe. Wærwulf makes his presence known, by directing Cinder directly at the mass of blades and horseflesh, and in no time at all, Lyfing and Icel have fought free.

Rudolf watches me approach, his seax ready in his hand, but with the halo of shimmering red that seems to adorn him, I'm unsurprised that the hesitant Raiders stay away.

"What?" he demands to know, chest heaving, perhaps anticipating a rebuke.

"The farm. We'll make our stand there. They're welcome to the damn bridge. It's in pieces. They can't make it inside Northampton, not without a swim, and then a steep climb, and then a gate that's not going anywhere, not again."

Ever vigilant, we quickly evade the rest of the enemy, and then I turn Haden, but not before noting that the fire has all but consumed the main farm building. We won't have the much-needed light for long. We need to kill the Raiders quickly.

"What's this about?" Edmund rages.

"We need to give them a focus, and there's fuck all reason for skirmishing with the river at our back, risking a dunking in the bastard water. The bridge is gone." The news seems to steady him, and a thin smile touches his lips.

"So we just invite them here, do we?"

"I don't think they'll take much inviting, but yes. We want the Raiders where we can control what's happening, especially with so many of them compared to us."

"So, there's no one else coming?"

"No, Haden just made it, and he had to take a running jump. Otherwise, you'd be on your own."

I can't tell whether the news pleases him or not, and I don't have time to press the matter.

"I once faced sixty enemies, and there were no more than five men, besides me." Icel offers the history lesson, as he moves Samson between Haden and Jethson, and I don't know whether he does it to be helpful or to infuriate. "Not that the other five were much use." And Icel startles me by roaring with laughter.

I feel a grin slither onto my face, and I start to chuckle at the incredulous looks that suddenly turn to glare at Icel. Rudolf's jaw has dropped entirely open, and even Pybba is smirking. Damn the man. There's a reason why Icel is such an essential member of my warriors, and why his absence has been so sharply felt.

I gaze out at the Raiders who wish to kill us. They're beginning to realise that we've all gathered together beside the farm. I think they thought we were retreating, and some of the Raiders have dipped low to check on prone comrades, blades and weapons catching the glint of the lowering fire.

But some are beside the river, perhaps thinking we've forsaken the inhabitants of Northampton. Cries of dismay follow the sound of a heavy object hitting the water, perhaps tumbled down the steep bank without realising the bridge is more than half gone. I hope the horse survives. The Raider is welcome to a watery death.

And then there's a ripple effect, a cacophony of calls between our enemy, and all eyes suddenly settle on my small band of warriors, atop their horses. This is what I want to happen.

I don't glance along my line of men, horses shuffling gently forward and backwards, breath fogging before them. I know what they're capable of achieving. I trust them as implicitly as they do me.

I take the time to try and determine how many Raiders we face, and where their leader might be, only for another to beat me to it.

"Sixty, or thereabouts, and there," and Rudolf points away from the river, closer to the woodlands where I hid not so long ago. "Is the man who commands them."

I peer where he points, but I can't make out more than the haze of the trees, swaying energetically in the gathering wind. It seems that Estrith wasn't in overall command. That only adds weight to my belief that she acts under the instructions of another, for all she claimed the opposite.

"Only about twenty of them are mounted."

"So it's about equal then," I offer, a shrug of my shoulders reminding me of my old wounds, and alerting me that I might have already gained some new ones.

"They're going to form a shield wall."

I've decided the same, even as Icel speaks.

I feel Haden still beneath me. We've encountered such tactics many times before. The mounted Raiders mill behind the shield wall. They mean to tackle us once the Raiders on foot have hacked at our horses, and we're as exposed as their shield-brothers are now.

"You know what needs to be done," I caution my warriors.

"Aye, My Lord," Ælfgar replies, his voice laced with resolve.

No one else speaks, although a few are adjusting harnesses and saddles, eager to ensure they don't lose their seat in what's about to happen.

"Attack." I feel Haden's powerful rear legs bunch beneath him, and almost in an instant, we've gone from motionless to a full gallop. The air whips the parts of my face that are exposed, around my mouth and just below the cheekpieces. I have no weapon to hand. I won't need it. Not just yet.

I spare a thought for Rudolf, suddenly realising that he's only ever practised such a move, but there's no time to change my mind, not now.

The shield wall stretches almost to the river, but my men and I are concentrated at its middle. This is where we'll strike first because this is always the chosen position of the most skilled warriors; those who probably could skewer a horse through their neck. But I'm not about to let that happen.

The roll of the advance fills my ears, flooding me with a sense of purpose.

I crouch low over Haden's neck, ready for what will happen next, even as the shield wall seems to shimmer with indecision. Perhaps there are those amongst them who realise we're not about to do what they think we are. Or maybe they're just terrified, pissing their trews and praying to their fucking Gods.

But, they'll get no fucking help from them.

Haden rushes closer and closer, the darkness spreading the further from the fire we travel. But I don't need to be able to see to direct Haden to what we're about to do. Truthfully, I probably don't need to offer him any instructions.

When I can smell the bastards, I gently touch Haden's side with my knees, squeezing him just the once, even as those in front of me, shudder backwards, unprepared, despite their earlier bravery, to face a charging horse. I imagine they brace, perhaps waiting for us to soar over their heads.

Abruptly, Haden's forward momentum stops, my low position ensuring I remain on his back, and then he rears, forward hooves kicking out, one after another, and then again. Damn the brut. He manages it three times before he's forced to touch the ground once more. Quickly, I relinquish my hold on his reins, my right hand reaching for my seax, my left for my sword. I would have liked a spear, but it's too late for such thoughts.

The sound of twenty hooves clattering against the shields of our foe fills the air, and then I'm stabbing and slashing, weaving Haden one way and then another, his own experience meaning we both want the same result.

An easy path opens up before me, men tumbling left and right, and even one straight down, so that Haden serenely walks over his splayed body.

The sound of slaughter fills the air even as I keep my gaze immediate to my endeavours, lashing out, left and right, wherever the bastards happen to be.

My seax slices arms, necks, noses and exposed foreheads, my sword stabs down, beneath byrnies and metalled tunics. There's so much blood muddying the air; it appears as though the fire has dimmed even more.

But then I'm through the shield wall, ready to face the mounted Raiders. These warriors, I predict, will be more challenging to defeat than the shield-foes. And they outnumber us, two to one, and that's not easy to overwhelm, despite my words to the contrary.

I seek out my first target, not so much by appearance rather than by the simple fact that the white horse is easy to see in the gloom.

Haden steps eagerly to follow my commands. I'm not alone behind the shield wall, but neither has the line of defence entirely collapsed. Not yet. I catch a glimpse of Icel, as he batters his war axe against an exposed head, the sound of the weapon embedding itself through the skull, reaching me despite the roars of battle and the shrieks of the dead and dying. It grates, and I grit my teeth. The sound is far from pleasant.

When will these fuckers learn to leave Mercia alone?

I palm my sword into my right hand, having wiped my seax blade down the leather of my byrnie. Not all of the ruddy mixture disperses, but I slick the weapon back on my belt all the same.

My foe eyes me with a downturned expression on the part of his face I can see. A thick beard covers his chin, his lips barely visible. I aim my sword at his neck, the slash wide and seemingly impulsive, and the man ducks out of my reach, or at least tries. His severed beard sheers free, parts of it borne away on the stiffening breeze, while some of it merely tumbles to the floor.

Fierce eyes glance my way, and then a war axe is being levelled at me. I'm forced to knee Haden aside, or risk being impaled by the lethal-looking weapon. Fuck that.

Haden responds quickly, stepping backwards and sideways at the same time, and while the man flails, his balance affected by such a huge attack, I risk rushing in closer, thrusting my sword before me, hoping to impale him.

But he's a wily old fucker, and this time, it's his horse that makes the life-saving move.

I'm breathing heavily, trying to determine what happens all around me, even as I face my opponent. I want the fucker dead. But equally, I don't want to be caught by any opportunistic bastard coming at me from behind. And that's precisely what happens.

While my sword manages to pierce the man's byrnie, a hand reaches for me from my left side, trying to tug me free from Haden's back. I grip his sides tighter, anchoring myself with the stirrups, as I thrust my elbow out, hoping to catch the fucker's nose.

But my aim is wildly out, and the mounted warrior realises I'm beset and comes toward me with his axe once more.

"Fucking bastards," I huff, sweat stinging my eyes.

Abruptly, I direct all of my attention at the warrior on foot. He'll be the easier of the two to kill. Swinging my sword over my head, I stab downwards, the effort far from secretive, and yet it slicks home, all the same, slicing clean through the man's byrnie, forcing him to skip out of my reach.

His shriek of rage emboldens me, and I rotate Haden, forgetting my first opponent, for the time being, giving the shield-warrior all of my attention.

His byrnie gapes open at the front, revealing a matted chest of dark hair, and the tell-tale silvery thread of a long-healed scar. A thin trail of blood has sprung up on his skin, but the weapon's done little other damage.

So far, I've killed a beard and a byrnie. Not my finest battle-glory to date.

The warrior leers at me from the ground, thrusting his shield at me, showing me the darkened paint with some sort of animal at its core, only it's impossible to determine what it is. Perhaps red paint on brown, or some other dark colour, on black. It might work during the daytime, but right now, it tells me nothing of his loyalties.

His weapon of choice is also a war axe with an elongated handle. It gives him a more extended reach than I might like. And I'm not at all convinced I can attack him from Haden's saddle.

With decisive movements, I rip my right leg free from the stirrups and slide to the ground, four quick steps putting me directly in front of the Raider. And he's trapped. He's managed to walk his way into the back of the shield wall. While his comrades fight for their lives, they're not about to help him.

Not that it seems to concern him. He swings his war axe with his left hand, thrusting the shield into my face, and I'm forced to scamper to the side of the shield, and only then attack with the thrust of my sword. I've removed my seax from my belt, now that I don't have a rein to hold. Both weapons have taken their fill of kills, but I'm sure they're not sated yet.

Blinded by his shield, the man doesn't notice my circuitous movements, until my seax slices into his upper arm, encountering some resistance, but not enough for the weapon to have been stopped by his protective leathers.

His breath steams in the air, a cry of terror rippling through the air, and I think I've got him, only for movement behind me to alert me that I'm no longer alone.

I stoop, more by instinct than any real knowledge of what's there, and as I do, I take three squat footsteps. When I stand again, both Raiders are watching me, their eyes perplexed.

But this isn't the mounted warrior I first battled. No. Somehow, I've become part of the shield wall again, and that's not what I had planned. Not at all.

Haden remains close to me, and I could just mount him, and flee the two men, but my pride won't let me. Both of them nearly drew blood, while my original opponent watches on with a half-amused expression on his face, his hand reaching for his beard, only to encounter nothing. I smirk at him as he looks down, confusion quickly turning to fury.

"Lost something?" I call, but he doesn't understand my words.

"Angreb," he spits, and the shield-warriors share a quick look, and then approach again.

Two against one. I'd call it unfair odds, only I've seen something that lends urgency to my actions.

Quickly, I stab, left-handed, with my seax, into the man who tried to upend me from Haden. I'm too fast for the warrior, and before he can swing his shield in front of him, my seax has found a home at the top of his bearded chest, and there I leave it, a final thrust assuring me that while the man might still stand, it won't be for long.

The second man is armed with a spear. He jabs it at my legs even as his companion slumps to the ground.

I rush into the attack, taking the length of the spear shank on my shoulder, and appreciating the man's great strength. If he'd managed to get close enough, it could have been a killing strike. Instead, his drive goes wild, forcing Haden to move aside to avoid its barbed point. Haden neighs, his complaint easy to hear as he stamps the ground, and steps behind me. Damn Bastard. He could kill the fucker with a well-aimed blow from his hoof, but it seems I'm to protect him this time with my iron.

While my opponent tries to regain control of his spear, I launch my seax, now in my right hand, at the exposed left side of his body. He wears a decent enough byrnie, but even it has weaknesses, and I've killed enough fuckers to know where to aim.

It cuts deep, into his armpit, and although it's not a killing blow, it stuns him enough that I can turn and check the first man is entirely dead.

His eyes condemn me in the dim light, but it's the white horse behind him that worries me most. I spare a glance for the rest of my warriors, but it's impossible to determine the flow of the battle from my current position. I can hear Hereman as his war cries reverberate through the air and I can see Pybba as he stabs down into the back of an oblivious shield-warrior, but nothing else.

I need to finish this myself, and I need to be fucking quick about it.

Reaching for Haden, I slip my foot back into the stirrup, turning to slice across the skewered man's throat almost as an afterthought before I return to the first enemy I wanted to kill.

The Raider is ready for me, and I consider why he's not already attacked me, or even come to the aid of his comrades. Not that it doesn't make it easier for me, but all the same, it begs the question.

His war axe is ready for me, held tightly in one hand, while he seems to weigh it in the other. I've never understood the need for such an action. Surely all warriors must know their weapon intimately. And if they don't, then they're more fucking contemptible than I thought possible.

I meet his eyes, testing the tenacity in them, and trying to keep my eyes from fixating on his savaged beard. It seems, from this angle, as though my cut wasn't straight, not at all. Now, he has more beard on one side than on the other. It's not a good look.

I encourage Haden on, my seax ready to drink once more. Despite the cacophony of noise all around me and the sense that the shield-wall is about to submit entirely, I don't break eye contact. The mounted Raiders are the problem. They could escape far too readily compared to the men on foot.

Only my foe doesn't do the same, the white horse standing still, perhaps refusing to move, I can't quite make out the movements the rider's legs make.

"Right," I huff, realising that I'm going to have to force the altercation. It wouldn't be the first time.

I direct Haden to a gallop, and he covers the distance quickly, as I determine where to aim my attack. Neck, armpit, the top of his leg, all of them are enticing targets, but while the man hesitates to renew his assault, I make a snap decision, twisting Haden slightly, and launching my seax as though it were a spear.

It wavers in the air, the reflected flickering flames showing me its path, and I think the warrior will see it and move aside. Only he doesn't. And my throw is accurate, the seax landing cleanly to slice through the upperpart of his lip as though it were little more than a slab of cheese, and the blood wells immediately.

The man's eyes furrow, and then lose focus, the blood flow increasing to a deluge that swamps his open mouth. He's dead, even if he's still mounted for now.

I reach across the divide, place my hand on the seax handle. But, he's not quite dead yet, and some part of his mind must still be focused on his initial task. His hand folds around mine, the latent strength making me wince, but my gaze seeks out his other hand, the war axe aimed toward my chest. My other hand thrusts out, knocking the war axe aside, the strength abruptly gone from him, and in the space of one breath, the war axe thuds to the floor, his hand relinquishes its hold on me, and I have my seax back.

I turn aside, surveying the battlefield. I don't need to see another warrior fall to the ground. I think I've had my fill.

I rotate Haden, peering at the shield-warriors. There's only one patch of fighting now; Ælfgar and Hereman keeping the Raiders at bay. But, it seems that the amount of mounted warriors has only diminished by three, perhaps four.

They still outnumber us.

Icel is engaged in a bloody fight against a tall warrior on the back of a roan coloured horse. I think them an even match until Icel takes a swipe at the Raider's reaching arm, and I think he'll quickly be the victor. The white horse crosses my vision, riderless now, but there are not many animals in such a state.

Pybba battles a mounted Raider, Rudolf coming to his aid, whether Pybba wants him to or not. Edmund is far in the distance. Almost in the tree line, but I'll always recognise the way he wields his sword, even in such low light, as he battles two mounted opponents.

Wærwulf twists his grey mount to direct it toward a knot of fighting that involves three Raiders, Gyrth and Lyfing, and I almost go to lend them my aid, but I've seen something, in the woodlands, behind Edmund, that unsettles me.

"Come on." I encourage Haden to move closer to the tree line, making it appear as though I seek out a solitary Raider, sitting atop his horse, fixated on Northampton, and not the battle ensuing around him.

But really, I want to know if what I think I've glimpsed is genuinely there, or if it's a figment of my imagination. I fucking hope it is.

I could do with Edmund at my side, but he's busy battling his foe. Both Raiders fight with shield and war axe, the horses spinning time and time again, under the command of their warriors.

From here, it's not possible to tell who will triumph, but I know it will be Edmund, all the same.

Still some distance from the lone Raider, I bring Haden to a stop. I pretend to survey the scene before me, where men battle for their lives, the sound of iron on iron ringing harshly, the shrieks and grunts of warriors fighting for their lives, a thundering counterpoint. But really, I'm determining whether the densely-packed trees harbour more of my enemy.

It wouldn't surprise me, and yet equally, I would want to question why they're not yet engaged in the battle. I consider who might command them, and I worry that while Jarl Guthrum can't possibly have made it here in the intervening time, and across a river in full spate, it might well be Jarl Anwend who cowers in the trees.

How the fuckers have made it to this side of the Nene worries me more than anything. Are they elsewhere in Mercia as well? I pray they're not.

But yes, my eyes catch on something that almost sparkles beneath the wind-tossed trees. How many more of the bastards are there? I'm just about to warn my warriors, when I catch sight of Edmund, encouraging Jethson on, his chestnut hide slick with sweat or blood, as he careers after one of the warriors they were battling, who now aims for the sanctuary of the woodland.

"Fuck. Hereman, Pybba." Both men raise their gaze from their latest kills to glance at me.

"The trees. There's more in the trees." I don't care who hears me; in fact, I need everyone to listen to me, including those who cower there.

"Follow Edmund," this I direct to Hereman, and he quickly turns Billy, and streaks after his brother. I manage a final sighting of Edmund before the impenetrable darkness of the interior swallows him. I fix his position in my mind, even as I move to gather the rest of my men.

With detachment, I slice my seax across the throat of the Raider whose gaze has remained on Northampton. He offers no resistance, and I only realise why, as I glance down. The man is dead already. He didn't need another cut. A spear protrudes from his belly, and it's this that keeps him upright, the sharpened spike just missing his horse, wedging on the stiff leather of the saddle. I kick the man aside, the horse momentarily startling before bending to tug at the tufty grass on the ground. It's oblivious to the death of its rider.

Pybba has taken it upon himself to round up Rudolf and Ælfgar fells the one remaining shield-warrior before mounting up to join them. Lyfing and Wærwulf still war against the enemy, but Gyrth peers into the tree line. Ingwald and Icel are together, surveying the scene before them, and I raise my voice to beckon them closer.

"The wood?" I jut my chin toward the path Hereman has just taken. "We need to follow Edmund and Hereman, and I don't know how many Raiders are in there."

"It'll be even more difficult to see," Icel's words fill me with foreboding, and yet there's little choice but to follow the other two.

"We have the advantage of having spent some time in there,"

I try to coax, forgetting for a moment that Icel wasn't with us then. "Stay with me," I urge him, and he nods, although he looks far from happy about it.

"We ride in groups of three. I'll have Icel and Wærwulf. Rudolf, Pybba and Ingwald form a group. Lyfing, Gyrth and Ælfgar, you're the other group. Stay close, and stay tight. If you encounter no one after a reasonable amount of time, come back to the river."

"We don't know how many of them there are. The aim is to kill them all, not chase them into the interior of Mercia. Remember that." The promise of Watling Street might be too much for any attempting to escape, and there are too many settlements along Watling Street that are currently unprotected.

My warriors all look my way. I notice the exhaustion on their faces, the slashes of maroon that show their skills, and the passionate determination that reflects in their stances. I try not to see the winces that reflect some wound they're not about to reveal to me.

"Just another fucking night as a member of my warband," I try and crack a smile but only Rudolf seems to appreciate the intent, well Rudolf, and the damn horses. They're still fresh, keen for more carnage, and so I give it to them.

"Stay alive," I growl, the words never getting old to me, and then I urge Haden on. The fight isn't fucking yet over, even if we've won the battle of Northampton.

CHAPTER 13

It takes all of three steps beneath the swaying bows to reveal to me how impossible this new task is. It's blacker than charcoal, and I'm forced to rely entirely on Haden's ability to see. If I direct him, we'll walk straight into a tree, and maybe never find our way clear from the dropping bows.

Wærwulf stays close to Icel, just behind me, and yet I sense that the pair of them would be better at leading than I am.

But within those three steps, the fierce breeze stops, and although the trees shimmer and shake above me, the penetrating cold is held at bay.

I can make out the sound of further hoof-falls over the spongy surface, but not for long. It's as though I'm blind, relying on my senses, and Haden's skills more than mine.

"Shitting bollocks," I exclaim, lifting my hand, and yet unable to see my fingers.

"We should wait until daylight," Icel rumbles, but I'm shaking my head, only to realise he can't see it.

"No, we do this now, before they have the chance to retreat."

"We could walk right fucking passed them and not even realise," a slither of fury infuses his voice, but I appreciate it for what it is, fear. I've never known Icel to fear anything, but his time away from us has changed him in ways that are only just making themselves known. He sounds, and speaks as he once did, and mostly acts the same as well, but his unfailing belief in his abilities has been dented. I pity him. No man should ever live to doubt himself, not when he's done no ill.

"Well, let's shut our mouths then, and listen for their heavy breathing."

For a moment, I feel remorse for pushing Icel when he's uncomfortable, but then he speaks again.

"Why don't you shut up, and then I can hear."

I snap my mouth shut on any retort. Icel remains behind me. What more can I ask from him?

I strain to hear, appreciating that I can no longer perceive the two other groups of men. Neither does the sound of Hereman pursuing Edmund reach my ears.

The start of an idea forms in my mind, and the longer I consider it, the more I know I'm right.

"We need to go to our old campsite," I pause, swivelling to seek our Wærwulf's eyes.

"How will we find it?" He makes a valid point. "We can't just meander around here looking for it?"

"No, no, we can't."

"We should wait until sunrise," Icel tries once more, but I don't know when that will be. At this time of the year, it's dark for far longer than it's light. And I want the Raiders to know that they're being hunted.

"We press on. Search for anything you recognise and shout up if you see something. If we encounter the others, we'll tell them the same." It's hardly a satisfactory outcome, but without light to see by, it's the best I can do. I'd sooner we floundered around than made ourselves a target by lighting a brand.

Yet I can't shake the unease that we're being watched, perhaps even herded towards a larger group of Raiders. Was this all foreseen? Again, I just can't reconcile it with what's happened so far. The Raiders didn't know that we'd built a second, interior wall to prevent them gaining access to Northampton, neither did they know about the problems with the bridge, nor that we'd prevent more significant numbers from gaining admittance. And certainly, they can't have predicted that only eleven of us would make it free from Northampton to harry the Raiders on this side of the Nene.

No, I don't think it's a trap. But, it could still become one.

Haden picks his way unwaveringly through the tree trunks. He seems to sense where the branches can't be passed and where trees block the route. I lift my hands from the reins and allow him to do what needs to be done. Instead, I focus on every sound, and my hand slips to my seax, as Haden's ears perk up, his head rising from where he plods along. Only then I realise it's Rudolf I can hear, but only faintly. I imagine he and Pybba are arguing about something. It pleases me to know that they must be heading in the same direction as us, even if they're too far away to see, or risk hailing.

The sigh of the branches overhead quickly covers the noise, and Haden lowers his head again. Icel and Wærwulf don't so much as speak, and at times, I can't hear the hoof-falls of the horses either, so I feel entirely alone.

The sensation is far from pleasant.

I stifle a yawn, fearing that I might fall asleep in the saddle, and try to rouse myself. I squint more intently at the impenetrable gloom that surrounds me, seeking out the shadowed shapes of the trees, and eventually, I too can see, my eyes finally adjusting to the reduced light.

Yet, my view remains obscured. I can only perceive so far in front of me, or to the side, and behind me, I can't even determine the objects I've just passed.

When Icel speaks, I startle in my saddle, and Haden lifts his head with a soft nicker, as though he reassures me.

"We're no longer alone." His voice is ominous, and yet I sense no malice.

"Where?"

"Behind us, I believe." His voice reflects neither concern nor happiness, and for a brief moment, I believe it might just be the rest of my warriors, somehow muddling their paths, so that we all meet up. Only then I hear the slither of a weapon being drawn from a scabbard, and I know better. How the fuck we're supposed to fight in this, I have no idea.

"Arm yourselves," I almost whisper, ensuring Haden stays on his current path. It's one thing to grip a weapon; it's an entirely different matter to attack in such poor conditions. I'm not yet convinced that they will.

I ride more alert, eyes hunting the way we're going. I'm satisfied that our enemy is behind us. The longer they take to attack, the more chance there is of some light between the trees, even this deep inside the woodlands.

The noises of the night once more creep into my consciousness, the sway of the leaves, the call of forest creatures, and the plod of the horses. I think they'll override my awareness of the Raiders, but they don't, not at all.

Yet, I start to feel unease, and I rub my neck, wishing I could banish the knowledge that we're being observed, or at least, tracked. There's no way these Raiders would be able to see us. If I can't fucking see, then they sure as shit can't. Although, and here I realise I've erred in my judgement, I can see in front of me, just not behind me. Our foe might well be able to see more than I realised.

I slow Haden, while Samson and Cinder draw level with me.

"We need to attack them," I speak low, keeping my mouth closed, hoping the two men can hear me.

"You stay here," Wærwulf states. "Stay here, and I'll fall behind them. Take them from the rear. I can always offer some Danish if they suspect me." I can't deny the logic of his decision, and yet it frustrates me. It should be my risk and not his. However, he's gone before I can refuse him. I feel his absence, as he takes advantage of a wide-spreading tree to direct Cinder to the side. I would hiss and demand he returns, but it would only put him in greater harm.

"When it starts, I'll go left, and you go right," I inform Icel, and he grunts softly, his breath coming a little too fast. I'm surprised that he's still so uncertain. I would have thought he'd have become used to the situation by now.

Haden ambles on, but I'm overly alert now, just waiting for a cry of surprise or the soft shush of a body tumbling to the spongy ground, riddled with exposed tree roots and pine cones. Haden's wider hooves can cope with the obstacles. I know I'd have fallen on my fucking arse by now.

But the crash doesn't come, or at least, it's inaudible to my ears, and my hand slips more and more often toward my seax, only then Wærwulf reappears, a soft murmur to alert me to his presence.

I can't see his face.

"Five of them. Daft bastards. Dead now."

His words should reassure me, but they don't—five of them, against three of us.

Only then the rush of the river percolates my thinking, and I turn my head, as though scenting it. Haden does the same, the jingle of his harness alerting me after the fact.

It seems that we've strayed from our course, and yet I'm not upset by it. Perhaps we should have followed the Nene all along. It would have made it easier than fumbling in the dark, as we've been doing.

"This way," I instruct, reaching out to pull Samson's head to where I want him to go. I have a feeling that Icel sleeps, or has slipped into some sort of trance, half awake and half asleep. I feel him startle, and his head swivels.

"This way," I instruct him, Wærwulf already in front.

"Aye," he rumbles, his voice laced with fatigue. Fuck, I've forgotten that he's been ill, and taken months to recover. I wish he'd stayed within Northampton, but more, I fucking wish I'd remembered. Time and time again, I expect too much from my warriors. What sort of leader am I? Clearly not a very thoughtful one.

The rush of the river grows as Cinder leads the way. Haden's steps double, perhaps the beast is thirsty, or maybe, and I believe it to be the truth, he doesn't like to be led by another. Damn beast.

The cloying branches that have tugged at harness, horse and tunic, slowly spread out, and then Cinder stops, Wærwulf waiting for me. It's lighter here, but only a little, the moon still obscured by heavy cloud, the scent of cold assaulting my nostrils. I shiver, wishing I had more than a tunic and byrnie to cover me. But, no man can truly fight in a cloak. It only gives the enemy something else to grip onto, like a beard. Stupid fuckers who decide to fight with a full beard and cloak. I'd sooner be cold for the duration of an altercation, than dead and cold forever.

Icel sidles up beside me, and the three of us just stare, both upstream and down, and even peering to the far side. The water glints with menace, the promise of a frigid swim far from inviting. But, if we needed to, we could escape that way. But that would only be in the direst circumstances. I can't see that happening.

"Where are we?" I ask, even though I know it's an absurd question.

"Some way from the campsite," Wærwulf offers all the same. "I recognise this place. We can risk travelling beside the river, almost in the open, if you want."

I want to because it's much easier to see, but it'll also make us targets.

"Just inside the tree line," I advise. I don't want to relinquish the advantage we currently have, but equally, I don't want to abandon the river, not now we've happened upon it.

"But first we all need a drink."

We take it in turns to water our horses, and ourselves, kneeling on the muddy banks, trying not to fall into the rushing water. Its sharp tang wakes me quickly, even if it's so cold, it makes my teeth ache.

When we're ready, Haden rushes forward, and I suppress a smirk. He makes it clear he wants to lead the other horses, and so I direct him to where I want to be. I keep the glimmer of the river in sight. Only this time, we move more quickly. The horses can see better as well, and their movements become more fluid.

Icel is just behind me, Wærwulf to the rear, and I consider that Wærwulf appreciates Icel's exhaustion. I wish he'd fucking warned me.

Yet, Icel's not alone in nodding in his saddle, and I startle awake sometime later, surprised to realise the light is growing, and even I can see the straggling roots underfoot and reaching branches overhead.

I swivel in my saddle, pick out Icel's white face, and behind him, Wærwulf's fierce gaze. Icel barely acknowledges me, although Samson seems well. Wærwulf nods his head at me, and I huff my appreciation. Before I turn back, I hear a strangled cry, and immediately, my exhaustion leaves me, and I'm peering into the depths of the woodlands. From where has the sound come? And who is under attack?

"There." Icel points further inland. I follow his directions, and I'm spurring Haden to greater speed even before I've truly realised what I'm seeing.

I've realised whose voice it is. Rudolf.

"Come on," I urge Haden, hoping that Icel and Wærwulf follow behind me.

The scene that greets me between the tightly-packed tree trunks has me reaching for my seax, even as I kick my feet free from the stirrups and slither to the ground.

My warriors are under attack, by at least nine Raiders, perhaps more. I can't see beyond the glint of iron.

Pybba fights from the back of Brimman, but Rudolf and Ingwald have both dismounted. I quickly realise they've been caught resting, and I don't blame them. It's been a long few days. I'm fucking exhausted. The bastard enemy have seen what they think is an easy means of attack, but it isn't anymore, not now we've arrived.

I slink in beside Rudolf, where he faces a grinning Raider who towers over him. The fucker thinks it'll be easy to kill my one-time squire. But he doesn't expect my reinforcement. Without even considering it, I rush the fucker, shoulder down, driving him from his feet. While I fumble to get my seax in the correct position to kill the bastard, Rudolf has already crouched and thrust his blade through the warrior's splayed armpit.

The fucker's not dead yet, but he will be soon, as blood sprays and quickly trickles onto the leaf-strewn floor.

I can hear Rudolf puffing.

"My thanks," he breathes, but I'm already moving to take the next Raider.

Wærwulf has joined Pybba, and the pair of them face four mounted opponents, while Icel is assisting Ingwald to beat back a further three.

Everyone is outnumbered, apart from Rudolf and I, who now face one Raider each.

My foe turns his head and spits, and I think he'll try and dance with me, but I've had more than enough. I must have been fighting for an entire day. I thought I'd been fucking clever with my tactics, but evidently not.

I jab forward with my seax, aiming for his elbow, keen to knock his war axe to the floor. It's an unusual line of attack. I think it'll work, only the bastard grips his weapon even tighter, swinging the axe toward me. I thrust my seax upwards, absorb the force of the blow and just keep moving forwards. He's going to die today, whether he realises or not.

While he tries to bring his war axe back under control, I move both my seax and my other hand. I grip his right arm tightly, holding him close so that he can't evade my assault, not this time.

It brings me no pleasure to thrust my seax into the side of his neck. He's just a fucking impediment that needs dealing with.

I spare a thought for Rudolf, finding the time to admire his fast-moving feet and economical use of his seax. Again, his foe is dead. He just needs to realise that.

I return to Haden, slipping my foot into the stirrup and encouraging him to where Wærwulf and Pybba still battle three Raiders. The riderless horse has meandered away, keen to be free from the threat of attack, and I offer him a hearty slap to his backside as I pass, just a little more encouragement to get out of the way.

Two Raiders beset Pybba, and although they both carry wounds, it's Pybba who's most at risk. I take stock, assuming that Wærwulf has already felled his first opponent. I take the man to Pybba's right. His horse flicks wild-eyes my way, but it's the warrior I want to kill, not the beast.

This Raider has a deep cut along an un-bearded chin, and blood drips down their front, but it's not a killing blow, far from it.

"I'm here," I mutter to Pybba and he moves Brimman aside, allowing Haden the room he needs to allow me to counter one of his opponents.

The bloody-chinned warrior growls low in his throat; no doubt pissed off by the interference. Perhaps they sensed success. It spurs me on. My seax darts out, as though to aim for their chin, but then I drop it low at the last moment, aiming instead for the savaged tear I've spied through their leather byrnie. There's no bloody mark to show a previous wound, and I consider that the poor bastard has borrowed another's byrnie, and it's not about to end well.

My seax easily slips between the leather to either side, only there it stops, no matter how much I try and hammer it home. Does the warrior wear two byrnies, one on top of another? It would be unusual, and bloody hard to move easily in, but it's a possibility.

"*Skiderik*," the fucker spits into my face while attacking me from the left with a seax. I see the blade glint as it aims for my left arm, and for no more than a heartbeat, I'm unsure how to counter the attack. My seax is still wedged against the Raiders chest. And there's no weapon in my left hand. And the bastard senses my confusion, the assault seeming to come even quicker. And then they slump, their weapon missing my arm easily, and I gasp in surprise.

Edmund's eye greets mine, fury on his face.

"Fucking kill the bastards, don't look at them."

I realise that Hereman is there as well, assisting Icel and Ingwald. Both Pybba and Rudolf have killed their opponents. It seems that I was the only one still fighting.

"What were you doing?" Edmund demands to know hotly.

"I was trying to kill the fucker, but there was something

beneath their byrnie that tempered my blow." As I speak, I'm sliding from Haden's back, keen to see what prevented me from making such an easy kill.

"What happened?" I ask him, as I turn the body, ignoring the unseeing-eyes that peer at me, as I explore the slit in the byrnie. My hands touch iron.

"A necklace," I explain, pulling the object through the space. It just about fits, and my eyes fasten on a heavy-looking hammer, a pagan symbol.

"The cunt thought they had Thor on their side." I dredge a smile to my face, and then stand, hands on knees, to gaze at my warriors.

They're all knackered. Completely done in.

"What happened?" I repeat.

I think Edmund won't reply.

"We killed him. They've made a camp. At our old campsite. We were coming to find you." I'm grateful to Hereman for responding, even as I watch Edmund for some sign he's unhappy with his brother. But there's nothing.

"They have two ships in the river, and some horses, but they're not all mounted."

This confuses me.

"Did they bring the horses on the ships?"

"I can't see it," Hereman states, Edmund still refusing to speak or meet my eyes as he works on cleaning his weapon.

"So, they've planned this?"

I look to Rudolf. He's the one who knows the most about the rivers of Mercia.

"Where has the ship come from?"

"The Wash."

"So, not from Grantabridge then?"

"No, but it could be the same Raiders. They'd have needed to venture back to the North Sea before coming down the Nene."

"Did you recognise anyone?" I direct the question to Edmund, although I'm aware that Hereman will answer.

"Too fucking dark," he grunts. "We could see 'em, but not see them, if that makes sense."

I peer to where I think our old campsite must have been. Only for Rudolf to step close and offer softly. "That way, My Lord," and he points behind me.

"Fuck," I growl, but my warriors are smirking, and it's good to see them smile. Well, all of them apart from Icel. He stands almost frozen in place, and a thread of unease percolates through my body. It's not like him, not at all.

And then he surprises me by speaking.

"Edmund, tell me of the verse you composed for me? When you thought me dead."

Of all the things he could have said, I would never have expected this, and it's evident that Edmund didn't either.

He stiffens, his remaining eye flashing to Icel, his mouth falling open in shock.

"Come, it's not a difficult thing for you to remember. You have perfect recall. I am merely curious."

As he speaks, Icel moves closer to Edmund, and I'm aware of Pybba wavering uncertainly behind them. Some of the others, Wærwulf and Ingwald, have bent to riffle hands through the possessions of the dead. I'm not surprised. This is going to get uncomfortable.

"I." I don't think I've ever seen Edmund falter for words. "I." He tries again.

"I know you composed one. I would hear it now." And Icel ends his sentence with an unexpected, "Please." I feel my head swivelling between the two. We're soaked in the blood of the dead, chests heaving, faces pinched with exhaustion, the farts of the dead filling the air, and my warriors are about to have the most intense conversation I've ever witnessed.

"It would be wrong," Edmund stutters.

"Wrong?" Icel presses.

"To sing of a man's death, when he yet lives."

"But you've sung the song, and everyone has heard it, apart from me." Icel is persuasive, and yet I think Edmund will still refuse. Only then he begins to speak.

"Bitter in battle, with blades set for war.
Attacking in an army, cruel in battle.
They slew with swords, without much sound.
Icel, pillar of battle, took pleasure in giving death."

I'm unsure where Edmund summons his usual tone and stance from, but he does, and in fact, he honours Icel more than I could ever have imagined with just such simple words. My warriors watch Edmund, although I keep my focus on Icel.

The flurry of emotions that covers his face is unsettling. There's fury, sorrow, anger, frustration, and an element of pride that makes him stand taller, Samson beside him mirroring his movements.

Silence rings through the woodlands at the end, and I appreciate that it's finally light enough for everyone to be able to see.

Icel nods when Edmund finally looks at him.

"My thanks, old friend," he offers, and then turns to mount Samson. The rest of my warriors are doing the same, the bodies already moved to one side, a pile of flesh for the lucky forest inhabitants to gauge on between now and the time the bodies are interred beneath the rich soil. White flesh, blue-tinged lips and gaping wounds are hideously exposed as a single beam of rich sunlight finds its way between the reaching branches and sodden leaves still hanging on to the skeletal branches.

This is what it means to make war and deal death.

And we've got more to fucking do yet.

CHAPTER 14

I want to tell my warriors to rest, but I know they won't, not after what happened to Pybba, Rudolf and Ingwald. We're being hunted, just as much as we're hunting. And Lyfing, Gyrth and Ælfgar are still to track us down.

I feel surprisingly exposed, and when Hereman meanders up to my side, I know what he's going to say.

"What the fuck was that all about?"

"I don't know. I really don't."

"No man should know his scop song before he dies."

"No, he shouldn't. I agree."

Edmund hasn't spoken again since he delivered the last word of his song, whereas Icel is more expansive than I've seen since his homecoming. It's almost as though Edmund's words have returned Icel to us, and yet, I'm not sure that they have, or even, why they would.

"I don't like it."

"I don't, either." And that's where our conversation ends because Edmund comes to join us as our beasts pick their way back toward the river. They need to drink, and so do we. It's been a fucking long night. None of us has eaten, but we can make do with cold water. It'll revive even the most exhausted of us.

Not that Edmund speaks. His head is down, almost lower than Jethson's, and I sense that the words he was forced to share weigh him down. Since Icel's return, he's not spoken about what happened to Icel. None of us has, not really. It was simply too good to have him back with us, to know he yet lived, even though he took himself away from Northampton quickly enough.

Wærwulf reaches the tree line first and dismounts to ensure there's no one watching, before returning to Cinder.

"All clear," he calls, leading Cinder. Haden finds a burst of speed, and the daylight floods my senses. It feels as though it's been dark for days, only now, even the thick rain clouds have moved on, and there's the snap of cold in the air. Walking free from the trees makes me feel suddenly exposed, and while Haden drinks his fill, perched on the steep incline, I peer behind me, seeking out the gaze of any watchers.

But there's no one.

"Drink, I'll watch." Hereman offers, and only then do I bend, remove my gloves and cup my hands to quench my suddenly rampant thirst. The water is so cold it makes my teeth ache, but it invigorates me, as I knew it would, only for the sound of hands reaching for seaxs, to intrude into my consciousness.

Rising swiftly, I too reach for my weapon, before settling again.

"I might have known you'd be here," Gyrth calls, the hint of a smile on his strained cheeks.

Ælfgar and Lyfing are with him, but Ælfgar rides heavily in his saddle, and it's evident he's taken a wound.

"The finest ale," I indicate with my hand, and even Lyfing smiles, although Ælfgar's gaze is shot with pain.

"Come, drink," I instruct them, walking to Ælfgar's side when he makes no effort to move.

"What ails you?"

"Nothing, My Lord, nothing." But I've spied the maroon stain low on his side.

"A belly wound?"

"No, a stab wound. Shallow but long. It just fucking aches." He tries to infuse his voice with strength, but I can see that even that discomforts him.

"You should have seen the bastard that did it. He's got more than a belly wound," Lyfing consoles.

"Have you cleaned and bound it?"

"No, nothing, not yet." I want to know when it happened, but it's not my immediate concern.

"Right, you need to dismount, and we'll see what we can do for you."

"But, My Lord, there are Raiders."

"Yes, there are, but you're no good to me like this, more a liability than an asset. Come on; I'll help you. Maybe, we can get you across the river, and you can return to Northampton from there."

Immediately, Ælfgar kicks one foot loose from his stirrup, his pale lips fixed in a grimace. For an old sod who once decided to spend the rest of his life at Kingsholm, he's become stubborn of late. I admire him. Well, I do before he more falls on me, than dismounts.

"Bloody bollocks," I expel, trying to keep him upright.

Rudolf is there to lend me his strength, and between us, we get Ælfgar lying down, while his mount noses the dank earth and then saunters to take her fill of cool river water. I try not to see the shimmer of maroon that covers Poppy's coat.

"Show me," I demand, and he fumbles at his right side, trying to pull his byrnie high. When it seems only to hurt him more, I reach in.

"Here, let me."

His byrnie shows a small wound, but beneath it, his tunic is sodden with blood, the wound much longer than such a tiny tear might imply. The flesh is jagged, the cut more than my hand's length.

Hereman appears, his helm brimming with water, and I rip the tunic and dribble the water into the wound. Again, the poor bastard hisses, but I've got nothing to give him to ease the pain.

Pybba stands behind me.

"It'll heal," he advises. "But it'll hurt before it does." I agree with him. Ælfgar has been scored just above his hip, and all the way around to this back, no doubt he was moving to evade the attack.

"Whatever you wear, it's going to rub on it," I advise. "Riding will be painful."

"I fucking know that," he exclaims.

"Does anyone have a piece of linen?" I think it a stupid question, and I'm surprised when Icel hands me a piece of soft fabric, but I don't question where he obtained it.

Deftly, I finish cleaning the wound, and then pack it with a small piece of the fabric, before fashioning a bandage that can fit just under the top of his trews.

"You don't have to come with us," I caution him, even though I know he won't accept my dismissal of him.

"I know," Ælfgar offers, taking my hand to level himself up, before staggering to his feet.

"I don't have to do any of this, but I fucking want to kill them all. Now, I need a damn drink."

While Ælfgar takes his fill, I evaluate the state of my warriors.

There aren't enough of us to beat back the Raiders. But that's never stopped us before, and we're not about to start running away from a fight.

I direct my men to travel along the edge of the river. Now that it's daylight, we can see the Raiders just as easily as they can see us. On a bend in the river, I turn around, hoping to catch a glimpse of Northampton, but we're too far away. I fancy that I can see a thin trail of smoke in the leaden sky and hope it signifies a cooking fire, and not the place burning.

My plan is simple. Find the bastards and kill them. But I know that nothing is ever that simple.

Ælfgar rides in front of me, and I try not to wince in sympathy when Poppy missteps and a hiss of agony erupts from his lips. The daft fucker. He should have taken the swim to the other side of the Nene and returned to Northampton. But when did my oath-sworn men ever do the sensible thing? If they did, I'd have no one to fight at my side.

Edmund remains sullen, but we're all quiet, trying to listen for the enemy over the hoof-falls of our mounts.

And why have I chosen the river route? I want to see the ships. I want to see for myself how many Raiders there might be, this close to Northampton. I've always suspected it was strange that the Raiders came mounted, not on board a ship. Now I want to know that I was correct to be suspicious.

My thoughts return to the unexplained events of recent months; the lone warrior on the far side of the Trent when I killed the escaping horseman; the understanding that a traitor shelters within Northampton, and of course, whatever happened to Icel while he was apart from us. Are these things connected? I want to say they're not, but I think that's just wishful thinking. I don't know who lurks in the woodlands, at our old campsite. Is there some new enemy that I don't even know about?

Has there always been someone other than Jarls Halfdan, Oscetel, Guthrum, Anwend and of course, Sigurd, ransacking Mercia?

"My Lord," Ælfgar returns me to the here and now, his eyes fatigued, but curious.

"What?" I ask, but there's no need for him to reply because my eyes fasten on the object he wishes me to see.

Just ahead, on the shimmering waters of the Nene, there are two Raider ships. They wallow in the water, moored to this side of the Nene, although, if they were end to end, across the river, I'm sure they'd act as some sort of bridge. I gasp in admiration of their size and menace, the burnished wood taking on the properties of gold even under the weak winter sun.

"They're empty," Gyrth, from the front of my line of warriors, offers the observation, and at the same time, I know our arrival has been noted.

"Weapons," I instruct, my voice low, but carrying all the same. I risk a glance behind me, eyes seeking out Hereman's who rides to the rear. He peers into the fastness of the trees, but he doesn't seem overly concerned. That means we're being watched from elsewhere.

My fingers itch to grip my seax, but I keep my hands slack on the reins instead.

"There," it's Rudolf who points out our overseer, and I stifle a smirk. It's merely an inquisitive bull on the far side of the river. I'd expect the huge bugger to be sheltering inside, but he's tugging at the stray river grasses, almost a bemused expression on his intelligent face at finding an audience to keep him amused.

"Right, under the trees," I command, grasping that we've been given a brief respite. I'll not be caught out again.

As much as I appreciated being out of the gloom of the trees, it's comforting not to feel as exposed as before. I strain to hear the sound of warriors at their camp, and to begin with the noise is so slight, that I don't appreciate it for what it is. Only when Gyrth calls a halt, his hand in the air to indicate we should both stop, and shut the fuck up, do I understand that the soft sounds aren't those of the forest dwellers, but instead of a group of warriors exerting themselves over the natural surroundings. Well, there's that and the more obvious scent of burning wood. I'm surprised I've not smelt it sooner, but I've not been alone in my oblivion.

Yet, I can't see the Raiders. Not yet.

I gather my warriors around me. This feels like our altercation in the woodlands close to Warwick, only there were more of us there. We beat the Raiders on that occasion by using our horses and our superior skills, as well as the fact, they were ripe for killing. I've no idea if these Raiders will be the same. None at all.

I don't want to risk splitting my small numbers. Not when we could be about to face nearly a hundred Raiders, and possibly more if those ships were fully crewed.

My men are alert, just waiting for my instructions, but I'm torn. Should we just ride at them, and react to what comes, or should we be a little more devious, perhaps wait for the shipmen to be separated? Maybe one ship will sail away, while the other holds the camp?

I stifle a yawn. I need to factor in just what my warriors and I have endured in the last few days. Our reflexes might be dulled; our aim may not be accurate.

Fuck. I thought I was hunting a handful of stray horse-warriors, not two fucking ships full of ship-Raiders.

I've never been one for indecision. Never.

"Everyone remain here. Edmund, you come with me, and Rudolf, I need your eyes. Stay alert," I instruct, determined not to see the confusion on the faces of my men. Surely, they didn't expect me to just ride in there without so much as a thought for surviving the coming attack?

Or maybe they didn't. Have I genuinely become so reckless, or is it just that they're surprised by my growing caution?

As I move through the trees, allowing Rudolf to guide my steps, I'm aware that I recognise where I am. I expected every tree to look like every other tree, but they don't, and I can even see where we previously dug latrine holes and filled them in. I avoid them. I don't need to advertise my presence by stinking of shit.

In no more than fifty steps, I get my first glimpse of the campsite, and I don't much like what's on display. There are many Raiders, all of them busy at some task, even if it's only eating or cleaning equipment. I don't detect any more horses. It seems we've stumbled upon an entirely new force. I hold out the hope that we've tracked down every stray mounted Raider.

Rudolf skips from tree to tree, getting so close, even Edmund hisses with fury, and yet he's not discovered. I remain where I am, happy to see more without the risk of getting caught.

"Seventy-three," Edmund offers even though I've not asked him. Seventy-three against eleven of us. Even I hesitate at such a considerable number.

"We should come back another day, bring more warriors."

His silence tells me what he thinks of that.

And then Rudolf returns, his face red with his exertions for all he doesn't breathe heavily. It must be the cold.

"About seventy-three. There's one tent, the rest sleeping on the floor."

"Who's in the tent?"

"I couldn't see who it was, although I could hear voices. But I couldn't make out enough to know what they said to ask Wærwulf. I think they've been here a while, although it's not easy to tell because the camp overlays our previous one."

"Did you see weapons?"

"Seaxs and war axes, yes, the odd spear, but nothing else. I don't even think they had shields."

I feel my forehead furrow at such a statement.

"They have four men on guard duty, or at least, I think that's what they're doing, but they have a fire to keep them warm, so they're not skulking in the shadows. I think they're waiting for someone."

I fix him with a stern stare.

"What do you mean, waiting for someone?" I barely speak above a whisper, but he hears me all the same.

"There's no purpose to their actions. They're not getting ready to fight or preparing to leave. They just seem to be trying to keep warm. Some of them are even playing games." Rudolf's surprise pitches his voice too high.

I feel Edmund's gaze more than see it. He wants to attack, despite the overwhelming numbers. It's not like him to want to be so provocative, but even I feel a stirring in my gut. This might be too good an opportunity to miss. But how the fuck are we to take on so many ship-men without being overwhelmed?

"We ride at them," Edmund states when we've retreated to the others. "Eleven horses will sound like a hundred. They'll panic, and run for it."

"Perhaps," I muse. The longer I delay, the more likely it is that we'll be discovered, but even so, I don't rush to decide.

"We should scuttle the ships, make sure they can't escape." Lyfing's suggestion holds merit, and I nod.

"Ingwald, Lyfing and Gyrth, go and do that if you can. If they can't escape on their ships, then they'll have to fight us, or die trying."

"And what are we going to do until then?" I'm so surprised

that it's Icel who questions my decision, that I almost find myself explaining even though there's no need for it.

"We rest. Half of us sleep, the other half stays awake. Hopefully, we'll all get some sleep, and then we'll tackle them, and bring about their deaths." I test the resolve of my warriors, as I do before every altercation. I find none of them wanting, even Ælfgar, and I dredge a grin to my tired face.

"I hope you're all keeping count. I'll reward the most prolific of you."

I manage to sleep a little and feel reinvigorated by the time the saboteurs return. Not that I set out straight away. I know I risk their handiwork being exposed, but they need to sleep, just as much as we do.

Rudolf and Wærwulf spend the time hunting for something to eat amongst the vibrant trees, and they return with gleaming red berries and handfuls of equally vivid mushrooms. I eye them with unease, only for Rudolf to pop one into his mouth and chew vigorously.

"Bloody lovely," he belches, dividing up his supplies so that we all get something to eat, even if the berries are a bit hard, and the mushrooms merely remind me of the smell of decaying flesh. Still, I feel better with something in my belly, as we make ourselves ready.

"We're going to strike together, in a long line, one after another. We run them down, and we hunt them down. They don't have horses or shields. Lyfing, Ingwald and Gyrth found all the shields on the ships. They have seax and war axes, and a few have spears. They'll try and run for their ships. We'll follow them. Once they get there, they'll have no means of escape, none, and we can scythe them down, as though it's the harvest."

Edmund scowls at my words, but I expect him to do so. I turn to Pybba, weighing his response. It'll be far more telling. He doesn't grimace, but neither does he look overjoyed. Rudolf, on the other hand, grins with delight. Was I ever as young as him? Were the rest of the warriors? It seems impossible, and yet, we've had our reputation for longer than Rudolf's drawn breath, and back then, we must have been young. Well, they were. I was off, elsewhere, my brother leading them. What I concerned myself with is not really fucking important anymore, and never was to anyone other than me.

"When?" Hereman asks.

"Now. Let's do this, and do it quickly. I'd like something to eat that's spent time close to a fire."

Hastily, everyone mounts up, even Ælfgar. Some sleep and some mushrooms have reinvigorated him. Even I don't feel quite as achy as I did, although my body thrums and I'm going to be felled when I finally have time to rest.

"I'll take the rear," Icel informs me. He doesn't ask for permission, and I want to refuse him, but I don't, perhaps because Edmund glimmers with rage at the audacity. Maybe, just because I don't want to upset Icel.

"As you will," not so much an agreement as an acceptance.

Above my head, far above the nodding heads of the trees, the day is moving quickly, the air temperature beginning to dip. Soon, I imagine, darkness will begin to fall, and this needs to be done long before that. I've had more than enough of fighting under the moon and stars.

"Come on, boy," I direct Haden where I wish to go, only for Rudolf to come beside me, Dever angled differently.

"This way, My Lord. That way, you'll end up in the middle of the woods searching for your arse in the darkness."

A chuckle from Pybba assures me that others have heard Rudolf's cheeky response. If he were my squire, he'd be the one on his arse, but he's not.

"Were any of you going to fucking tell me?" I demand to know, only for more laughter to ripple around me.

"Your daft bastards," I huff, Haden eager to overtake Dever.

"This way?" I point, just to be sure. Rudolf nods, eyes alight with mischief. "Then you have my thanks," I condescend to offer him, inclining my head, and now he stills in seriousness.

"Aye, My Lord." His voice is firm, no hint anymore of the

strange trills and dips that affect all youths as they become men.

"Come on," I give Haden his head, fixating on a tree in the far distance, from which a thin line of smoke seems to emanate. Provided I keep my eyes on it; I'll not go astray, not again.

Weapon to hand, I ride smoothly in my saddle, Hereman directly behind me. I spare one look, to make sure that everyone is obeying me, and my eyes alight on Samson. The horse eagerly follows those before it, his patchwork covering making it appear as though he moves from darkness to light, although he does nothing of the sort. I blink and clear my eyes of the illusion.

Turning back, I realise I don't need the trail of smoke to guide me anymore, because I can see the ship-men now. I watch how some bend low over games, while a few shelter around a fire, sticks showing where they roast whatever fish or beast they've managed to slaughter for their meal.

Rage ignites within me. Once more, the fuckers have made themselves at home in my kingdom. How dare the bastards? Do I travel to their homelands? Do I rush to steal their land and resources, or do I remain in Mercia?

I would wish I had enough warriors to reverse these attacks, to make these fuckers worry for their families, their women and their harvested goods. But I don't, and even if I did, could I afford to risk their lives in such a way? I don't think I would. I could never risk a life so carelessly for such little gain.

I squeeze Haden tightly, encourage him a little with my heels, and soon he's spurred to a quick canter, and then ever faster. And yet, none of the ship-men seems to hear us. Only when Haden's gait changes, his legs outstretched as far as they can be in the woodlands, galloping towards the camp, does anyone even look up.

A cry of surprise reverberates around the enclosed space, panicked eyes seeking me out in the gloaming; the sky cut off overhead by the trees, the ground deeply matted with the leaf matter of many years. It's too late for those who are supposed to stand a watch to take any sort of action. Haden leaps the small flames from their pitiful fire, and my seax takes the dazed ship-man to my right, his eyes wild, as my blade slices deep into his neck.

I leave the other three for those who come next, and aim Haden towards the central part of the camp, wildly hacking as I go. Fragments of blood flee through the air, the cold air holding them for the blink of an eye before they tumble to the floor.

Haden allows me to take two more ship-men on my right before I'm forced to slow him for fear of galloping straight through the camp, and out the other side.

I want whoever shelters at the centre of the camp, within the dirty, stained tent, only a flood of ship-men have rushed to protect it. I can see nothing beyond their bodies, and certainly not whoever is within. The high tip of the structure seems to taunt me, and I growl with frustration.

Those furthest from our point of entry, have abandoned all of their possessions, and rush to make it back to their ships, the dubious chance of survival enticing them to greater and greater speed. Haden follows them, even without my command. He knows what I expect from him. He's not exactly new to waging bloody death on our enemy.

Another two men fall victim to my cuts and jabs, and then I'm forcing Haden back toward the main body of the fighting.

Hereman has impaled a man on his long spear, but the swaying body refuses to slip free, even as his foe's eyes lose all focus. With disgust, Hereman is obliged to discard the weapon in favour of his war axe. The long handle of his spear wobbles where it's wedged within the dying man, his hands gripped around it, while blood burbles free from the savage wound. Rudolf has had more success, his blade moving in a whirl of motion, first one ship-warrior and then the next, tumbling to the floor.

But my focus is on the tent, and I'm not alone in being so consumed. Edmund and Icel are the same.

A good number of our opponents have all rushed to protect the inhabitant of the tent, even those who could have made a bid for freedom toward the ships. That arouses my intrigue. I also notice that here, at least, they have some shields, if not enough for one each.

But, I can't get to the structure, not yet, because three ship-warriors face me. I have time to focus on the three men. I can see how strong they are, their upper bodies heavily muscled, necks wider than I might imagine, and fury in their eyes. They don't wear byrnies, but they do have thickened tunics, perhaps needed for the colder weather. Whereas a shield-warrior might wear an emblem of Thor or Odin, maybe even an inked image running along their arms, these men have none of the same embellishment. I think it a wise decision. Why risk a chain around their necks to weigh them down should their ship sink in the icy depths of the whale-road?

Lyfing grins at me from behind my foes, the imprint of the dent he obtained fighting Sigurd, just about visible on his iron helm, for all a seasoned blacksmith has hammered out most of the damage.

He lashes out with sword to take one of the ship-men trying to attack me, leaving me just the two. I spare a glance for Ælfgar and realise that he wars beside Gyrth. I hope the two look after one another. But then I'm consumed by the task before me.

I have two opponents. That doesn't overly concern me.

The one swings a long war axe toward Haden's front leg; the other holds a seax he wants to stab at my legs. The pair of them broadcast their intentions so broadly that it's easy to counter them both. I urge Haden closer to the seax ship-warrior, the war-axe man's swipe going wild. I thrust my seax handle into the first ship-warrior's nose, blood fountaining, to drip over his gaping mouth, and it's easy to thrust the blade inside.

The scrape of iron over teeth has me gritting my teeth and clenching my buttocks. Abruptly, Haden rears, compelling me to grip his reins tightly, my hands on the saddle, as he kicks out with first one leg, and then the other, to leave the first warrior a crumpled mess on the floor. It seems the fucker pissed off my temperamental beast. He really should have known better.

Edmund and Hereman direct their attention towards the

mass of ship-men surrounding the tent. I hunger to join them, but Pybba and Ingwald are engaged in a heavy attack, Pybba somehow unhorsed, and I know that he must be the priority. Either that or Rudolf will never forgive me.

And Rudolf can't help his ally, not at the moment, as he expertly beats back a wild-eyed ship-warrior who's armed with both a seax and what seems to be clumps of horse manure. I admire his attempts, but he probably doesn't realise just how impervious to the stuff my young warrior has become, as they thump against his byrnie. I wouldn't be surprised if Rudolf could no longer scent the stuff.

"This way," I point Haden toward Pybba, and my horse eagerly rushes forward, not bothering to avoid the bodies he tramples. A cry of pain, and a sharp snap, and I turn aside and spit the bile from my mouth. I almost know a flicker of pity for the poor fucker.

Only then Pybba's cry of pain seems to bring everything to a standstill, all apart from me. Haden spurs to such a turn of speed that I'm aware of weapons flying slowly through the air, as others battle for their lives. Somehow, Haden makes it beyond the three opponents getting ever close to Pybba, turning to stand between the man and the enemy.

Sharp movements see me impale one of the men on my seax, even as Ingwald directs his sword into the back of one of the others. That leaves just one, or it should, but a sudden rushing sound, has everything snapping back into the real passage of time, and now there's another opponent to defeat. Somehow, he's closer to Pybba than I am.

"Mount up," I roar, fear making me shout so loudly, they probably hear me in Northampton. But Pybba can't mount up. His missing hand usually is no impediment, but one of the fuckers has managed to land a blow on his remaining, left hand. Even I can see how deep the wound is, the flow of blood making his hand too slick, the pain making it impossible for Pybba to retain the hold on his seax, even though he keeps trying.

"Shit." I jump from Haden's back, a thwack on his back to

force him to shield us. I don't like to risk my horse. Neither will I allow Pybba to be skewered by the prick who's found a spear. Trusting Haden to protect himself, I concentrate on Pybba.

He turns pain-hazed eyes my way, a look of utter despair on his lined face, even as he desperately scrabbles for Brimman's back.

I shake my head at the bastard who tries to deprive me of one of my most valuable warriors. I'll not have it. I really fucking won't.

"*Skiderik*," I bellow at the man, keen for him to see me and be distracted so that Pybba can either escape or at least, make an attempt. Still, the fucker is fixated on my injured warrior, giving no indication that he's even heard me.

"Bastard," I try, bending to flick a lump of green horse shit at his ear, but still the ship-warrior doesn't turn aside, even as the shit hits his neck with a satisfying squelch.

"Is this really the hill on which you wish to die?" I demand to know, but of course, he doesn't understand my words, and they have fuck-all impact on him.

I rush him then, seax on my weapons belt, not prepared to have it turned against me in the coming fight or to have the foe's spear any closer to Pybba or Brimman.

I thrust my fist into the ship-warrior's lower back, and as he buckles, I deal the same to the back of his neck, reaching around him with my left hand to wrestle the spear from him. Even as he falls to the floor, he keeps a firm hold on his weapon, and I admire him. It seems I was hoping for the usual sort of knee-jerk reaction, but it appears that hauling an oar teaches a man better than to release his grip, no matter what's happening.

Despite being splayed on the floor, the spear is still levelled toward Pybba, where he's held in place and unable to move, perhaps an enemy coming at him from the other side of Brimman as well. I just can't see.

"Fucker," I snarl, keen for the man to be dead, as I fumble for my seax, crouching low, and prepared to hold him with my knees if I must.

But he's just too damn fast. He rolls before I can react, seeming to bounce back to his feet, the spear a mere hands-width from Pybba's chest.

"I really wish you'd just fucking die," I huff.

I lash out at his back, my seax eager to shed yet more blood, but even though I gouge a sizeable chunk from his byrnie, revealing a slither of skin, he still doesn't turn to defend himself.

"What the fuck have you got against Pybba?" I question, wishing that Pybba would move and that the bastard would turn and face me, that Ingwald would reach Pybba before I can.

I think he'll skewer my friend, only then he thrusts back with his arms, and I jab my hand through the arch that his elbow makes. I hold it there so that even as he tries to land a killing blow, he can't. He jams my left arm as he attempts to stab forward, and it hurts like a bastard, because he's strong but, just as before, when he didn't react to my attempts to defeat him, my involvement doesn't stop him from trying. Time and time again, he jabs forward, and I feel as though my arm is caught in a vice.

"Fuck's sake," and I manoeuvre from behind him so that even though I'm half bent, I can stab upwards, towards his face.

He doesn't even flinch, even as his other hand fumbles for the almost useless spear. I finally manage to land a blow, on his broad, flat nose, so that blood cascades down his chin. But the bastard doesn't even seem to notice. Certainly, it doesn't slow him down.

I can't risk looking up, to check on Pybba, but I sense he might have finally moved. I hope he has because this bastard isn't going to give up. I wish I knew why he'd directed so much rage at Pybba, but it doesn't matter. All that's important is stopping him.

With my right hand, I again aim my seax, hunting for the flashing skin beneath his tunic. It reveals itself quickly, but I can't quite reach it, not wedged as my arm is.

"This better fucking work," I growl to myself, as I slip my arm free from the vice of his grip. I rush around to the front of him, angling my seax down so that it easily pierces the skin, and then burrowing it as deep as the hilt. Still, the determined brute, able to move his trapped hand again, lunges with the spear toward Pybba.

I half-turn, angle my elbow back into his chin, feeling the snap of his teeth crashing together, catching sight of a whirl of fabric, that I take to be Pybba, grateful when the relentless fuck finally stills in death.

Not, it seems that I've killed the ship-man. Instead, he's skewered, having the same done to him as he tried to inflict on Pybba.

"Hereman," I shout, both wanting to thank and berate the lucky bastard, but he doesn't respond. And I'm not surprised. I don't know where they've come from, but the number of ship-warriors seems to have swelled.

"Get on Brimman," I hastily instruct Pybba, thrusting him upwards, trying not to look at the mess of his remaining hand.

"My thanks," he huffs, even as sweat beads his face, and an anguished shriek erupts from his lips as Brimman takes his weight, his wounded hand accidentally brushing the saddle.

"We need to get you out of here," but as I hastily take in the view, I know it's impossible. While many of my warriors still surround the tent, the enemy has slipped in behind them. There are few enough of us not trapped, and I think they might be leaving Pybba alone because they realise he's half-dead anyway.

How the fuck did this go so wrong?

Mounting Haden, I flick my gaze around the clearing. We've made a good number of kills, and so far, all of my warriors yet live, although Lyfing and Gyrth are hard-pressed as they fight off at least seven ship-warriors, weapons glinting with menace.

Other than that, Edmund, Hereman, Icel, Ælfgar and Wærwulf are all trying to assault the ship-warriors who protect the tent at the centre of the camp. Rudolf and Ingwald attempt to get to them, to add their skills to the attack. I can't call them back, it would be too risky, but neither can I watch them all being overwhelmed.

"Fuck," Pybba's face is white and drained, blood dripping from his wound.

"Here, I'll bind it." I reach across, and as gently as I can, I strap it tightly together using a piece of fabric from Pybba's saddlebags. The deep cut runs down the length of the back of Pybba's left hand, and I'm sure that the tip of his middle finger is missing. A lucky attack by the bastard, but one that's going to be painful to heal.

"Can you move it?" Sweat drips from his nose as Pybba tries to do just that, but his hand moves only a little, and his fingers tremble with the exertion.

"No, then." This leaves me in a quandary, and Pybba knows it. I need to support the rest of my warriors, but Pybba can't defend himself, not without the use of his hands. Not that he won't have some success with Brimman's hooves and his own feet.

"I'll be fine," he huffs, but I've not just risked my life to save his, only to abandon him again.

"No, stay with me. I'll fight for both of us."

"You can't fucking do that," Pybba mutters, but I can already see that the knowledge I won't abandon him has filled him with renewed determination.

"I can do what the fuck I want, remember. I'm your damn king."

"We're going to Lyfing and Gyrth. I'll kill the fuckers, and then we can help the others." Without giving him time to argue, I knee Haden forward, aiming for the smouldering remains of a fire, trusting Brimman to follow behind.

Lyfing and Gyrth fight side by side, and they're winning, but it's too damn slow. I need them now. I ride Haden into the fray, trampling one ship-warrior beneath Haden's heavy hooves, and taking another through the neck as he turns to aim a war axe at Haden's right front leg. I can hear Pybba attacking someone behind me, the huff of his air making me wince, because it's ragged with agony, and yet he persists, all the same, using his feet, and his elbows, and probably his head.

I sight the reaching hand of a foe from behind Lyfing and lash out with my seax, the satisfying sound of the weapon falling to the floor, followed by a heavier sound, and gushing blood dripping to the ground. I wince as I realise my blow was poorly aimed, and the warrior is now missing a hand. Taking pity on him, I persist, taking him with a well-aimed impact through his neck. It'll be quicker than bleeding out through his lost hand. I'd have hoped some fucker would have done the same for Pybba if we'd not been the victors.

By the time I've finished with the handless ship-warrior, Lyfing is checking on Pybba, while Gyrth is on the floor, stabbing down to end the life of one of his foes who twists in agony, his hands trying to hold his belly in. It seems I'm not the only one who takes no joy in prolonging the suffering of my enemy. Better dead, than half-dead. There's just more finality to it.

"Now we need to reach Ingwald and Rudolf."

I turn Haden towards the mass of ship-warriors, trying to determine how many of them remain. Perhaps I was mistaken about the number increasing. Or maybe not. It's impossible to tell. Maybe I just felt overwhelmed when Pybba was threatened.

Rudolf has managed to force a path through the shield-warriors. I almost wish he hadn't, because now there are more of my men with enemies at their backs as well as in front of them.

"What now?" Pybba asks.

"The shield-warriors don't want us to reach the structure. Look. They're all protecting it now. We can focus on that. Pick the bastards off one at a time. Pybba, stay close to me."

I ignore the searching look from Lyfing at my insistence that Pybba fights on. He should know that I have fuck all control over what my men decide to do. I'd like him to get him to retreat. Chance would be a fine fucking thing.

"Let's get this done as quickly as we can." We've done nothing but leave a trail of bodies since we left Northampton, and it's far from over yet.

I slick my seax through my gloved hand, keen to remove as much of the sticky blood as possible. I grimace at the torrent that pours to the ground, the scent of the leaf-litter combining with it to make a smell that speaks only of the slaughter-house.

Pybba, as I knew he would, directs Brimman close to where Rudolf labours. I spare a glimpse for him, marvelling at his skills. He doesn't seem beset by fatigue, and more often than not, he lands his attack, even while turning Dever to prevent the ship-warriors from attacking his animal.

I choose the most awkward position, beneath the reaching arms of a low hanging branch, where it makes it difficult to swing my seax well.

Lyfing and Gyrth take the rear, and then I lose sight of my men, my focus exclusively on hacking my way to join my warriors, relying on them to stay alive, until we can all fight side by side once more.

But I'm worn out by the constant battling. Haden lashes out with teeth and hooves, even on one occasion, thrusting his arse into one of the bastard's faces and emitting a foul-smelling fart that makes our foe gag and then cough. It's almost too easy to stab down, through the top of his exposed mane of brown hair. But I feel the strain in every part of my body.

Maybe I'm getting too old for this shit.

Perhaps it's time for me to sit in Worcester, with my ealdormen and bishops surrounding me, and direct other men to fight for the future of Mercia.

The sound of battle, of men and some women, fighting for their lives, slowly recedes from my consciousness, and my movements become instinctive. Thrusting, cutting, slicing, protecting my horse, and myself. Not that I remain unhurt. Far from it. I feel cuts open on my legs, significantly just above my high boots, and along my forearms, and even one fucker who manages to slice a chunk from my cheek, but I know I'm slowly diminishing the number who attempt to stop me.

And then I find myself with my seax dripping wetly down Haden's black and white side, both of us, chests heaving, but with no enemy to fight.

I risk removing my helm and under-cap, wiping the sweat and blood from my face, wincing as the rough fabric of my tunic

THE LAST ENEMY

brushes the cut, while I consider how the rest of my warriors fare.

Pybba still lives, thank fuck, and he fights side by side with Rudolf, kicking and spitting, and using his elbows to stun those who try and attack him. His wound must hurt like a bastard, but he doesn't stop.

Hereman and Edmund are close together, just a thin layer of ship-warriors to get through before they reach the tent the enemy have all been labouring to protect. Lyfing and Gyrth have no more than five warriors battling against them, while Icel and Wærwulf have only a few more. Ælfgar has retreated behind them, face white with pain, and I appreciate that he's done all he can, for now. I can see where his byrnie has darkened with blood, and I hope the fucker hasn't done too much. My men. They'd fight even as their bodies wept their blood into the ground, perhaps even as blue-tinged their lips and their last breaths left their mouths.

Only then, with such a thin band of the enemy to protect the solitary structure, does someone emerge from it, just as a piercing whistle echoes through the air. I glance to the person who's stepped from the now open doorway, even as I'm listening to see if the sound means anything. Are there more ship-warriors out there? Will they come running at the noise, or is it entirely unrelated?

I thrust my helm back onto my head, not prepared to take the risk, as I instruct Haden so that I can see the enemy more easily.

Who is it? I think I've never seen them before, but perhaps I have. It's impossible to tell when warriors wear their war gear. And certainly, they're dressed for battle. An elaborate helm covers their head. It glints both gold and silver, but more impressive are the bristles sticking from its crest. Not red, as my ceremonial helm which the bishops placed over my blond hair, but black as night, and they're much shorter. Yet even I can see the shape of the animal being depicted. An ugly boar, stubby snout over the warrior's nose, with thick silver plates that cover the neck.

"Who the fuck is that?" I hear Pybba demand to know.

"I wish I fucking knew," I reply, licking my lips and thinking that whoever kills such a foe will be prosperous for the rest of their lives. The byrnie, rather than being made of leather, glints with the skills of a metalworker whose managed to weave iron as though it were no more taxing than stitching a collar, and the legs are sheeted in iron as well.

Whoever this is, they have the best equipment I've ever seen, and that's before I even consider the sword that glints maliciously from the weapons belt or the seax whose hilt is similarly covered with silver with an animal depicted on it. I can't make out the details from where I stand, but I'm sure it must be a boar. How can it not be?

The figure beneath the armour is strong and well-built, eyes blackly glinting as he surveys the scene before him, the hint of amusement playing over the small parts of the face that are visible.

I don't know who this warrior is, but they show no dismay at our endeavours, and that, even more than the immaculate warrior's-garb sends a shiver of worry down my sweating back.

He oozes confidence, and that can only come from believing a battle won, even before he's lifted his sword or seax. With so many of his ship-warriors dead, he still thinks he can win.

I knock aside an opportunistic slash with a blade from one of the shield-warriors who bleeds profusely from an open wound running from shoulder to elbow. The man stumbles and falls to the ground. I don't know what killed him but imagine a poorly discarded seax or sword was to blame, that, or he carried another injury that I'd not seen. But I keep my gaze focused on the warrior before me.

He lifts his sword high, and my eyes travel the length of the weapon. The small skirmishes have all come to an end. Now my warriors face just the one man, and yet, there's no fear or unease on that face, as another piercing whistle echoes through the suddenly soundless woodland.

What is this?

"Who the fuck are you?" I demand to know when none of my warriors speaks, not even Edmund.

Slowly, the head turns, and settles its gaze on me, the superiority in such an action making me swallow down my question. Why would a warrior of such renown fight only with ship-men? Surely, such an outfit calls for mounted warriors and more than a hundred of them?

Only then do I detect the thunder of those missing mounted warriors. I force my gaze away from the disdain of that contemplation, to peer through the tree trunks and try and determine where the direction of the riders. It's evident to me that they must be rushing to rescue their beleaguered leader. But from where?

Haden moves unhappily beneath me, his ears alert to the same sound, as do the rest of my warriors. My breath is harsh in my parched throat, my stomach complaining that mushrooms and berries are not enough to maintain this long-drawn-out fighting. Edmund meets my eyes, and I feel the heat of the searching glances of the others as well, but I'm watching someone else.

Icel has brought Samson to just the far side of the open space. His byrnie is sheeted in blood, his saddle shimmering darkly, his helm wedged slightly to one side, but it's the look on his face that's arrested me. I might have no idea who the fucker is that struts before me, like a peacock, but it's evident that Icel knows who it is only too well.

He slips from Samson's back, the horse not even seeming to notice, and takes calculated steps toward the warrior. And the Raider seems to welcome his scrutiny, a smile still playing around his lips. I swallow my unease, trying not to focus on the threat of more mounted Raiders coming toward us.

I know I should order my warriors together, perhaps even try to achieve a quick escape, but I don't. Icel consumes me, and I'm reminded of the words Edmund composed about my friend when he thought him dead. They've never seemed more apt than the way Icel reveals himself to me now.

He stands alone, but seemingly shrouded by more and more manifestations of himself. I see him as I first knew him, not young, but not aged either; as he has been when facing the usurpers of Mercia during the long hot summer, and then as he is now; changed but the same. I hear Edmund's words repeated, even though he doesn't speak them.

"Bitter in battle, with blades set for war.
Attacking in an army, cruel in battle.
They slew with swords, without much sound.
Icel, pillar of battle, took pleasure in giving death."

"Jarl Olafr," Icel's knowledge of the man's name has no impact on him. It's as though the stranger expects others to recognise him.

"Who is he?" I demand of Icel, but I get no reply.

"Form up," I belatedly instruct, wanting my warriors closer to me, even if we linger behind Icel, prepared to support him because one thing is obvious. Whoever this man is, Icel has a personal connection with him, and this battle will be fought between the two of them. I dare not interfere.

"Riders are coming," Lyfing worries.

"I know, but if their leader is dead, it won't matter." Icel's voice rumbles with the sound of falling rocks, and although I feel myself the object of Lyfing's stare, I hold my tongue.

"Hurry the fuck up." Hereman has no such compunction, and yet Icel is oblivious. So too is our enemy.

Jarl Olafr stands, surrounded by the dead and dying, all he once laid claim to becoming nothing, and yet he doesn't even seem to notice. Instead, his keen eyes are fixed on Icel, although I sense no recognition there. How then, can Icel know who this man is? And then I understand.

"Fuck," but it's too late. Icel has taken six steps forward, and with his seax ready, begins his approach. I don't expect him to rush. This is something that's been driving him on since his recovery. This is something he will savour.

"My Lord," Edmund questions my decision without even voicing the words.

"This is Icel's fight," I assert. "Stay alert for the Riders." This doesn't please my warriors, but nor does the clang of iron on iron as Jarl Olafr and Icel finally clash, sword to sword. The sound seems intensified between the tree branches far overhead, and the matt of bodies and leaves below, making it sound as though giants battle, and not mere men.

Icel moves quickly, his sword almost a blur, as Jarl Olafr counters each move with languid ease. I can't tear my eyes away. I have to watch.

Jarl Olafr has a shield to hand, and he uses it against Icel's every other blow, and in between, the two swords shimmer and strike one another. Icel has no shield, and I wish he did. Jarl Olafr's has been bleached white, an image of a boar depicted in detail on it, and when Icel pauses between blows, Olafr thrusts it outwards, forcing Icel to sidestep, unbalancing him. But Icel is determined. No trace of exhaustion marks his movements, which are fluid and determined, even as his opponent attempts to unsettle him.

"My Lord," Rudolf shouts for me, and I flick my eyes toward him.

"Bollocks," Pybba's eyes have rolled in his head, and he slumps over Brimman's back. I make to go toward them, only for Lyfing to demand my attention once more, his voice filled with worry.

"My Lord, they're coming." I know what he means, but Pybba isn't fit to fight, whereas Icel does fight.

"Hereman."

"My Lord?" He surprises me by speaking softly.

"You have Icel's back," I inform him. Of all my warriors, he's the one with the most similar build to Icel. Should Jarl Olafr succeed in felling Icel, which I just can't envisage, Hereman will fill the void. I feel Edmund's seething frustration that I'd risk his brother, but really, what choice do I fucking have?

Pybba and Ælfgar are wounded. Icel engaged in a battle that will only end with his death or that of Jarl Olafr's, and I have few enough men as it is.

"Ælfgar, get the other side of Pybba. Assist Rudolf. Wærwulf, protect them all."

That leaves me with Edmund, Ingwald, Lyfing, and Gyrth. It's not many, not to counter the threat about to emerge through the gloom, but it's all I have to offer.

I force my warriors close to me, ensuring the rest are shielded. I vow then that we'll all ride from this fucking woodlands. All of us, or none of us, but all of us is my preferred option. Obviously.

"Fucking fools," Edmund curses, and I don't know whether he means us, or the Raiders, and I don't want to know either.

Behind me, I can hear Rudolf speaking to Pybba, trying to rouse him, and the response is weak, reedy and barely heard above the clash of weapons and the approaching thudding hooves.

I straighten my shoulders, prepare to once more wield my seax in support of all that I hold dear, and only then risk glancing to where the others look. I can see the horses coming towards us not by the glint of metal or the flash of piebald or chestnut, but rather by the darkening of the tree line close to the ground as they gather speed.

They don't come in a long line, but rather between the tree trunks, so that it all merges to double the number, and I can't look away, even as I hear Icel's grunts and his enemy's answering snorts.

"Kill them," I instruct, dredging resolve from deep inside me. I could curse my luck. I could demand to know why this is not easy? I could even rail at my God for sending so many of the cursed bastards to infect my realm, but what would be the fucking point?

I can only thwart what's happening. I can only do my fucking best, and then the riders are before us. Rather than screaming for my warriors to oppose the attack, I feel a furrow of consternation forming over my eyebrows, and I turn to Edmund, the question half on his lips already.

"What the fuck?"

Before anyone can reply, I perceive the sound I've been dreading, the cry of anguish from Icel, a rare enough occurrence, and one that I won't allow. Not even the realisation that Hereman has already hurried into the fray, as instructed, can stop me from rushing to his aid.

With concise movements, I dismount from Haden, and stride to where Icel is bleeding into the ground, desperate to get to his feet, a deep wound exposing too much of his thigh. The boar warrior exudes arrogance and confidence, even as Hereman blasts him with his sword, racing from left to right, from left to right.

"No," Icel screams, his face tight with pain where his helm's been knocked askew.

I offer Icel my hand, taking all of his weight as he stumbles back to his feet. I can't see the bone, in my swift examination of his wound, but the torrent of maroon is enough to make me realise that Icel will struggle to stand straight even when it's healed.

Yet, his furious steps take him beyond me. To my amazed eyes, he lashes out at Hereman, hooking him around his upper arm and pulling him away, the action only just not resulting in Hereman being the next to feed Jarl Olafr's blade, as he batters the other warrior aside.

"What the fuck?" Hereman roars, and I'm forced to restrain Hereman, one arm around his neck so that he has to still or risk being choked by my hold.

"I don't fucking know," I gasp. It's all I can say. "I don't understand. But Icel needs this."

"Fuck that," Hereman defies my orders, wriggling free from my grip because I'm distracted by Icel's current predicament. Hereman goes to Edmund's side. He shakes his head, spittle flying through the air, and we can all hear his words, even if he has only offered them to his brother.

"Fucking mad cunt."

I do not disagree with him, and I turn to meet Rudolf's horrified eyes. This is not our way. It has never been, yet Icel is once more attacking his opponent. His movements quicken, and while I watch, Jarl Olafr seems to weaken visibly. For a moment, I worry it's a ruse, but it isn't. It's evident Icel isn't the only one to carry an injury.

Pybba calls weakly to me from where he too watches what's happening.

"My Lord, help him." But I shake my head.

"He needs this," I call, swallowing the distaste the words form in my mouth.

I've never seen such rage, such fury, such naked necessity to accomplish the death of another.

I've fought a lot of fucking bastards, all of them seeking my death, and yet, rage is never the way to go, not if you want to live through the battle. And what boils my piss, is that Icel knows this. If anything, he's the fucker who taught the most valuable lesson I've ever been forced to learn.

Fight with skill, fight with precision, but not with the rage of a personal vendetta. It's why we've always managed to beat our enemy. They've always hated us and despised us for being better, for being meticulous with our movements, for killing as easily and quickly as we can.

But that's not what Icel is doing.

Yet, his opponent is faltering. The boar shield seems to rise only so high now; the sword blows that Icel thunders against his foe's blade, making the straining arm tremble. All the time, those swipes reach ever closer to their target of ending the man's life.

Only then, the thundering hooves that we've heard for some time come to a complete stop. Jarl Olafr finds some new incentive, his attack even speedier than before, his chest heaving beneath the weight of iron that he carries, and my ears pick up a conversation taking place behind me.

A conversation, not a battle.

I risk a glance, a smirk stealing over my face at those I encounter there.

They're not the fucking Raiders. It couldn't be further from what I thought. Instead of twenty or even thirty mounted

THE LAST ENEMY

Raiders, there are twelve Mercians, led by Wulfsige, a look of contentment on his face for finding his king. I'd go to him, give him my profound thanks, both for turning up just when we need him, and also for not being our enemy on mounts; only Rudolf shrieks my name.

"Coelwulf." The sound rings too loudly, seeming to repeat under the canopy of the trees, as though the words are held in the confined space. I twist my body, unsure what I'll see, but knowing it will be terrible.

And it is. Icel is down on the ground once more, his leg flailing uselessly beneath him as Jarl Olafr hammers him with a war axe, Icel's sword discarded on the ground. Blood and flesh pollute the air, and each blow makes me wince, even as I hurry toward the pair of them.

I can hear others doing the same, Hereman's voice the loudest of all as he rebukes, "the daft bastard." But I'm going to get there first, I know it. I was the closest, and I'm also the quicker of Hereman and me.

Icel's arms are in front of him, no longer attacking, but defending himself. I see his flesh open under the onslaught, blood running freely down his arms, where he tries to protect himself, but his foe is getting closer and closer. Any moment now, I expect the killing blow to land, depriving me of Icel one more time, and this time forever.

I run so fast that I feel as though I'm almost out of control, hand on my seax, ready to counter the fucking bastard who pounds against Icel. Only, it's all happening too quickly and too slowly. I see the war axe take more flesh from Icel's forearms yet, and then they slump to the ground, perhaps a muscle torn or wrenched apart, something so terrible, Icel can no longer prevent the attack.

His bloodied leg flails on the ground, as he attempts to find his feet, his boots moving in a mesmerising circle, but he can't get to his knees, let alone stand. He's too weak, and the enemy too strong, and then Icel arches backwards, the seax impaling his undamaged leg, and at that moment, I know what the Raider will do because Icel's neck is exposed, his helm almost touching the ground.

"Fuck," I huff, the sound spurring me on and on. There's only one option available to me, and I have to do it. If I don't, Icel will be gone, for all time, and I'm not about to allow that. Not when it's within me to stop it.

My seax is held rigid against my chest, I thrust myself between Jarl Olafr and Icel, even as I hear Icel's cry of outrage.

I feel war fluid covering my hands, and know that my blade struck true, but suddenly there's too much blood, the scent sweet, my hands sticky. My head feels too heavy, and something is tugging at my throat, a pain so raw I have no words to explain it. I try to move my head, ensure that Icel is well, that Jarl Olafr is dead, but it's as though I'm being ripped in two, and my vision fades into spots.

I form words in my mind, but they don't make it to my lips.

And then I know nothing else.

CHAPTER 15

"Be fucking careful," I recognise the voice, surprised it seems to come from so far away.

"I am being fucking careful. You need to watch what you're doing." Again, a voice I know exceptionally well.

"Will the pair of you just shut the fuck up and do what you've been told to do." I want to tell them all to shut the fuck up, that I need to sleep, but something holds me back, my thoughts muddied. Instead, I latch onto the continuing argument.

"Will you lift your fucking end up, Hereman. Do you want him to have no bloody head?"

"You can talk, Edmund. Look, his foot trails on the ground. He won't get far if he's missing his left foot, will he?" Fury, and something else I can't decipher, laces through those words. I try to determine what it is, undoubtedly, it's not something I've ever heard before, but whatever's happening, something knocks me, and once more, my vision clouds.

"Whose fucking idea was this?" I'm somewhere else, I can tell even through my sealed eyelids. It's lighter here, the scent of clean water tickling my nose. But, the argument continues to rumble.

"It's the only way we can do it. We all agreed if you remember."

"I don't remember agreeing to any such thing."

"Well, you've always had that particular skill, haven't you?"

Another voice joins the debate, and I wince at the fury in Pybba's voice.

"What does that mean?" Edmund demands to know.

"I think you fucking know. But if you want me to make it clear to you, you always could only hear things you want to hear. We all know it. Coelwulf knows it as well."

"And are you any different?" Edmund's response elicits a huff of annoyance.

I wish I could open my eyes. I wish I knew what was happening to me.

The sound of running water grows, but that's not what concerns me. Why am I being carried, and what is it that holds me flat?

I want to lift my hands, work our why my neck is weighed as well, but my body doesn't want to respond to my commands, and then something smashes against my side, and I know only blackness again.

"It was your fucking fault." I'm aware once more of my warriors talking above me. I don't much like it. I'd struggle to stand, but it's just too much effort.

"It was no one's fault." A calm voice seeks to bring about some sort of peace, but I already know it won't work.

A strained silence follows, the sound of water all around me. Am I onboard a ship? Why would I be onboard a ship? I try and open my eyes, but the lids refuse to obey my instructions. Neither can I move my arms or legs, but I don't think it's because my body won't allow it. Not this time. Instead, it feels as though I've been secured to something, perhaps to stop me from moving. If I didn't recognise the voices of my loyal warriors, I'd been concerned that the Raiders had caught me, but no, the voices are well-known to me, even if I've no idea what's happening to me.

I try and recall why I might be in such a position. No, it wouldn't be the first time that I've been entirely at the mercy of my loyal warriors, but it's certainly the first time where I have no recollection of why.

I try to think, to find some clarity to explain my perplexing situation, but it's all too much effort.

"Fuck," the word reverberates through my head, and yet I know I don't speak it aloud because if I did, I'd expect one of the bastards to have stopped doing whatever it is they're doing. The pain is intense, almost making it impossible to think about anything other than the throb that runs down the left side of my body.

There are too many voices to focus on, but all of them filled with either frustration or worry, and then I hear one that almost makes my heart stop beating.

"Stop arguing amongst yourselves, and get him inside. You might not think you're killing him with your bickering, but you might just be." My Aunt's voice is tight with both frustration and concern, and yet all I can worry about is why she's on a boat with me? How did that happen? Again, I try and make some sense of what's occurring to me, but there's nothing but the shards of pain that seem to stab me.

"Careful," she snaps, her bark waking me once more when I'd not even realised that I slept. Not that my eyes open. Or perhaps they do, and it's merely too dark to see anything.

I think I'm being lifted, prone, from the belly of the ship, but I'm too confused to be able to make sense of it all. What I do know is that I can feel every little knock and bump from where I'm being hauled like little more than a sack of grain, and every one of them is agony.

I wish I could make them hear me.

Probing hands wake me, and I'm sure I cry out with pain, but it does nothing to stop the examination I'm enduring. There's something on my neck, or rather, it feels as though there's something inside my neck. I've never felt anything like it before.

I sense, more than see, that I'm inside because there's no wind or stray drops of rain falling on my face. Yet I can still hear my warriors squabbling. Someone needs to tell them to shut the fuck up, and I don't believe it's going to be me.

"Penda, help me." My Aunt's voice is soothing, even as she administers to me. I don't want to think about what she needs Penda's help to achieve. I'm pleased he's here, with her, all the same. He's reliable.

"I can do it," Rudolf's voice is much too close to me, and I almost flinch at the rawness of his words.

"You need to sleep," my Aunt instructs him. "And bathe, and not be in the way." I hear a slap of flesh hitting flesh, and I'd wince for him, but I can't. "And when you've done all those things, you can ensure Haden is well."

"Wulfhere is looking after Haden," Rudolf sounds aggrieved and exhausted. I wish I could speak to him, tell him that I'm fine, but another wave of pain engulfs me.

"He should be awake." Ealdorman Ælhun must think he speaks softly, but he wakes me all the same. I can smell the smoke from the fire, and pottage, or perhaps roasting fish, but I'm not sure.

"He'll wake when he's ready," is my Aunt's assured reply.

"Then he better be ready soon."

"Why, what's the rush? The Raiders are all dead or fled. Northampton is safe. Mercia is safe. Storms will keep even the hardiest of the Raiders at bay."

Ealdorman Ælhun's long delay in responding would bring a smile to my face if I had such control over it.

"He should be awake," he merely repeats, and I hear him moving away.

There's little sound but the crack of logs falling into the fire, and then my Aunt begins to speak.

"I know you can hear me," she surprises me by saying. "I know you can, and I know you'll fully wake when you can, but please, not yet. I'll not deal with your testy temper and complaints. The wound will heal. I know it will, and under my ministrations, how can it not? But it will take time. So sleep, and heal, and listen, as well, because you need to know what's happened while you've been recuperating." I think she'll say more, but instead, I feel fingers around my neck, digging and probing, and the pain is too much for me once more.

"It's not your fault," my Aunt's voice thrums with annoyance.

"How can it not be. Jarl Olafr was mine to kill. I should be lying here, not King Coelwulf." Ah, Icel, his words drip with sorrow. I'm almost glad my Aunt must be the one to speak to him.

"And what, you expect your king, your oath sworn-lord, your friend, to allow you to die when he can save you?" I don't expect to hear the sudden understanding in her voice.

"I." A pause. "I." And nothing further.

"He was mine to kill. He was mine to seek revenge on."

"It little matters who made the killing blow, provided he is dead, and your ill-considered vendetta at an end."

"She saved my life."

"I don't deny that, but she should not have forced such an oath on you. You owed your oath to King Coelwulf already."

"He left me for dead."

"No, we've been through this. They returned for you, and you were gone. They came to bring you back to Kingsholm."

"Perhaps." I sense Icel's huge shoulders shrugging as he makes the concession. "But it is still my fault."

"It's no help to anyone to assign blame. What's done is done. He'll recover, in good time, and he'll expect you by his side."

Silence greets those words, and it's laden with too much for me to ignore it, even though I'd quite like to sleep once more. My neck aches, but it's not the debilitating pain that it has been.

"I suspected your intentions, but now it seems they're confirmed to me."

"I can't serve him now."

"Why? What would stop you?"

"He nearly died."

"Yes, he did. But he didn't. And there's fuck all reason for him to have risked his life, and that of the king of Mercia's, if you're going to be so careless of that in leaving him, now." The rage in my Aunt's voice is more shocking than her language. Once more,

I'm reminded of what a formidable woman she is.

"The others expect it of me."

"I don't believe they do, but if they did, when has that ever forced your hand? Never, is the answer you're trying not to offer."

I can picture the scene now. Icel, fierce and proud, stance wide, fingers on his weapons belt, as he confronts my Aunt. If he'd genuinely wished to leave me, then he'd never have spoken to her about it. I allow the fact to comfort me.

"Why did you encourage him to stay if he was merely going to be his usual unhelpful self?"

"I didn't encourage him. I told him what was expected of him, but yes, it was to make him stay."

"But it's his," and here Edmund stumbles, "fault." I don't imagine my Aunt appreciates his slight slip.

"It was no one's fault, other than the Raiders. You should know that."

"I know it wouldn't have happened if Icel hadn't made such a fuss about being the one to face Jarl Olafr, alone."

"We all carry our burdens," my Aunt mollifies, and in her words, I detect something else. I suddenly have the feeling that Edmund knows exactly of what she speaks, although I have no idea of what she alludes.

"Will he recover?" His words barely reach me, and I hear a sharp slap, and imagine my Aunt has made her feelings about his question well known. Yet Edmund doesn't move away. Perhaps this is their way.

"He. Well, I've never told him how much I appreciate everything he did after the death of his brother." The words are little more than a whisper. "How he's always accepted everything about me, and never tried to make me any different."

There's a silence, and I think my Aunt will ignore those words, only then she speaks.

"Then, when he wakes up, I suggest you speak to him about your true feelings. He'd probably appreciate knowing that you don't think he's a complete failure."

"Failure?" I imagine Edmund's furrowed brows.

"You're not the only one to keep their true feelings locked up tight, for fear someone might see through the façade." I want to hear more of their conversation, but when next I'm alert it's another who speaks.

"Lady Cyneswith," Rudolf's words are soft, as though he hardly dare speak.

"What is it?" My Aunt's voice is laced with fatigue.

"I just came to ensure you had everything you needed."

"I do, thank you. Penda and Hiltiberht have been assisting me." Her voice is filled with sympathy, so different from the way she speaks with the other men.

"He will be fine," she goes so far as to reassure. "He must rest and sleep. The wound is clean and healing well. It's just that it takes a great deal of a body's strength, and it was a deep cut. He was lucky it missed his air tube."

"I would not know what to do if he didn't wake."

"There's no need for you to worry about such things. In a few days, he'll be up and about, plotting more far-fetched attacks on the Raiders, and it will be as though he was never injured."

It seems my Aunt has just as much of a soft-spot for Rudolf as I do.

"Sit with him for me," and I can hear her rising. "I have a few tasks to complete."

Silence fills the space around me, and I decide it must be night time or very early morning. No doubt, everyone sleeps.

"My Lord," I wish I could make some movement, assure Rudolf that I hear him, but it's impossible. Lethargy drags at me, threatening to send me once more to sleep, and I don't want to sleep, not yet.

"I wanted to thank you, for all you've done for me. I was nothing. I had no expectation of wearing a byrnie and carrying a seax and sword, of protecting Mercia from the Raiders, and her other enemies, but you made it possible." Rudolf's usual cheer is missing, and it's strange to hear such serious words from his lips. He's always been light-hearted, filled with his own belief.

"When you left me behind, with Pybba, and went to Repton, I believed you thought I wasn't ready to fight yet, but then you listened to the idea Pybba, and I had, and you allowed me to be involved. You made me a true member of your war-band then, and I'll never forget it."

If I were awake, I'd have no choice but to deny his words. I've never made a youth a man, they've always done that on their own. Before Rudolf, there was Sæbald and Lyfing, and before them, a handful of others, gone now, lost in the escalating battles. I miss them all. I feel the weight of their loss.

"Here, drink this," my Aunt is back, her voice brokering no argument, and I'm not surprised when Rudolf doesn't speak again. I imagine she's up to her old tricks again, of making foolish men, who don't appreciate their exhaustion, sleep again.

Silence falls, and I allow myself to be swept along with it.

"My Lady."

"Pybba." I know my Aunt's lips are pursed at yet another interruption, but Pybba won't be put off.

"Your lord and king will recover, as I keep telling everyone." There's a trill of frustration in my Aunt's voice. I doubt she's used to having so many doubt her skills. I would certainly never be so bold.

"I know he will. I merely came to see for myself. The others come here, speak with you, and can tell me nothing about how he fares, how the wound heals, or even what colour his skin is. It's as though they don't even notice."

My Aunt's unexpected laughter rings through the room.

"Well, I think they come more for themselves than Coelwulf. It's often the way."

"Selfish lot, aren't we?" And the humour ripples through Pybba's words. "But, I imagine we all have things we've never told the cranky old git, and now those matters plague them."

"So it seems, yes. Why what plagues you?"

"Nothing, well, perhaps an appreciation for how he brought

me back to myself after I lost my hand."

"The loss of a limb need not be fatal," my Aunt offers. "It is life-altering, yes, but it's not life-destroying, or need not be. It is, unfortunately, a common injury amongst men and women who make war on their enemies."

"I imagine few of them fight again."

"Perhaps not, but, I understand that it's hardly diminished your skills."

"No, but I am reliant on others to fight with me, and of course, at the moment," and I hear fabric straining, "I'm doubly-hampered."

"The other wound will knit. You won't lose any mobility, provided you keep your hand active."

"I do, My Lady. I do."

"Then, it's your motivation and not his encouragement."

"There, I must disagree with you. Without Coelwulf, I'd have fallen into my dark thoughts and never fought again."

"Then, I suppose you must tell him, as well."

"I believe he knows," and again, my Aunt laughs, the sound softer this time.

"You're a wiser man than others."

"I am many things that others aren't," Pybba acknowledges, and then the conversation falls away from me once more. I doubt I'll remember these things when I wake.

"Wake the fuck up," I know the voice, but I don't appreciate his rough hands on my arms.

"What are you doing?" My Aunt's voice is filled with fury.

"He needs to wake up, so I'm telling him that," Hereman growls, and I sense an edge of desperation to his words.

"He will wake when he must."

"Well, then inform him that he must wake now. He's needed." Only then do I become aware of a thrum running through the air. I can't determine what it is, or what causes it, although I know I should. I'm just relieved that Hereman no longer batters at me.

"Why? What's changed?" I don't understand the question.

The delay in Hereman's reply stretches, and I think I've probably fallen asleep again, only then he speaks.

"We need him. To show his face. To send the bastards running once more. The Raiders grow more and more daring."

"It's been no more than three days, only two since he was last seen. There's time yet."

"And how would you know?" Fury floods Hereman's words.

"We've been doing this for too long, Hereman. We know what they're like. We know what Mercia's enemies have always attempted to do. We don't normally quell before them, and there's no need to on this occasion."

I can sense that the answer is both reassuring and yet, not at all what Hereman wishes to hear. I'm not surprised when my Aunt perseveres.

"The walls are stout, and there's no way for them to come through the tunnels, is there? They've been blocked off once more. They can do little but shout curses and ride their horses around in circles."

"But there are so many of them."

"When has having a bigger number been an advantage? The king has never been able to overwhelm the enemy, only to undermine them. Remember that."

"They threaten to ride into Mercia, to Warwick, or Worcester or Repton, once more."

"And we all know how that will end. If they threaten Worcester or Gloucester, then they'll be faced with the Gwent Welshmen as well. They don't know of what they speak. If they were successful warriors, then they wouldn't be shouting up at you while we shelter behind well-built defences."

"And there is the problem of London." Now my Aunt sighs, and I feel her breath on my face where her fingers uncover my wound. I remember it now. Damn, it fucking hurts.

"London will wait. It has its own walls as well, and Bishop Smithwulf is not a man to capitulate easily."

"And what of the threat from Wessex?"

"There's no true threat. Their king is just as threatened as King Coelwulf, and doesn't have the advantage of quite such a distinguished reputation."

"All the same, he needs to wake."

"All the same, he needs to heal. Now, begone about your business. Take your worries and concerns elsewhere. They're not to be mentioned here again. I won't have him waking too soon."

Now, as the conversation comes to an end, I understand the noise I'm hearing. It's mounted Raiders, no doubt, attempting to intimidate from beyond the walls. But they won't. My warriors are stauncher than that, and far more assured in their belief of an independent Mercia. No matter Hereman's worries.

"Tell me," I push the words beyond my dry tongue and the shard of pain that threatens to pierce me. I don't recognise my voice.

"What would you know?"

"What has happened to me?"

"A neck wound, a slice, or a slither. A long wound, and a little deep, but you're head remained firmly on your shoulders. It will mend."

"And how long have I been here?"

"Four days, perhaps five by now, I can't determine whether it's morning yet."

"And Northampton?"

"Safe and secure."

I want to ask more, but just that has exhausted me.

"Tell me," I'm aware it's lighter as my eyes flicker open, and I focus on my Aunt.

"I've already told you."

"Then tell me more."

"I'll not waste words. What do you wish to know?"

"Mercia is safe?"

"For now, yes."

"My warriors?"

"Will heal."

"The Raiders?"

"Outside Northampton."

"When will I be well enough to stand?"

"Soon."

"He must wake."

"Then wake him." My Aunt's voice is spiked with tightly held fury and fatigue. I consider how many times she's been asked the same question. Only, this time, her response surprises me.

"Really?" It's Edmund whose voice shows such surprise.

"I can't keep you away from him forever. I've done what had to be done. The rest will be for him to decide."

"I'm awake," I mumble, wishing I could cough, and yet appreciating that it's going to hurt like a bastard if I do. "Water."

There are strong hands beneath me, Edmund and Hereman working together, as they slowly lift me. I can feel my wound tugging tightly, the sensation that my skin has been slit and is now trying to knit together, far too overwhelming. I could vomit, but I appreciate that will also fucking hurt, so I try to keep hold of whatever I've drunk in recent days.

My Aunt presses a beaker into my right hand, her other hand clasping it tightly so that I don't drop it. The water is chilled and contains nothing, and she arches an eyebrow at me, as though aware of my sluggish thoughts.

"How long?"

"A handful of days. Not long. Not really, although your men have made it feel like an eternity." Her waspish tone brings a rueful smirk to my face.

"My apologies."

"It's not for you to apologise," she informs me, only then looking away from me, no doubt to quell some poor sod with her most formidable gaze.

Then I lift my hand to my wound, keen to know it's extent.

"Don't touch it," my Aunt speaks even though she's not looking at me. "Leave it alone. Don't befoul it."

The room wobbles a little in front of me and then coalesces

into a more familiar scene, flooded with concerned looking faces. I try a grin, but notice Rudolf shaking his head at me, caution in his wise, young eyes. What must I look like?

"Alright?" I ask, not sure who I expect to answer.

"I think we should be fucking asking you that?" Wulfstan huffs.

"What's boiling your piss?" I demand to know, the question aimed at Hereman, for all I think it was Edmund who tried his hardest to pressurise my Aunt into allowing them to wake me.

"Kingdom to run, Raiders to kill."

"Yes, yes, but what else? Something's going on. Tell me."

"Jarl Guthrum is beyond the walls." I can always rely on Rudolf to tell me the truth. I admire him, even as others hiss, although why the fuckers insisted I woke if they didn't want me to know, I've no idea.

"All hot air, and fuck all skill." Wulfstan comments, and now I do grin, and I don't care whether I look gruesome or not.

"Well, tell him to back the fuck off."

"And you think we didn't try that?" Edmund is back to his usual self, his voice dripping with scorn.

"He won't leave, not until he sees you."

"So the walkway's been rebuilt then?" It seems that the few days my Aunt informed me I'd been unconscious for might not be the actual truth.

"Aye, and it's bigger and much better," Icel rumbles. I'm pleased to see him there. I know it can't be easy for him.

"And."

"And what?"

"Oh, come on, we'll show you. If you can walk."

I spare a thought for my Aunt, but she's standing ready, a thick fur cloak in her arms, and as she fastens it around my neck, I appreciate that it's been made with an exceptionally high collar. It covers my wound well, and while the weight is uncomfortable, it's bearable. Just.

"Don't move your head too quickly. It'll take time—more time than you're going to want to admit. And don't go getting into any fights. Not yet." I feel chastised, and I think she realises. A wicked glint enters her eye.

"You're a lucky man to hold the esteem of your ungainly lot. I think you know that, but I'm only just beginning to realise." And she turns aside, seemingly dismissing me as she begins to tidy her supplies. I focus on her back.

"I've long appreciated your skills," I offer, and I feel her shoulders tighten at my words, her hands still, until she seems to recover herself and resume her original task.

"I can walk alone," I inform the hovering Hereman and Edmund, but with that first step, I realise that I need to piss.

"You can go on the way," Edmund assures me as I make my need known. I take my first step, and then my second and third. By the time I'm up to my sixth, I think my Aunt was over exaggerating, but then I take my seventh, overbalancing slightly, snapping my head back, and a shard of fire ignites around my neck.

"Fucking bastard," I complain, sweat beading my forehead. "Fucking, fucking bastard."

Then I'm outside, the bite of a crisp winter day making my breath swirl before me. I risk a glance down toward the gateway and bridge, pleased to see it firmly in place, a handful of alert men standing guard. I see a flicker of movement before me, and turn, full-bodied, in surprise, as Haden peers at me. How the damn brute knew I was up and about, I have no idea. He lifts his long neck, nickers a soft greeting, and then turns aside, Hiltiberht and Wulfhere both grinning at me. I raise my hand to hail them, and they scurry to be about their duties.

I turn aside, hurry to the latrine, the stench of my water almost making me gag.

"Now, what is it you want to show me?" I call, emerging from behind the wooden structure.

"You need to see it," Edmund evades.

"Fine. Let me see it."

And I do, even before I've come out from the warren of buildings, the scent of wood smoke strong in the air.

There was, before the Raiders destroyed it, more by chance than any great skill, a wooden walkway at the top of the wall, allowing sight of what was happening beyond. That's been replaced, by young wood, the yellow almost too bright on such an overcast day, but the planks of timber extend far beyond anything that stood before.

"What the fuck?" I gasp, turning my body, not wanting to risk just my neck, as I see how far along the length of the wall the walkway now extends.

"It's not complete yet," Edmund hastens to inform me.

"But it will go all the way?" I ask, just to be sure.

"Almost. It'll stop before the gateway. Something to do with weight and balance, and some other shitting bollocks that made sense to those who nodded their heads and gave their consent to the plan."

"Not a builder, are you?"

"No, I'm a killer. I destroy. I don't fucking create." Such satisfaction rings through Edmund's voice that I don't even try and deny his assertion.

I set my foot on the first step, eyes staying forward. I want to look up, but from such a position, it'll be too acute, and I don't want my neck to hurt any more than it already does. It's not a dull throb, as other wounds have been, but a searing heat. It's not pleasant. I appreciate my Aunt's warning.

Only now do I realise that the sound that's been humming in the background is coming from beyond the sturdy walls. I can't make out individual voices, but I can detect a wave of hatred. I grin. Jarl Guthrum's about to get a fucking shock.

But first, there's another one for me.

Ealdorman Ælhun eyes me with pleased surprise as I crest the final step.

"Ah, My Lord King. It's good to see you up and about."

"It's good to be up and about."

"Before you face the Raiders, you should see what we have planned for them, now that you're awake."

He indicates several elongated wooden crates and then bends

to lever the top from one of them. I grin at the glinting menace from inside.

"A fine greeting," I confirm, and allow him and Wulfsige the time they need to distribute their treasure.

"From the ships?" I ask of Edmund.

"Yes, a fine gift, for Mercia's king."

The walkway is filled with Mercians and my warriors alike, and all of them stand ready. I meet the eyes of as many of them as I can, a nod, or a grin, or sometimes, just a glance, and only then do I take the steps that reveal me to the Raiders bellow the sturdy walls.

There's a large group of them, perhaps even more than last time, with their campsite set further back from the ditch, glistening with dirty water, some of it frozen. I must assume that they've come from Grantabridge. Damn the fuckers. When will they learn?

Yet, if I'm dismayed by seeing them, it seems they're dismay at seeing me, is even more significant.

"Jarl Guthrum," I allow Icel to summon the Raider for me, aware my voice still cracks and aches uncomfortably.

"Lord Coelwulf," the cur doesn't give me my title, but I'm not concerned, not with the knowledge I carry.

"It seems that you've been incorrectly informed of my death," I manage to voice those words, refusing to shout, and trusting to the fact that the crisp day will ensure my words reach him.

It amuses me to watch the disappointment that quickly slides onto Jarl Guthrum's face. He truly looks devastated, and he's not alone.

I pause there, just to make sure that all of the Raiders not only see me but appreciate that their jarl has lied to them. Their friends and comrades have died and sweated, been injured, or simply disappeared, and yet Guthrum has accomplished nothing. I'm still inside Northampton, and Mercia remains under my control.

When I'm sure that my survival is appreciated and well

understood, I step back from the parapet and turn my back on my enemy. But I'm quickly replaced by the Mercians and my warriors. The air is filled with the hum of a hundred spears flying through the air, and the screams and shrieks that greet the act make me chuckle, the sound making my neck ache, but I don't fucking care.

HISTORICAL NOTES

The events which occur in this book, are entirely fictional. As I've said before, some would refute the suggestion that Coelwulf was more than a 'foolish king's thegn,' (as he's described in the Anglo-Saxon Chronicle). I would argue with that.

The more I study the time period, the more questions I have, and as a writer of historical fiction, and not 'fact' (non-fiction doesn't seem the correct word to use), I get to play with what I think might have happened.

But to address the source material from the past, I will say that I believe the words written by our ancestors should never be dismissed, but they should be understood. It does no one any good to merely accept the words of the Anglo-Saxon Chronicle, or any other source, at face value. A good historian will question absolutely everything that is available to us from the time period, be it the words themselves, the nature of their survival, the reason for their survival, the way the words have been translated to English, or even why past 'historians' have interpreted them in the way that they have. Bias is not new, and neither is the art of 'claiming' a victory over an enemy and rewriting their story to fit a new narrative.

Neither, in light of current affairs, should we disregard the old 'north/south' divide that infects England, whether people want to accept it or not. The accepted means of understanding the Early English period is that there was a gradual movement of smaller kingdoms coalescing and then kingdoms having dominance over others – starting in Northumberland, then moving to Mercia and then onto Wessex, who then slowly subsumed the other kingdoms, until one king ruled all of 'England.' It's about time that this generalisation was understood better, and that everyone realised none of this was inevitable. England was not always going to be England. Wessex wasn't always going to 'win.' The Vikings were not always going to be beaten. Mercia was not always going to fail!

And neither was Coelwulf.

I would also note that the term Viking, as we know it, is generally incorrectly used. People went Viking, they weren't Vikings. The use of Raider attempts to resolve the issue.

For any concerned with the use of the term Anglo-Saxon for this time period, I have adopted 'Early England,' even if it's not entirely accurate either. I also refute the idea that this was the Dark Ages (and if you do use the term, it should be to describe the events between the end of Roman Britain and the emergence of the first written records of the period.) The images conjured by the Dark Ages are entirely misleading, as it refers simply to a lack of written records.

While writing this book, I had a hemi-thyroidectomy (which was benign). It was an interesting experience. My consultant informed me beforehand that I was being cut with a knife across my throat, and to appreciate what that actually meant. It was a much-needed warning, and accounts for Coelwulf's injury. I can't imagine how painful such a wound must be without the aid of some bloody wonderful pain-killers.

Coelwulf will be back soon, AD875 beckons.

CAST OF CHARACTERS

Coelwulf's Warriors

Ælfgar – one of the older members of the warband
Athelstan – killed in the first battle in The Last King
Beornberht – killed in the first battle in The Last King
Beornstan
Coelwulf – King of Mercia, rides **Haden**
Edmund – rides **Jethson**, was Coelwulf's brother's man until his death. Brother is **Hereman.**
Eadberht
Eadulf
Eahric
Eoppa – rides **Poppy**, dies in The Last Horse
Gardulf – first appears in The Last Horse – Edmund's son
Goda
Gyrth
Hereman – brother of Edmund, rides **Billy**
Hereberht – dies at Torksey, in The Last Warrior.
Hiltiberht - squire
Ingwald
Icel – rides **Samson**
Leonath – first appears in The Last Horse
Lyfing – wounded in The Last King
Oda
Ordheah
Ordlaf
Oslac
Penda – first appears in The Last Horse – Pybba's grandson

Pybba – loses his hand in battle, rides **Brimman** (Sailor in Old English)
Rudolf – youngest warrior, was a squire at the beginning of The Last King, rides Dever
Siric – first appears in The Last Horse
Sæbald – injured in The Last King, but returns to action in The Last Horse
Tatberht – first appears in The Last Horse, normally remains at Kingsholm. Rides **Wombel**
Wærwulf – speaks Danish, rides **Cinder**
Wulfstan
Wulfhere – a squire, grandson of Tatberht, rides **Stilton**
Wulfred – rides **Cuthbert**

The Mercians

Bishop Wærferth of Worcester
Bishop Deorlaf of Hereford
Bishop Eadberht of Lichfield
Bishop Smithwulf of London
Bishop Ceobred of Leicester
Bishop Burgheard of Lindsey
Ealdorman Beorhtnoth – of western Mercia
Ealdorman Ælhun – of area around Warwick
Ealdorman Alhferht - of western Mercia
Ealdorman Æthelwold – his father Ealdorman Æthelwulf dies at the Battle of Berkshire in AD871
Ealdorman Wulfstan – dies in The Last King
    His son – (fictional) dies in The Last King
    Werburg – his daughter
Ealdorman Beornheard – of eastern Mercia
Ealdorman Aldred – of eastern Mercia
Lady Cyneswith – Coelwulf's (fictional) Aunt

Vikings
Ivarr – dies in AD870
Halfdan – brother of Ivarr, may take his place after his death

Guthrum - one of the three leaders at Repton with Halfdan
        His sister
Oscetel - one of the three leaders at Repton with Halfdan
Anwend – one of the three leaders at Repton with Halfdan
        Anwend Anwendsson – his fictional son
Sigurd (fictional
Olafr (fictional)
Estrith (fictional)

The royal family of Mercia

King Burgred of Mercia
    m. **Lady Æthelswith** in AD853 (the sister of King Alfred) they had no children
Beornwald – a fictional nephew for King Burgred
King Wiglaf – ninth century ruler of Mercia
King Wigstan - ninth century ruler of Mercia
King Beorhtwulf – ninth century ruler of Mercia

Misc

Cadell ap Merfyn – fictional brother of Rhodri Mawr, King of Gwynedd (one of the Welsh kingdoms)
Coenwulf – Coelwulf's dead (older) brother
Wiglaf and Berhtwulf – the names of Coelwulf's aunt's dogs, Lady Cyneswith
Wulfsige – commander of Ealdorman Ælhun's warriors
Kyred – oathsworn man of Bishop Wærferth of Worcester
Turhtredus – Mercian warrior
Eanulf – Mercian warrior

Places Mentioned

Northampton, on the River Nene in Mercia.
Grantabridge/Cambridge, in eastern Mercia/East Anglia
Gloucester, on the River Severn, in western Mercia.
Worcester, on the River Severn, in western Mercia.
Hereford, close to the border with Wales

Lichfield, an ancient diocese of Mercia. Now in Staffordshire.
Tamworth, an ancient capital of Mercia. Now in Staffordshire.
Repton, an ancient capital of Mercia. St Wystan's was a royal mausoleum.
Gwent, one of the Welsh kingdoms at this period.
Warwick, in Mercia.
Torksey, in the ancient kingdom of Lindsey, which became part of Northern Mercia
Passenham, in Mercia
River Severn, in the west of England
River Trent, runs through Staffordshire, Derbyshire, Nottingham and Lincolnshire and joins the Humber
River Avon, in Warwickshire
River Thames, runs through London and into Oxfordshire
River Stour, runs from Stourport to Wolverhampton
River Ouse, leads into the Cam/Granta, runs through Bedford (Bed's Ford)
River Nene, runs from Northampton to the Wash
River Welland, runs from Northamptonshire to the Wash
River Granta/Cam, runs from Cambridge to King's Lynn (East Anglia)
River Great Ouse, running from South Northamptonshire to East Anglia
Kingsholm, close to Gloucester, an ancient royal site
The Foss Way, ancient roadway running from Lincoln to Exeter
Watling Street, ancient roadway running from Chester to London
Icknield Way, ancient roadway running from Norfolk to Wiltshire
Ermine Street, ancient roadway running from London to Lincoln, and York.

MEET THE AUTHOR

I'm an author of fantasy (viking age/dragon themed) and historical fiction (Early English, Vikings and the British Isles as a whole before the Norman Conquest), born in the old Mercian kingdom at some point since AD1066. I write A LOT. You've been warned! Find me at mjporterauthor.com and @coloursofunison on twitter. I have a newsletter, which can be joined here.

Books by M J Porter (in chronological order)

<u>Gods and Kings Series (seventh century Britain)</u>
Pagan Warrior (audio book coming soon)
Pagan King
Warrior King

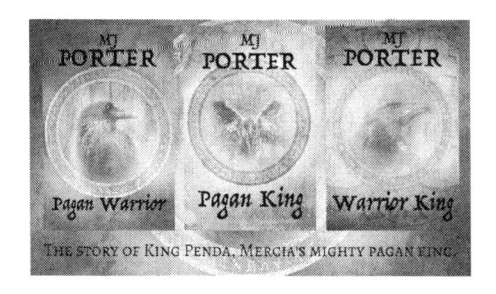

<u>The Ninth Century</u>
The Last King (audio book coming soon)
The Last Warrior

The Last Horse
The Last Enemy

<u>The Tenth Century</u>
The Lady of Mercia's Daughter
A Conspiracy of Kings (the sequel to The Lady of Mercia's Daughter)
Kingmaker
The King's Daughter

<u>Chronicles of the English (tenth century Britain)</u>
Brunanburh
Of Kings and Half-Kings
The Second English King

<u>The Mercian Brexit (can be read as a prequel to The First Queen of England)</u>

<u>The First Queen of England (The story of Lady Elfrida) (tenth century England)</u>
The First Queen of England Part 2
The First Queen of England Part 3

<u>The King's Mother (The continuing story of Lady Elfrida)</u>
The Queen Dowager
Once A Queen

<u>The Earls of Mercia</u>
The Earl of Mercia's Father
The Danish King's Enemy

Swein: The Danish King (side story)
Northman Part 1
Northman Part 2
Cnut: The Conqueror (full length side story)
Wulfstan: An Anglo-Saxon Thegn (side story)
The King's Earl
The Earl of Mercia
The English Earl
The Earl's King
Viking King
The English King (coming soon)

Lady Estrid (a novel of eleventh century Denmark)

Fantasy

The Dragon of Unison
Hidden Dragon
Dragon Gone
Dragon Alone
Dragon Ally
Dragon Lost
Dragon Bond

Throne of Ash (coming soon)

As JE Porter
The Innkeeper

ACKNOWLEDGEMENT

I am once more indebted to my beta readers, EP, ST, CH, AM and CS who continue to inspire me to write bigger and better for Coelwulf and his comrades.

And to my readers. Thank you for embracing my loveable rogue. He's a joy to write.

THE NINTH CENTURY SERIES

Mercia lies broken but not beaten, her alliance with Wessex in tatters.

The Last King

They sent three hundred warriors to kill one man. It wasn't enough.

Mercia lies broken but not beaten, her alliance with Wessex in tatters.

Coelwulf, a fierce and bloody warrior, hears whispers that Mercia has been betrayed from his home in the west. He fears no man, especially not the Vikings sent to hunt him down.

To discover the truth of the rumours he hears, Coelwulf must travel to the heart of Mercia, and what he finds there will determine the fate of Mercia, as well as his own.

The Last Warrior

He sent a hundred men to kill two thousand. It had to be enough.

Mercia lies broken but not beaten, her alliance with Wessex in tatters.

Coelwulf, a fierce and bloody warrior, fears no man, especially not the Raiders claiming Mercia as their own.

Coelwulf must travel away from the heart of Mercia, hunting down the Raiders and what he discovers will determine the fate of Mercia, as well as his own.

The Last Horse

The Raiders have been routed from Torksey, dead, or escaped.

Mercia lies broken but not beaten, her alliance with Wessex in tatters, her new king a warrior not a ruler. And as he endures his coronation, as demanded by the bishops and ealdormen, there are stirrings from the east.

Coelwulf must again take to the trackways of Mercia. His destination, any place where the Raiders are trying to infiltrate the kingdom he's fought so hard to keep whole, losing beloved friends in the process.

The year is AD874 and Mercia lies threatened. But Coelwulf, and his loyal warriors, have vowed to protect Mercia with their lives. They're not about to stop now.

The Last Enemy

Mercia lies broken but not beaten, her alliance with Wessex in tatters, her new king a warrior, not a ruler. And Coelwulf has done little but fight against overwhelming numbers since being declared Mercia's king, and it's far from over.

Northampton is secure, but the Raiders persist in infiltrating Mercia. Coelwulf has enticed them away from their stronghold at Grantabridge, and now he must rout the Danish Jarl, Guthrum, once and for all.

The year is AD874 and Mercia lies threatened, but Coelwulf and his loyal warriors have vowed to protect Mercia with their lives.

BOOKS BY THIS AUTHOR

Pagan Warrior

Britain. AD632.

Penda, a warrior of immense renown, has much to prove if he is to rule the Mercian kingdom of his dead father and prevent the neighbouring king of Northumbria from claiming it.

Unexpectedly allying with the British kings, Penda races to battle the alliance of the Northumbrian king, unsure if his brother stands with him, or against him as they seek battle glory for themselves, and the right to rule gained through bloody conquest.

There will be a victor and a bloody loser and a king will rise from the ashes of the great and terrible battle of Hædfeld.

Pagan King

The year is AD641 and the great Oswald of Northumbria, bretwalda (wide-ruler) over England, must battle against an alliance of the old Britons and the Saxons led by Penda of the Hwicce, the victor of Hæðfeld nine years before, the only Saxon leader seemingly immune to his beguiling talk of the new Christianity spreading through England from both the north and the south.
Alliances will be made and broken, and the victory will go to the man most skilled in war craft and statecraft.

The ebb and flow of battle will once more redraw the lines of the petty kingdoms stretching across the British Isles.
There will be another victor and another bloody loser.

Warrior King

The year is AD655 and the great warrior king, Penda of Mercia, stands in a position of power, with allies in every kingdom, from the northern Pictish lands to the southern kingdom of the West Saxons, from the British states to the West, to East Anglia where its king now rules with his backing.

Just one kingdom stands aloof, just one realm chafes against Penda's influence, Bernicia, ruled by Oswiu, the brother of the long dead Oswald of Northumbria, who, in the fourteen years since his brother's death, has failed to claim the combined Deiran and Bernician kingdoms for himself, but who schemes for a unified Northumbria, despite Penda's desire to truncate those wishes.

As Penda and Oswiu align themselves for one more final battle of survival and supremacy, alliances will be made and broken, and the victory will go to the man most skilled in war craft and statecraft. Or will it?

The ebb and flow of battle will once more redraw the lines of the petty kingdoms stretching across the British Isles.

There will be a victor and a bloody loser.

Printed in Poland
by Amazon Fulfillment
Poland Sp. z o.o., Wrocław